OUT OF THE DARKNESS

OTHER TITLES BY ROBERT D. MCKEE

Killing Blood (2016)
Dakota Trails (2017)

OUT OF THE DARKNESS

ROBERT D. MCKEE

FIVE STAR
A part of Gale, a Cengage Company

GALE
A Cengage Company

Farmington Hills, Mich • San Francisco • New York • Waterville, Maine
Meriden, Conn • Mason, Ohio • Chicago

LIBRARY OF CONGRESS CATALOGING-IN-PUBLICATION DATA

Names: McKee, Robert D., 1948– author.
Title: Out of the darkness / Robert D. McKee.
Description: First edition. | Waterville, Maine : Five Star Publishing, [2017]
Identifiers: LCCN 2016057801 (print) | LCCN 2017005914 (ebook) | ISBN 9781432834197 (hardcover) | ISBN 1432834193 (hardcover) | ISBN 9781432836924 (ebook) | ISBN 1432836927 (ebook) | ISBN 9781432834173 (ebook) | ISBN 1432834177 (ebook)
Subjects: LCSH: Frontier and pioneer life—Wyoming—Fiction. | City and town Life—Wyoming—Fiction. | Public prosecutors—Fiction. | Physicians—Fiction. | BISAC: FICTION / Historical. | FICTION / Legal. | GSAFD: Legal stories.
Classification: LCC PS3613.C55255 O88 2017 (print) | LCC PS3613.C55255 (ebook) | DDC 813/.6—dc23
LC record available at https://lccn.loc.gov/2016057801

First Edition. First Printing: June 2017
Find us on Facebook– https://www.facebook.com/FiveStarCengage
Visit our website– http://www.gale.cengage.com/fivestar/
Contact Five Star™ Publishing at FiveStar@cengage.com

Printed in the United States of America
1 2 3 4 5 6 7 21 20 19 18 17

For Kathy

★ ★ ★ ★ ★

PART ONE:
CHESTER'S DECISION

★ ★ ★ ★ ★

CHAPTER ONE

Micah McConners had been back in his hometown of Probity, Wyoming, less than fifteen minutes when the peaceful afternoon was cracked open by a gunshot. He could tell it came from around the corner on Main Street, so Micah, being curious, edged in closer to the buildings and started in that direction. The second shot, though, brought him to a stop. By the sound of it, the gunfire was getting closer, and his natural curiosity began to drain.

It was August 1900 and central Wyoming was mostly civilized. From time to time a band of young Indians would ride around the countryside raising a little havoc, and trains were robbed often enough to cause the railroad barons back East some sleepless nights, but the land's wildness, for the most part, had been tamed.

Micah's father, John, used to tell stories of the old days when about everyone wore a sidearm. During those unruly times, gunfights in the streets were not uncommon, but now, times were modern, and such things were rare. After all, it was almost the twentieth century. Some wrongly believed the new century had begun on January 1, 1900, but Micah knew it wouldn't really start for another four months.

As Micah reminded himself that times were less wild now than in his father's day, he heard a third shot, and that pretty much took away whatever curiosity he had left. He decided it would be wise to duck between the buildings until he could determine what was going on. As that prudent thought came to mind, a riderless horse raced around the corner at full gallop.

"What the hell's going on?" Micah asked out loud, and as soon as he said it, he saw. He wasn't certain what he was seeing, but he sure knew what it was that made that horse run.

A man on a large blue bicycle was coming down the middle of the street, and he was gaining on the galloping horse. Micah had never seen a bicycle move so fast, but its speed was not the only wonder of it. Micah blinked to make sure his eyes were working, and then he looked again. His eyes had not lied. The man astride the bicycle was not moving his legs. The cycle was not being pedaled. The sound of a million bumblebees came from the two-wheeled contraption. A fourth bang disrupted the peaceful afternoon, and a puff of blue smoke erupted from beneath the bicycle's seat.

A group of a dozen men, women, and children rounded the corner down the street. Some were shaking their fists; others were cheering. One irate man shouted, "Doc, damn your hide. If that horse gets hurt, I'm-a gonna take you apart."

Doc?

Micah couldn't tell by looking because the man wore a long duster, a small-billed cap, and huge goggles over his eyes, but, yes, causing a panic in the middle of downtown was something Micah's best friend, Chester Hedstrom, M.D., was apt to do.

Micah stepped into the street and waved his arms. The man must have seen him because he brought the cycle to a quick stop on the dirt street and sent a plume of dust twenty feet into the afternoon sky.

"Chester?" Micah asked, trying to peer into the goggles. "Is that you inside there?"

The man pulled a lever on the machine's cross bar, causing it to sputter, gasp, and fall silent.

"Micah." The rider swung his right leg over the rear of the

cycle and lowered a stand. He pulled the goggles to the top of his head and grabbed Micah in a bear hug. "You made it. Hooray." He spun Micah around and did a little jig. "Home at last. Home at last," he sang.

Micah and Chester had corresponded earlier in the month. It had been arranged that Chester would meet Micah at the train station upon his return, and Micah would stay at Chester's house until he could find a place of his own. Micah had been admitted to the bar two days earlier, and he was returning to Probity to begin his career as an attorney-at-law.

"Sorry I wasn't there when the train pulled in," Chester said, "but I went for a ride and lost track of the time." He gave Micah one more spin and set him down. Micah hurried to straighten his suitcoat and hat. He was no dandy, but concern for his appearance became habitual after three years in the offices of the fastidious Judge Roscoe Pullum. It was under the tutelage of Judge Pullum in Cheyenne that Micah had read for the bar.

At six feet two, Chester was taller than Micah by almost three inches. And Micah figured Chester must outweigh him by at least forty pounds. Chester was a big, friendly man who didn't know his own strength, and he was always whacking people on the back hard enough to knock off their hats or grabbing them around the shoulder and twisting their clothes.

Chester slapped Micah's back now. "How was your trip?" he asked, but before there was time to answer, he moved on to another topic. Keeping up with Chester's conversation always required a fleet mind. "What do you think?" He extended both hands, palms up, toward the bicycle. "It's a beauty, isn't it?"

"Yes," Micah said, "it is. But what is it?"

"Why, it's a moto-cycle, of course. Haven't you ever heard of moto-cycles?"

Micah had read quite a lot about the new internal combustion engines being used to power carriages, and now that he thought about it, he remembered reading something about the engines' also being attached to bicycles. But he'd never seen one, and little Probity, Wyoming, was the last place he ever expected he would.

By now the crowd had caught up, and the man who'd threatened Chester a moment earlier shouted as he ran by. "As soon as I catch that horse, Doc, I'll be back." He jabbed a thick index finger in Chester's direction. The man was barrel-chested and way too heavy. As he ran, a purple blood vessel pulsed between his eyes.

"He'll be back," Chester said with a chuckle, "if he doesn't die of apoplexy first."

The rest of the people milled around the moto-cycle, but no one, not even the children, ventured too close.

"Step aside, folks," Chester said, shooing them away. "There'll be time enough later for all of you to see this fabulous machine. But right now Attorney McConners and I have an important appointment, and we mustn't be late."

Chester lifted the cycle off its stand and threw a leg over. With a smile, he patted the cross bar and said, "Al-l-l aboard."

"What?" Micah wasn't sure he'd heard right. "You expect me to get on that thing?"

"Of course."

Micah felt his eyes widen, and he shook his head.

"Oh, come on, Micah. You need to be open to new experiences. It's a new age. Prepare yourself for it."

"Yes, climb on," someone shouted. "Give 'er a try." The rest of the group then chorused their encouragement.

Holding to his chest the carpetbag that contained everything he owned in the world, Micah inched himself side-saddle onto the moto-cycle's center rail. Chester pulled down his goggles and pushed off.

There were conventional pedals on the contraption, but Chester only had to pedal them a half-dozen times before the motor beneath his seat caught and the machine lurched forward, giving Micah a stomach-churning rush.

Micah squeezed his eyes closed, but he could feel Chester, who had always been a showman, turn the thing around and ride back past the cheering onlookers.

"I can't believe I'm doing this," Micah said, once he'd mustered the courage to speak. There was a vibrato to his voice that had nothing to do with the moto-cycle's shaking.

"What do you mean you can't believe it? Why, it's exhilarating. Open your eyes, for God's sake. Stop being such a coward."

Micah had never thought of himself as a coward, but maybe that was what he was. If being a coward meant keeping his eyes closed while sitting on this fool's device, he was more than prepared to live with the burden of cowardice.

"Micah," Chester said, "if you don't open your eyes, I promise you, I'll see how fast this thing can go." Micah felt Chester reach beneath him and push the cross bar's speed lever forward. The motor sputtered and fired off another of its bangs, and the machine sped up.

"All right, all right," Micah said. "I'm opening them." And he did, with reluctance, one lid at a time.

"There now, that's not so bad, is it?"

The buildings sped by. Micah had gone that fast on horseback, and trains went that fast and more, but on this small contrivance it was different. After a bit, though, his heart skittered down to a more normal rate, and he admitted, "No, I guess it's not so bad. Where'd you get it, anyway?"

"My Uncle Oscar in Brooklyn builds them. He's talking to a fella out of Springfield, Massachusetts, about building them for sale. When I was back East earlier in the summer, he let me ride one. It was such a thrill, I made him promise to build his next one for me. So he did and shipped it out. It arrived this morning. I had to install the wheels, but that was no problem."

Chester veered to avoid a rut, and Micah almost toppled off. "Damn, Chester, be careful!" he shouted.

"Sorry," Chester said with nonchalance. "Uncle Oscar expects to be producing them for the open market within the next year or two. I've already invested."

Chester's parents had left him a sizeable inheritance. Investing portions of it in hare-brained inventions was something Chester did with regularity. He once lost five thousand dollars in an electric machine that was supposed to milk a cow. When the prototype was built and attached to the cow's udders, it sent out such a jolt of electricity that ol' Bossie keeled over dead on the spot. To make matters worse, the falling cow landed on the machine and smashed it beyond repair.

Putting money in an engine-powered bicycle seemed less insane than many of Chester's investments.

"I suppose something like this could have some commercial success," Micah allowed, "at least until the fad wore off."

"Fad!" Chester's shout into Micah's ear was almost loud enough to drown out the buzz of the engine. "Motorization, Attorney McConners, is the coming thing. Believe me, this is no passing fad." He shook an index finger at the heavens for emphasis and almost lost control.

"Keep," Micah said through clenched teeth, "your hands on the handlebars."

At the moment he said that, a small bulldog ran from the sidewalk and began snapping at Chester's ankle.

"Get away, damn you." Chester kicked at the dog, but the more he kicked, the more the tiny dog snapped.

"Chester," Micah said. "Uh, Chester?"

"Back. Get back." Chester kicked again.

In his attempts to discourage the dog, Chester had allowed the moto-cycle to drift to the right-hand side of the street, and they were now headed toward a large watering trough.

"Chester, for God's sake, look out."

But it was too late. They struck the trough head on, and Micah was catapulted, arms flailing, over the handlebars and into the water. He came up sputtering, not believing what had happened. Chester had been thrown from the machine as well but landed to one side of the trough and was dry and unhurt.

"Well," Chester said, lifting his goggles, "that was exciting, wasn't it?"

Micah said nothing as he stood and stepped from the trough. The brim of his hat hung in front of his eyes. With every step, he felt a squish inside his boots.

"Wait, Micah," Chester called, "you forgot this."

Micah turned and saw Chester push his sleeves up, reach down into the water, and pull out the carpetbag.

"My," Chester said, handing it over, "that's a bit of a mess, isn't it?"

Still Micah said nothing. He took the bag, walked to the boardwalk, and sat down.

The moto-cycle's engine had stopped, and it lay lifeless on its side. Chester crossed to it with small, tentative steps, as though approaching an injured pet. After a moment, he said, "Well, good news." There was a joviality in his voice that Micah resented. "Except for a slightly bent front wheel, everything looks fine. I can fix the wheel easily enough." He shook his head and clucked a couple of times. "It's not rideable right now, though."

"Gosh," Micah said, pouring water from his boot, "that's too bad."

Chester must have recognized a tone in Micah's voice. "Now, no need for sarcasm. This sort of thing could happen to anyone."

Micah glanced at the group that had begun to form around the trough. At first they'd shown concern for the men's safety, but now, as Micah knew they would, they began to snicker.

Chester had that effect on people. Although he was well respected in the community, he was always making people laugh without intending to.

Micah wrung out his socks and draped them over the tops of his boots. He'd been about to ask Chester where they were going when the dog came at them; now he did ask.

Chester, who was bending over his moto-cycle, stood without saying a word. He was as stiff as a two-by-four.

"Chester," Micah repeated, "what was this engagement you said we couldn't be late for? Where were you taking me before you decided we should stop off for a swim?"

Chester cleared his throat, then stroked his chin. "It's, er . . . a . . ." he stuttered, "supposed to be a surprise."

"Seeing the bottom of that horse trough was surprise enough for me, thanks. Where were we going?"

"Well, if you insist on knowing," Chester said with indignation, "the city council got together and decided to throw you a welcome-home party. They've planned a picnic in the park and invited over fifty of the most prominent citizens in the county." He pulled his watch from his vest pocket, shook it, and held it to his ear. "And we better get a move-on, too. They'll all be waiting."

CHAPTER TWO

Micah ignored, as best he could, the embarrassment of marching into the park wearing a soaking-wet wool suit. It was far from how he'd envisioned his first encounter as a young attorney with the citizenry of Probity, but there wasn't anything he could do. He had nothing to change into; everything he owned was drenched. He had considered going right to Chester's house and locking himself inside, but as much as he would've liked to have done that, he couldn't overlook the fact that all these people had turned out to welcome him home. Instead, he sauntered in as though not a thing was out of the ordinary. When the mayor asked him about his soggy condition, Micah merely rolled his eyes, jerked a thumb toward Chester Hedstrom, and everyone in the crowd gave out an understanding chuckle.

At first Micah had been furious with Chester, but now, as he milled about in the warm afternoon sunshine, his chill dissipated and so did his anger. That's the way it had always been. He might often get angry with Chester, but he could never stay angry with him long.

Micah scanned the crowd. There were a lot of people here. He recognized almost everyone. All the local officials were present. Reginald Barker, who was chairman of the county commissioners; Henry Thompson, mayor; Brad Collins, the sheriff; and Earl Anderson, the county attorney. Plus there were bankers and businessmen, farmers and ranchers—everyone Micah had known since he was ten years old. But he didn't kid himself. Most of these people were here because they had known his father. John McConners, who had opened his general store in 1886 when the town was new, had been one of the best-liked men around. He'd died four years earlier, but folks in Probity didn't forget.

Micah spotted Chester at one of the barbecue pits talking to Max Heinrich, the town butcher, and Charlie Bannock, the baker. Despite everything, it was good seeing Chester again. They had corresponded often while Micah was away. And earlier that year, on his trip back East, Chester had stopped in Cheyenne for a few days' visit. As boys, and even as young men, Micah and Chester had been almost inseparable.

Micah started toward the barbecue pit where Chester was having his discussion with Max and Charlie. On the way, he was stopped by Thomas Blythe, one of Probity's three attorneys.

"Micah," Blythe called out, "come over." He waved in a regal manner, inviting Micah to join him and Probity's two other attorneys at one of the tables.

Micah knew these men by reputation only. He buttoned his still-damp coat and climbed the grassy hill to their table.

"Have a seat, Micah." Blythe made a flamboyant, sweeping gesture to an empty spot at the table. He motioned to the other two men. "Earl Anderson. Jackson Clark."

"Nice to meet you," said Micah.

Anderson only nodded, but Clark said, "Yes, you too."

"By the way, congratulations," said Blythe. "It's always a pleasure to welcome a newcomer into the bar."

Both Anderson and Clark seemed to accede to Blythe's leading the conversation. Clark, about sixty years old, was tall and thin. He'd been an attorney much longer than either Blythe or Anderson, but Thomas Blythe had, without question, the most successful practice around. No other attorney in the county, no matter how long he'd been lawyering, could command either Blythe's statewide acclaim or his substantial fees.

"Thanks, Mr. Blythe," Micah said as he sat next to Anderson.

Earl Anderson, the county attorney, was a foppish little gnome. He was maybe five feet tall, and maybe he wasn't. Micah couldn't tell for sure. Around his neck he wore a monocle on a long, gold chain. "That was quite an entrance you made, young man." Although he put a special inflection on the words "young man," Micah doubted Anderson was more than eight or ten years older than he was.

"Wasn't it, though?" agreed Blythe. Blythe was not yet fifty, although, like Anderson, he appeared older than his years. They were both condescending, but Blythe's condescension was less blatant than Anderson's. Still, it seemed to Micah that both men were play-acting, cultivating mannerisms to make themselves appear more . . . what? Micah couldn't quite put his finger on it. Sagacious maybe. More solid and trustworthy. Micah wasn't sure, but whatever it was, he hoped it wasn't the way folks expected attorneys to be.

"You were in an embarrassing situation, yet you did not allow it to get the better of you," said Blythe. "You handled the problem with a subtle, quick-thinking gesture. Very clever."

"I promise you, Mr. Blythe, there was no cleverness involved. If I'd been clever, I expect I'd've thought of some way to attend this shindig in a dry suit."

"Don't be modest, Micah," Blythe said, shaking his finger like a scolding father. "Your cleverness is instinctual." He raised an eyebrow and looked toward his colleagues. "That's the most valuable kind. Right, Clark?"

Jackson Clark didn't respond. Instead, he asked, "Care for a beer, Micah?" Before Micah had a chance to answer, Clark lifted a pitcher and poured him a glass.

Micah doubted if any of these men had ever said a dozen

words to him, or even noticed his existence, for that matter; now they were all sharing a beer. At least he, Clark, and Anderson were sharing a beer. Thomas Blythe drank lemonade.

"The ability to think quickly," Blythe continued, his voice taking on the tones of a professor, "is an attorney's greatest asset, particularly if he intends to do trial work. Do you intend to do trial work, Micah?"

Micah smiled. "Trial work is what I hope to do." He lifted his glass and took a sip. "But I suppose I'll do whatever work I'm offered. I'm in no position to be choosey."

"Choos . . . ey, . . . yes." Blythe drew the three syllables out in such a way it suggested that being unable to choose was a concept that just now occurred to him. "I suppose that is true." He stared for a moment into the clouds of his lemonade, then looked off toward the men at the barbecue pits. "I wonder when the food is to be served."

"I was wondering that myself," said Anderson, following Blythe's gaze.

Blythe, speaking to both Clark and Anderson, said, "Perhaps you gentlemen wouldn't mind finding out. I have something to discuss with young McConners here, and then I'll be right over."

"Of course," Anderson said, standing. Clark rose more slowly.

Once they were gone Blythe said, "It looks to be an excellent party. Everyone has worked very hard to make it a success, particularly your friend Dr. Hedstrom."

"Chester has?" Micah asked.

"Very much so. In fact, it is my understanding that the doctor planned the menu."

Micah found that hard to believe. As far as he knew, Chester had never even heated a can of beans. Planning a menu to feed more than fifty people sounded way beyond Chester's skills.

"Are you sure about that?" Micah asked. He didn't even try to hide his disbelief.

"Oh, absolutely. The good doctor is always full of surprises."

"That's true." Micah had to agree with that. "He is."

Blythe took on a confidential air. "I hope you don't mind my asking, Micah, but what are your feelings with regard to divorcement proceedings?"

"My feelings?"

"Do you have a moral compunction against divorce?"

The truth was, beyond reading the statutes and a case or two, Micah had never given a moment's thought to divorce one way or the other. "No, it has its place, I suppose. I can imagine a number of situations where it might be necessary." He wondered if there was a right or wrong answer to the man's question. Had he espoused some radical point of view that would get him ostracized from the legal community before he'd even begun?

"Excellent, my boy. Excellent. I had hoped you would feel that way. I am, as you might imagine, in a position to, from time to time, refer you clients."

"Yes, sir." Being close to broke, Micah liked the direction the conversation was beginning to take.

"And it so happens I know of someone who is interested in obtaining a divorce. I, as do you, feel the proceeding, regrettably, has its place in our society."

In some ways Blythe reminded Micah of Judge Pullum, the man under whom Micah had read for the bar. Both men had a remarkable ability to insert adverbs and parentheticals into every sentence.

Blythe took a sip of his lemonade, then pulled a handkerchief from the breast pocket of his coat and dabbed at his mouth. Compared to his earlier sweeping gestures, the act was almost dainty. "I, however, being a deacon in the Baptist church—and if I might be so bold, a moral leader in our community—must decline the case. I thought perhaps you might be interested."

"Of course, I'd be happy to. Having neither religion nor any

21

particular reputation for morality provides me the freedom to do most anything."

A blank expression crossed Blythe's face. After a short pause, Micah laughed, letting the older man know it was a joke. Blythe then laughed too, but it was a dry kind of laughter. "Yes," he said. "Yes, of course. Very good. Very good." His eyes scanned the crowd. "Here, come with me." He set down his lemonade and stood.

Micah followed Blythe to a table where half a dozen women sat talking. When they arrived, Blythe said, "Mrs. Pratt, may I have a word with you?" As soon as he spoke, four of the women rose and scattered.

A girl of maybe eighteen, small and pretty, started to leave as well, but the woman to whom Blythe was speaking stopped her. "No, Polly, stay," she said.

The woman looked at Blythe, but she didn't stand, nor did she offer him a seat. "What is it?" she asked. Her tone was blunt.

"I wondered if it was your intention to continue with the course of action we discussed in my office last week."

"It is," Mrs. Pratt said. "Polly and I have rented rooms at Mrs. Jordan's boarding house." She was a handsome woman of maybe forty who looked to have at one time been beautiful. There was a firm set to her jaw. Her nose was a bit too large, but it fit well with the structure of her face. Her eyes were a shade of gray Micah had never seen before. A kind of pewter.

"If that is the case, then allow me to introduce Mr. Micah McConners." He turned to Micah. "Mr. McConners, this is Mrs. Cedra Pratt. I suggest, Mrs. Pratt, that you discuss your circumstances with Mr. McConners. I have mentioned to him that I knew of someone interested in divorcement proceedings but gave him no more details than that."

Mrs. Pratt offered Blythe a stony look, then directed her gaze at Micah. He felt his temperature rise in the heat of this woman's scrutiny.

"Do you have an office address as yet, Mr. McConners?" she asked.

"No," Micah said. "I'll begin searching for office space tomorrow."

"Very well," she said, "if you don't mind, perhaps we could go over some things right now."

"Yes, of course. That would be fine."

"That is," she added, "if Mr. Blythe would excuse us."

Blythe cleared his throat. Micah doubted the man was accustomed to being dismissed in such a fashion. "Certainly, Mrs. Pratt. If I can be of further assistance, do let me know." He took the brim of his Homburg, lifted it a couple of inches off his head, gave a little bow, and walked away.

The woman, watching Blythe leave, said, "What a pompous ass."

Micah hoped he was able to hide his shock. He'd never heard a woman use such language.

"The reason I went to him in the first place is because Jackson Clark is a drunkard and Earl Anderson is a fool. I trust you're neither of those things."

"Well," Micah said, "I'm not a drunkard."

Her left eyebrow rose an inch, and she smiled. When she did, the hard set of her features eased some. "Please, Mr. McConners, have a seat." She turned to the young woman and said, "Polly, fetch the gentleman something to drink."

"Yes, ma'am," the girl said. She was pretty but frail-looking. Her skin was as white as writing paper. "What would you like, sir?" Her voice was soft, almost a whisper.

"A beer would be fine. Thank you."

The woman placed her hand on the girl's forearm. "You get it and come right back," she said. When the girl was gone, the woman turned to Micah. "I am married to Emmett Pratt. Does that matter to you?"

Micah shrugged. Of course he knew Emmett Pratt, or knew of him. He was one of the largest landowners in the county. He had homesteaded here in the mid-seventies and now controlled tens of thousands of acres. It was said that during the late troubles in Johnson County, Emmett Pratt's place had been a favorite stop-over for the Cattle Grower Association's "enforcers" as they traveled from Cheyenne to Kaycee and Buffalo. "It doesn't matter to me," Micah said. "How does he feel about the divorce?"

"He doesn't want it."

"Why do you?"

She paused and looked away. "I no longer have—" She seemed to search for a word "—respect for him." After a quick beat, she added, "Nor, it seems, does he for me."

"Well," said Micah, "the sum of my experience in these matters is zero, Mrs. Pratt, but I can tell you divorce is not an easy thing to obtain. The law lists ten or eleven very specific causes that allow a divorce to be granted, and if your situation doesn't fall within those causes, there can be no divorce. I would have to reread the statute, but I doubt loss of respect is listed among the grounds. If it were, I'm sure there'd be many more divorces in this country than there are."

"My reason for wanting a divorce is because it's the right thing to do if we are not going to live together as husband and wife." She looked to where Polly had gone for the beer. The firm set of her jaw that Micah had seen soften when she watched her daughter earlier now seemed to soften even more. "And we'll not be living together as husband and wife ever again."

"How many children do you and Mr. Pratt have?" Micah asked.

"Although Polly has taken the name Pratt, we have no

children together," she said. "We've been married only eight years. It's the second marriage for both of us. My first husband was killed in a hunting accident when Polly was three. Emmett's wife died of cancer ten years ago. Emmett has a boy, Sonny, from that marriage. I don't want anything from Emmett, Mr. McConners, if financial support for children is what you're considering."

"That is what I was considering, but even without that, there are provisions for alimony."

"I have no interest in alimony."

"You have invested eight years of your life in the marriage, Mrs. Pratt. Don't you think you should be allowed something for all that?"

"I have my reasons for wanting out of this marriage, Mr. Mc-Conners. If the law does not recognize those reasons as legitimate, so be it. I shall get out of this marriage with or without the law's blessing. But I was not seeking Emmett Pratt's money when I married him. I'll not be seeking it when I leave him."

"There are practical considerations, ma'am. You have a daughter. How will you survive?"

She sat up straighter, her back stiffening. "I was a teacher before I married. I expect I can return to that occupation."

It was clear Cedra Pratt was a strong, proud woman. Micah suspected that once she had committed herself to a marriage, she wouldn't let go of it without good cause. Whatever Pratt had done to bring her to this state of mind must have been serious.

"I hope," Micah said, "to have an office rented by the end of the week. Look me up, Mrs. Pratt, and we'll discuss this further. Perhaps divorcement is available. You may have some cause that fits within the statute."

Polly returned and placed a glass of beer in front of Micah, spilling a bit as she set it down. "Momma, look," she said, and there was a note of desperation in her tone. She nodded toward a well-dressed young man about fifty yards away. He was leaning against a tree, sipping a beer. There were other young men involved in animated discussion all around him, but he paid none of them any attention. Instead, he stared across the picnic area at the three of them.

It was rare to have a congregation of more than five people in Probity without someone making a speech. Some activity appeared to be about to begin at what was serving as the main table. The mayor and a few local bigwigs were milling around.

"So, I saw you conferring with your fellow attorneys a little while ago," Chester said.

"Yes," said Micah. "I think I got my first client."

"You think? Shouldn't a well-trained professional like yourself be able to tell if you have a client or not?"

"Well, I haven't received a retainer yet."

"Aha," said Chester, "already thinking like a lawyer. So were you impressed with the other members of the Probity bar?"

Micah shrugged.

"I guess they're all harmless enough," Chester said, "except for that little weasel Earl Anderson."

"You have no fondness for the county attorney?" Micah asked.

"He wears a monocle," Chester pointed out.

Whatever bias Chester's dislike of Anderson's monocle represented, it made sense to Micah.

"Besides," Chester added, "I've never met a more ambitious, do-anything-for-a-vote scoundrel in my life. He's not too fond of me, either."

"Not fond of such a loveable fella as you? Why, Chester, I can't believe that."

Chester gave Micah a scowl. "Still a smart aleck, I see." He turned his gaze to where Anderson was sitting. "He doesn't like me because when no one around here would oppose him for county attorney, I made no secret of the fact that I had gone to Casper in an effort to recruit a new lawyer to move in and run for the office."

"I can see how that might not endear you to him."

"You can also see how successful I was," Chester said. "When I couldn't find anyone who wanted the job, I started writing letters to the newspaper encouraging people to not vote for the office of county attorney at all. I suggested they leave that column blank. Turned out Anderson got barely fifty-one percent of the vote, and he was running unopposed."

"You have a gift for knowing how to win friends in high places, don't you?"

"The man's a louse."

"What did he do to cause you to dislike him so?" Micah asked.

"He's very discriminating about who he chooses to prosecute and who he doesn't. During his first term in office he launched a campaign against prostitution and drunkenness, which is all well and good, I suppose."

Micah felt himself smile. He knew that Chester was not much offended by either of those vices.

"But," Chester continued, "at the same time he was defending our morals, he was turning a blind eye to a consortium of wealthy landowners who'd gotten together and stolen the water rights from three farming families west of town. He'll prosecute to the fullest some poor drunk or vagrant and allow his cronies to get away with anything. Whatever happened to the days when people like that were run out of town on rails? It makes you want to pluck a chicken and heat up some tar."

Chester had always maintained there hadn't been a decent politician since Lincoln, and he wouldn't waste his time with any of them. "My God, Chester," Micah said with a laugh, "I never knew you to be so political."

Chester smiled. "Surprising, isn't it? I guess Earl Anderson brings out the politics in me."

Micah nodded toward the tables that held the food. "You seem to be full of surprises today, aren't you? This is quite a to-do."

Aside from the pies, cakes, and a dozen or so large bowls containing vegetables and various kinds of salads that had been prepared by the town's ladies, the food was unidentifiable. Large trays were stacked high with fare the likes of which Micah had never seen. Huge containers holding something else as unrecognizable were set next to each of the trays.

Before anyone could begin eating, they had to stand around the tables waiting for the dignitaries to speak—or that was the pretense. Micah suspected the truth was that no one wanted to be the first to sample whatever it was that Chester Hedstrom had concocted.

Mayor Thompson stepped to the main table and clanked a beer pitcher with a knife. "Could I have your attention, everybody? I'm not going to take much of your time. I'm sure everyone's real hungry and eager to, uh—" His eyes dipped down to the trays in front of him. "—dig right in. But before we do, I want to say welcome home, Micah. We all knew and respected your father for a whole lot of years, and we wish he could be here to join us in our celebration."

"Thanks, Mayor."

"I'm certain you'll be a credit to John as well as yourself and your profession. We wish you the best. Let's now turn everything over to Dr. Hedstrom. Doctor?"

Chester stepped to the table carrying something three feet long under his arm. It was flat and wrapped in butcher paper.

"What's that in your armpit there, Doc?" someone from the

crowd called out. "Not something else you're going to try to feed us, I hope."

"No, no," Chester said, smiling. "It's a gift for my good friend." He handed the package to Micah.

Micah rushed to unwrap it, and what he saw once the paper was off wrenched a smile to his face. It was a sign—a shingle. Chiseled on oak in beautiful script were the words, "Micah Mc-Conners, Attorney-at-Law."

When he thanked Chester, his voice came out raspier than he would have liked.

"Now," said Chester, rubbing his hands together, "all you folks are in for a treat. In my travels back East this year I made some discoveries, great discoveries, two of which are on the tables before you."

He reached to one of the large bowls and extracted something small, white, and roundish. He held it up so everyone could see. "This I ran across in Saratoga Springs, New York," he said. "It's a white potato, sliced as thin as paper, and fried in a special way." He bit into the thing, and Micah could hear it crunch from ten feet away.

Chester lifted the bowl and held it out to some children standing in front of the crowd. "Here," he said, "give 'em a try. They're called Saratoga chips. Some folks call them potato chips."

With caution, one boy, a little older than the rest, reached into the bowl and picked one out. He brought the thing to his nose, smelled it, then took a tentative bite. Astonishment washed across his face. With wide eyes, he gobbled it down and reached into the bowl for more. This time he brought out a handful. When the other kids saw that, they too made a grab for the bowl.

"Slow down," Chester said. "Not so fast. There's plenty for everyone." He took another for himself and popped it into his mouth. "Yes," he said, "tasty. Very tasty."

He moved down the table to one of the trays. "But this is the best of all." Chester pointed to the back of the crowd and said, "I have to thank Max and Charlie back there for helping me with this item." The butcher and baker both gave halting waves. Micah wondered if they weren't standing in the back in order to make a fast getaway should the need arise. Being involved in one of Chester's schemes could be a risky endeavor.

With both hands Chester lifted one of the objects from the tray and held it high for everyone to see. It appeared to be a small six-inch loaf of bread, sliced down the middle. Tucked inside was some kind of meat. The strangest thing about it, though, was that the meat was long and tubular.

"This," said Chester, "I also discovered in New York, in New York City, where it's all the rage."

There was the same pride in his voice that Columbus must have had when he reported back to Isabella.

He shoved the end of the thing into his mouth and took a huge bite. The pleasure on his face was obvious. "It's called," Chester said, "a hot dog."

A lady behind Micah whispered to the woman next to her, "Sadie, did I hear him right? Did that young man say *dog*?"

CHAPTER THREE

Chester Hedstrom had a beautiful house. It was located on North Sixth Street, the most fashionable area of Probity. At three stories high, the house was the tallest building in town. It was painted a sparkling white and boasted porches and gables and gingerbread trim.

The library was the first room Micah saw upon entering, and despite its opulent furniture, carpeting, draperies, and row upon row of leather-bound books, the place was a pigsty.

"Good God, Chester, how can you live like this?"

"Like what?"

"Look at this place." Micah motioned toward the litter of magazines and pamphlets, handtools, and debris. There was a long table at one end of the room, and on it were piled dozens of objects in various stages of disassembly. "If your parents were still alive," Micah said, "they'd both drop dead."

"It is a little cluttered with my projects," Chester allowed.

Micah walked to the table. It was a chaotic mess. "What is all this stuff?" he asked.

"A few things that've caught my interest."

Micah picked up a rectangular wooden case. The thing was covered with tiny, numbered keys. He turned it over and saw that the bottom had been removed and nothing was inside. He had no idea what he held, and he gave Chester a quizzical look. "This?" he asked.

"Why, it's one of Mr. Burroughs's adding machines, of

course." Chester's tone suggested that Micah was a little slow for not knowing. This might have bothered another person, but it had been years since Micah felt self-conscious because Chester was interested in something Micah had never seen before.

"Adding machine?" he asked. He poked one of the buttons. Even more so than with the moto-cycle, Micah had heard of this device. There were a few in Cheyenne, but he'd never actually touched one. They weren't common in lawyers' or judges' offices. "So I guess you push these keys and the machine will add the figures?"

Chester took the box from Micah, and with a shrug said, "Well, it did." He placed it back on the table next to the jumbled pile of tiny wheels, levers, and gears that Micah assumed once made up the machine's innards.

The table was strewn with a dozen similar projects.

"I see," said Micah.

Chester had always had a compulsion to take things apart. He was never without a pair of pliers and a screwdriver tucked into his back pocket. As a boy, he'd dismantle the household clocks to see how they worked, but always struggled to put them back together—sometimes with success, more often not.

Once when Chester's parents were away on a trip to Omaha, Micah watched in amazement as Chester disassembled the brand-new coal-burning cookstove his father had ordered from Chicago.

"I don't think you should do that," Micah had warned. And as it turned out, Micah was right. Before they were done, it took not only Chester, but Micah, the local blacksmith, and the blacksmith's apprentice to get the thing together again. And even with all that, for years afterward, on a windy day, the kitchen would have a thin haze of black smoke.

Chester took Micah's still-damp carpetbag and called to the back of the house, "Mrs. Eggers." Then to Micah he said, "We'll, give these things to Mrs. Eggers to wash."

"Eggers? What happened to Anna?" Anna had been Chester's housekeeper, secretary, and assistant in his surgery ever since Chester had graduated from the Columbia College of Physicians and Surgeons.

"Her son-in-law was killed in the Philippines in 'ninety-eight. As soon as she heard, she moved to Lander to be with her daughter."

Micah felt a twinge of guilt. He always felt he too should have gone to fight the Spaniards, but he was well into his studies when that short one-hundred-and-fifteen-day war broke out and he couldn't give up his position with the judge. Micah's only hope of becoming an attorney had been to study while at the same time working for Judge Pullum.

"That's too bad about Anna's having to leave," Micah said. "She was quite a hand."

"She was, indeed," agreed Chester. "I miss her. Mrs. Eggers is the third woman I've had work here in two years." He added under his breath, "And I'm not sure how long she'll be around."

As Micah started for the stairs, a large woman in her mid-fifties entered the room. She had huge breasts that sat upon her ample middle like melons on the back of a cart. Her face was florid and fat, with tiny, deep-set brown eyes. Her hair was a reddish blond. It was so severely pulled back in a bun that it caused the corners of her eyes to lift.

"Good evening, Mrs. Eggers," Chester said. He motioned to Micah, who stood at the foot of the stairway. "This young gentleman is my friend, Micah McConners. I mentioned to you a couple of days ago that he'd be staying with us until he can find a place of his own." He handed her the carpetbag, which she held as though it were a dead animal. "Please clean his clothes, if you would. Micah here is a clumsy oaf and he dropped the whole outfit into a horse trough."

Micah gave him his coldest look.

"He'll be takin' his meals here too?" she asked. Her voice was hoarse-sounding and wet. Hearing it made Micah want to clear his throat.

"Of course," Chester said. "He's a lout and a bore and not at all bright, but, please, despite all that, do your best to make him feel at home."

She left the room stirring some verbal stew under her breath. It sounded as though the phrase, "Twice the damned work," was somewhere in the mix.

Once she was gone, Chester smiled and said, "Yep, I miss Anna more every day."

Micah nodded in agreement. "I can see why."

Chester pointed to the wide staircase. "Your room's the second door on the right. Take off the clothes you're wearing so she can clean those as well. I'll bring you one of my dressing gowns."

Micah was glad to get upstairs and undress. His suit had dried, but it would feel good to take it off.

Micah appreciated Chester's putting him up like this, but he hoped his stay would be brief. Chester was as free a spirit as Micah had ever known. And even though they'd been friends for years, Micah knew living with him could be overwhelming. Chester had an all-consuming exuberance for life—particularly modern life, as Chester liked to call it—and everything he did, he did with an energy that exhausted anyone foolish enough to try to keep up.

With the exception of the library, which Chester never allowed his housekeepers to touch, the house was immaculate. The room Chester had given to Micah was spotless. Micah crossed the thick carpet and sat on the bed, bouncing a couple of times to test the mattress. Not bad. It was much more comfortable than the cot he'd become accustomed to in his sparse rooms in Cheyenne. The outside wall of the room was banked with three large windows. They provided a view of the hills east of town. The draperies had been opened to allow in the light, and Micah could see a group of a half-dozen antelope grazing not a hundred yards from the house.

By the time Micah undressed, there was a knock at the door. "Yes?" he said.

"It's me." Chester poked his head in. "Here," he said, tossing Micah a robe.

"Thanks." Micah caught the robe, pulled it on, and tied the sash around his waist. He reached up and felt the lapel's material with his thumb and forefinger. It was thick and plush. He had always been fascinated by the luxury Chester seemed to take for granted. It wasn't envy; it was fascination. Luxury itself was not something Micah craved, but because his own upbringing had been modest, he couldn't help but notice when he was exposed to the finer things. Chester, who'd been surrounded by luxury all his life, seemed to pay it no mind at all.

"When you're ready," Chester said, "come down to the parlor. I'll open a bottle of Glenlivet. We'll see if I can still drink you under the table."

He stepped back out and closed the door behind him. As Chester went downstairs, Micah heard him shout, "And hurry up, damn it; I am a thirsty man."

By the time Micah entered the parlor, the Scotch had already been poured. He took the glass that Chester extended and whiffed its contents. "It's always been more pleasant drinking your whisky than my own," he said. "Yours is so much better."

"So *that* explains why you were always hanging around sniffing at Pappa's liquor cabinet." Chester opened a heavy wooden box. "Cigar?"

Micah shook his head and pulled a package of Cyclones from

the pocket of the dressing gown. He placed one of the cigarettes in his mouth, and Chester lit it for him. Chester then snipped the end from a cigar and lit it as well.

It had been a long day. Micah leaned back on the sofa and took a sip of the expensive whisky. He could feel the smooth liquid trail its way down his throat.

"It's good seeing you again, Chester," he said. With first the adventure on the moto-cycle and afterward the picnic, they'd not had an opportunity to visit.

Chester folded himself into a chair across from the sofa. "Same here," he said. He was having a hard time keeping the cigar going, and he fired another match and lit it again. With his eyes on the flame and the now glowing tip of the cigar, he asked between puffs, "How've you been feeling?"

Micah smiled at the casual way the question had been tossed out. Chester Hedstrom was flamboyant and blatant in every way. But Dr. Hedstrom possessed a bedside manner that was offhanded and subtle.

"I'm feeling well," Micah said. "I'm feeling very well."

Chester cocked his eyebrow and scrutinized Micah through the cloud of smoke.

"All right," Micah admitted, cringing a bit at the sound of his defensiveness. "The blue devils still knock at the door from time to time."

"There's nothing to be ashamed of, you know." Chester said this as he flicked the spent match in the direction of the ashtray. He missed by six inches. "Melancholia's an illness like any other."

"Yes," said Micah, "I know." And he did know. He should. He'd heard it from Chester a dozen times before. "But it has gotten better," he said, and that wasn't a complete lie. The depression came less often than in the past. When it came, it was worse than ever, but it was coming less often. "Perhaps I'm outgrowing it."

Chester nodded. "I suppose that's possible. Hell, anything's possible. There's plenty we don't understand. But there's a lot of work being done with this sort of thing in Europe these days. Particularly over in Austria." He raised his glass. "To your health, sir," he said, taking a sip.

"And yours." Micah tipped his glass in Chester's direction and took a drink as well.

Chester examined his cigar, which seemed to be burning nicely now. A two-inch gray ash extended from the end. Chester took another puff and the ash tumbled to his lap. Chester paid it no mind. Micah assumed it wasn't hot, but he kept an eye on it anyway.

"There are office spaces to let on Third Street," Chester said after a bit. "The old Stimpson property."

Micah was interested. "Is that right?" He was familiar with that building. It had three rooms and was across the street from the county courthouse, which was located on the second floor above the First National Bank. That would make it convenient for any hearings he might have in front of the Justice of the Peace. When the District Court Judge came to town on his circuit ride out of Casper, court was held at Bury's Opera House. The opera house was nicer and much roomier than the small space allotted the JP. That was a situation, Micah recalled, that had been brought to the attention of the county commissioners more than once by the Justice of the Peace, who felt he was being given short shrift. If Micah could afford the rent, this would be a fine location for a lawyer's office. Except for First Street down by the depot, that area of Third and Main had become the busiest spot in town. "I wonder what the rent is," Micah said.

"It shouldn't be too bad. Stimpson's nephew has it now. He doesn't drive as hard a bargain as the old man did." Chester huffed a blue smoke ring toward the ceiling.

"I'll look into that first thing tomorrow. By the way," Micah said, "thanks again for the shingle. It'll look good hanging beside my office door. That was a fine gift. I don't suppose you made it yourself."

"Good God, no," Chester said with a laugh. "The only time I use a saw is when I hack off someone's leg. I hired Harvey Pecker to make it."

"Is that right? I haven't thought of him in years. I heard he'd he moved to Sundance."

"He did, but he came back a few months ago."

"How's he doing?" Micah asked.

"Very well. He's become a fine finish carpenter." Chester placed his feet, boots and all, on the ottoman in front of his chair. "Damn, but we used to make his life miserable when we were boys, didn't we? You more than any of us. You were always the worst about that sort of thing."

"With a name like Harvey Pecker, what should he expect?"

Chester held up a finger as though he'd been struck with a brilliant idea. "Perhaps now that you're a prosperous attorney you should make up for your past sins by offering to do a name change for the poor bastard free of charge."

"You know," Micah said, "you're right. I'll do it. What do you think of the name Dick Pecker?"

For some reason Chester found that funny. He laughed so hard he dropped his cigar to the carpet. It rolled beneath the sofa, and Micah bent and retrieved it before it burned the house down. He placed it in the heavy ashtray that sat on the cocktail table between them.

"The truth is," Chester said after a while, "Harvey's become a real success. He has a well-equipped shop down on First, south of the old stage headquarters. He has all the latest equip-ment—very progressive."

"Who would've thought Harvey Pecker would ever be called a progressive?"

"He is, though. You wouldn't believe some of the modern tools he has down there. And more are coming. There'll be a time in the not-too-distant future when electrical saws, sanders, and all sorts of devices will be available to make carpentry much easier and more exact."

Micah had often heard Chester's thoughts on the future of electricity. Electricity, according to Chester, perhaps even more than the internal combustion engine, would change the world. Already Chester had a kerosene-powered generator behind his house. The only room wired to it was the library, but when he ran the generator, Chester could, with the mere flick of a switch, fill the room with light.

"And it's not only in carpentry or the other trades, no, sir," Chester continued. "Change is in the wind. We're about to see great advances in every field. In a short four months, it'll be 1901, and we'll have entered the twentieth century. Mark my words, Micah, the twentieth century will be a renaissance, a time of wonder, man's greatest·adventure."

"God, Chester," Micah said with a grimace, "you're the one person I know who could turn the pleasure of sipping eighteen-year-old Scotch into pure misery."

"Misery? What do you mean, misery?"

"Precisely what I said. For years now, ever since you started subscribing to those scientific periodicals of yours, and—worse yet—started reading that Wells fella and the other one, the Frenchman—"

"Verne."

"—Verne, yes—ever since you began reading all of that stuff you have had nothing on your mind but gadgets and electricity and gasoline, and God knows what all. You think of nothing else. You've turned into a real wind-bag." Micah added that wind-bag remark mostly for his own amusement. He recognized there was some truth in all Chester said, but he couldn't resist laying it on as heavy as he was because there was nothing in life he liked better than baiting Chester Hedstrom.

"Go ahead," Chester said, "scoff, but it's coming. I promise you. This new century offers the human race the greatest opportunity in history. It's a new age." He tapped his temple with an index finger. "Our intellect, Micah, can turn this planet into a paradise. We'll have the means to end hunger and poverty. We can free ourselves from the sickness and drudgeries of life so we can evolve into something better. Perhaps we can even eliminate war. Can you imagine that? An entire century without war. There is that potential in the twentieth, and it's thrilling. The human race has a chance to become something more than it's ever been. I'm telling you, this new century will give us the chance to step out of the darkness and into the light." Chester gave an awkward little smile at his grandiose turn of phrase, but it was clear he meant every word he said.

Micah seldom turned down the opportunity to debate. In most instances he didn't even care which side of an issue he was on. The debate itself was the important thing. And he especially enjoyed the mental jousting he and Chester had always engaged in over drinks. Micah's first impulse was to go at it with Chester now. He was tempted to argue that man instead of ending war might well find more horrendous ways to wage it, but he stopped himself. Tonight what he wanted was to relax. All he said in response to Chester's excited and optimistic rant on the wonders of the twentieth century was, "You, my friend, have much greater faith in humanity than I do."

Chester frowned, "My, my," he said with a tone of sadness that might have been feigned, Micah couldn't quite tell, "you have become a horrible cynic in the years you've been away."

"All part of my intensive legal training." Micah lit another cigarette, and they sat without speaking, enjoying their Scotch and smokes.

"So," Chester asked after a bit, "when do you plan to see her?" Chester was a master at approaching from the blind side.

Micah didn't answer right away. He blew a small ash from the sleeve of the robe, set his drink on the table, crossed his legs. "No plans," he finally said.

"Did the two of you correspond while you were away?"

"A little nosey, aren't we?"

"Curious, only curious."

"Well, if you must know, no, we didn't. We have not communicated in three years. Before I left, she said she didn't want that. She felt we should make a clean break."

"Why do you suppose she'd say something like that?" Chester asked. The bottle of Glenlivet was beside him on the table, and he freshened their drinks.

"The reason she said it is obvious; don't you think?" Micah said.

"Yes, it is obvious. She wanted you to tell her how wrong she was."

Micah shook his head. "You're full of insights tonight, aren't you?"

Chester blew a stream of smoke toward the window.

It was after eight-thirty, and the sun was below the hills to the west, but the sky was still light, and gold trimmed the bottoms of the clouds.

"All these years," Chester said, shaking his head, "I tried my best with you, Micah, I see now how much I've failed. Imagine my disappointment."

"There was no hope for us. You know that. Even if we didn't have the obvious problem, she was too, I don't know, sensible— too practical to put up with someone like me."

"You really don't know much about women, do you? You two

had problems. So what? There was no reason to avoid keeping in touch."

"We couldn't be together, and neither of us wanted to sneak around anymore. It was time for it to end. My leaving for Cheyenne provided us the opportunity to end it. It was a mutual agreement."

Chester scoffed. You're a fireball, Micah, or at least you were back then. You should've swept her off her feet and taken her with you."

Micah searched Chester's face for the usual signs of joking, but this time none were there. Despite that, Micah said, "You're not serious."

"All right, maybe taking her to Cheyenne might've been too much. That's my own fiery side speaking. My own passion is always warring with my practical side. I agree, you weren't in a position to support a wife then. But what's to keep the two of you apart now? You still love her, don't you?"

"No," Micah said, "I don't. It was difficult, but I've let it go."

Chester sat forward in his chair and gave Micah a skeptical look.

"Damn it, Chester, why are you doing this? You and I both know it's impossible. She knows it's impossible. Hell, she knows better than anyone how impossible it'd be."

Chester leaned back. "There would be difficulties," he allowed. "That's true."

Micah snorted a derisive laugh.

"But it could be that those are the kinds of difficulties that'd bring the two of you closer."

"I did love her," Micah admitted, "but I'm past that now." He didn't know why it was important to make Chester understand, but it was. "And I've taken my lead from her. She's the most sane, practical girl I've ever met. She always knows the right thing to do, and I promise you, Chester, when I left three years ago, we were both in agreement that our ending it was the right thing to do."

Micah felt his emotions rise, and he hated that feeling. It was the sort of thing over which he was trying to gain control. This time, though, he wasn't sure what he felt. It wasn't anger, although he suspected it could quickly turn to anger. Perhaps he felt resentment. Things were always so much easier for Chester. It might've been that Chester's romantic and practical sides were always at war, but he wasn't fooling Micah. Chester always knew where the battle lines were drawn. For Chester all lines were clearly drawn, and it was impossible for him to accept that for the rest of humanity lines were often blurred.

Micah was about to point this out when, without knocking, Mrs. Eggers came into the room. Her already sanguine complexion seemed even redder than before. She made no apology for her interruption. "Doctor," she said, "there's a woman at the door. She claims to need your help."

Micah and Chester followed Mrs. Eggers from the parlor into the foyer. The front door stood open, and standing on the porch was Cedra Pratt. Her features were pinched and carried the look of worry. But it wasn't Cedra that caught Micah's eye. Standing beside her mother, her head leaning against Cedra's shoulder, was Polly. And it was Polly's face that drew Micah's attention. Her right eye was swollen shut. There was a two-inch cut along her left cheek. Blood sheathed the side of her face and covered the front of her dress.

"Now, Doctor," Cedra said, her lips a thin line beneath her patrician nose, "will you please, *please* help us?"

"Here, Micah," Chester said, "get the door." There was a screen on the front door, and Micah held it open as Chester stepped out onto the porch and took the girl from her mother. He placed his right arm around Polly's shoulders and walked her into the foyer. She staggered as they stepped through the threshold, and when she did, Chester scooped her up and carried her.

The girl was not unconscious, but it was clear that she was in shock. Although some blood still oozed from the wound on her cheek, for the most part the bleeding had stopped, and it was drying in dark, thick streaks down her face and neck.

"Light the lamps in the examination room, Mrs. Eggers," Chester said. The woman, who appeared only now to be aware of the injured girl, stared at him dumbly.

Micah touched Mrs. Eggers's forearm and got her attention. "Please, Mrs. Eggers." He jerked his chin toward the back of the house. With that, she turned and disappeared into the shadowy hallway. If Chester questioned this woman's value as a cook and housekeeper, he must have grave concerns regarding her abilities as a nurse.

Cedra followed Chester into the house, and Micah closed the doors behind them.

Chester's clinic was located on the Main Street side of the house. Micah knew that earlier, when Chester first opened his practice, he'd had an office downtown, but he disliked the noise in the daytime and the inconvenience at night, so after a couple of years he had the ground-floor guest rooms in his home remodeled and moved his office there.

Mrs. Eggers did not move quickly. She was still lighting the lamps when the rest of them made their way into the room. Micah took a match from his pocket and lit the four lamps above Chester's examination table.

These lights showed Micah more of Polly's face than he wanted to see. The flesh around her right eye looked like ground meat. The eye was swollen to the point where only a slit remained between the upper and lower lids, and through this slit Micah could see that the eye itself was as red as the blood that seeped from the wound on the girl's left cheek.

Mrs. Eggers stood with her mouth agape.

"Mrs. Eggers," Chester said, "don't stand there staring. Get me some water so I can wash up and clean these wounds." The woman didn't move. "Now!" he snapped. Mrs. Eggers jumped, her hands leaping to her breast like two fat quail startled into flight; finally, she left the room.

"Polly," Chester said, his tone the opposite of what it had been a moment before with Mrs. Eggers. "I know you're in pain, and I'll give you something for it in a bit, all right?" There was a softness to Chester's voice that Micah had never heard.

Polly didn't answer.

"Polly," he said again, "can you hear me?"

"Yes," she said. A tear leaked from the narrow slit of her eye.

"Do you know who I am?" Chester asked.

"Yes," she answered. "Dr. Hedstrom."

"That's right. I'm going to fix you up, but you have to tell me everywhere it hurts. Will you do that?" All the while he was talking, Chester was feeling her head, neck, and shoulders. His hands moved down her arms, along her breasts and ribs. As his hands moved, his eyes never left Polly's face. All the while, he spoke in that soft, musical voice, which, to Micah, sounded alien to the Chester he'd always known.

"It hurts here." Polly's fingers moved toward her face, but Chester caught her hand.

"Anywhere else, Polly? Does it hurt anywhere else?"

"I—I don't think so, no," Polly said. Her hands drifted down to her abdomen and she held herself. "Just my face. My eye and jaw."

"Does this make it hurt more?" he asked as his fingers explored her jaw line and throat.

"No, not more."

Mrs. Eggers came into the room carrying a steaming pan of water. She poured some of the water into another pan on the table beside Chester, and she took the remainder to the counter on the far side of the room and placed it next to a basin.

"All right, Polly," Chester said, "you lie still for a moment. As soon as I wash my hands, we'll get you cleaned up."

As he turned to go to the basin, he asked Cedra, "What happened here, Mrs. Pratt?"

Chester asked the question as though it held no more significance than an inquiry about the weather, but Micah could hear something more in Chester's voice. It was unspoken, but there was another question beneath the surface. Micah had no idea what Chester was asking, but he knew it was there. And he knew he was not the only one aware of it. When Chester asked the question, Micah saw the knuckles of Polly's fists whiten.

"We were leaving Mr. McConners's party," Cedra said, nodding in Micah's direction. "Polly and I had stayed to help clean up."

From the table came a whispered, "No." Micah, who was now standing closest to the girl, expected he was the only one who heard it. It was less than a whisper. It was as much a groan as an articulated word.

"As we were leaving," Mrs. Pratt continued, "I stopped to talk to one of the women. Polly wasn't feeling well, so she walked on ahead."

"No." The sound was louder this time, although not much. Polly was watching her mother with an intense expression, but Micah saw that Mrs. Pratt, whose attention was focused on Chester, hadn't noticed.

"She was on Fourth Street, between the park and Mrs. Jordan's boarding house, when he attacked her—"

"Momma, *no.*" Polly came up from the table. Her good eye was wide and filled with panic. "No, no!" she screamed. "You can't tell anyone! He warned me. *No!*"

Chester whirled around and came back to the girl. He put his arms around her and said, "It's okay, Polly. Shhhh. It's all right."

Polly bared her teeth and kicked the heels of her shoes against the table so hard that two of the buttons on the right one popped open, and the shoe came halfway off. Micah grabbed her feet and was amazed at the slender feel of her ankles. The bones were thin and fragile. They were so light, they felt hollow like the bones of a bird. But she was strong.

"Fetch the ether, Mrs. Eggers," Chester said. He held the girl's arms and shoulders. She strained against him so hard that cords the size of pencils stood out in thick relief along her neck.

"No, no!" she screamed over and over. Tears mixed with the blood on her face, and lines of thin red soup ran onto the linen that covered the examination table. "Nooo!" she wailed. "Momma, nooo! Nooooo!"

Mrs. Eggers returned to the table carrying a gauze mask in one hand and a tin container in the other. She handed them to Chester.

"Here, Mrs. Pratt." Micah nodded for the woman to take Polly's feet, and he went to the head of the table and held the girl's arms. Chester turned his head and poured a small amount of the container's contents onto the mask. In an instant the room filled with a heavy, medicinal odor. Chester placed the mask over Polly's mouth and nose. The moment he did, her struggling slowed. In another moment, it stopped altogether, and the room was silent except for the girl's smooth, even breathing.

When it was clear she was sleeping, they let her go. Micah looked down at the battered, injured girl and wondered what kind of man could do this sort of thing. Polly, a small young woman, appeared even smaller and more fragile as she lay before them unconscious.

Cedra, standing at the foot of the table, said, "Oh, Polly." The woman's long, trembling fingers rose to her lips. Without blinking, she stared down at the face that a few hours earlier Micah had noticed was so pretty. He watched now as Cedra's eyes filled, brimmed, then overflowed. "My baby," the woman whispered. "My little girl."

Chester bent over the table and tied off the last of the catgut sutures he'd used to close the wound on Polly's cheek. Once the knot was tied, he trimmed the end with a pair of chromium scissors. When he was done, he stood erect, winced as he rubbed the small of his back, and said, "She'll have a scar." He handed the scissors to Mrs. Eggers. "But it's along one of the natural lines beneath the eye, and it won't even be noticeable."

Mrs. Eggers put the scissors away, then poured the dirty water into the basin. Chester continued to rub his back as he said, "After you've disposed of that water, Mrs. Eggers, you may call it a night."

"All right, doctor," she said, and left the room.

"The anesthetic will wear off within the hour," Chester said. "When she comes around, I'll drive the two of you to Mrs. Jordan's in my buggy. Polly'll still be a little groggy, and I expect she'll sleep well tonight. Tomorrow, though, she may have some pain." He went to a cabinet in the corner of the room and took down a small pasteboard box. "If so, give her one of these tablets." He tapped the front of the box with an index finger. "But don't exceed the dosage printed here." He handed the box down to Mrs. Pratt, who sat in a straight-backed wooden chair. She had sat in the chair without speaking during the entire course of Chester's cleaning and suturing her daughter's wounds.

"All right, doctor," she said. "Thank you." She had regained her composure. To Micah she seemed too composed. She was now stiff, formal, and overly polite.

Chester crossed to Polly and lifted her left eyelid. He looked at the pupil and allowed the lid to drop. "All right," he said, turning around and facing Cedra, "would you like to tell me what happened?"

The woman gave a curt shrug and said, "She was beaten." Without saying more, she crossed her legs. When she did, her dress rose above her ankle. Mrs. Pratt was at least sixteen years older than Micah, but he couldn't help but notice what a handsome ankle it was.

"It's obvious, Cedra, that she was beaten," Chester said. Exasperation ruffled his words. "Now if you'll tell me by whom, I'll have Brad Collins throw the man in jail. I'm sure Earl Anderson would be happy to prosecute whoever beat the hell out of Emmett Pratt's daughter."

"Stepdaughter. Soon to be ex-stepdaughter," she said.

"Yes," said Chester, "so I've heard. You're planning to sue Emmett for divorce."

Cedra looked at Micah. "As soon as your lawyer friend here can draft the papers."

"Divorce is a serious business, Cedra. I don't have to tell you that. You're an intelligent woman. I'm sure you've given it considerable thought and you have your reasons. But your relationship with your husband is not what concerns me. My concern right now is for your daughter. Now tell me who is responsible for this beating she received."

"Well, Dr. Hedstrom," Mrs. Pratt began, "Polly's terrified of what the man will do if anyone finds out, but, despite that, I will tell you." She raised a finger for emphasis. "I'll not, however, tell Sheriff Collins. He would never have the courage to make an arrest, anyway." She placed her hands in her lap and laced her fingers together. She turned her gaze to the floor and drew in a deep breath, held it, and exhaled. Without looking up, she said, "The person who beat my daughter was her stepbrother, Sonny Pratt."

Micah could see the surprise flash across Chester's face. He wondered if by Mrs. Pratt's answering that question, she had also answered the unspoken question he'd heard Chester ask her earlier.

She had responded to Chester in a matter-of-fact voice, without emotion. Now she lifted her gaze from the floor, and when she did, she appeared more like the woman Micah had met at the park that afternoon. She pinned her powerful gray eyes to Chester, held him fastened, and said, "But you didn't ask who beat her, did you, doctor? You asked who is responsible for her beating, and the answer to that question is you."

Micah had no idea what she was talking about, and he looked to Chester, expecting some reply.

But Chester only returned the woman's hard gaze with a look tinged with sadness. "Micah," he said without taking his eyes from Cedra, "would you mind leaving us alone?"

Chapter Four

When Chester Hedstrom graduated from secondary school at the age of sixteen, he wanted more than anything to become an engineer. He was fascinated by machinery of all kinds. He loved their function, their form, and their power.

At the age of twenty, Chester graduated *cum laude* from the Colorado School of Mines with a degree in mechanical engineering and was immediately hired by a firm in Pennsylvania that was in the business of manufacturing locomotives.

Chester's first month on the job was exciting. The engines produced by the factory were beautiful. And to Chester, equally beautiful was the machinery used by the factory in the production of those engines. It was as though the factory itself was a huge machine, and all the machines used within the factory were components of that greater machine.

The smells, the sounds, the power that surrounded the place were all exciting.

But by his sixth month, he realized he'd made a terrible mistake. He still appreciated the theory, the mathematics, the physics of engineering, but he discovered he had no talent for what he was doing. He'd even become a joke. He heard the snickers of the workmen as he walked past them on the factory floor. And he knew everything they whispered was true. Chester had the skill to master the concepts of engineering, but he lacked the ability to translate those concepts to the cold, three-dimensional world of steel.

By his eighth month he had submitted his resignation and applied for admission to the Columbia College of Physicians and Surgeons. After all, Chester told himself, the human body was a machine. Like any engine, the body required fuel, maintenance, and repair. As it happened, Chester found that his aptitude for medicine matched his aptitude for engineering, but with medicine he had the ability to translate that aptitude into everyday life. He accomplished this by possessing a sensitivity to the needs of his patients.

At least until now he had believed he was sensitive to the needs of his patients. But maybe Cedra Pratt was right. There was a lot he didn't understand. It could be he was responsible for what happened to Polly tonight—not because of something he'd done, but because of something he had refused to do.

What they asked of him, though, was too much.

"I'm sorry, Cedra."

"Sorry?" Cedra said, looking past him at her daughter. "That's a wonderful word, isn't it? *Sorry.*" She turned her gaze back to Chester and, with a look that seemed to drop the room's temperature she said, "No matter what you do, if you're sorry, and you tell the person you've wronged how *sorry* you are, then you're absolved. It's magical. What power there is in that one word, *sorry.*"

Chester had known Cedra since before she married Emmett Pratt. He'd always admired her strength. After the death of her first husband, she had returned to normal college and obtained her degree. She had become an excellent teacher. And she did all this while raising her little girl.

"What would you have me say?" he asked.

"That you'll reconsider."

He shook his head. "I can't do that."

"Why?"

He stood, shoved his hands in his pockets, and walked to the window. He stared out into the night. There was no moon, and the darkness was heavy.

"Why?" Cedra repeated. "What happened to Polly is not her fault, Chester."

"Of course it's not her fault. Neither is it my fault. It's Sonny Pratt's fault. I think we should notify the sheriff and Sonny should be punished."

"Sonny wouldn't be punished." She said this without explanation. She didn't need to explain. Chester knew what she said was true. It wasn't only that Sonny's father was a powerful man. He was, but the sons of powerful men and the powerful men themselves had faced justice in this county before. Not in recent years, perhaps—not since Brad Collins and Earl Anderson had begun to administer the law. They were both more concerned with the feathers in their own nests than with justice. But it wasn't that Emmett Pratt wielded influence. In fact, Pratt's influence was minimal. He was powerful and well-to-do, but most people in the county thought both Pratt and Sonny got by with way too much.

The biggest reason Cedra was right when she said Sonny wouldn't be punished was because Sonny Pratt was smart. Chester knew Sonny well, and Chester was certain there would have been no witnesses to his beating Polly. Chester expected Sonny would have even arranged an alibi. In the end, it would be Polly's word against his. Besides, it was clear from Polly's reaction earlier that she would be unwilling to testify against her stepbrother.

There was prairie and cedar-covered hills outside the window, but it was impossible to see into the inky night. Instead, what Chester saw was his own reflection, and below his shoulder he could see Cedra sitting in her chair, her hands folded, watching him.

Cedra was fourteen years older than Chester and had always

been a beauty. As a teen he'd had a boyish crush on her. In those callow years he would have done anything she asked.

Now, though, the only time she had ever asked him for anything, he had told her no.

Did he resent her for what she wanted from him? Many people had to face what she and Polly were facing. Perhaps this situation was more complex than usual. Chester realized its complexity when Cedra answered his question about who had attacked her daughter. Still, it wasn't fair that she would lay this burden on him.

He watched in the glass as Cedra stood and crossed to the table where Polly lay. She took the girl's small, limp hand in her own. "When I said it wasn't Polly's fault, I wasn't talking about what happened tonight. I was referring to the other thing."

He nodded. "I understand. When I asked who beat her, I was sure the answer would also tell me who the father was. I guess I'm not surprised it's Sonny. He's always had a way about him."

With that Cedra looked toward the ceiling and laughed out loud.

"Chester," she said, wiping an eye, "this is not the results of some little affair. It did not happen that way. Polly did not become mixed up with some boy."

With effort Chester forced himself to turn from the woman's reflection and face the woman herself. "No," he said, "not *some* boy, her stepbrother."

Cedra lowered her head and pinched the bridge of her nose. She looked older and very tired. "No, Chester," she said, looking up. "Polly didn't have a romance with Sonny Pratt or anyone else. This situation is not because of *anything* Polly did. That's what I am telling you."

Chester was confused, and it must have shown, because in a tone of bitter exasperation, Cedra said, "Chester, Polly is—" She stammered. "She's expecting because Sonny and two of his friends carried her down by the river two months ago and spent an afternoon taking—" Again she stammered. "—taking advantage of her."

She stepped around the table and came toward him. "Sonny Pratt is responsible for what happened to Polly at the river," she continued, "but you, Chester, are responsible for what happened tonight."

"Because I wouldn't perform the surgery you requested?" he asked, knowing what her answer would be.

"Precisely."

"That's ridiculous." He wasn't going to let her do this to him. He felt bad enough without assuming the responsibility for Polly's beating.

"We've already moved out of Emmett's house. If you had been willing to end her situation, my daughter and I could have begun our struggle to get over this nightmare. As it is, there is no getting over it, not ever. Both Polly and I will be dealing with this for the rest of our lives."

"What you ask me to do is a criminal act," Chester said. "You came in here last week wanting me to commit a crime, Cedra. Now you tell me it's rape, but even that doesn't change anything. The law doesn't make allowances for rape. As a matter of fact," he added, "even your seeking an abortion is a crime. Merely asking for it carries a six-month jail term."

Her jaw set and her lips disappeared. "I don't give a damn about what is or is not a crime." She flung her arm in the direction of the table and said, "My daughter was beaten tonight, Chester, *beaten,* and it is only going to get worse. This happened because Polly approached Sonny at the picnic today and told him of her condition. Yes, it was a stupid thing to do. Sonny had threatened her before, right after they'd finished with her. She was still lying in the weeds on the river bank, and he stuck a knife under her chin and said if she told anyone what had happened he would cut her throat."

Chester suddenly felt tired. He crossed to the chair where Cedra had been sitting earlier and dropped into it. "Why would she tell him?" he asked. "What did she want him to do?"

"I'm sure she didn't know. Polly's beside herself over this. She can't sleep. She can't think straight. She told Sonny she would make him pay for what he'd done. She said she was going to the sheriff, and even if the sheriff refused to arrest him, she would still tell everyone in town."

"That's exactly what she should do," Chester said.

"I agree. I've tried to get her to do that very thing, only report it to the marshal in Cheyenne, not Collins. But she won't. I would do it myself, but she becomes hysterical every time I mention it. You saw how she was tonight. What she said to Sonny was an empty threat. In truth she's terrified of him."

"Why would she provoke him like that then?"

"Anger. Humiliation. The frustration of having no control. Most of all, the horror of bearing a rapist's child. I think a part of her wanted him to kill her right there. It would be quick and over with. And I've known Sonny since he was ten years old. I'm surprised he didn't."

Chester didn't say anything, but he had to agree that Sonny Pratt was capable of murder.

"But he won't be able to risk the truth coming out once people know of her condition," Cedra continued. "When Polly starts to show, I'm convinced Sonny will kill her."

Chester could feel the muscles in his shoulders tighten. Like thunder preceding a storm, this tightening meant within the hour he'd have a headache that would lay him low.

He rubbed the back of his neck. As he did, he heard a rustling, and he turned toward the sound. Polly, her face now swollen almost beyond recognition, pushed herself to a sitting position. Chester stood and was about to go to her, but after a step he stopped. She leveled her one good eye at him and stared across the room without speaking. He returned her gaze, and he could see her sadness. Her hopelessness and despair made him ache. As he searched that wounded face, he saw that although at eighteen Polly still had her youth, this girl who clung to his examination table was no longer young.

CHAPTER FIVE

Jackson Clark was not impressed with Chester Hedstrom's hot dogs. He'd eaten half of one, tossed the rest in a garbage barrel, and went back to drinking beer. Once the picnic broke up, Jackson had made his way downtown to Buck's Saloon, where he spent the next six hours socializing with the boys. Now, as he pushed himself back from the bar, his legs felt a tad wobbly, and he told himself it must be because—like a fool—he'd skipped his supper.

He drained the last bit of suds from the bottom of his mug, blotted his mustache with the back of his hand, and tossed Buck a two-fingered salute from the brim of his derby. "I'll be seeing you, Buckley," he said as he turned toward the door.

"Where you headed, Jackson? It's still early yet." Buckley Daggett was a ruddy-faced fellow with a thick chest and a gut that hung low over the front of his white apron. He was originally from Tennessee and had come to Wyoming as a young trooper in the army. Although sizeable and healthy-looking, Buck was an infirm man whose left arm was drawn up and shrunken. He had been stationed at Fort Fetterman during the Indian hostilities, and once while out on patrol, he'd taken an arrow in the shoulder. It was a painful and unpleasant experience, and his arm had never been the same since.

As a result, Mr. Daggett had no fondness for the red man. Many times he'd asked patrons whose features were darker than average, "You ain't an Injun, are ya, mister?" He was mindful of the Wyoming Statute prohibiting the sale of spiritous drink to Indians. And he took it as his duty to warn any customers of that law whose appearance suggested an ancestry on this continent that might predate the Mayflower's famous voyage. He would give them this warning with a wicked smile while jabbing the thumb attached to his good arm toward a sign behind the bar that proclaimed in blood-red letters, "No Indians Allowed."

Except for this prejudice, he was a friendly enough man with a personality suited to the dram-shop trade.

"You're welcome to one on the house," he called out to Jackson. Buckley was a shrewd businessman and often coaxed his customers into having just one more. But Jackson Clark always stayed until he was done, then, even with the promise of a free drink, he would leave.

"No, sir. Thanks, though," he said. "Except for half of some kind of sandwich that defies description and two of those vinegary eggs of yours—" He pointed toward a large jar of hard-boiled eggs at the end of the bar. "—I've not had a bite to eat since breakfast. It's time I was on my way." He bade farewell to all his cronies and stepped out into the night.

Once outside, Jackson pulled his watch from a vest pocket. He held it out the full length of his arm, both in an effort to catch the light that spilled from the barroom window and to bring the numerals, which seemed to get smaller every year, into better focus.

Not quite ten.

He wondered if Lottie's would still be open. He craned his neck in an effort to see up Second Street, but he couldn't tell if her lights were lit or not.

Lottie's Café was not officially recognized as offering the best food in town. That reputation went to the restaurant in the Glendale House Hotel. But let the travelers and passersby do their dining there. The locals and the railroaders alike knew the truth: Whether all you wanted was a steak and potatoes, or some of that strange Louisiana French stuff she liked to serve, Lottie Charbunneau's was the place to eat in Probity.

Jackson made his way down Second, and once there, he saw lights were still burning; but when he tried the front door, it was locked. He rattled the knob a couple of times trying to find the right degree of jiggle to communicate an eagerness to come in without being brusque. He prided himself on his ability to walk thin lines between getting what he wanted and accomplishing it without seeming pushy. He liked to think he acquired that characteristic as part of his lawyerly training, but he knew in truth it was one of the many traits that kept him from success. The most successful lawyers didn't give a whit if someone thought they were pushy. Many of them honed their pushiness skills both night and day.

After a bit, Lottie herself, wiping her hands on a rag, came out from the back of the café and cracked open the door.

"Lottie, dear," Jackson said, giving her his most pitiful but charming smile, "I realize you're closed for the evening, but what's the chance you could fry me up a steak? I'm starving, and you're my only hope."

Jackson had known the woman ever since she'd landed in town eighteen years before. Lottie, her husband, Gaston, and their daughter had been traveling from Louisiana to the Yellowstone country Gaston loved so well. They had made it as far as Probity when Gaston took a slight fever. It didn't seem serious at the time, but a week later the Frenchman was dead. Jackson Clark had openly questioned the Gallic ability to ward off disease ever since.

"Are you drunk, Jackson?" the woman asked in her scolding Southern drawl. She was small and thin, but she had the voice of a woman twice her size.

"Drunk? Why *Madame* Charbunneau, you know I would never attempt to enter your premises while intoxicated."

She cocked her head and looked him in what he suspected were his bloodshot eyes. It was his eyes that often gave him away. "Don't you lie to me, lawyer," she said.

Shamed, he lifted his thumb and index finger and held them an inch apart. "All right," he said, "maybe this much."

She nodded. "At least that much and more, I'd wager." But she opened the door wider and allowed him in. She often bent her rules for Jackson. He'd helped her establish herself in this community when no one else would. "Lock that door after you," she said as she tightened her apron. "I'll fix you up a steak—a small one—but if you ain't done by the time I'm finished my cleanin', you'll be leavin' anyway, and what's left of your supper'll be goin' to Rufus." Rufus was the small terrier that always slept under the table at the rear of the café. It was a table reserved for Lottie to do her books and was never used by customers.

"Lottie," Jackson said as he slid into a chair, "you're a lifesaver. A Samaritan. A—"

He was about to go on, but the tiny woman stopped him with an arched eyebrow. "I don't want to hear it," she said. "I know that almost never stops you, Jackson Clark, but it's late, and I've had myself a long day."

"Well, then, my dear, with that you may count on me to remain as quiet as a mouse. I'll not say a word. Silence shall become my motto. If I—"

She gave him a look, and he ended his sentence by clearing his throat.

He enjoyed teasing Lottie, but he knew he could only go so far. Although he'd never asked, he guessed that Lottie was not yet fifty. Though she was not unattractive, he had to admit she looked every bit that old. But she'd had a hard life, one full of labor. They were friends, and she had told him some about her early years.

She'd been born a slave in Iberia Parish, Louisiana, and had lived as one until Mr. Lincoln had signed his proclamation and beyond since the war raged on as it did. During her slavery days, she'd taken a husband and born him two sons. Reconstruction was not well accepted in south Louisiana, and Lottie's husband had been an outspoken sort of fellow. Outspoken Negroes did not endear themselves to the local population, and one night their house was set afire and the husband and both boys died. Lottie might have died too, but at the time she was a live-in maid at a mill owner's home outside of New Iberia, and she spent only one night a week with her family.

She was twenty-two when that happened. The day after the funerals she asked the mill owner for her pay, and she left Iberia Parish and moved to New Orleans. It was there while working in a restaurant she met Gaston Charbunneau.

He was a Frenchman who had immigrated to Canada and after a bit came to America by way of the Rocky Mountains. He loved the high country, but he'd always longed to see the city of New Orleans.

"We was in love from the second we laid eyes on each other," Lottie had once told Jackson. "We was married in a week, and nine quick months later we had us a baby girl."

They continued to live in New Orleans for the next five years, but their lives were hard. Folks did not take to a white man, even a Frenchman, marrying a colored. Eventually Gaston had enough. "He'd always promised to show me the geysers, so one day we jus' picked up and headed north for the Yellowstone. Left Loosi-anna forever, and good riddance to it," Lottie had said.

She pulled an onion from under a cupboard and sliced it into the frying pan. "I reckon you'll be wantin' onions on top of this steak and some potatoes on the side as well," she said in a put-upon voice.

"Well, Lottie, I am mighty hungry," Jackson admitted. "I haven't had much in the way of food today."

"If you paid as much attention to your eatin' as you do your drinkin' I expect you'd be a whole lot fleshier."

"I'd planned to eat, Lottie," Jackson said, defending himself. "It's not like I forgot. I went to a picnic Dr. Hedstrom put on up at the park. I was going to eat there, but you would not believe what that man was serving. Long skinny sandwiches with the strangest meat you ever did see."

Lottie laughed. "That Dr. Hedstrom, he is the beatin'est, ain't he?" She flipped Jackson's steak and stirred the onions. "This afternoon one of my customers said he saw the doctor ridin' some kind of motor-powered bicycle right down the middle of Main Street. He had horses and people runnin' every which way." She took a pot from the stove and poured Jackson a cup of coffee. "What was he havin' a picnic for, anyway?"

"It was a welcome-home party for his friend Micah McConners. Seems I have some new competition in town." He lifted the cup and took a sip. "Micah was admitted to the bar a couple of days ago. He's come home to practice law."

As he said that, Jackson felt eyes on him, and he looked toward the far end of the room. Lottie's daughter stared at him from the doorway that led to the back. Jackson was always pleased to see the girl. She was bright, pleasant, and, at least to Jackson's way of thinking, the prettiest girl in town. "Why, hello there, Fay, darlin'," he said. "I didn't hear you come in. How long've you been standing there?" The girl didn't answer. She stared at the old lawyer without answering. "What's the matter, girl?" he asked with a smile. "Has the cat got your tongue?"

CHAPTER SIX

He would hate to do this sort of thing every day of his life, but Micah had to admit he enjoyed manual labor. A little of it was good for the soul—not too much, but a little. For his tastes, Micah had been doing more than a little for the last five days, but he was about finished, and he was pleased with his efforts.

Micah had rented the Stimpson property the first morning after arriving back in Probity, and he'd been fixing it up ever since. The first thing he did was clean the place from top to bottom. Joseph Hoover, the fellow who had rented the property prior to Micah, was fond of chewing tobacco. And though Mr. Hoover was a gentleman in most respects, he was negligent with his aim and rarely hit the spittoon. The floors of all three rooms were glazed with dried tobacco juice.

After the cleaning, Micah had to repair the lath and plaster in a couple of places and put on a fresh coat of paint.

It was a long, narrow building divided into three rooms. He made the room closest to the street into a waiting area, although it was hard to imagine he would ever have clients enough that waiting would be a problem. The second room he made his private office. And the room in back was where he meant to live.

Two days earlier he had applied at the First National for a loan of five hundred dollars. This morning the check had come through, and he had already spent the entire amount down the street at Collier's Furnishings.

For the first room, he bought three chairs. If the day ever came when he needed more chairs than that, he expected he would be able to afford to buy them. He furnished the third room with only a bed and a small chiffonnier. He also bought a scattering of accessories: tables, lamps, and pictures for the walls. But it was in the second room where he'd spent the bulk of the money. He had purchased two sets of book cases—of course, he had not yet purchased the books to go in them—two chairs for clients and one for himself; and the pride of his shopping spree, a dark oak desk manufactured by the Merle and Heaney Company of Chicago, Illinois. It was the finest desk Mr. Collier had. Although it cost more than he should have spent, Micah had coveted the beautiful desk from the moment he set eyes on it. And in his effort to become more pragmatic, he reminded himself he'd be spending the largest portion of his life sitting at a desk, it might as well be the finest.

Now he had only one thing left to accomplish and he'd be ready for business. He carried a stepladder out to the boardwalk, climbed it, and drilled four small holes on the outside wall to the left of the front door. He lifted the sign Chester had hired Carpenter Pecker to build—Micah smiled when he thought of that—pulled four screws from his pocket, and stuck them into his mouth.

He was finally going to hang his shingle. This was a big moment, he told himself. One that deserved a fanfare with trumpets and drums. There should be a Greek Chorus behind him, filling the afternoon with its voices. The hanging of this shingle was, Micah mused, the culmination of years of dreaming and hard work.

He closed one eye as he aligned the holes in the sign with the ones he'd drilled. It was awkward balancing on the ladder, keeping the screw holes lined up, and at the same time trying to get the first screw started. He could use an extra pair of hands.

As he told himself this, he felt the ladder wobble. His stomach lurched, but, luckily, as he was about to fall, he caught himself—or, at least, he thought he had. A half-second later the ladder shook again, and he knew in one sick stomach-dropping instant he was going down.

The shingle and screwdriver clattered to the boardwalk, and as he spit out the screws, he shouted an obscenity that was seldom heard on the streets of Probity. He pin-wheeled his arms, scooping the air in an effort to regain his balance.

At the moment he reached the point of no return, he felt one hand on his leg and another on the ladder. As quickly as the ladder had started to go, it was now steady again, and the rungs were solid under his boots.

He grabbed the wall and exhaled in a gush. "My good God, that was a close one," he said. "Thanks a lot. I nearly broke my—" He stopped when he realized he was staring down into the dark, bottomless eyes of Fay Charbunneau.

She checked the ladder to make sure it was secure, and through her dimpled smile she said, "I should think, Mr. McConners, an attorney, a man versed in the law, would know better than to break the most basic law of all."

Micah stared at her stupidly. She was even more beautiful than she had been three years before. Her brow was ruffled as she looked up at him, and the slanted light from the afternoon sun accentuated the height of her high cheekbones and the fullness of her lips. Micah swallowed away the lump clogging his throat and mumbled, "What law would that be, Miss Charbunneau?"

"Why, the Law of Gravity, of course." She turned up the heat on her smile, flicked a strand of her thick, curly hair behind her, and stepped off the boardwalk into the street. "It's good to see you back, Micah," she said over her shoulder.

He clutched the wall as he watched her walk away. She was a

small woman, but her shoulders were wide. Her back tapered into a tiny waist, and her hips flared, pushing against the thin cotton of her summer dress.

He closed his eyes and took a deep breath; when he opened them again she was gone.

Micah decided he would ask Chester to help him put the shingle up later. Right now, feeling his heart thump against the inside of his chest, he eased himself down the ladder.

CHAPTER SEVEN

Chester sat in a rocker at his bedroom window sipping from a tumbler of milk. The only sounds were the metronomic tick of the clock and the counterpoint squeak of the chair. Chester was a poor sleeper, and often he'd wake in the night. He hated lying in bed, so in the winter he'd get up, stoke the fire in his bedroom hearth, and sit and watch the flames. In the summer, he'd move his chair to the window and stare into the night. Usually the combination of a half hour's worth of rocking and a warm glass of milk would make him drowsy enough to get back to sleep, but Chester knew that would not be so this time.

There were lights across the way in the dark pasture. They were shining, disembodied little orbs that floated a foot or less above the ground, soaking up the soft glow cast by the moon and stars and transforming it into something more than it was. They were eyes, of course—the eyes of predators: raccoons, skunks, foxes. These were animals with eyes evolved to a higher level than man's, capable of cutting through the gloom, making the darkness irrelevant.

In many ways Chester envied those creatures. They knew their motivation. They were well cast and comfortable in their roles. They never questioned their blocking nor brooded over their lines.

He exhaled a noise that was part snicker, part sigh. He had carried that metaphor about as far as he dared. But it was true; sometimes he did envy the lower creatures' lack of self-awareness. They played no conscious part in their own evolution, and Chester was convinced that humans did. We had choices. Now—or soon—we'd have more choices than ever. And with those choices there was responsibility.

Polly and Cedra were coming into the office this afternoon so he could remove Polly's stitches. He hadn't seen them since the night Polly was attacked, but they'd filled his thoughts almost every minute since.

Choices.

The eastern sky was turning a pinkish gray, and the glowing eyes of the small creatures were beginning to dim. Chester drank the last of his milk, pushed up from the rocker, and crossed to his wardrobe. He took off his dressing gown and night shirt and dressed in jeans, shirt, and leather vest. He pulled on an old pair of boots and left the room. He stepped quietly on the landing so as not to wake Mrs. Eggers, whose room was at the far end of the hall. The walls of Chester's room had been confining, and he ached to be outside. Once he got to the foot of the stairs, he hurried to the foyer, grabbed his riding cap and goggles, and left the house.

A warm breeze wafted in from the west, and Chester filled his lungs with the clean morning air. He loved the fresh smells of Wyoming. That was the thing he'd missed most during his years of living beneath the sooty skies back East.

He went around to the carriage house, opened the door, and walked in. It was dark inside, but Chester didn't need to light a lamp. He knew what he was looking for and where he had left it. He crossed toward the double doors to where Uncle Oscar's moto-cycle leaned against the wall. He pushed open the doors and rolled the machine outside. He had repaired the bent wheel a couple of days before but had not had a chance to try it out.

Although it was still dark, the sky was a little brighter, and there was enough light to ride by. He straddled the seat and shoved off. After three quick pumps of the pedals, the motor caught. Chester pushed the speed lever forward, and the cycle accelerated with a head-snapping jerk. It was not the lumbering rise in momentum felt on a train, nor the loping acceleration of a horse. This acceleration was pure and smooth, unlike anything else. He pulled his cap down a notch along his forehead and increased the speed. The feeling of it, the pure joy, pulled his lips into a smile.

He rode down Main toward the river faster than he knew he should, but he couldn't resist. He didn't even try. Riding the moto-cycle was like flying a magic carpet two feet above the ground. He loved the feel of the road beneath his wheels, the bounce and spin of the hard rubber tires, the blur of the buildings on either side.

He crossed the bridge west of First Street and, beneath the buzz of the motor, he could hear the North Platte—low now in the late summer—lap against the bridge's pilings. Past the bridge, the road became rougher, but Chester handled the moto-cycle with skill as the tires clawed at the ruts.

The land rose as it moved away from the river, and Chester climbed toward the foothills that lay at the base of the Laramie Mountains. Two deer munching grass beside the road looked up in apparent bewilderment as he rode past, their graceful necks lifting high above their shoulders, their ears pricking toward a sound that no deer in this part of the world had ever heard.

Chester was amazed at the freedom the moto-cycle provided. And, as he rode farther into the hills, he realized this freedom—this *kind* of freedom—was more than a word or even a concept. It was also a feeling, an emotion. The rush of air past his face opened his senses. It blew away the dust and cobwebs that had of late collected in his head.

Still Chester increased his speed, leaning into the road's wide curves, feeling the weight of the machine roll from side to side beneath him. He rode for another five miles and came to a stop at the crest of a tall hill. He shut the motor down, and the silence filled the morning, wrapping around him like a cloak. He propped the cycle against a large boulder and climbed to the top of the boulder and looked out at the world.

To the south were the serrated aretes of the Laramie Mountains, with Laramie Peak itself, at over ten thousand feet, rising high above the rest. To the east he looked down onto Probity, and beyond that, the prairie stretched wide toward the horizon.

Still buzzing from the moto-cycle's vibrations, he tried to rub the tingling out of his arms. But it wasn't unpleasant and, after a bit, he shoved his hands into his pockets and allowed the feeling to fade on its own.

He realized as he looked down on Probity that the ride up had been the first time in days when his thoughts hadn't been full of Cedra and Polly. At first he'd been angry with them for what they wanted. What they asked of him was criminal. But now his anger toward them lessened, and he focused it on the fools who would write a law banning abortion and make no allowance for rape. Even if abortion itself was immoral, and Chester thought it might well be, ending a pregnancy that came about as Polly's had was not immoral. But, intense as it was, that anger, too, began to dim.

He breathed in the crisp, damp air. The day would be warm later, but right now he could detect a hint of autumn. He looked forward to it. Spring and autumn, the seasons of change, were the times Chester enjoyed the most.

No, he was not angry any longer. Anger was not an emotion Chester could hold on to. Now he realized that as far as his role in all this was concerned, it had nothing to do with Cedra or even Polly. And it certainly had nothing to do with the band of buffoons who met in the capitol down in Cheyenne and drafted their narrow legislation. His decision had only to do with him, Chester Hedstrom, and his view of the world.

He would not be shamed into helping Polly by the guilt Cedra Pratt tried her best to inflict. Nor would he be prohibited from helping her by a law drafted by idiots.

As the sun lifted above the horizon, the shadows lengthened. Traffic began to stir through the streets below. And Chester watched as the town stretched, rubbed its eyes, and woke, preparing itself for another day.

Polly winced as Chester plucked the last stitch from her cheek. "There," he said, moving his thumb along the thin scar. "It's red now, but that'll fade with time. In a few months you won't even notice it."

Polly didn't respond, but Cedra, who stood behind the chair in which Polly sat, said stiffly, "Thank you, doctor."

There was bruising on the girl's face, but the swelling was gone, and it was clear to Chester that Polly would be pretty again.

Perhaps.

At least she *could* be pretty again if it were not for the severity that edged her eyes and the corners of her mouth.

They were in Chester's private office. It was a small room down the hall from the examination and treatment room where he had last seen the girl and her mother. He often tended to patients with minor complaints in here. It was more comfortable and less intimidating.

Chester washed his hands and blotted them dry on a towel. He found he had been washing his hands a great deal in the last few days. Without turning, he said, "Things are not as simple as they once were, Cedra."

"No," she agreed, her words seasoned with weariness, "they're not."

He turned to face them. "I've been considering what you said the other night." Cedra stood more erect, and Polly seemed to slump. "Fact is, that's about all I have been doing." He tossed the towel to the counter. "This is quite a problem we have here." He walked to Polly and lifted her chin. It was the same gesture he had used earlier when he was examining her injuries, but this time he was looking at deeper wounds. "They've hurt you, girl, and the truth is there's not a thing in the world anyone can do about that. Only time can fix it."

She pulled her chin back from his hand and looked down at the floor. There was no rudeness in the gesture, merely a drifting away.

"I know it doesn't seem so now, but trust me," he said, "time's an effective medicine. The body's been designed to heal wounds wherever they are. Whether here." He pointed to the scar beneath her eye. "Or here." He lifted his hand and touched the backs of his fingers to her brow. "At least it's been designed to heal almost anything as long as complications don't set in. You're a strong, healthy young woman, Polly. And I know you could overcome what these boys did to you if it weren't for what's come along with it." He raised his eyes to Cedra. "It's a sad thing, but the loathsome manner in which this impregnation came about is a complication and not only because of what Sonny Pratt might do, although there certainly is that, but also because the pain of that horrible event will never allow all the wounds to heal." He was looking at Cedra as he spoke, but he could sense Polly wince when he mentioned Sonny's name.

Cedra's eyes began to fill, and a single tear wedged its way out and leaked onto her cheek.

Chester turned and crossed to the door. "Sometimes when complications set in, for the good of a patient, we have to perform aggressive therapies we might not otherwise perform. What's wrong in one situation isn't necessarily wrong in another."

He opened the door and called down the hall. "Mrs. Eggers, would you come in, please?" He stood at the door waiting. When the woman arrived, he said, "Please, Mrs. Eggers, prepare the surgery."

There was nothing scheduled, and the woman looked puzzled. "Now, doctor?" she asked.

"Yes, please," he said, "now."

When she was gone, Chester turned back to Cedra and Polly. "We do have a complicated and difficult situation. One filled with hard choices. But I have to do what I feel is necessary for the welfare of my patient."

Cedra wiped the tear away, cleared her throat, and said, "Thank you, Chester."

He responded with only a nod.

"No," she said, not allowing him to dismiss it. "I mean it. Thank you."

"We've not grown up in a very flexible age, Cedra, none of us. Perhaps that's the American race's only real shortcoming, its tendency toward rigidity. But things are more complex now. What's right is not always so obvious. Sometimes the rules have to be bent so they fit around more complicated situations." He paused for a second and looked over at Polly. She looked nervous, but the lost expression she'd had earlier was gone or at least beginning to fade. "These," he added, "are unique times."

He was glad his choice was made. The law was what it was, and maybe it was an appropriate law in most cases, but not in all.

Both of the women smiled across the room at him. He saw their great relief at his decision, but he sensed their surprise as well. He doubted they had ever expected him to agree. Despite their relief, they looked at him as though he were some uncommon sort of creature.

And along with their relief and surprise, Chester saw something else on their faces: bewilderment. They reminded him of the deer he'd encountered on the road earlier that morning.

With that thought, Chester was smiling too.

CHAPTER EIGHT

Emmett Pratt had not been involved in his own haying in a long time. That was what he had a grown son and a bunkhouse full of hired hands for. But since Cedra left, he needed more to occupy himself than riding around on horseback watching other men work.

"Pump some water, Sonny," he said, pointing toward the pump handle. Sonny did as he was told for once, and Emmett leaned out over the trough and felt the well-water splash across his head and the back of his neck. It was icy cold, but it felt good. Emmett was hot. He might even have a touch of sunstroke coming on, and he needed cooling off fast.

He allowed as how stacking hay might not be a job for a man almost fifty years old, especially one who wasn't used to it.

"Damn, ol' man," Sonny said with a snigger. "You look like you've about had it."

"Keep cranking that handle," Emmett said. He let the water wash over him a while longer, then tilted his head and drank some. He stopped himself before he swallowed too much. When he stood erect, he felt some better, but it was clear to him that piling up winter feed on a hot August afternoon was a chore he'd been better suited for in younger times.

He pulled a kerchief from his rear pocket and wiped his face and neck. The boys were still out in the field cutting, but, though Emmett hated to admit it, he'd had enough. It had been a long, hot week, and he'd worked right alongside every twenty-year-old on the place.

He'd never liked the practice of farming his feed anyhow. He was a cattleman, not a damned sod buster. When he'd first come out to this country the prairie grass was higher than a tall man's ass. A fella's cattle could eat their fill summer or winter wherever they found it. Hell, one spring he'd located a bunch of his cows nearly sixty miles to the east. It was an open range in those ancient days, and they'd wandered that far over the course of the winter hunting grass not covered in snow. But that was fine by Emmett. Rounding them up in the spring was part of it. It was a lot better than fences, and it was a whole lot better than keeping them penned all winter and feeding them hay. To Emmett Pratt's cow-savvy way of thinking, cattle should be able to come and go as they damn well pleased; that's why they wore brands. But, of course, the open-range days, like plenty of other good things, were gone forever.

Emmett tied the wet kerchief around his neck and looked across the trough at his son. Sonny was a handsome kid, nearly six feet tall, lean and hard. He had strawberry blond hair like his mother and eyes the color of an old pair of jeans. But the boy didn't have his mother's disposition, never did. Emmett Pratt had been a lucky man at finding good women. They didn't make them any better than Alice, his first wife, nor Cedra, his second. He lost Alice to a cancer, and Cedra . . . well, he wasn't sure what it was he'd lost Cedra to, but he guessed it was to the loyalty a man has to show toward his son.

"What're you doing in from the field, anyhow?" he asked. "Why aren't you out there with the rest of the crew?"

"Come in to change my shirt," Sonny said. "Me and the Joneses are headed into town."

That was what Emmett had figured before he had even asked. "God-damn it, Sonny, it's the middle of the week and there's haying to be done."

"It's getting done," Sonny said, jerking his thumb back over his shoulder toward the crew in the field.

His loyalty was not fading, but Emmett was beginning to admit to himself—if not to anyone else—that Sonny had grown to be a disappointment. The boy had always been a little wild, even before his mother died. Now, though, he'd become more than wild. He was mean. Emmett knew that. But there was still some good in him. Sonny wasn't as bad as Cedra believed he was. And as much as he loved that woman, Emmett couldn't accept as true what Cedra said. Sonny would never harm his stepsister. Never. It came down to Sonny's word against Polly's and Cedra's, and in the end, Emmett had to go with his son. That was how it had to be. Even if it cost him what he knew had been a happy marriage to a fine woman, there was nothing else he could do.

"You're not going into Probity tonight," Emmett said. He figured telling Sonny that would cause some ruckus, but before his son could answer, they heard horses coming down the road. Emmett turned in time to see Hank and Lester Jones ride into the yard.

"Heya, Sonny," Hank called. "Mr. Pratt." He made a gesture toward his hat.

Hank was twenty, the older of the two brothers, and right at Sonny's age. Hank and Lester's parents had both passed on, and the two boys were left to run their small ranch out on La Bonte Creek. From what Emmett could tell, they were pretty much running it into the ground.

"Mount up, Sonny," said Lester. "Let's get-a going. Time's a wastin'." Lester was a dull-looking kid of about eighteen. His teeth were terrible. What few he had left poked out in every direction and were black around the edges.

Hank took off his hat and whacked his brother in the face so hard it left a welt across Lester's cheek. "I don't know what your hurry is," he said. "That whore Becky'll be spending her night screwing every cowboy and thimble rigger in the county before you get a chance at 'er."

Lester gave his busted picket fence grin and said, "Ah, hell, she'll make time for me, Hank. That girl loves me dearly." He rubbed the red welt with dirty fingers, but didn't complain to his big brother about it. This was likely not the first unexpected smack to come Lester's way.

"Loves you," Sonny said with a laugh. "She'll love you as long as you got yourself a couple spondulicks you ain't got a problem with handing over to that whore-keeper Adelaide." Adelaide was Probity's bawdy-house proprietress.

Emmett suspected his son was more than a little familiar with the inner workings of a bawdy house.

Sonny climbed aboard his sorrel.

"Sonny," Emmett said, "you heard me. You're staying home tonight."

"Well, sir," Sonny said, reining his horse's head toward the gate and the road beyond, "I reckon you're as wrong about that as you can be, ya ol' coot." He gave out a high-pitched laugh, gigged the sorrel, and led the two brothers off in a lope.

Emmett Pratt had little experience with having his wishes ignored, but it seemed he exercised less and less influence over his son. He knew he was to blame for the way Sonny turned out. The boy was ten when Alice died, and Emmett had never been much of a father. But deep down where it counted, Emmett still believed Sonny was a good boy.

From the shadow's slant, it figured to be around five o'clock. He'd hoped to get all this field cut by the end of the day so they could get started on the field by the river tomorrow morning. It didn't look like that was going to happen, though, now that Sonny was quitting early.

Emmett looked around and found his straw hat on the

ground beside the trough. He picked it up and placed it on his head. He considered going inside for a rest, but with Cedra gone, the house was an empty place. Besides, he felt better now. The hot spell that had come over him earlier had passed.

He pulled off the kerchief, pumped some water over it, then tied it back around his neck. Yes, sir, he told himself as he headed off to the field to give the boys a helping hand, his son could be ornery, but at heart Sonny was still a good boy.

CHAPTER NINE

That man must take me for a fool, Mrs. Eggers told herself. A blind fool at that. She was standing in the kitchen peeling a potato and watching through the window as the doctor and that Pratt woman helped her young strumpet daughter into Hedstrom's buggy. Did he think she didn't know what he'd done that afternoon? How stupid did he think she was?

She had never liked this job, and she had never liked this Dr. Hedstrom, either, with his strange ideas and his foolish little gadgets. She'd taken the position only because the pay was good and it provided a place to live. Those were the only reasons. She was a housekeeper, not a nurse. She had never wanted to be a nurse, but in this job she was forced to be both.

Hedstrom helped the women into the seat of the buggy and climbed up beside them. He snapped the reins, and the three of them drove off. Mrs. Eggers could see Polly's head loll against her mother's shoulder. Hedstrom was giving them the ride because the little harlot was too groggy from the anesthesia and weak from the surgery to walk the few blocks to Mrs. Jordan's boarding house.

She didn't care what butchery he practiced in his surgery, but she resented being taken for a fool.

In a burst of anger, she threw the potato to the counter. It bounced against the wall and rolled onto the floor. She started to retrieve it, but stopped. The devil with it.

She left the kitchen and went into the parlor. She opened the

81

liquor cabinet and poured herself a brandy. Mrs. Eggers had developed a fondness for brandy before when she was working as a maid in a school for wayward girls in Omaha. It was in those days she had begun keeping a bottle hidden in her room. There was a bottle in her room now, but why drink her mediocre stuff when she could enjoy the wealthy doctor's best?

Mrs. Eggers had been around the girl Polly enough to suspect her situation. She became even more suspicious when Hedstrom unexpectedly had her prepare the surgery—more suspicious yet when he did his procedure without having her assist. But the oddest of all, he cleaned his own mess, something the man was never prone to do. She'd gone in, though, afterward, and she saw what implement he'd used. That was when she knew. Despite her distaste for the nursing profession, she had learned some things in the doctor's employ. He had used the curette, a spoon-like instrument designed for scraping the uterine wall.

She took a long drink of the brandy. She loved the sting of it in her throat and the warming once it hit her belly.

Hedstrom would not be gone long. It wouldn't take twenty minutes to deposit the little whore in her bed. She tossed back the last of her drink and started for the kitchen to wash the glass before he returned. She was nearly to the parlor door when she came to a stop.

She had seen abortions before, Mrs. Eggers had. She'd performed three herself during her days at the school in Omaha. With two of them she hadn't received much pay for her services—the girls had very little—a locket here, a gold bracelet there. But the last girl, a year or so after leaving the school, had married a well-to-do businessman, and Mrs. Eggers had siphoned a goodly sum from that one before she was done.

Yes, the woman thought. A goodly sum indeed.

She held the crystal snifter up and looked through its smooth surface. Perhaps she needn't rush to wash the glass after all. With a smile, she decided another slosh of the brandy would really hit the spot.

She returned to the liquor cabinet, took down the decanter, and poured herself another drink. Glass in hand, she sat in the doctor's overstuffed chair and lifted her feet to his ottoman.

The little tramp in Omaha who married well had been eager enough to pay to keep her handsome new husband from learning the truth. Mrs. Eggers expected that with the possibility of prison staring him in the face, the haughty Chester Hedstrom would be willing to pay as well.

Yes, she mused, she expected that he would.

She sipped from the snifter more slowly, letting the warm liquid trickle down, and felt herself smile again with the thought of how surprised the good doctor would be when he learned she was not the fool he had taken her for after all.

CHAPTER TEN

Micah plucked his hat from the rack by the front door, stepped out onto the boardwalk, and locked the door behind him. He had not been outside his new office in a day and a half. That both infuriated and frightened him.

He would not allow the blue devils to take him over again. There was a time when the melancholia would lay him so low he couldn't get out of bed for days. It was like falling. Slipping and falling into a well, tumbling deeper and deeper down. But lying in bed had not been an option in his years with Judge Pullum. In time, Micah discovered that forcing himself to perform regular activities would usually help some. Not always, but usually, and not a lot, but some.

It did feel better to be outside. It was warm but breezy, so the heat wasn't bad. A million stars salted the black sky, and there was no reason—not one in all the world—that he should feel low.

But he did.

He set out down the boardwalk, and the clomp of his boots drummed a hollow cadence.

Was it Fay, he wondered, who brought this spell on? He knew it would be unfair to blame his depression on her. Over the years he'd suffered hundreds of bouts with low spirits that had nothing to do with Fay. But he couldn't discount the effect she always had on him, both good and bad. Even long ago when they would see each other, there was never a time when the sight of her didn't cause something inside him to move. They might be separated by a crowd of people, and with a sidewards glance she could cause his internal geologic foundations to shift—collide like tectonic plates in an earthquake.

Fay Charbunneau was an intoxicant to Micah; that was a fact he'd learned to accept. He was certain this effect was not something she plotted, although he was also certain she made no attempt to lessen its impact. He had tried to explain it to her once, and she'd laughed. She didn't laugh in an unkind way, but she'd laughed nonetheless, so Micah had never brought it up again. He had devoted many hours to pondering this ability of hers to make him drunk, but he didn't understand it any better now than he had the first time one of her smiles had caused his head to swim.

When he turned the corner on Main, he could hear the piano music coming from Buck's. It sounded as though the town revelers were having a fine time. Any other night, Micah might have joined the fun. Tonight, though, he kept walking. He wandered all the way down Main, across the tracks to the river. In the darkness, the North Platte looked like a channel filled with paint, black and viscous. He continued north along the river's east bank. Occasionally he'd stop long enough to toss a stick into the water and watch it turn lazily, as though it was reluctant to begin its long journey to Nebraska and beyond. He'd spent many summer afternoons sitting on this bank. He would jam the butt of a fishing pole into the rocks and lay back and watch its line strain against the current.

He continued upriver a ways, climbed the rise, and walked toward the station. His father used to say every major event for the last seventy-five years, in one way or another, had begun at a train depot. Micah expected things to continue that way forever, but now the station was as quiet as stone.

That was when he saw them, Lottie and Fay, side by side,

walking from the café toward their small house on North First Street. His inclination was to step back down the rise toward the river, but he didn't.

Later he tried to lie to himself. He pretended not dropping out of sight had been a conscious decision, that doing so would be childish and would merely delay the inevitable. But he knew the real reason was much simpler than that.

Though Fay was at least fifty yards away and the night was a dark one, already Micah was too drunk to move.

"Micah McConners, is that you over there staring at us from the darkness?" Lottie bent forward and squinted into the gloom.

"Yes, ma'am, Mrs. Charbunneau, it is." Micah was doing his best to keep his eyes on Lottie, but it wasn't easy. Like metal shavings to a magnet, they were drawn to the young woman by Lottie's side.

"Well, I'll swun," Lottie said. "Jackson Clark was in to the café t'other night, and he said you was back in town."

"Yes, ma'am. I've been here a few days now."

"And you haven't been in for some of my pie?" They were beside him now and she reached over and smacked his hand. "Shame on you, boy. Did you take on some of them strange Cheyenne ways since you've been gone?"

"Now, Momma," Fay said. There was a faint tinge of the South around the edges of her voice.

"I tried my best not to become too strange," Micah said. "And I did miss your pie, Mrs. Charbunneau. There's none like it anywhere that I know of."

"So what's been keeping you away, boy?"

"I opened an office, and I've been fixing it up."

"Ah, yes, you're an attorney-at-law now, aren't you?"

"That's right."

"Well, good for you, Micah. Good for you." She turned to her daughter. "I'm headed on now, girl," she said. "I'm tired to death. Are you comin' or are you goin' to stay and visit?"

Before he could catch himself, Micah said, "Please, Fay. Could you stay for a bit?" He'd been avoiding her for at least as long as he had been back in town, and if this situation were a case at bar, any lawyer worth his salt could argue that Micah had been avoiding her for the last three years; but now, when faced with watching her walk off into the night with her mother, Micah stopped her before he could even think.

"All right, Micah," she said. "A while."

"Don't you be too long, now," Lottie said.

"No, Momma, I won't."

"And don't you be makin' yourself so scarce, you hear, Micah?"

"Yes, ma'am."

Micah and Fay watched without speaking as Lottie walked off. Once her mother was out of earshot, it was Fay who broke the silence. "I missed you, Micah," she said.

And with that, Micah wanted to grab her. He wanted to pull her to him and crush her into his chest. He wanted to smother her with kisses, and in a torrent of words tell her how he'd spent every waking moment thinking of her, and how every sleeping moment, she had filled his dreams. He wanted to shout that for three years he had missed her too, that he ached with missing her, that there had been times when he thought the pain of missing her was going to drive him insane. Those were all the things he wanted to say. What he said was, "Yes, it has been a long time, hasn't it?"

But Fay would have none of it. "You are such a fraud, Micah McConners," she said with a laugh, and she turned and flounced down the embankment to the river.

"A fraud? What do you mean?" he asked, following along behind.

"Exactly what I said." She stopped at the bank's edge and

Robert D. McKee

looked out over the dark water. What little moonlight there was soaked into her and made her glow.

"I am *not* a fraud," he said, but when she turned and fixed him with her smile, he had to laugh. He was laughing not at his own absurdity—although that was funny enough—but he was laughing at how this woman amazed him. He was amazed by her beauty. He was amazed by her intellect. But most of all, he was amazed by her skill at reading him. "All right, damn you, Fay. You're right. I'm a fraud. I am the most fraudulent man I know." And he pulled her to him and kissed her. He kissed her long and hard. And as he held her in his arms and pressed her lips into his, he felt as though he were falling into the sky.

★ ★ ★ ★ ★

Part Two:
Polly's Decision

★ ★ ★ ★ ★

CHAPTER ELEVEN

As Chester pulled into the carriage house, he was pleased the ordeal was over. There had never been an occasion when he'd had more difficulty deciding the best thing to do. But now that it was done, he knew the choice he'd made was the right one.

He unhitched Mary, took off the harness, and led the mare to her stall. He grabbed a brush and gave the horse a quick rub.

"Good girl," he said. Mary answered with a soft snort, shoved her nose into the bin, and folded her lips around some oats.

Under the circumstances Chester had no regrets. Unpleasant and difficult as it was, it had been right to do it, and sometimes the right thing was not the easy or pleasant thing. Chester was convinced that if more people accepted that idea as true, the world would be better off for it.

The whole thing—all of it—had been hard on Polly, and it would take time for her to get better, but at least now she *would* get better.

For a while he'd considered going around Polly and Cedra to the law. Sonny Pratt deserved to be brought to task for what he had done, but finally Chester had decided against it. That would not help Polly. It might have made things worse.

Chester hung up the harness and threw a cover over the phaeton. Before he blew out the lamp, he glanced into the corner where the moto-cycle leaned against the wall. It made him feel good to look at it. Shiny and blue. Uncle Oscar was going to make a fortune on these things. This Sunday Chester would take Micah for a ride. Maybe they'd go into the mountains. If Micah resisted, Chester would berate and humiliate him until the poor wretch gave in.

With a smile, he told himself how nice it was to have his friend back home.

As Chester walked up the path toward the house, he realized he was hungry. He'd had little appetite the last few days, but now he was starved. He wasn't sure what Mrs. Eggers was cooking for supper, but whatever it was, he expected he'd be piling on double portions.

The door from the back porch led into the kitchen, and Chester was surprised when he came in and didn't see Mrs. Eggers at her cooking chores. It was already late. They always ate well before now.

"Mrs. Eggers," he called out. When there was no answer, he left the kitchen and walked into the hall. He could see a light coming from the parlor, and he headed in that direction. "Mrs. Eggers," he called out again. Still there was no response, but when he rounded the corner into the parlor, he saw her. She was sitting in his good chair, the one he'd had Mr. Collier order from the factory in North Carolina. Her feet rested on the ottoman, and she held a snifter of brandy.

"Well, Mrs. Eggers, taking a little rest, are we?" He pointed to the decanter on the table beside her chair. "That looks to be just the thing. I think I'll join you." He crossed to the cabinet, took down another snifter, and poured himself a drink.

"I hope you don't mind me helping myself to your fine liquor, Doctor," the woman said.

"No, not at all." Chester knew Mrs. Eggers drank, but he'd never noticed his liquor supply diminishing, so he suspected she kept private libations in her room. It didn't matter to him what she did. She was a terrible employee, but that wasn't due to strong drink.

He lifted his glass. "Cheers," he said.

Mrs. Eggers nodded and said, "Same to you." She took a drink, staring at him over the rim of the glass as she did. "You've had a busy day, haven't you, Doctor?"

"Yes, very," he said.

Every morning after breakfast, Mrs. Eggers walked to the post office for the mail. Today's was on the writing table in the corner. Chester thumbed through the letters as he spoke. "So what's on the menu this evening, Mrs. Eggers? I'm famished."

"I haven't decided yet," she said.

Chester glanced at the wall clock. "You haven't decided?" He assumed she was making a joke—although she never joked—and he punctuated his question with a quick laugh of disbelief.

"That's right." She snuggled herself down deeper into the easy chair. "For you, I'm thinking crow."

Chester leveled his gaze at the woman, and for a long moment their eyes held. "What are you saying, Mrs. Eggers?"

"I'm saying you made a terrible mistake today, young doctor. You were thinking dumb old Mrs. Eggers was too dim-witted to know what you were up to, but you had better give your thinking a second thought; that's what I say." She took another long pull of the brandy.

"What the devil are you talking about, woman? Put that glass down."

She lowered the glass and a snarl curled her lips. "Don't you take that tone with me," she said. Her feet came off the ottoman, and she sat forward in the chair. "You *abortionist.*"

When Chester didn't respond, Mrs. Eggers leaned back in the chair and replaced her feet on the ottoman. She took a dainty sip of the brandy and blotted her lips with a fingertip. "You scraped that little tramp's baby out of her today, and you thought no one would be the wiser. Well, sir, there's laws against that sort of thing. Laws with harsh penalties, too, I expect."

Still Chester said nothing, but he crossed to another chair and sat down.

"I don't reckon a fellow with your fine sensibilities would fare too well in the state penitentiary. The majority of the folks who populate that institution aren't prone to gentlemanly behavior." She smiled and replenished her snifter. "I doubt the warden is one to let you have all your books and little gadgets in your cell, either. Yes, sir, your manner of living is apt to go through some serious changes real soon."

Chester set his glass down and cleared his throat. "Well," he said, "it sounds as though you've come up with some sort of plan, Mrs. Eggers, in the time you've spent not cooking my supper."

"That's right," she answered, "I have. Being an honest citizen, Doctor, it pains me to have heinous crimes and criminal activities taking place in the house in which I lay my head every night. I feel it's my duty to inform the county prosecutor of your misdeeds. My guess is he would like nothing better than to get his hooks into you, you working against him the way you did in his last election and all."

"I imagine you're right about that," Chester admitted. "Earl Anderson has no fondness for me. That's for sure."

"Hate for you is what I hear," Mrs. Eggers offered with a smirk.

"So, let me guess, you have some idea as to how we might avoid involving Mr. Anderson in all of this. Am I right?"

"You're a regular mind-reader, aren't you, Doctor?"

"No clairvoyance needed to read your mind, Mrs. Eggers. What is it you want?"

"A sum of money would do nicely," she said. "A sum of money, and I'll be on my way, never to trouble you again."

"What sum were you thinking?"

"Ten thousand dollars is nice and round, isn't it?" Like a coy girl, she cast him an innocent smile.

"Yes, it is. All those zeroes make it very round, indeed."

She finished off the last of her brandy, set the snifter aside, and stood. "So ten thousand is what it will be," she said, her innocence gone. "Ten thousand dollars cash money, or I fix it so you go to prison. Those are your choices, *Doctor.*" She spat out his title.

Chester slapped the palms of both hands down onto his knees and pushed himself up. "Well, Mrs. Eggers," he said, "it appears you have me."

"I'll say I do." She waggled a finger at him. "You figured me for a fool, and that's where you went wrong."

"I expect you're right about that," Chester agreed. He dug his right hand into his trousers' pocket and pulled out a medium-sized wad of bills. He peeled a ten-dollar note from the outer fold, crossed the room, and handed it to her.

Mrs. Eggers took the bill and looked at it as though she'd never seen one before. "What's this?" she asked.

"I'm not positive," Chester said, "but I believe a decent room at the Glendale House goes for about three dollars a night." He took her gently by the upper arm and led her out of the parlor, through the foyer, and to the front door. "Ten dollars should be more than enough to see you through till tomorrow. I'll have your things packed and brought to you in the morning. I'll also figure what salary you have coming and send that along as well, plus two weeks' severance." He gave her an easy nudge across the threshold onto the front porch. "Good-bye," he said.

The woman's mouth was moving, but no sounds came out.

He started to close the door but stopped himself. "By the way, Mrs. Eggers," he added with a smile, "I'd suggest you not use me as a reference."

She was staring at him, her mouth agape, as he pushed the door closed.

CHAPTER TWELVE

Micah saw Fay the moment he stepped into the general store. The Bell sisters, Edith and Arlene, were at the counter paying Mr. Tucker for the goods they wished to purchase, and Fay stood back away from them waiting her turn. At first Micah thought she held only a bag of flour, but with a smile, Fay lifted a six-inch strand of red ribbon. It was a joke between them how well Micah liked her hair pulled back and tied with a red ribbon.

When Micah came in, Mr. Tucker glanced up from his pencil-work. He always provided his customers with meticulous receipts. "Morning, Micah," he said in his crisp New England tones. He had arrived in town three years before when Micah put the store up for sale, and Mr. Tucker, who had experience in Vermont at the storekeeping profession, bought the store and all of its inventory without any haggling at all. Micah offered it at a fair price, but he had expected at least some negotiation. It seemed Mr. Tucker was more skilled at selling than he was at buying.

The women at the counter turned at the storekeeper's greeting and chimed, "Good morning, Micah."

Micah smiled and nodded to Mr. Tucker. To the women, he took off his hat and said, "Ladies." He turned to Fay. "Good morning, Fay," he said. "You're looking well."

"Mr. McConners," she answered, dropping her eyes. There was always more of the South in Fay's voice when she spoke in public than there was when they were alone. Micah couldn't understand why she did that, and once he mentioned it to her. All she would say was, "The whites expect it."

Micah had come in to buy cigarettes, and he was in a hurry. Cedra Pratt was due in his office in less than fifteen minutes. They were to discuss the filing of her divorce.

"Now are you sure you ladies can carry all that?" Mr. Tucker asked. "I'd be glad to have Jamey take it to your house." He jerked his head toward the hired boy who was in the corner stacking shelves.

"That won't be necessary," Edith said. Edith was the more talkative of the two spinster sisters. "We have our basket." She patted the handle of a large wicker basket she had resting on the counter. "We'll do fine."

Micah stepped to the tobacco counter, picked up two packages of Cyclones, and started back. It would be more economical to buy tobacco and rolling papers, but Micah liked the convenience and the snug packing of the factory-rolled cigarettes.

As he made his way to the front, the Bell sisters were leaving, and Mrs. Henry Thompson came in. "Why, as I live and breathe," she said, "if it isn't Edith and Arlene." Mrs. Thompson was the mayor's wife and among the elite of Probity society. "We missed the two of you at the box luncheon after church last Sunday." She shook her finger at them. "Reverend Boyson took me aside personally and asked me wherever could the Bell sisters be."

"Oh, Muriel," Edith said, "we hated to miss it, but we had to leave right after the sermon. Arlene, the poor dear, was having terrible . . ." She glanced around, leaned forward, and whispered in Mrs. Thompson's ear. From all the way across the room, Micah could see Arlene Bell redden.

"My, my," said Mrs. Thompson, giving Arlene a consoling

touch on the shoulder, "I do so hope you're feeling better now."

"Yes," Arlene said in a near whisper. "Thank you."

As the women conversed, Fay placed her flour and ribbon on the counter. Mr. Tucker hefted the bag of flour onto his scales. "All right," he said peering over the tops of his spectacles, "that's right at five pounds of flour." He folded the top of the bag over and put it back on the counter. "And one piece of ribbon. Will there be anythin' else for you, girl?" Tucker asked.

"No, sir, that's all."

Tucker was adding it up when Mrs. Thompson bade her farewells to the Bell sisters and came to the counter. "Good day, Mr. Tucker," she said. Looking past Fay, she said, "Micah."

Micah nodded.

"Would you please fill this list for me, Mr. Tucker?" She handed him a piece of paper that was covered in her swirly cursive.

Tucker took the list. "Of course, Mrs. Thompson. I'd be glad to." As a rule, customers gathered their own merchandise and brought it to the counter to pay. Some patrons, though, chose to have it done for them.

"And if you don't mind," Mrs. Thompson said, "I am in quite a hurry." She stepped from the counter to examine the bolts of material stacked on the shelves along the far wall.

Tucker turned to Micah. "What do you have there, Micah," he asked, "two Cyclones?"

"Yes, I do, but—"

"I'll need a few minutes to fill this order. Go on and take 'em. You can pay me when you come in next time." He ducked his head to the list and made his way around the counter toward the back of the store.

"But, Mr. Tucker," Micah said, "Miss Charbunneau was—" He stopped when he felt Fay's hand on his forearm. He turned to look at her. Her face was stern.

"Hush, Micah. It's all right," she whispered. "I'm not in any hurry. Please, let it go."

CHAPTER THIRTEEN

It was perfect. Ideal. It couldn't be better. These were the thoughts that raced through Earl Anderson's mind as he and Sheriff Collins walked through the door of Chester Hedstrom's clinic. As far as Anderson was concerned, the Eggers woman coming to his office that morning had been like a gift. Now the self-righteous doctor was finished.

And as a bonus, not only could Anderson bring the loathsome Dr. Hedstrom to justice, he could win the favor of Emmett Pratt at the same time. Everyone knew the Pratts were about to become involved in a case of divorce. And although Anderson had no intention of bringing charges against Cedra Pratt, she no doubt was in this with Hedstrom up to her eyebrows. Once that got out, Mr. Pratt's position in the divorce proceedings would improve greatly. Being the man responsible for that improvement might come in handy when Anderson began collecting campaign contributions for his reelection.

Yes, indeed, this showed every sign of working out well.

When Anderson and Collins entered the clinic, Dr. Hedstrom walked into the reception area from one of the back rooms. He was with Flan O'Toole, an Irishman, who, the best Earl could tell, was ninety-five if he was a day. The old coot inched his way across the floor, steadying himself with a cane. But to his credit, Earl allowed, he was moving under his own power. Earl held open the door, nodded, and gave the codger a gracious smile. It was his most practiced smile, the one he used on the constant blur of fools he was forced to encounter every day.

Neither O'Toole nor the doctor acknowledged his or Collins's presence.

"Now if that hip keeps giving you trouble, Mr. O'Toole," the doctor was saying, "you send someone over to let me know. I'll come out to see you. I don't want you on it any more than you have to be for a while."

The man nodded without speaking. He seemed to focus all his concentration on the simple act of executing the three steps that led from the clinic's porch to the ground below. Hedstrom walked beside Mr. O'Toole all the way to the man's wagon and helped him up into the seat. Hedstrom then unwrapped the reins from around the brake handle. "Here you go," he said, handing the reins over. "You sure you can handle this team all the way to your place?"

"Aye hitched 'em up, an' Aye drofe 'em in," O'Toole said in his thick brogue. "Aye reckon Aye'll b'able ta dwit a-gin."

"All right," Hedstrom said. He'd been standing on the hub of the front wheel, and he hopped down and gave a wave. "You take care of yourself now, Mr. O'Toole."

The man snapped the reins, and the wagon lurched away. Hedstrom watched for a bit as the old Irishman moved into the center of the street, then turned left on Fourth and headed out of town. Once O'Toole was out of sight, Hedstrom turned back to Earl and Collins, who were standing on the porch. He climbed the steps and walked between them back into the clinic.

"How old are you, Earl?" he asked.

Earl and Collins followed him back inside. "Thirty-seven. Why?" Earl could not stand this man, and he was wary of anything Hedstrom had to say.

"When you're Mr. O'Toole's age, the year will be nineteen fifty-nine. Imagine that. The new century'll be more than half over. Think of all the wonders you will have seen. Hell, by then, they may have even developed a cure for stupidity."

Earl felt his skin flush and his fury rise. Seeing Brad Collins cup a hand over his smile didn't help, either. He gave the worthless sheriff a look hot enough to burn the smirk off his dull face.

"You can make your jokes now, Hedstrom. That's fine. But you may not think things are so funny once you realize why we're here."

Two leather sofas were set at right angles against perpendicular walls of the waiting room. Hedstrom dropped down on one and crossed his legs. He gestured for the men to have a seat on the other. Collins started to do so but stopped when Earl said, "We didn't come here to visit."

"No?" said the doctor. "Golly, Earl, I'd so hoped you had. I was about to offer you gents a cup of tea."

"Everything's a joke with you, isn't it?"

"Not everything," Hedstrom corrected. "Your being in a position of public trust, for instance. I can't find one single thing amusing about that, although, God knows, I've tried."

Earl gave him his mean smile. It was the smile he saved for those he particularly disliked. "You might be finding it even less amusing here in a bit."

"I cannot imagine," said the doctor, "how that could be possible."

"I received a visit from one of your acquaintances. She was sitting in the hallway outside my office when I came to work this morning."

"Don't tell me. Let me guess." The doctor stared at the ceiling and tapped his chin with an index finger as though he was pondering all the many possibilities. Finally, he said, "Could it have been a Mrs. Eggers, late of my employ?"

"Exactly," Earl confirmed.

"Well," said the doctor, clapping his hands together, "what a lucky guess."

Earl dug his fingernails into the meat of his palms. Even when Hedstrom was not attempting to humiliate him, the man's very manner made Earl furious. This time, though, Anderson would not allow him to get away with his arrogance. He puffed out his chest. "If the vaudeville is finished," he said, "perhaps we can get on with the business at hand."

Earl lifted the monocle that hung from a gold chain around his neck and inserted it over his right eye. "Mrs. Eggers has made the accusation that you performed an abortion yesterday afternoon."

"My, my, what a concerned citizen Mrs. Eggers has turned out to be."

"Yes," Earl said, "I think so too." Anderson was not a stupid man. The doctor's attempt at irony regarding his ex-housekeeper was not lost on him, but Earl knew something the doctor did not. In front of a jury, it could easily be made to appear as though Mrs. Eggers's actions were, indeed, those of a concerned citizen.

"So, what now?" asked the doctor. "Do you drag me away in chains?"

Now they were in Anderson's domain, and he was beginning to feel more in control. He gave a friendly chuckle, allowing the monocle to flick from his eye. "Chains? You do have a flare for the dramatic, don't you? You really should have gone on the stage. These accusations have been made. We are obliged to look into them. Of course we want to hear your response, if any."

"So, if I deny what she says, you'll leave. Is that it?"

"Well, I shouldn't think it would all go away that easily," Earl said with honesty.

"No, I shouldn't think so, either."

"I expect we would have to question the Pratt women. Perhaps investigate their involvement as well."

"All right, what do you want to know?"

"Not so much. We're curious to know if what Mrs. Eggers says is true. Did you perform an abortion on Miss Polly Pratt yesterday afternoon here in this clinic?"

"Yes," Dr. Hedstrom admitted without any hesitation. "I did."

For a moment Anderson was stunned into silence. He couldn't believe what he was hearing. He'd never doubted this sanctimonious know-it-all had committed the crime. Playing God was the sort of thing he would do. After all, people like Hedstrom always felt they were above the law. But Anderson could not believe the fool was witless enough to admit it.

Earl felt his mouth stretch into a wide, natural smile. It was one that came from his core. It was not a smile designed to communicate anything in the world short of the purest of pleasure. "Then, sir," he said, making no attempt to hide his enjoyment, "with that, I shall order Sheriff Collins to place you under arrest and to take you to his jail."

Earl turned to the sheriff and said, "And I'd suggest you use the handcuffs. You never know what a desperate criminal might do."

CHAPTER FOURTEEN

Chester had always envied his father. Maxwell Hedstrom had been large and powerfully built. With his broad moustache and thick mane of hair, he'd been imposing in a way that caught the attention of the ladies and other men as well.

He had been a creature of great innate dignity—a kind of dignity that Chester knew he had not inherited. Where in an instant Max Hedstrom could win the respect of a group of people merely by striding into a room, if Chester were to obtain their respect at all, he had to strive to earn it—a process not measured in seconds, as was true with his father, but measured in months or years.

Although the man had been dead almost a decade, it was his father and his father's dignity that Chester thought of now as Anderson and Collins paraded him down Main, his wrists chained behind his back. The two men walked on either side of him, each with a hand on one of his elbows, leading him like an animal to a pen.

Chester could feel the shocked wake of silence the three of them left behind as they made their way to the jail. Busy people who a moment before had been going about their business, now stopped and stared.

As Chester, Anderson, and Collins rounded the corner on Third Street, Mrs. Elkins and her daughter Missy stepped out of Blakely's Candy Store. Missy's pink fist was clamped around a cinnamon stick. At first Missy seemed startled when the men, marching three abreast, had stopped short to keep from running her over, but with quick recognition the little girl said, "Oh, hi, Dr. Hedstrom. Look, Mommy, it's the doctor."

Mrs. Elkins, a large, ruddy-faced woman who always wore a smile, said, "Why, hello, Dr. Hed—" But with a second look, her smile faded, and she yanked her daughter back into the candy store's doorway to allow the men to pass.

As they walked on, Chester overheard the girl ask her mother what those things were on the doctor's wrists.

"Hush, Missy," her mother whispered. "You hush up right now."

Earl Anderson snickered.

Back at the clinic when Anderson had asked Chester whether he had performed the abortion, Chester had been forced to make a quick decision. He could have lied. Although he couldn't remember the last time he had told a lie, he was not so pure as to be above such a thing. Perhaps in this situation it would have been the smart thing to do. Even if Anderson had questioned the Pratt women, Cedra was strong enough and smart enough to handle the little prosecutor. In the end it would have come down to Chester's word against Mrs. Eggers, and Chester doubted the prosecution would have gone very far with that and nothing more.

But why should he lie to this weasel? To Chester's way of thinking, in a kind of perverse way, lying to someone implied respect. He would never lie to Earl Anderson.

The jail was on the other side of the street, four doors down from Micah McConner's new office. As they stepped off the boardwalk to cross over, Chester glanced toward Micah's office but could see no activity through the front windows. That was fine. He preferred Micah not see him like this.

Micah had fixed the place up nicely. The shingle looked good next to the front door. Very professional. Yesterday morning

Chester had come over and helped Micah hang the sign.

Had it been only twenty-four hours? Chester wondered. A lot had happened.

With his arms pulled back, Chester's shoulders began to cramp, but he ignored the pain and kept his head up.

Chester was amazed at the effect his passing in irons had on the townsfolk. It was as though, upon seeing him, the citizenry was frozen. A man rushing down the street on horseback reined in sharply and allowed them to walk in front. Although the rider said nothing, Chester could feel the heat of the man's eyes.

"You'll have the whole cell block to yourself, Doctor," Collins said. "Bashful Paxton's been the only prisoner I've had for weeks, and of course once he sobers up I always let him go."

Bashful was a barber who worked the second chair in Guthrie Bowls's shop. Unlike most barbers, Bashful was not the talkative sort. In fact, six days a week he would hardly say a word even if spoken to. Every Saturday night, though, he would get drunk, and when Bashful got drunk, his personality underwent some changes. He'd been known to stand in the middle of the street and shout obscenities at everyone within earshot. There was hardly a Saturday that Bashful didn't pass the night in one of the sheriff's cells.

Collins had no deputy, so he had to lock up the office when he left. Chester watched as the tall, lean sheriff pulled a key from his pocket and opened the front door. Collins stepped aside so Chester could go in. "I reckon I can handle it from here, Mr. Anderson," said the sheriff, "if you need to be getting back to the courthouse."

"No, no," said Anderson. "I wouldn't dream of leaving you alone with this criminal until you have him secured in his cell." He followed Chester through the door, adding with a laugh, "You can never be too careful."

They crossed Collins's office and walked through a door that led to a large room in back. The room held four empty cells, two on each side, with an aisle down the middle. Collins nodded to the second cell on the right. "I'll put you in here, doctor," he said. "It's got the newest mattress." He opened the cell door and followed Chester in. He pulled a small key from his vest pocket and undid the handcuffs. He draped the chain of the cuffs over his shoulder and stepped back into the aisle, locking the door behind him. To Anderson, he said, "I got some paperwork I need to do."

"Fine, sheriff," Anderson said. "I'll be right out."

Both Chester and Anderson watched as the sheriff returned to his office. Once he was gone, Anderson began to pace. For a full minute without speaking he walked back and forth staring in at the doctor. When he stopped, he leaned toward the bars and jutted an index finger toward Chester's chest. "I got you now, you son of a bitch. I got you now." The little man looked very pleased. "Do you know what you did back there? Do you have any idea?" He gave his head a shake as though astonished. "You admitted in the presence of the prosecuting attorney and the county sheriff to committing a major felony. That was the dumbest damn thing I have ever seen in my life. Yes, sir. The dumbest by far."

Chester didn't respond.

Anderson shone his unctuous smile into the cell for a bit longer. He then turned and started for the door. Halfway there, he stopped. It seemed to Chester that Anderson was having such a fine time, he didn't want to let go of the moment. "Hedstrom, your fascination with the new century is well known. You're always showing off your new toys and making your silly predictions." He moved back toward the cell and looked up through the bars. "Well, here's a prediction for you. I predict you'll be spending the first fourteen years of your exciting new century at the Wyoming State Penitentiary swinging a sledge hammer at some very large rocks." He tapped the end of his pointed nose. "That's *my* prediction for the future." With a laugh loud enough that it sounded as though it came from a man twice his size, the prosecutor departed.

During the walk from home and throughout Anderson's little speech, Chester had forced himself to remain impassive. Whatever feelings might have wanted to rise to the surface, he'd grabbed by the neck and shoved back down. He'd be damned before he showed Earl Anderson any weakness.

Now that he was alone he looked around at his bleak surroundings: the rough cement floor, the brick walls, the steel bars. Even now he fought to hold back the fear he felt bubbling inside. Perhaps this time he'd taken on too much.

He took a deep breath and crossed the cell to the pathetic bunk. He lowered himself to a sitting position, dropped his head into his hands, and thought about his father.

CHAPTER FIFTEEN

Micah slid the summons, complaint, and filing fees across the counter to Sue Anne Flagstone, the deputy clerk of the district court. He was in the clerk's office filing his first action as an attorney. The case of *Pratt versus Pratt*.

"Oh, my," hummed Sue Anne in her sing-songy voice, "this is exciting, isn't it?"

Sue Anne was a thin woman whose eyes were a little crossed. The right eye always looked askance, as though whatever minor god was assigned the task of assembling faces had misaligned the threads when he screwed the eyeball into its socket. Micah was never sure which eye he should look into.

"Our newest attorney filing his very first law suit."

She was right; it was exciting. After Cedra came to see him early this morning, he'd spent all the rest of the day holed up in his office drafting his pleadings, making sure everything was right. Every *t* crossed, every *i* dotted.

But as much as Micah wanted his first case to be a success, he was not optimistic. It was very difficult to obtain a divorce. Marriage was sacrosanct, protected by culture, custom, and law.

The statute allowing for divorce laid out eleven very specific causes for its granting. Adultery, physical incompetence of one of the parties, a spouse convicted of a felony and sentenced to prison, desertion for a minimum of one year, drunkenness, extreme cruelty, a husband failing to provide his wife the necessities of life, either party offering such indignities as to render life intolerable, a husband's vagrancy, conviction of a felony prior to the marriage of which the aggrieved party was unaware, or, finally, a wife's pregnancy at the time of the marriage by a man other than her intended husband and without the intended husband's knowledge.

Solid proof of at least one of these causes had to be provided to the court or the case would fail. The parties couldn't even stipulate that one of the causes existed; evidence by independent means had to be shown.

Micah believed society had it backward. It should be as difficult to get married as it was now to get a divorce, and it should be as easy to get a divorce as it was now to get married. With that change, marriage would become a much happier institution.

But until that day arrived, Micah had to deal with the law as written, and based on the information Cedra had provided, it didn't look good. From what she said, the conditions of her marriage did not fit within any of the eleven causes.

The one possibility, as Micah saw it, was the situation of Emmett's refusal to do anything about his son's violent behavior. After all, Micah himself had witnessed the results of Sonny's brutality at Chester's house his first night back from Cheyenne. So, based on that, Micah pled his case under cause eight, intolerable indignities. Rumor had it, though, that Benjamin Walker, the district judge from Casper who covered Probity, held a narrow interpretation of "intolerable indignities." He resented lawyers using that as a catch-all for whatever took their fancy.

"Where's Mr. Dunn this afternoon?" Micah asked Sue Anne. Marcus Dunn, the clerk of court, was a man Micah had known for years. Mr. Dunn and Micah's father had been Masons together and the best of friends. When Micah was growing up, Mr. Dunn had been like an uncle to him.

Sue Anne file-stamped and dated the documents as she spoke. "Oh, my, he's very busy today, very busy. He's out, and I don't know when he'll return. It's been so hectic. I hardly ever work past noon, but Mr. Dunn insisted I stay late while he and a couple of errand boys rounded up the grand jury."

"Grand jury?"

"Oh, my, yes, As soon as Mr. Dunn can get everyone located and brought in, Mr. Anderson is calling a special session of the grand jury."

"Why's that?" Micah asked. "Do you know?" Proceedings before a grand jury were supposed to be confidential, but Micah suspected Sue Anne had some knowledge. Courthouses were notorious gossip mills.

"Well, I don't know for sure, but my guess is it has something to do with the arrest that was made today." She handed Micah his stamped copies and a receipt for his filing fees.

Micah slipped the papers into his satchel. "What arrest was that?" he asked as he buckled down the satchel's flap.

"Oh, *my*," Sue Anne said. The sound of her disbelief caused her voice to rise an octave. "You mean you haven't heard?"

When Micah entered the sheriff's office, Brad Collins sat with his boots propped up on his desk reading a two-month-old issue of *Harper's Weekly*.

Collins peered over the top of the magazine. His eyelids were heavy with laziness. "You need some help?" he asked without taking his feet down.

"I've come to see Dr. Hedstrom," Micah said without further greeting.

Collins nodded toward the door to the cell block. "I expect you'll find him that way," he said with a smile and returned to his reading.

Chester was lying on his bunk, his hands folded across his

chest. He sat up when Micah came in, but he didn't stand.

Micah walked to the far end of the narrow aisle between the cells where Collins kept a straight-backed wooden chair. He dragged the chair over in front of Chester's cell, then straddled it, leaning his forearms across the top.

For a long moment neither of them spoke. It was Micah who broke the silence. "I admit to being new at this," he said, "but I think it's customary to send for your attorney when you get in trouble with the law."

Chester said nothing.

"It looks like Anderson keeps a grand jury impaneled in this county all the time. He's having them rounded up right now. My guess is we'll be seeing an indictment by noon tomorrow. Are you going to tell me about it, or do I have to wait to hear the barroom version over at Buck's with everybody else?"

Chester shrugged. "Not much to tell," he said. "I did an abortion on Polly Pratt yesterday. Mrs. Eggers told Anderson about it this morning—" He looked about at his surroundings and waved a hand taking it all in. "—so here I am."

Micah scratched the side of his face with his thumb and murmured, "Damn. Do you do that sort of thing often?" he asked.

"Never before."

"It's been a while since I've read that statute," Micah said, "but as I recall the only time an abortion is legal is if the pregnancy gets all fouled up and you need to do it to save the life of the mother."

Chester shook his head. "That's not the case here."

"So why'd you do it?" Micah asked. When Chester didn't answer, Micah asked again.

Finally, Chester responded with, "I had my reason."

Micah studied him through the bars. He knew his friend well, and he was certain Chester did have what he considered a valid reason for doing what he'd done. He also knew if Chester in his stubbornness decided he would not tell what that reason was, nothing Micah could say would change that. But, he told himself, he needed to try.

"Are you going to tell me what that reason is?" he asked.

"Nope," Chester said. "I'm not."

Micah didn't push it further. He knew it didn't make a whit of difference what the reason might be. Short of a mother's dying if the abortion was not performed, there was no defense to this crime. None.

"Do you have any idea how much Eggers told them?"

"No," Chester said. "But it couldn't have been much. I didn't allow her into the surgery while I did the procedure. And for the most part I was the one who cleaned things up afterward."

Micah sat up straighter. "Well, it could be they don't have much of a case."

"No," Chester said. He stood, moved to the cell door, and leaned against the bars. He gave a half-frown. It was the kind of look Micah had seen Chester give his parents many times when he and Chester were in their teens and Chester had taken something apart and not been quite able to get it back together. "I'd say they have a pretty good case."

"Why's that?"

"I confessed."

Micah felt himself flinch. It was as though they were actors in a play and he was sitting in the front row watching them deliver their lines.

"You did what?" Micah heard the actor playing him ask.

"I admitted to Anderson and Collins that I had done it."

Micah looked up into Chester's wide eyes. "Good Christ, Chester, why would you do that?"

"He asked, and I told him. Let Anderson do his worst. I wasn't going to lie to the little son of a bitch."

Micah yanked the hat from his head and slapped it against his thigh. "Who said you had to lie? You didn't have to tell him a God-damned thing. You could've kept your mouth shut; did you ever think of that?" Micah stood and turned away from Chester. He gave the chair a shove with his foot. He walked to the cell across the aisle. He had to think, and he was certain his brain worked better when he was on his feet. But it didn't seem to be working too well now. "This carries a maximum sentence of fourteen years," he said. He turned back to Chester and repeated himself. *"Fourteen years."*

"Yes," Chester acknowledged, "so I've heard."

The indictment was served on Chester in his jail cell late the next morning. Micah was with him when the sheriff brought it in.

After giving the papers to Chester, Collins turned to Micah and said, "They say they can set the arraignment in front of Porterhouse at two this afternoon if you're willing."

"I expect we will be," Micah said. "I'll let you know here in a minute."

"Good enough," said the sheriff as he went back into his office.

"What does he mean, 'if we're willing?' " Chester asked without looking up from the papers he'd been given.

"They can't arraign you in less than twenty-four hours after you've been served unless you're willing to waive that right."

"So what do you think? Should I waive?"

Micah cupped a hand around his ear as though he hadn't heard. "What's that? Are you asking my advice about something here?"

"Sure. Why not? There's no law that says I have to take it, is there?"

Micah ignored that question and answered the first one. "I

can't see any reason to wait on the arraignment. They'll do it sooner or later. We need to get bail set, anyway." He looked toward the clock on the cell block's far wall. It had been less than twenty-four hours since the arrest. This Earl Anderson was an eager prosecutor.

"So what is an arraignment, anyway?" Chester asked.

"A short hearing where the judge explains the charges to you and asks how you plead. On an indictment, it's usually held in front of a district court judge. Since Walker's not around, it looks like we're getting Porterhouse." Micah pointed toward the papers that were still in Chester's hand. "Are you finished reading those?"

Chester handed them through the bars. "Yes," he said. "Go ahead." Standing, he shoved his hands in his pockets and walked around the cell. "So they're already going to ask me how I plead, huh?"

"That's right," Micah answered while he read. He was learning a lot about Anderson by the flowery language of the man's pleadings.

"Well, that's easy," Chester said. "I'll be pleading guilty."

Micah finished the sentence he was reading before he realized what Chester had said. "What? Pleading guilty, did you say?"

"That's right."

Micah gave a quick, stunned laugh. "The hell you will," he said, coming to his feet.

Chester turned to face him. "What are you getting so huffed up about?" he asked.

"You'd be insane to plead guilty today."

"Micah, did you forget? I've already admitted to Anderson and Collins that I did it."

Micah nodded. "That's true," he said, "you're right. You've already proven you're insane, but let's not make it any worse by pleading guilty."

"Well," said Chester, flopping down on his bunk and resting his legs on the cross-piece of the bars, "that's what I'm going to do."

"No," said Micah, "you're not." He tried to sound assertive despite knowing no one had ever asserted much control over Chester Hedstrom once his mind had been made up.

Chester rose to an elbow. "What do you mean I'm not? Have I even hired you as my attorney? I don't remember hiring you as my attorney." He lay back down. "I'm sure that's something I'd remember."

"Whether you know it or not, and whether you like it or not, I am your damned attorney. At least I am until I see another one in here with you. And I'm telling you, you are *not* going to go in there and plead guilty—not today, anyway."

Chester was lying on his back looking up. "Why prolong the inevitable?" It sounded as though Chester was not asking this question of Micah, but more to himself, or the ceiling beyond the cell, or whatever it was beyond the ceiling. After a moment, he turned to Micah again and repeated, "Micah, I am pleading guilty today and getting it over with."

Micah's quick temper suddenly took over, and he was furious. "For *Christ's sake!*" he shouted. Despite his inexperience, Micah knew even as the words came out how unprofessional he sounded—how young and even frightened he sounded. "Will you *please* listen to reason, Chester?" He wondered if he might have better skills at client control with a defendant who wasn't his best friend.

If he was going to succeed in this business, he could only hope.

Chester put on a flippant air, but Micah knew better. He could see from the dark circles beneath Chester's eyes and the slight tremor in his hands how Chester was being affected by all this. It was almost enough to make Micah agree and give Chester's pleading guilty his blessing. There was something, though, that held him back.

"Chester," he said, trying to take the edge out of his voice, "you can always plead guilty later. Let's at least wait and see if we can't work out some kind of a deal."

"Anderson will never deal," Chester said. "He'd never settle for anything less than the maximum sentence, and he knows Judge Walker'll give the maximum if it goes to trial and I'm found guilty."

Chester was right about that. Benjamin Walker was a fair jurist and an honest man, but he was known to be harsh at sentencings.

"There's no rush to plead guilty, though, Chester. The trial won't be for at least another three months. And if Anderson won't offer us anything, by God, why not take him to trial? That way, we can make him work for his fourteen-year sentence."

That argument seemed to brighten Chester up a bit. "It does seem a shame to play dead, doesn't it?"

"It does, indeed."

"On the other hand," Chester went on, "forcing a trial would drag Cedra and Polly into the mess further than they already are. I won't do that, not when there's no point to it. I'm guaranteed to be convicted."

It was hard for Micah to argue with that. "But that's not a decision we have to make today," Micah said.

Chester ran both hands through his hair. He looked very tired.

"I'll have to think about it," Chester said.

"Think about it? Come on, Chester, what's there—"

"No," Chester snapped. "No more, Micah. I've got to think about it. That's all there is to it."

★ ★ ★ ★ ★

"All rise," shouted the bailiff as Justice of the Peace R. Mc-Craken Porterhouse ascended to his bench. Actually, it was less of an ascent than it was a squeeze. Judge Porterhouse was a large man, famous for being proud of his girth. According to the scales down at the sale barn, he weighed three hundred and forty-seven pounds. At least that was what he had weighed four years earlier when he'd bet Mr. Barrows, the editor of the local newspaper, one hundred dollars that he weighed more than three-fifty. Micah suspected Judge Porterhouse would be a hundred dollars richer if the wager were held today.

The county courthouse was on the second floor of the First National Bank Building. At one end of that floor were the offices of the county clerk, treasurer, and assessor. At the other were the offices of the county attorney and the clerks of the justice and district courts. What little was left over—a room about twenty feet by twenty feet—was the courtroom. When the tiny room was stuffed with all the parties necessary for an action at bar, plus a three-hundred-and-fifty-pound judge, it took on congested proportions.

"You folks sit down," grumbled Porterhouse. There was an old shibboleth that all fat people were jolly. Porterhouse proved it was wrong to generalize. "Court's in session. We're here for an arraignment on an indictment handed down from the grand jury this morning against Chester Hedstrom, M.D. I'm Judge Porterhouse, justice of the peace for this county. Since the district court judge was here last week and won't be back around for another three months, I'll be handling this hearing today in my capacity as Judge Walker's court commissioner."

Porterhouse wore small wire spectacles that were almost swallowed up by his huge eyebrows and bulging cheeks. "I note the presence," he said, "of the defendant, Dr. Hedstrom, along with his attorney, Mr. McConners. The state's represented by the county attorney, Mr. Anderson."

The judge, who seemed to be winded, breathed through his nose, and with each breath there was a whistling that sounded like a signal from a distant locomotive. "Have you received a copy of the indictment, Mr. McConners?"

Micah stood. This was a week of firsts. He was about to address his first judge in a courtroom as an attorney. "Yes, Your Honor," he said, "we have." He felt his stomach flutter.

"Have you discussed it with your client?"

"Yes, sir. We've gone over it in detail."

Porterhouse directed his gaze at Chester. "Stand up," he said. When Chester was on his feet, the judge asked, "Is what your lawyer said true? Have you gone over the indictment with him?"

Chester nodded. "Yes," he said, "I have, just before coming in here."

The room was warm, and Micah could see kernels of perspiration in a row across the judge's brow. "You're a smart man," Porterhouse said to Chester, holding the charging papers up for all to see, "and I'm not going to take the time to read this whole thing to you." He jerked his head toward the prosecutor, and when he did, his jowls waggled. "Anderson here is a long-winded sort of fella who takes ten words to say what most folks could say in three. I've tried to break him of it, but it doesn't seem to work. It's a flaw in his character, I suppose. But what this thing says is that you performed an abortion upon the person of one Polly Pratt on the twenty-seventh day of August, 1900, right here in this town and this county and this state."

Porterhouse turned around, reaching for his statute book on a shelf behind the bench. As he turned, his chair gave a plaintive creak, and Micah had a vision of the poor, abused piece of furniture finally giving up and shattering into a hundred pieces. But, as the judge turned back to face them without incident, it appeared the chair would survive at least for a bit longer.

The thick statute book he took down was bound in beige calf skin, and it had gold letters against a red background on the spine. Porterhouse flipped through it, stopped, and began to read. Micah noticed as the man read to himself, he mouthed the words.

"Yep," said the judge, "that's what I thought. Fourteen years. That's what you stand to get if you plead guilty or are found guilty of this crime. Do you understand that, Dr. Hedstrom?"

"Yes, sir, I do."

"All right," said the judge, "Chester Hedstrom, how do you plead to the crime of performing an illegal abortion on the person of Miss Polly Pratt—guilty or not guilty?"

Micah swallowed hard. Unable to look at his friend, he stared up at the judge.

Judge Porterhouse was not a patient man. "Well, sir, let's have it," he urged. "How do you plead?"

Chester cleared his throat, and in a strong, sure voice he said, "My lawyer says I ought to plead not guilty, Judge."

"Yes?"

"So," continued Chester, "I guess that's what I'll do."

"You had me worried there for a minute, you stubborn son of a bitch," Micah whispered from the corner of his mouth to Chester as they sat back down.

"Golly, Mr. McConners, you don't think I'd do anything contrary to your sagacious advice, do you?" This was the first time Micah had seen Chester smile since the arrest.

Porterhouse was writing something in Chester's file. When he was finished he looked up. "So," he said, "what about bond?"

Micah said, "We'd request a personal recognizance bond, Your Honor."

"Mr. Anderson?" The judge turned his tiny eyes toward the prosecutor.

"The state resists that, Your Honor."

"Why's that, Mr. Anderson? Do you expect the doctor here to be a flight risk?" Micah couldn't tell if the judge was putting the sarcasm in his voice on purpose, or simply making no effort to hide the sarcasm that was always there.

"Well, sir, of course there is that possibility. This is a heinous crime, Your Honor. The defendant knows the caliber of the state's case. We have an eyewitness and a confession. I believe that flight is a very distinct possibility." Anderson removed his monocle in what Micah was sure was a practiced flourish. "And there is the other thing, Judge."

"What other thing might that be, Mr. Anderson?"

"I fear for my witness, sir. When Mrs. Eggers approached the defendant with her concerns about what he had done, he threw her from his house without even allowing her an opportunity to collect her possessions and threatened her physically if she said anything to anyone."

"That's a lie," Chester muttered under his breath.

"Quiet," Micah said.

"She is concerned for her safety," Anderson continued, "and frankly, sir, so am I."

Porterhouse turned to Micah. "Response, Mr. McConners?"

"Well, Your Honor," Micah said, standing, "this is the first we've heard anything about threatening the witness. I've not even had a chance to discuss it with my client. I guess my initial reaction is to question the accuracy of the allegation. If there is a confession, as Mr. Anderson says—and we are not conceding that at this point—but if there is, it seems strange to me that an individual who is willing to confess would threaten to harm some woman to keep her from divulging the very facts he is confessing."

Porterhouse seemed to ponder that for a moment, then said, "Very well, I'll set the bond at ten thousand dollars, personal recognizance. That means, doctor, that you are released from jail without posting any money, but if you flee the jurisdiction of the court, when you're caught, you'll owe the State of Wyoming ten thousand dollars. Do you understand that?"

"Yes, sir, Judge, I do," Chester said.

"I'll also put in the order that you're to stay away from the state's witnesses, whoever they may be."

"I'm sure that will be no problem, Judge," Micah said.

"Court's in recess," Porterhouse said. With a groan, he hefted himself from his chair and left the courtroom.

Seeing Brad Collins come up to the defense table, Micah said to Chester, "You'll have to go back with the sheriff until the paperwork's done. Once that's completed and filed, you'll be free to go."

"All right." As Collins led him away, Chester turned and said, "Thanks, Micah."

Micah nodded. "Don't worry, Chester. Everything's going to be all right." He wasn't positive, but he thought he made it come out with more conviction than he felt. He hoped so, anyway.

Collins took Chester out the door next to the bench. Once they were gone, Micah turned to see Anderson leaving through another door at the back of the courtroom. "Mr. Anderson," he called, "do you have a minute?"

Anderson stopped and waited for Micah to walk over. "Yes, young man?" he said in the same condescending tone he'd used at the park the first day Micah was home.

"Could we talk?" Micah asked.

"Of course we can, my boy. I expect you wish to make a deal. Am I right?"

Micah was a bit disarmed. He expected Anderson to show more guile. He didn't believe for a second the man was without guile, but he hadn't expected him to be very good at it. "Well," he said, looking down at his boots and scratching the back of his head, "I'm realistic, Mr. Anderson. I'd be a fool to deny you have a strong case."

An odd smile crept across the little man's face. "Yes," he said, "you would be, wouldn't you?"

"But you and I both know this was an isolated event. Dr. Hedstrom is not an abortionist."

Anderson held up a slender index finger. "Wait," he said. "Excuse me for interrupting, but the man performed an abortion on an eighteen-year-old girl. That does not make him a deacon, young man. That, as I understand the term, makes him an abortionist."

Micah had known of the problems between Chester and Anderson but did not realize until now how difficult that animosity was going to make things. "Yes," he conceded, "perhaps it does." Micah leaned against the flimsy courtroom bar and felt it rock under him. He quickly took his weight off the rail and stood up straight. "I think we should start this off by being honest with each other. I know there's no love between you and Dr. Hedstrom."

"On the contrary," Anderson said. "I've always considered the doctor a fine man." The eyebrow above the eye not holding the monocle lifted a quarter of an inch. "To be sure, we don't always agree on things, but I would never begrudge any man his opinion. Until now, I've had the deepest respect for the doctor. You can imagine my shock when I learned he had committed this horrible crime."

Micah could see now why Chester disliked Anderson so. "Yes," he said, "I suppose in your line of work you often encounter things that would shock a person of your fine sensibilities."

Anderson paused a beat. Micah assumed he was trying to determine if Micah was being serious. "Well," Anderson said, "we all must do whatever it takes to do our duty."

"Yes," Micah agreed, "which is what I'm doing now. It would do no one any good for this matter to go to trial."

"Particularly your client," Anderson pointed out.

"Well, the community too. It would be unfortunate to have this become some sort of public spectacle. Dr. Hedstrom has many friends. He's well liked."

"He might be less so once people see him for the killer of babies that he is."

"Oh, come on," said Micah. "Don't you think that's overstating it a bit?"

"No," Anderson said, "I do not. And I'll tell you right now, I expect to put on testimony to describe in vivid detail exactly what takes place in one of these brutal surgeries. The jury will have no doubt in their minds when they retire to deliberate what sort of crime your friend, the good Dr. Hedstrom, committed when he performed his abortion."

Micah stared down at Anderson until the little man began to squirm, but Anderson did not look away. "You seem to have strong feelings about this, Mr. Anderson."

"I do, sir."

And Micah realized by the expression that shadowed Anderson's face that the prosecutor was enjoying all of this. There could never be a deal with this man. Never. It was pointless to even try.

"So," Micah said, unable to resist, "I guess this means you won't recommend probation."

Two lines formed between Anderson's eyebrows as he considered what Micah had said. He then burst out laughing. He roared and slapped Micah on the shoulder. "Well, I must say, you and Hedstrom share the same conceited sense of humor. You truly do. Which is good. You're both going to need it before this is finished."

He was still laughing as he turned and left the courtroom.

Chapter Sixteen

Micah was having a cigarette in the alley behind his office. He leaned against a water barrel and blew smoke toward the stars. It was the last day of September, and there was a chill in the night air, but Micah wore only his suit jacket. He always waited until he had no choice before he took to wearing his winter coat. It was as though the simple act of putting it on was admitting something he didn't wish to admit.

He had celebrated his first month as a practicing attorney a few days before, and, God knew, except for Chester's troubles, it had been an uneventful month. Not counting Chester and Cedra, Micah had acquired only two other clients. One, a man running a logging operation in the mountains around the Esterbrook area had struck a bargain with a local landowner and asked Micah to draw up a contract. It was a complicated affair made up of lease holdings, rights of purchase with options on certain parcels that were to be exercised within one period of time, and options on other parcels that were to be exercised at different periods of time. Micah had worked hard putting the deal together, and he felt good about the document he had devised.

The other client was, in a roundabout way, none other than Bashful Paxton. Bashful's pattern of being drunk and disorderly was consistent, as was his Saturday night of sleeping it off in Collins's jail. But for some reason known only to Judge Porterhouse, the judge wearied of throwing Bashful in jail for only one day a week and took to throwing him in for two. Now this meant that Bashful missed Monday at the barbershop, which infuriated Guthrie Bowls, the shop's owner, because every day that Bashful was out of the shop was money out of Guthrie's pocket. Guthrie, being a prudent man, realized that in the long run this was not a paying proposition, so he was willing to invest a little to get Bashful—who everyone knew was the best barber within miles—back in the shop on Monday. It was Guthrie who ended up paying Micah's fee to accomplish this, but it was Bashful who was Micah's client.

Micah felt he'd done an excellent job of presenting Bashful's case. Although there was no law on his side, Micah argued that a man had the right to count on what punishment he was going to receive for a specific crime. And for about as long as anybody could remember, Bashful's punishment for being drunk and obnoxious on Saturdays had been one night in jail, no more and no less. It wasn't as though on recent Saturdays Bashful had been any drunker or any more obnoxious. Hell, Bashful's manner of obnoxiousness hadn't changed in years. All that had changed was his sentence.

When Micah completed his argument, Judge Porterhouse looked down at Bashful—who was by then asleep at the defense table—smacked his gavel, and said, "Two days in jail. Sheriff, take him away." Which Collins did by hefting Bashful over his shoulder.

Also in the first month there had been a motion hearing in front of Porterhouse, again sitting as Judge Walker's district court commissioner, regarding the sworn statement of Mrs. Eggers that Earl Anderson had taken and had typed up. He had hired Judge Walker's court reporter, Jebediah Blake—at county expense—to ride over from Casper to take Eggers's testimony. Anderson refused to provide a copy of the statement to Micah, so Micah filed a motion, argued it, and won. Anderson was not pleased, but he had no choice but to make the transcript available.

After reading it, Chester said the statement was about nine parts lie. All she got right was the fact that the abortion had taken place, but Micah knew when it came right down to it, that was pretty much all she needed to get right.

If those events—the motion hearing, the drafting of the contract, and the representation of Bashful—were taken out of Micah's first month of lawyering, things were very slow indeed. In fact, his days and nights were pretty much uneventful except for one thing.

Fay Charbunneau.

Micah waited for Fay now. A dirty alleyway separated the buildings on Second Street where Lottie's Café was located from the buildings on Third where Micah's office was. Every night shortly after closing, when Lottie did the day's books, Fay would sneak over to Micah's. This skulking about was the sort of thing that Micah had dreaded. It was what they had done before, but it could be no other way. Fay could still remember the life her mother and father had lived, and she didn't want that for them. Neither did Micah. But they couldn't let each other go. It was difficult, but they were trying to accept the way they had to live.

And too there was Lottie. Lottie understood Fay's fears. Lottie had lived the life Fay wished to avoid. And although Lottie liked Micah—she always had—being a religious woman, she couldn't accept Micah's and Fay's sins.

Fay would tell him of their conversations. "There are fine Negro boys workin' on the railroad," Lottie would point out. "Look at them, girl," she would say. And Fay would answer, "Yes, Momma." And every night when Lottie did her books, Fay came to Micah.

Micah dropped his cigarette to the dirt and crushed it under his boot. The evening chill was soaking through his thin jacket, and he was about to step inside when he heard footsteps. He squinted into the gloom, and, sure enough, it was Fay. She was still wearing one of her light summer dresses, but a shawl covered her shoulders. He moved to meet her, and they came together in an embrace. Fay held the ends of the shawl in each hand, and when she wrapped her arms around Micah, she brought him into the warmth of the shawl as well.

Micah bent and kissed her and, as always, he felt himself fill up.

"I can't stay but a minute," she said, placing her head against his chest. "There's still a customer, but I knew you'd be waiting."

Micah put his face into Fay's thick, wavy hair. It was soft, flowed past her shoulders, and smelled of lilacs. "I was hoping you could stay for a while tonight," he said. Some nights she would stay longer than others, and they would talk and make love for hours in his tiny bed.

"I don't think it'll be much longer, and I can come back. I spoke with Momma today."

"You did?" He didn't have to ask her what about. "What did you say?"

"I told her how we feel about each other, which she already knew, of course. And I said, 'Momma, Micah and I have enough problems in this world without you being one too.' "

"My, aren't we brave? And what did she say to that?"

"At first it was the usual. I let her talk as long as she wanted. I let her say everything she had to say. When she finished, I said, 'Momma, everything you said is the truth. Every word of it is God's own truth.' " Fay smiled. "Momma said, 'Thank you, Lord. Thank you, Jesus, for letting my baby see the light.' And I said, 'Momma, don't be thanking the Man too soon until you've heard the rest of what I have to say. What you said is the truth, but it doesn't matter.' I said, 'You act like Micah and I have a choice about how we feel. You think we can make it stop and go on about our business, but we can't.' " She lay her head back against him. "I said, 'We lost that choice years ago. Now all we are trying to do is cope the best way we can.' "

"What did she say to that?"

"Nothing. I wouldn't let her say another word. It was my turn to talk."

"You and Lottie are a lot alike," Micah pointed out.

Fay lifted her head and gave him a look that communicated danger. Luckily, except for the look, she ignored the remark.

"I told her we knew we could never have a normal life . . ." After a pause, she added, "A family. I promised we were being careful about that." She gave a little shiver when she recalled that part of the conversation with her mother. I told her that made us sad, and that we felt cheated, and that sometimes it made us mad too. But we can't change what is. We have to live with it."

She pulled him closer, snuggling them both deeper into her shawl. "Or," she added in a soft voice, one he had to strain to hear, "live around it."

They stood like that awhile, holding each other, not speaking. After a bit, Fay pulled away. "I can't be doing this," she said. "I've got to get back. Besides, I don't like leaving Momma alone with that man."

"Who's there?"

"It's one of the Jones boys. Lester. He's drunk as usual."

"Where's Hank?" Micah asked. "You don't often see one without the other. Or without Sonny Pratt, either, for that matter."

"I'm not sure what happened, but there was some kind of fight. I get the idea that Sonny and Hank beat the devil out of Lester."

"Oh?"

"Lester came in about thirty minutes ago wanting coffee—well, he was so drunk, first he wanted whiskey, but when I told him we didn't have any, he settled for coffee. His face was all bruised and his lip cut. He said Hank had knocked out one of his teeth, but for the life of me, I can't imagine how he could tell."

"I expect Lester can count to at least four, so he should be able to keep track of his teeth. Now if his toes started falling off, he might be in trouble. What was the fight about, anyway?"

"Who knows? *They* probably don't even know. It could be anything with those three."

"Was Sonny part of it too?"

"It sounded like it."

That didn't surprise Micah. Although Sonny Pratt was much smarter than either of the Jones boys—or the two of them combined, for that matter—they were always together.

Fay stepped back and pulled her shawl tighter around her shoulders. "Autumn is in the air," she said, looking up at the gray swipe of Milky Way that spanned the opening between the buildings. "It won't be long before the cold's here to stay."

"I hate that," Micah said. He had spent his earliest years in Amarillo, Texas, where it got plenty cold, but in the Panhandle winter started later and spring started sooner than they did in Wyoming. He'd sometimes considered moving to warmer climes, but Probity was his home. His father was buried here. He looked at Fay. This was where he wanted to be.

"I'll go and shoo Lester away," Fay said. "I'll be back as soon as I clean things up. Will you still be awake?" she asked.

Micah, who didn't want to make promises he wasn't sure he could keep, said, "I'll leave the door unlocked."

Fay smiled, and Micah felt something inside him collide with something else. She stepped back over and gave him a quick kiss and said, "You do that. If you're asleep, I'll wake you in a nice way."

She turned to go but stopped herself. "You know," she said, "Lester did say something when he first came in that was a little strange."

"Lester Jones, say something strange?" Micah put the perfect note of disbelief into his voice.

"I mean strange even for Lester."

"What was that?" Micah asked.

"He was kind of mumbling to himself, but I swear it sounded like he said he wasn't going to have any part of murder, no matter what Polly Pratt told the law."

CHAPTER SEVENTEEN

Micah stood across the street from Lottie's waiting for Fay to send Lester out. He shook another Cyclone from his package and lit up. He hadn't used tobacco much before moving to Cheyenne. Once every week or so he'd have one of Chester's cigars—the taste of it mixed well with Chester's fine Scotland whisky—but he never smoked any other time. It was the thing to do in Cheyenne, though, and he had taken it up. At first a packet of Cyclones would last him almost a week. Now he was lucky if one lasted even two days. It was strange, but it seemed the more you did these things, the more you wanted to do.

He saw movement behind the curtains, and a moment later, Lester staggered out. It didn't seem the coffee had done much to sober him up. His footing was wobbly, and he muttered to himself in a slurred soliloquy. Micah tried to make out what he said but was too far away to hear.

Lester started toward a horse that was tied to a rail a couple of doors away, and Micah crossed the street at an angle to cut him off.

"Lester!" he called out. "Lester Jones!"

Lester stopped where he was and peered into the dark street. "Whozat?" he said as he pushed his hat up on his brow a notch with his thumb.

Micah stepped up on the boardwalk, and Lester's eyes followed him. They were glassy but focused. Micah was close enough now to see caked blood in the stubble of the boy's scant beard.

"Who're you?" Lester asked. The tone of his voice didn't sound as though he was up for friendly conversation.

"Name's McConners," Micah said. He stuck out his hand, but Lester only looked at it without extending his own. Micah wasn't sorry Lester didn't want to shake his hand. Even in the dim light, Micah could see the grime between Lester's thumb and index finger. "My father used to own the store over on Second and Walnut. When we were all kids you and your brother would come in from time-to-time, and he'd give you both a lemon drop."

Lester squinted as his mind ratcheted over. After a moment he said with a vacant smile, "I recall you. Your daddy was nice. He even give Hank and me some peppermint sticks once."

The Jones family had been well known around Probity. The mother had been slow to the point of hardly being able to function, and the father had been mean. Micah winced at the thought of how the gift of peppermint was maybe one of the few high points in Lester's childhood. "Pop sure liked to feed candy to kids," Micah offered with a laugh.

Lester joined the laughter. "Well, sir, you couldn't never feed me and Hank too much candy. That's for sure."

"Where's Hank now?" Micah asked. "I don't know as I've ever seen one of you Jones boys without the other."

"Hell, I don't know where they got off to. I don't care, neither. I'm done with 'em. I might head out for Colorado. They's hiring folks in them mines west of Denver. There was a harness salesman come through about six months ago told me all about it. Yes, sir. A fella can make him some money down in Colorado. That's what I hear."

Micah pointed to Lester's face. "Looks like you've been roughed up some there, Lester. Who did that to you?"

"Ah, Sonny Pratt," he said. In a quieter voice as though he was embarrassed to admit it, "And Hank done some too."

Micah pulled out his pack of Cyclones and offered one to Lester. Lester looked at it as though he'd never seen a ready-rolled cigarette before.

"Thanks," he said, shoving it into his mouth. He fumbled through his pockets for a light, never coming up with one.

"Here you go," Micah said. "Let me get that for you." He struck a match, and the yellow glow of it showed Lester's face was worse than Micah first thought.

"Damn, Lester," he said. "They sure did work you over."

"It ain't so bad," Lester said, exhaling a gray flood of smoke. "I've had worse, and I've give worse too."

"I bet you have." Micah shook out the match and tossed it into the street. "But it seems strange coming from your own brother and best friend. You must've done something pretty bad to make them that mad at you."

"They's the ones that does bad things, not me." He took another pull on the Cyclone, held it up, and eyed it. "These ready-rolleds is good and tight, ain't they?" he said. "Not like when you twist 'em up yourself."

"Here," offered Micah, pulling the pack from his pocket, "take them. I have more." He handed the cigarettes over.

Lester looked as though he'd been presented a great gift. "Damn, store-bought smokes. Thanks, Mr. McConners."

"Hell, Lester, don't mention it. You've had a bad night."

Lester rubbed his swollen jaw. "What time do you reckon it is?" he asked.

It was too dark to see his watch without striking another match, so Micah made a guess. "I don't know. Must be about ten-thirty."

"I wonder if Becky's got herself a customer over at Adelaide's."

"Who's Becky?" Micah asked.

The boy seemed to perk up at the question. "Why, Becky's my girl. We's in love."

"Is that right?"

"Yes, sir. Sometimes in the middle of the week like this, when it gets on around eleven or so, if Becky don't have a customer, I can come into her room and we can be together." His gaze drifted up the street in the direction of Adelaide's Bawdy House. "Becky's a sight, Mr. McConners. She has long yellow hair and the greenest eyes you ever did see."

"Sounds like a beauty."

"You ever go into Adelaide's?" Lester asked.

"No, can't say as I have." Micah gave a quick laugh. "I've thought about it a few times but never made it in." Lester Jones might be the only person on earth Micah would be willing to admit that truth to.

"You should go," Lester urged. "It's a fine place. It's got thick carpets and velvet curtains. Adelaide has three piano players on the payroll, so they's music goin' night and day. And in the parlor, she's got this big light what's hanging down from the ceiling, and I swear, it looks like it's made out of diamonds." He turned a sly grin to Micah. "And the girls is somethin'. Adelaide says she's got the prettiest girls around. It's the truth too. And my Becky's the prettiest of the batch." Lester's voice dropped, taking on a confidential tone. "Now, Becky's large, mind ya," Lester added. "She's a large, full girl, but I like my women on the fleshly side, don't you, Mr. McConners?"

"Well, I've seen some large women that I thought were real appealing, Lester. I surely have. But I expect if you're in love, it doesn't matter whether the girl's large or small."

Lester snapped his fingers and slapped his knee. "By golly, you're right, damned if you ain't. And me and Becky are sure in love; yes, sir, we are. There ain't no other woman for me—not another one at Adelaide's, nor anywheres else neither. I don't never lay with any woman 'cept for my Becky. Why, I never even touched a beauty like Polly Pratt, no, sir. And I had me the chance when—" Suddenly the smile left his dull face. "I gotta be goin'," he said. He began to sidle off the boardwalk toward his horse.

"What was that, Lester?" Micah asked. "You didn't touch Polly Pratt when?"

"Nothin'," Lester said. "Never mind." He turned toward his horse.

Micah wasn't sure where Lester had been going with his last comment, but it was clear the boy had let something slip that scared him. Micah decided to jab him a little. "You were with Sonny last month when he beat the hell out of Polly, weren't you?" Micah wasn't at all sure that Lester had been, but it didn't hurt to throw it out to see what would happen.

"No," Lester snapped. "I don't know what you're talking about."

"I'm talking about the day of the picnic in the park. I saw you and your brother and Sonny Pratt all there together. Later on that night, Sonny Pratt beat Polly damn near senseless, and you helped him do it, didn't you, Lester?"

Lester turned on Micah. It looked as though he was going to charge, and Micah braced himself.

"You're a sneaky bastard, ain't ya?" Lester said. "You got a way about ya. I'll admit that. You give a fella free cigarettes, and get 'im talkin'." He pulled the Cyclones from his pocket and threw the pack at Micah.

Micah caught it and held it back toward Lester. "Oh, come on, Lester, settle down. Take the smokes back. If you say you didn't help Sonny hurt Polly, I believe you. Why would you lie to me? I'm not the law." He waggled the cigarettes a couple of times at the boy, and hesitantly, as though he were reaching out to pet a snake, Lester took them back. "Good," Micah said, "that's better." He stepped down into the street next to the younger man. "No, Lester, I'm not saying you had anything to do with it, but I know it was Sonny who worked her over that night, and maybe Hank too, the same way they did you tonight."

"It weren't me, though," Lester whispered. "Them two do things I don't like sometimes." He dug a line in the dirt with the edge of his boot. "I ain't never hurt Polly Pratt." He looked up, and even in the darkness, he found Micah's eyes. "I ain't bad, Mr. McConners." He shook his head and looked back down at the line he'd made. "I ain't sayin' I'm the best of fellas, no, sir." His head rose again. "But I ain't bad."

"Tell me why they beat her the way they did, Lester. They must have had a reason. Why would they do that?"

Lester backed away. He shook his index finger at Micah. "I ain't talkin' to you no more, Mr. McConners. No, sir. No more." His movements were surer now than they were when he first staggered out of Lottie's. He jerked the reins from the rail and threw his right leg over the saddle. He looked down at Micah for a quick second and, without saying any more, he whirled his horse and rode away.

Micah watched Lester ride into the darkness. Maybe Lester wasn't bad, but Hank was, and Sonny Pratt was. And there were strange things going on among the Pratt family: the divorce, the beating of Polly by her brother, the abortion. There was a lot about all of this that Micah did not understand. And he figured it was time he did something about that. Whether he wanted to or not, Chester was going to tell Micah what the hell was going on.

CHAPTER EIGHTEEN

"Please, sir, have a seat." Earl Anderson extended his arm, palm up, toward the heavy leather chair in front of his desk. "This is quite an honor," he said. Anderson had been beside himself ever since the messenger boy brought the note informing him that Emmett Pratt would be in this afternoon "to discuss some matters of importance."

Pratt, holding his hat and dressed in a suit and string tie, sat without saying a word.

Anderson circled behind his huge oak desk, sat in his own leather chair, and leaned forward, his weight on his forearms, his fingers interlaced. "I can't tell you how pleased I was," he said, "to receive your note this morning. It's an honor to meet with Probity's distinguished citizenry. It's not only my duty as your representative in the halls of justice, but my pleasure as well. Now, sir—" He beamed his brightest smile. "—what is it I can do for you? Anything. Anything at all."

Pratt tossed his hat onto Anderson's desk, hitting a bottle of ink as he did and almost toppling it over. "The first thing you can do is stop that blasted chattering. I don't have much to say to you, Anderson, except that it may be you're the dumbest son of a bitch that God ever let breathe air."

Earl felt his smile melt away.

"You may know that Thomas Blythe is my personal attorney, and he informed me yesterday that your reasoning for the prosecution of Dr. Hedstrom was that you thought you were doing *me* some kind of favor." With every word that left Pratt's mouth, his complexion grew redder. "Perhaps you would like to explain what favor you are doing me by destroying a good man and dragging my wife and stepdaughter through the mud."

Earl tried to swallow, but something felt as though it was plugging his throat. "Well, I—I—" he stammered. "With the divorce proceedings and all, I assumed—"

"You assumed too God-damned much, little man. I'll tell you that right now." Pratt's anger was rising to the level of fury. He jerked himself from the chair and began to pace in front of Anderson's desk. "First of all, I don't want a divorce. I've never wanted a divorce. I've done everything I can to prevent my wife from obtaining a divorce, up to and including having Blythe refer her to that know-nothing little pup of a lawyer McConners. I've worked my entire life to protect my family from hardship and disgrace, and now you bring criminal charges against a man who's done nothing but risk his career and his freedom to try to help the people I care about most in the world. And, as if that's not bad enough, you have the God-damned audacity to suggest you did it because you thought you were doing me a favor. Well, sir, you have done me no favor." He paused. "But you will." During the course of his tirade, Pratt had leaned across the top of Anderson's desk and placed his nose scarcely six inches from Earl's own. "And do you know *why* you will?"

"No, sir—I mean—"

Pratt stood up straight and once again began to pace. "Year before last I spent ten thousand dollars of my own money trying to get a friend of mine elected governor. But I don't have a great deal of political influence, despite what some fools who don't know what the hell they're talking about might think, and my friend lost by a landslide." Pratt stopped pacing and leaned again toward Anderson. "But I will tell you something, you Nancy-boy little prick: You will either fix this mess you've made

141

or I will spend twice ten thousand to see that you're not only run out of this town and this state, but the whole God-damned West. Now, maybe I can't get someone elected governor, but I'm willing to bet twenty thousand dollars that I can handle a little shit like you. What do you have to say about that?"

"Well, of course, sir. I'll d-d-do anything I can, but there has already been an arraignment, the trial date has been set, the press—"

Pratt dropped back into the chair in front of the desk. "I've talked to Blythe about this, and although it's within your discretion, he acknowledges it would be awkward for you to dismiss the charge. Judge Walker would be asking questions that would be difficult to answer."

"Yes, yes, he would."

"Blythe suggested some sort of plea agreement."

"It is my understanding the doctor would be willing to plead guilty," Anderson confirmed.

"If he did, a trial could be avoided, but I expect he would go to prison."

"There's no doubt about it. Judge Walker's fair, but his sentencing is harsher than some judges around the state."

"How long do you think Hedstrom might get?"

"The maximum is fourteen. If he pled guilty, I doubt he would get the maximum. But I can't imagine he'd get less than eight, perhaps as much as ten."

"My word," Pratt said as he stood and walked to Anderson's window. The afternoon traffic on Main rolled by. "Are you sure Hedstrom would plead guilty?"

"All I know, sir, is his attorney approached me after the arraignment and wanted to discuss that possibility."

"Eight, maybe ten years. That won't do. I cannot allow this man's life to be ruined." Pratt stood for a long moment staring out the window. "I want Thomas Blythe to prosecute this case."

"I beg your pardon?"

Pratt turned from the window and faced Earl. "Whether it goes to trial or whether he pleads guilty, either way, this man's going to be convicted of this God-damned crime you were stupid enough to charge him with. There's you on one side and McConners on the other. I want someone with a little brains in that courtroom—someone who might be able to exercise some influence when Judge Walker is making his decision on how many years to give the poor bastard."

Anderson stood now too. "But, Mr. Pratt," he said, "I'm the county attorney."

"I don't give three shits who you are. You appoint Thomas Blythe as some kind of deputy prosecutor, or I'm going to have your ass hanging from a stick."

He grabbed his hat from Anderson's desk, and when he did, he knocked over the bottle of ink. Both men watched as the black liquid spread across the desktop. "Damn," Pratt said, putting on the hat and heading for the door. "Seems you have a mess, Mr. Prosecutor."

CHAPTER NINETEEN

People looked at her in a different way now that they knew. The women were the worst. Women, in their own manner, could be crueler than men. Men's cruelty was physical. It was frightening, but she thought she understood it. Women could be cruel with their eyes and their whispers. And that was not a cruelty she could understand. It was one she could feel, though. It was as real as the hands of the men.

This morning was the first time Polly had been out of the boarding house in days, but she was going insane being closed up all the time. All her life she'd been a creature of the outdoors. She enjoyed horses and riding, and she missed the ranch with its thousands of acres of freedom. She had been happy there.

Polly was very young when her mother married Emmett Pratt. He was a stern man, but gentle with her, and over the years she'd grown to love him. Despite all that had happened, she still thought of him as her father. There had been a time in the early years at the ranch when she had even cared for Sonny. Sure, even in the good times he'd been an aggravation. When they were kids, he had teased her without mercy, but she had cared for him the way any sister cared for an older brother. It had been in her nature to be caring in those days. She wondered now if that was something she would ever feel again. Last spring Sonny had stolen the capacity for that from her.

She still wondered at what had happened. Sometimes she'd wake in the night, and for a moment she would have forgotten about it. For a brief moment in her half-sleep she would not remember. But then like a rock slide, the memory of that afternoon by the river would come crashing down on her. The feel of Sonny and Hank. The weight of them. The smell of them. All of it would be with her again in the night as real as it had been that day.

And the fear. Even in those rare moments when the memory of it was tucked into some dark corner of her mind, the fear was always present.

She'd had a chance in these months since to examine her fear. It was like a thing she could touch and see. She had gotten to know it. She had held it, turned it over, looked at it, lived with it. It had become a part of her. It was something alive, growing inside her in a way that no doctor could remove.

The fear came in many forms. She feared what Sonny would do to her. He would kill her without a second's thought; she knew he was capable of that. So there was that fear—the fear of death. But there was another fear as well. It was a kind of fear she had never known existed until that day at the water's edge when Sonny and Hank and Lester had dragged her down to the river. "Take her," Sonny had said to the Jones brothers. "She's yours. Do anything you want to her. She's a present from me to you."

Lester had looked confused, like he didn't understand what Sonny was saying, but Hank wasn't confused. "You mean right here?" he asked.

"Right here in broad daylight in front of God and everyone," Sonny said.

Hank's rubbery tongue rolled out and wet his lips. He was staring down at Polly, who'd been thrown to the ground. He was considering it; she could tell. "Well, Lester," he asked, "what do you think? You want some of this?"

Lester shook his head. "This ain't right, Hank." He looked to

Sonny. "You're jokin', aincha, Sonny?" he asked.

"Hell, no," Sonny said. "I been putting up with this little bitch for too long now. I say you do what you want, then let's gut her." He pulled a knife from a sheath on his belt. "I wonder how big a gut pile a little bitch like this would make. What d'ya think, Lester? Bigger than an antelope? As big as a deer?"

"Stop it, Sonny," Lester said, and there was a quiver in his voice. "This ain't funny. Polly here's your sister."

Sonny's fist lashed out and caught Lester on the tip of the chin. Lester was lifted in the air, and he came crashing down on his back. There was a whoosh as the wind exploded from him. In a cat-quick movement Sonny was on Lester's chest, his right knee buried in Lester's throat. Sonny's teeth were bared, and the flat of his knife was against Lester's upper lip, the edge under his nose. Lester's eyes were wide and crossed as he looked down at the blade. A flick of Sonny's wrist, and Lester's nose would be neatly shaved away. "That little bitch is not my sister. Her and her whore mother come into our house and they never left, but that doesn't mean she is anything to me. You got that, you dumb son of a bitch?"

"Yeah, Sonny, sure. Sure I do."

"Say it," Sonny ordered. "Say, 'She ain't nothing to you, Sonny.'" He wiggled the knife, and a trickle of blood leaked down the side of Lester's face. "Say it, you damned cockchafer, or I'll cut off your nose."

"Sure, Sonny," Lester said. "She ain't nothin' to ya. I know that. Nothin' atall."

Sonny slowly got up, never taking his eyes off Lester. Lester rolled over on his side, holding his throat and trying to get his breath.

"She ain't a God-damned thing to me," Sonny said, and he came over to Polly, pushing Hank out of his way. He reached down, grabbed the neck of her dress, and ripped. The material tore away, exposing her breasts.

"Hoo-wee," said Hank. "Look at them things. Ain't they pretty ones, though?"

Polly watched Sonny undo his gun belt and drop it to the ground. As he undid his pants, he repeated, "She ain't a God-damned thing to me. No, sir. Not a thing."

Now, as Polly walked down the street on that crisp, late September day, still she was afraid. She still feared that Sonny would kill her, and do it in some horrible way. But there was the other fear, too. A stronger fear. It was the fear of feeling again those feelings she'd felt that day. The fear of having no control. The fear of helplessness and being at the mercy of Sonny Pratt. Mostly, though, it was the fear of being made to feel like something less than human.

It was a warm day as long as she stayed out of the shadows. The sun was bright, and the sky was a thick blue.

She walked down Third, going nowhere in particular. She had nowhere to go. Hers and her mother's lives had been uneventful since those first two or three nightmarish days after Dr. Hedstrom's arrest.

The doctor's lawyer's office was down the street from where she was now. Mr. McConners seemed like a nice enough man, but Polly worried that he was too young and inexperienced for all of this. He was only eight or nine years older than she was.

She ached when she thought of the doctor's going to prison. It seemed strange, but he was taking it all very well. She and her mother had visited him a number of times since his arrest and release on bond, and although he wasn't pleased with the circumstances, still he made his jokes. He was no longer practic-ing medicine, which he admitted missing, but it allowed him more time to "tinker," as he called it. To Polly it seemed the doctor's tinkering was little more than his playing with his gadgets and machines.

Originally the doctor's trial had been set for the end of November, but due to Judge Walker's schedule, it was changed to the end of December. But as soon as the judge arrived for the trial, it was the doctor's plan to plead guilty. He said he would be convicted anyway. He might as well get it over with.

Polly could make no sense of any of this judicial business, none of it. Because the doctor's case took precedence over civil matters, the divorce trial of Polly's mother and Emmett Pratt could not be heard until the judge returned to Probity next March. Polly could not understand how people were supposed to set their lives aside until the system worked them into its machinery.

Despite all the eyes that followed her as she passed, the walk was invigorating. She was only a few blocks from the boarding house and already she felt better. But as soon as she realized she was feeling better, that caused her to remember again, and again the fear took hold. It was the same trap in which she always found herself. She spent her life in a maze. Every turn led back to the same place: her fear.

She hated Sonny Pratt. Despised him not only for what he had done to her, but for what he continued to do. Though she had not seen him since the beating the night of the picnic, he was with her always.

Sometimes she'd try to remember the Sonny from before— the twelve-year-old Sonny she had come to know when her mother first married Emmett. He was wild even then, but he was not evil. She was certain of that. But that Sonny was gone. There was a fire that had gone out inside that Sonny, and this new Sonny was dark and cold.

Polly walked past a group of women who stood in front of the haberdashery. As she neared, their whispering stopped and once she was past, she could hear it taken up again. She knew what they thought, of course: that she was a bad girl, that she had been with some boy and become pregnant, that she had gone to the doctor and convinced him to do what he'd done because she was ashamed.

And what Polly read in the eyes of these women was true, at least in part. She was ashamed. She was ashamed, not for what she had done, but for what she could not bring herself to do. She could not stand up to her stepbrother.

She was a coward. That was not a word often applied to women, but Polly knew it applied to her. She knew what Sonny and Hank Jones were capable of, and she feared for her life. It was as simple as that. If she told the truth about what had happened to cause her pregnancy, Sonny would kill her. And even if she did tell the truth, it wouldn't help the doctor. Dr. Hedstrom himself had told her that. She would be putting her life in jeopardy for no reason whatsoever.

No reason at all.

A group of people was milling around in front of the sheriff's office watching a couple of men untie a large bundle from the back of a pack horse. Polly couldn't imagine what could be so interesting about that, but she crossed the street anyway to have a look.

She stood at the edge of the crowd trying to peer between the arms and elbows of the men, standing on her tiptoes so she could better see. One of the men taking the bundle from the horse was Sheriff Collins himself and the other was a man she didn't know.

Once the bundle was untied and the two men were hefting it down, a third man, Lawyer McConners, stepped from the crowd and helped them. As they lay the bundle on the ground, the edge of the tarp that covered it lifted and fell away. There was a gasp from the crowd, but no sound came from Polly. No sound could come from Polly. It was choked off by what she saw.

Lester Jones lay in the dusty street. His eyes were glazed, wide, and lifeless. His face was a white-gray color, and tied around his neck was a black and red scarf. It was a deep red in the center, and black around the edges. It was an odd-looking thing. And no matter how hard Polly tried to make it look the way it was supposed to look, the way a scarf should look when knotted around a man's neck, it still was strange and not quite right.

It was at that point she realized what she was seeing wasn't a scarf at all. It was a wound. A cut. Like a toothless smile—this smile beneath his chin, rather than above—Lester Jones's throat had been sliced wide open.

No scream came from Polly, but her hand leapt to her mouth as she backed into the street. She turned away from the crowd and she saw, leaning against a building at the entrance to an alley, Sonny Pratt. Their eyes met, and as he stared at her, he lifted his head, chin up, and with a smile, he dragged his index finger across his throat.

Polly spun on her heel and ran. She sprinted, running like she had not run since she was a girl, pumping her arms and legs as fast as she could. In her panic, she ran without direction or purpose. She ran even without understanding why she was running. She ran hard and fast. She ran first one block, then another, and another, putting as much distance as she could between Lester and her—between Sonny and her. She ran, her eyes bleary with tears. Her head filled with her own screams and the feel of Sonny Pratt's breath in her ear. She ran, and ran, and ran, until she could not run anymore.

And then she stopped.

Pain stitched her side. Her lungs bucked and heaved inside her chest. Perspiration rolled down her brow, into her eyes, and mixed with her tears. She sucked in air, but it was as though she couldn't get enough. There wasn't enough air in the world to fill her up. She doubled over, holding her stomach, and dropped first to one knee, then the other.

Slowly the pain began to ebb, and it was replaced by a numbness. She felt nothing—no pain and no fear. She had seen Lester Jones lying dead in the street, his throat laid open—the lights out behind his eyes. And as horrible as that was, she felt nothing. If that was Sonny's worst, fine; there it was. She had seen it.

The cold numbness tingled out from the center of her to her arms and her chest and her head. It was a feeling that was almost as frightening as the pain and the fear that for so long had been a part of her.

But not quite.

"Polly, are you all right?"

It was a voice coming from behind. She was leaning against a white picket fence, and slowly she turned and peered up through the slats. It was Dr. Hedstrom. She looked around at where she was. In her mindless run, she had ended up on the doctor's street, in front of his house.

He wore old boots, jeans, and a work shirt. In his hand he held a rake. Scattered throughout the yard were piles of crisp, brown cottonwood leaves.

Again he asked her, "Are you all right?" He dropped his rake and stepped over the fence. He bent down and touched her face.

"Yes," she said. "I am all right. I'm fine." With the sleeve of her dress, she blotted the sweat from her forehead, and then she pushed herself up. The doctor stood with her. She lifted her eyes to his and said, "We need to talk." With that, she turned and walked to the gate, slipped the latch, and stepped into the doctor's yard.

"Talk, Polly? About what?" Chester asked.

"About what we are going to do," she said. "About what we

are going to do about the horrible things that are happening around here."

CHAPTER TWENTY

"Here, boy," Brad Collins said to the ten-year-old who was staring down at Lester Jones. "Back away from there." Collins fished in his pocket and pulled out a penny. He tossed it to the boy and said, "Go to the mortuary and tell Mr. Summerhayes what we got here. Tell him he better come on over."

Micah watched as the boy, without speaking, and without his eyes leaving Lester's throat, shoved the penny into his pocket. He backed off a few steps, turned, and bolted down the street.

"The rest of you folks move on too," Collins said. "We got us a dead man here. You seen him now, and there ain't nothing more to see." The people began to straggle away. "Go on, now," Collins said, hurrying them up.

Micah stood with his hands in his pockets.

"That goes for you too, lawyer," said Collins.

"I'd like to stay, if you don't mind, sheriff." Micah nodded in the direction of the short, fat man who had brought Lester's body into town. "I'd like to ask this gentleman a few questions."

"What's your interest in all of this, McConners?"

Micah shrugged. "Maybe nothing. Maybe something."

Collins, who had never been very friendly toward Micah, had been less so in the last few weeks. Micah expected it had to do with his representation of Chester. Chester's pending trial was big news in Probity. It was the sort of news that generated controversy. Lines had been drawn, and in many ways Brad Collins had been caught in the middle—not a place a sheriff prone to indolence liked to be. Micah would bet that Collins, if he could have any wish in the world, would choose to be invisible. Micah knew Collins liked things painless and uncomplicated, and already Micah was proving to be a thorn in the side of the sheriff and the prosecuting attorney as well.

The short, fat man who'd brought in the body was wiping down the side of his pack horse with a rag. A considerable amount of blood had leaked out of Lester onto the horse's right flank.

Micah extended his hand to the man. "Name's McConners," he said.

The man shoved the rag into the bib of his overalls, started to extend his own right hand, but stopped when he noticed it was smeared with blood. "Sorry," he said, and gave the hand a couple of quick swipes on his pants' leg and stuck it out again. "Matthew Wright. I grow wheat out east-a Lost Springs 'bout two mile."

"So what brings you into Probity, Mr. Wright?" Micah asked.

"I come in a couple, three times a year for supplies."

Micah pointed down to Lester. "Where'd you find the body?"

" 'Bout a mile out from town. He was laying in the ditch deader 'n hell. I tossed him on the back of Beulah here and brung him in." The man let go an amber stream of tobacco spit that hit the dust of the street and puddled into a ball of juice and dirt. He wiped the corner of his mouth with the back of his hand and looked up at the sun. "Whatsit, 'bout ten o'clock now?" he asked.

Micah pulled out his watch. "A quarter after."

"From the looks of him," said Matthew Wright, "I'd say he's been dead for ten, twelve hours. That the way you figure it, sheriff?"

Collins nodded. "I reckon."

"You see any tracks, or anything unusual around where you

found him?" Micah asked.

"They's tracks all over. Hell, man, it's a damned road. But I ain't seen nothin' unusual, 'ceptin' a dead man in the barrow ditch. That was unusual 'nough for me."

Despite himself, Micah smiled. Matthew Wright was a blunt man, and Micah liked that.

"How long you in town for, Mr. Wright?" Micah asked.

"A few of hours is all. I need to be gettin' back."

Micah jerked his thumb over his shoulder. "My office is down the street a ways," he said. "If you wouldn't mind, once you're ready to head out, maybe you could stop by and I'll ride with you to where you found the body. I'd like to take a look around for myself."

"I'll do 'er," Wright said as he mounted his riding horse and reached down for the lead rope of the pack animal. "I reckon it'll be two, maybe three o'clock. That okay by you?"

"I'll be waiting," Micah said.

As they watched Wright ride in the direction of the general store, Collins asked, "What the hell does Lester Jones being dead have to do with you, McConners?"

Micah took one more quick look at Lester's blank eyes. "Nothing, I hope," he said. But as he walked away, he was thinking that hope was pretty thin.

It was after five o'clock in the afternoon by the time Micah finished rubbing down Chester's bay. Since he didn't own a horse of his own, he had borrowed one of Chester's to ride out on the road with Matthew Wright. Once Micah was finished tending to the animal, he tossed some oats in the bin, gave the horse a pat on the rump, and headed for the house.

It turned out to be a waste of time going to the place where Lester's body had been found. Apart from some blood-soaked sand, there was nothing to see. A bad feeling gnawed at Micah about this though. He felt there was a connection between the murder and his and Lester's conversation the night before. It had been dark, and as far as Micah could tell, the street had been deserted. But who knew? It was possible Lester had been seen talking to Micah and had to pay a price. But that was nothing more than a guess, and Micah was tired of guessing. He was also tired of a client who refused to tell him the whole truth about what happened. As he headed from the stable toward Chester's house, he was determined to get to the bottom of what was going on.

Lights burned in the parlor, so Micah gave a couple of quick knocks to the back door, then walked in. "Chester," he called as he stepped into the kitchen, "it's Micah."

After a pause, Micah heard, "We're in the parlor. Come on in."

Micah walked down the hall, turned the corner, and saw Chester sitting with Polly and Cedra.

"So," said Chester, "the great detective returns." Chester lifted the glass he was holding as if in salute. "Care for a drink?" he offered. "Or a cup of tea?" He jabbed the glass in the direction of a pot and cups on the table.

"No," Micah said. "Nothing." He came into the room and sat down, nodding hello to Cedra and Polly.

"So, Mr. Holmes," Chester asked, "how are things on Baker Street?"

Micah was not in the mood. "Stop the shit, Chester," he said, snapping. Polly's eyebrows flew up. A smile flickered at Cedra's lips, but it lasted less than a second. Micah never used harsh language in the presence of women, but he expected that at least Cedra had heard the word before. If it was a new and shocking experience for Polly, he was sorry, but so be it.

"A young man died last night," Micah said. "I can't prove a thing, but I'm guessing he died at the hand of Sonny Pratt and maybe even his own brother, Hank Jones. It's been clear to me since the day they dragged you to jail that there are things you're keeping from me. Now it's time you told me the truth, all of it. What's going on here?"

Chester's eyes darted to Cedra and Polly. "Funny you should ask," he said, placing his glass on the table next to the tea service. "The ladies and I have been spending the afternoon discussing that very thing."

"I told Polly as far as my case is concerned what Sonny did to her doesn't matter," Chester said. "Am I right?"

Micah took a sip of the Scotch he had relented and agreed to accept. As always, his anger at Chester had evaporated quickly.

They had spent a half hour listening to Polly's story about her encounter with Sonny and the Jones boys by the river. Micah was numb from the hearing of it. And just as numbing was having his suspicions confirmed regarding the murder of Lester. Still there was no proof that Sonny had killed the boy, but Polly's description of Sonny's standing at the entrance to the alleyway earlier that afternoon and slicing his index finger across his throat chilled Micah to the marrow.

"Yes," he said, "you're right, Chester. It doesn't make a bit of difference as far as the statute regarding abortion is concerned. Even if we could convince a jury that Polly had been raped— and that's not very likely. Rape is a difficult thing to prove under any circumstances—it wouldn't make any difference. Aborting a pregnancy because it's come about as the result of rape is not a defense to the crime."

"Even if it can't be proven, I want them to know," said Polly. "I want the whole town—the whole county—to hear about it. I am not going to be frightened and shamed by this any longer. Even if there isn't enough proof to send Sonny to prison, I want everyone to know what kind of person he is. I want them to know what kind of an animal he is."

It was a difficult thing to believe that this was the same young woman as the terrorized creature Micah had seen in Chester's surgery only a month before. There was a different set to her jaw, a new glint in her eye. Micah could now see in the girl a resemblance to her mother that he had not noticed before.

"This is not a case we should take to trial," Micah said.

Chester leaned forward in his chair. "But you were the one who insisted I plead not guilty."

"That didn't mean I thought we should stand trial. We have no defense, and they have a witness and a confession." Micah swirled the liquor around in his glass until he had created a tiny tornado. "I'd say our legal position is not one to be envied."

"All right," asked Cedra, "let's get it out. What's the best thing for Chester to do? The best thing for Chester, I mean—no one else."

Micah lifted his glass with its whirling tornado and took a drink—too large of a drink. As smooth as the whisky was, it stung on the way down. "Of course, the best thing to do is make a deal, but Anderson isn't willing to bargain."

"So he's made our decision for us," said Chester. "The prospect of a trial doesn't bother me. It never did. I wanted to plead guilty in the hope of protecting Polly from that madman Sonny Pratt." He looked to the girl and smiled. "Now it seems maybe someone needs to protect Sonny from her." Polly didn't return Chester's smile, and Micah wondered how long it would be before she would.

"Besides," Chester went on. "I think that's a damned bad law, that abortion statute. It's high time someone took a position and pointed that out. It's an antiquated concept, and it should be changed." He shrugged and gave a resigned look. "I admit, rather than standing trial for the crime, I'd prefer to bring it to everyone's attention by going to Cheyenne next January and lobbying our elected buffoons, but it's too late for that now, isn't it?"

Micah had to agree. It was too late for many things. Even if Micah were an attorney with ten times his experience, there could be nothing gained in taking this case to trial. It was even possible that going to trial and losing—which was inevitable—might make matters worse. Everyone had a constitutional right to a trial by jury, but Micah suspected that a judge forced to sit through a jury trial of a defendant whose guilt was obvious would tend to hand down a harsher sentence than if the accused had pled guilty in the first place. That was not officially the case. In fact, it was never even hinted at, but Micah believed it was true.

"I'm worried," Micah said.

"You worry too damned much. You always have."

The first day of Chester's arrest had been difficult for him, but since that time Micah was amazed at how well Chester had been dealing with his situation. His mood now, though, could be described by no better word than ebullient. Micah could see the change in his expression, his smile, the way he sat in his chair. Chester Hedstrom was a fighter, and it was the fight and, even more, the message carried through the fight that mattered most to him. The idea that he was doomed to lose didn't seem to matter.

"Maybe I do worry too much," Micah said. "But better to worry too much than not at all."

"Well, that's a matter of opinion, isn't it? What nettle's in your boot this time?" Chester asked. He lifted the Glenlivet bottle and refreshed their drinks. He set the bottle down and wrapped his palm around the teapot to see if it was still warm.

"I'm worried about Polly and Cedra," Micah said. "Once the word gets out that Polly's prepared to testify, Sonny's going to be after her in earnest."

Chester's smile faded, and his eyebrows knitted together. He looked at the women and nodded. "He's right."

"Let him come," said Polly. And, though Micah admired the strength in her voice, that worried him too. Polly was finished with her fear of Sonny Pratt. She'd had enough. Now Micah was afraid she would become reckless.

Micah watched Polly, but he spoke to Cedra. "I think you'll be all right at the boarding house until we can make some other arrangements."

"They can stay here, of course," Chester said.

"No," said Cedra, "after the boarding house, this would be the first place Sonny would look."

"She's right," Micah agreed.

"Where then?" asked Chester.

Micah spun his glass again and watched the liquor swirl. "I have an idea where they can stay," he said. It was not an idea he liked, but it was the only idea he had.

Micah began the next morning by cleaning his rooms. When he wasn't seeing clients he needed something to stay busy, so he straightened things up and cleaned. Since for Micah seeing clients was a rarity, he figured he had the tidiest place in Probity.

He was in the back changing the sheets on the bed when he heard the jingle of the bell above his front door. He shoved the dirty linens into the bag that Sam Lung's Laundry provided its regular customers, and he stepped through his office into the reception area.

It was Thomas Blythe, wearing a wide smile and filling the small room with his regalness. "Micah, how good it is to see you again." He took Micah's hand and gave it one good, solid shake. He glanced around the office. "My, but you've accomplished a great deal in a short period of time. The offices look fine. Very fine, indeed."

"Thank you," Micah said. He was proud of what he'd done, and for a moment it pleased him to hear Blythe's compliments, but he remembered what a word-artist the man was and forced himself to deflate. "I think I'm about settled in."

"Good. Good." Blythe hung his Homburg on the rack and said, "I've been meaning to stop in for a visit for weeks now, but you know how it is." He held his hands out, palms up, and gave an expression and shrug that suggested he was a victim of his own success.

"Well," Micah said, "I don't know how it is, but I hope to someday." They both laughed louder than the little joke deserved.

"Do you mind, Micah, if we talk for a bit?"

"Of course not. Come into my private office." They stepped into the next room, and Micah felt a little awkward sitting in the large desk chair and motioning for Blythe to take the straight-back used by clients. For some reason Micah couldn't put his finger on, he felt it should be the other way around. It seemed if a room held a chair representative of authority, it should be occupied by the noble and distinguished buttocks of Thomas Blythe, Esquire, rather than his own paltry backside. He suppressed the smile that thought brought and said, "What may I do for you, Mr. Blythe?"

"Please, Micah," the man said, crossing his legs in a grand show of making himself quite comfortable, "call me Thomas. After all, we are now brethren in the same fraternity of attorneys." It was clear that Thomas Blythe enjoyed the sound of his voice, the flow of his words. "Not to mention that we are now adversaries in the same case."

"Yes," Micah said, "the Pratt divorce. I thought it was interesting, Thomas, that you were the attorney who filed the answer to my complaint in that matter when you referred Mrs. Pratt to me because you didn't accept cases of divorcement."

Micah thought for the briefest instant he saw a shadow pass over Blythe's bright smile, but the man's recovery was fast.

"It's not my practice to do domestic relations, but you must understand, Micah, over the years I've charged Emmett Pratt substantial fees in various matters. When he was served with a summons and complaint by his wife, and he came to me for help, I couldn't very well turn him away."

Blythe's explanation was quick and convincing. He was good. Micah had to give him that. A lot could be learned from this lawyer.

"But it's not the Pratt divorce to which I was referring, Micah, when I said we are now adversaries in the same case."

"No?" Micah was confused. His file drawer of cases was not so overflowing that he was likely to forget what attorney opposed him.

"Earl Anderson has requested my assistance in the prosecution of Dr. Hedstrom."

When Micah realized how long the silence was that followed Blythe's statement, he assumed it was up to him to fill it, but he was lost for what to say.

"You appear nonplused, Micah, and I assure you, that was not my intent. I can appreciate your surprise at this turn of events." He flicked an invisible piece of lint from his trousers' leg, then ran his finger along the crease. "It came as something of a surprise to me as well."

Once Micah found his voice, he asked, "Why would Anderson bring you in on this? It seems unlike him."

Blythe looked toward the ceiling as though his thoughts were written there and he was reading them aloud. "Mr. Anderson is blessed with an eagerness," he said. "In many instances—most instances—eagerness is a fine quality." Now he aimed his gaze at Micah. "But there are those who feel, and in my opinion rightfully so, that Anderson showed too much eagerness in his effort to prosecute the doctor."

Blythe was not a man of few words, but he offered Micah no more explanation for his involvement than that.

"So," Micah said, "which of you is lead counsel?"

"Mr. Anderson, of course. After all, he is the duly elected prosecutor for this county."

"Yes, so he is."

"I may be wrong, Micah, and, please, correct me if I am, but I infer that your question is not so much who is lead counsel but with whom are you expected to deal."

"All right," said Micah. He spoke with caution. Micah felt caution was necessary in a conversation with Thomas Blythe.

"I would never presume to infringe upon Mr. Anderson's authority, but let me assure you that any question you might have regarding our position in this case may be directed to me. In fact, it is only with me that I suggest you do deal."

Micah tugged on his earlobe as he considered what it was Blythe was saying. "That's twice, Thomas, you've used the word *deal*. I was under the impression from Anderson that there would be no deal."

"Yes, I am aware that he's given you that impression. All I can say is that Earl, in his eagerness to perform the duties of his office, spoke in haste. I feel confident we can work something out that is satisfactory to everyone."

Micah felt his stomach flutter. He couldn't believe what he was hearing. As a matter of law and as a matter of fact, his and Chester's position was untenable. They had nothing in their favor, and a trial would be a guaranteed conviction, even without Thomas Blythe assisting in the prosecution. With Blythe prosecuting, Micah wondered if the jury would even bother to retire to the jury room. Micah had this image of them reaching their decision right there in the box.

This talk of working something out was an interesting turn.

Micah did his best to keep his excitement from showing. "Did you have something specific in mind, Thomas?"

Blythe stood and with his hands behind his back began to walk about the room. "I did have something in mind, yes. I would love to make this case go away, Micah. I'll tell you that right now. If the situation was different, I would dismiss the charge. I have the greatest respect for Dr. Hedstrom and a real fondness for Polly Pratt. I do not wish to see harm or embarrassment come to either of them. But as you know, the mere filing of an action like this inflames a certain segment of the population. There are even people who feel the doctor has done murder and should be punished accordingly. It's true, that is a very small group, but nevertheless the group exists."

Micah knew what Blythe said was true. The attitude of the largest portion of the community was in Chester's favor, but there were a few who felt he should be hanged.

"The point to all that," continued Blythe, "is that this case, as much as some of us would like it to, cannot disappear."

Again Micah couldn't believe what he was hearing. Perhaps there was going to be a way out of this mess after all. The excitement began to churn in him, and it was difficult to sit still. He held himself at his desk, though, and watched as Blythe walked about the room.

"Dr. Hedstrom will have to serve some time," Blythe said. "I've thought about it long and hard, and there is no way around it. But if he is willing to plead guilty and we can avoid a trial, I'm prepared to recommend to Judge Walker that the doctor serve one year and no more. I will even recommend that he serve the time here in the county jail rather than the state penitentiary." He sat back in the chair and leaned toward Micah as he said, "I wish I could do better than that, Micah. I really do."

Now Micah was at a loss. He had no idea why Blythe was

making this offer, but he didn't care. "Do you think Judge Walker will agree to only a year?"

"I've been a friend of the judge for almost two decades. I'm confident he will accept my recommendation."

Ever since Micah learned of the charge and subsequent confession, he had felt that if he could keep Chester's sentence below ten years it would be a victory. Eight years would be a miracle. What Blythe offered was beyond anything he could have imagined.

"And," added Blythe as he raised an index finger to his lips and lowered his voice, "between you and me, Micah, after a few months, if you want to move the court for a sentence reduction, we will not resist. I won't guarantee Walker will go along with that, but he might. It's worth a try." He leaned back in the chair, folded his hands in his lap, and assumed the expression of a man who had successfully completed a chore. "I'm afraid that's the best I can do," he said. "I hope those conditions are satisfactory."

Satisfactory? Yes, Micah imagined they were quite satisfactory.

Micah sent messages to Chester, Polly, and Cedra asking them to come to his office at two o'clock that afternoon. When they arrived, he couldn't contain his excitement. In one torrential gush of words he told them of Blythe's involvement in the case, his visit to Micah's office earlier in the day, and the offer Blythe had made.

The women were also excited—Cedra in particular. First she gave Micah a hug, and then she hugged Chester. After holding Chester for a long moment, she pulled a handkerchief from her sleeve and blotted her eyes. For some reason, Micah found this strong woman's dabbing that lacy linen to her eye to be an especially beautiful act.

He cleared his throat and looked away.

Micah knew the jail time would be difficult. Chester was a man who relished his freedom. He always had, but perhaps even more so now. Every day Chester was spending more and more time on his moto-cycle, riding through the streets of Probity or traveling the rough county roads. Micah often saw him motoring along in his duster, floppy cap, and goggles. Even the local horses and other livestock now seemed accustomed to Chester's noisy contraption.

Not so long ago they'd been standing on the boardwalk outside Micah's office. Chester was on one of his rides, and he had stopped to say hello. They were looking down at the moto-cycle. It was up on its stand in front of the hitching post, and it seemed tiny next to an Appaloosa tied to the rail. Chester, with pride in his voice, said, "It's beautiful, isn't it, Micah?"

"Well," Micah allowed, "I got to admit it's an interesting thing, all right."

Chester smacked Micah on the upper arm with his leather gauntlets. "Hell, man, it's more than interesting, much more. It represents all that's new and ahead of us." He hopped from the walk down to the street, and with the sleeve of his duster, he buffed a spot on the moto-cycle's fender. "It's this device and a thousand other ingenious devices that'll make up the twentieth century. And it's not merely the devices themselves, but the attitude they promote. There's a new state-of-mind afoot, Micah. It's coming with the new century, and we have to be open to it. More than ever before, through his ingenuity, man is in control of the world around him. And all this will mean freedom, a new kind of freedom." He ran a hand along the handlebar in a gesture Micah could only describe as a caress. "There have been articles running in the newspapers all summer long about how the rail line is going to give a huge demonstration of its newest locomotive. Have you read them?" Micah said he had, but Chester continued telling him about them anyway. "They plan it for this coming New Year's Day, and they've given the locomotive the number twenty in honor of our new century. They claim it'll be able to travel from Casper to Cheyenne at an average speed of right at eighty miles per hour. Can you imagine that? In some stretches it'll exceed a hundred miles an hour."

"I've seen those stories," Micah said again, "and I don't believe a word of it. It's impossible."

"No, it's not. They're having to rebuild some of the track and reinforce it in places, but it's very possible. When I was back East in '93, locomotive Number 999 on the New York Line broke the hundred-mile-per-hour barrier. Of course, it wasn't close to the achievement this would be."

Chester was clearly excited about it. "I tell you, Micah, he went on, the twentieth century promises unlimited possibilities." He tossed his leg over the moto-cycle and sat down. "She's knocking on our door. All we need is to muster the guts to let her in."

Yes, it would be difficult for Chester to spend a year, or even a few months, locked away in some cell. But before Blythe's offer, the prospect looming out there of eight, ten, or fourteen years in prison was so horrible that Micah couldn't allow himself even to ponder it. Now the image was manageable. He could picture it now, and it was painful, but he knew it could be coped with.

It was likely this would cause Chester to lose his right to practice medicine. But if the state medical board decided to take his license, that too was something with which they could deal. They could argue their case in the district court and even appeal to the state supreme court, if necessary.

Micah never felt better. He never felt more capable. The potential damage of this horrible situation had been delineated, and he knew they could handle what lay ahead.

Although he hadn't said much, Chester seemed as surprised

as everyone else when Micah told them of Thomas Blythe's offer. Now Chester walked to the door, opened it, and leaned
against the sill. "It's a beautiful day," he said. Micah watched
from a chair next to the window. There was a touch of autumn
in the air, but as was common in the autumn in central
Wyoming, there was also bright sunshine. The sky held only a
few clouds, and those scudded along the horizon miles away.

As Chester looked into the street, watching the traffic and the
pedestrians pass, he began to hum an off-key rendition of the
chorus to *"On the Banks of the Wabash, Far Away."* He greeted
some of the passersby and nodded to others. Ricky Fallon, a
friend of Micah and Chester's dating back to their teen years,
stopped, and he and Chester talked baseball for a bit. The
season was drawing to a close, but mostly they discussed the
new American League that Ban Johnson out of Cincinnati was
putting together for next year.

It would be the first baseball season of a brand-new century.

As Ricky and Chester visited, Micah explained to Cedra and
Polly how nothing would happen with Chester's case until late
December, when Judge Walker came to town for the trial. Now,
though, instead of having the trial, Judge Walker would re-
arraign Chester, and Chester would change his plea from not
guilty to guilty. The judge would accept the guilty plea, then
sentence according to the terms of the plea agreement. The
whole thing would be over in fifteen minutes or less.

It was, Micah realized, an anticlimactic ending to a frightening ordeal.

"What do you think of all of this, Polly?" Chester asked.
Ricky had gone on about his business, but Chester had not
turned around. He still faced outdoors.

"Well, I think it's wonderful that you won't have to go to
prison and that the whole thing might well be over for you in

less than a year. Yes," she repeated, "I think it's quite wonderful."

Chester stepped back into the room and closed the door. "What about Sonny?" he asked.

"Sonny," said Cedra, who never hesitated to voice her disdain for her stepson, "will go on being Sonny until we get a sheriff or someone who's willing to stand up to him."

"That's my thought as well," Chester said.

Micah didn't like the expression on Chester's face. He had seen that look before. Apparently Cedra saw it too, because she asked, "What are you thinking, Chester?" There was a reluctant, uncertain quality to her voice.

"I was wondering if Polly wanted to miss this opportunity to tell everyone what Sonny Pratt has done to her." Polly didn't respond, and Chester continued. "There's a lot happening around here that I don't like, and I was beginning to look forward to the chance to get some of it off my chest."

Micah, seeing where this was headed, said, "That's ridiculous."

"Yes," agreed Cedra, "it is."

Chester's and Polly's eyes were locked. "What do you think, Polly?" he asked. "Do you think it's ridiculous to want to put a stop to Sonny Pratt?"

"I don't want to see you hurt, Doctor," Polly said.

"If I refused to plead guilty," Chester asked, "would you be willing to take the stand at my trial and tell your story?"

"Stop it, Chester," Micah said. "I am not going to let you do this."

Ignoring Micah, Chester still held Polly's gaze. "Would you?" he asked again.

"Micah is right, Chester," said Cedra. "You listen to him. We can tell the truth about Sonny Pratt without your doing this."

Still Chester's eyes held Polly. "We can tell them," he agreed, "but no one will listen. You know that yourself. At a trial they have to listen."

"Whether they will or whether they won't," Micah said, "doesn't matter. If you go to trial, you're going to lose, and then you're going to prison for a long God-damned time. Don't you understand that? It's not worth it. We have a way out of this thing, Chester. The hell with Sonny Pratt."

Chester, who even now had not released his gaze from Polly, said, "You found your courage earlier, Polly. Would you still tell them what happened?"

Cedra turned to her daughter. "Tell him no, Polly. Tell him you won't do it. Don't let him do this to himself."

"Or to you, Polly," Micah said. "Sonny Pratt is insane. You know what he's capable of. Before, we had no choice. We had to go to trial. Now, though, it's different. There's no reason to risk your life now."

"You know what's right, don't you, Polly?" Chester said. "Would you tell them, if you had the chance? Would you tell them, Polly?"

In a whisper, with her eyes still locked on Chester, Polly answered, "Yes, yes, I would."

★ ★ ★ ★ ★

PART THREE:
THE JUDGE'S DECISION

★ ★ ★ ★ ★

CHAPTER TWENTY-ONE

Christmas Day, 1900 fell on a Tuesday. Earl Anderson and Thomas Blythe assured Judge Walker that it would not take any longer than three days to try Chester Hedstrom's case, so even if the trial was not begun until Wednesday, it could still be given to the jury by Friday afternoon. The judge, though, being a man with a skeptical nature, brought the jury panel in on Monday morning. "We'll pick a jury," he said, "and recess for Christmas." Micah had heard stories of Judge Walker from Judge Pullum. Walker was a gentleman with a fondness for the intricacies of the law, but he had little regard for lawyers. He assumed they were all, for some nefarious reason, dedicated to wasting his time. "If we do *voir dire* on Christmas Eve," the judge had told the attorneys at a pretrial conference held a month before, "I expect it'll go a hell of a lot faster."

Micah sat in the back room of the small house on North First Street, going over his notes. He had eaten Christmas dinner with the others, but as soon as the last of Lottie's mincemeat pie was gone, he had returned to this room to prepare for the trial that would begin tomorrow.

Judge Walker had been right. The jury selection went quickly. They had chosen the twelve men by two o'clock yesterday afternoon. Micah suspected it went as well as it did for two reasons. One, because, as the judge pointed out, it was Christmas Eve and no one wanted to be there; and, two, both Blythe and Anderson knew they would get a conviction no matter who was in the box.

But Micah felt good about the jury. The twelve men selected seemed a reasonable lot. The oldest was a few years younger than the sixty-year-old maximum allowed by statute, and the youngest almost five years older than the twenty-one-year-old minimum. Micah wished he could have empaneled some women on the jury. Pregnancy—the avoidance of it, or the dealing with it once it came about—was a situation with which women were familiar, and Micah believed women would be more sympathetic to Chester and Polly. Wyoming had granted women suffrage twenty-one years earlier. It had been the first government in the world to take that step. In the earliest days, judges in Laramie and Cheyenne had allowed women to sit on juries, but it hadn't been long before judges in the smaller communities decided it was inappropriate and in time it wasn't allowed in any of the courts. A situation Micah hoped would someday change.

Micah snuffed out the butt of his Cyclone. The ashtray was full. He had smoked an entire package today, and his mouth tasted the way the ashtray smelled.

He stood and crossed the room to the vanity that held a basin of water. He washed his face and rinsed out his mouth. At Thanksgiving, Micah had decided he would stop smoking. He finished his open package of Cyclones but didn't buy more. At least he didn't until two days later. "I'll quit after the trial," he had promised himself at the time, but now that the trial was upon him he wondered if he would.

There was a knock on the door and before he could respond, Fay stepped in carrying a cup of coffee. The room contained a bed, a chair, the vanity, and the small table where Micah had been working. She placed the coffee on the table. "I made a fresh pot," she said. "How are you doing?" When he didn't answer, she crossed to him and pushed back a lock of his hair that had fallen over his forehead. As always, she smiled when it flopped right back.

"I'm tired," he said, and as soon as he said it, he wished he hadn't. He knew the response it would bring.

"You shouldn't be staying with us so much," Fay said. "With the trial coming, you should be at your own place where you can get some rest."

He pulled her to him and squeezed. Her body was small, yet strong. "I'm all right."

"We don't need you to protect us night and day, Micah. There's Chester and there's Jackson. And you know as well as I do that I can pull the trigger on that shotgun there—" She nodded to the gun leaning against the wall. "—as well as any of the three of you."

The truth was she could do it that well or better. Fay, using the very gun in this room, had killed the two Canada honkers they'd eaten earlier for Christmas dinner.

This was not a new topic of conversation. "If Sonny tries anything," Micah said for what seemed the hundredth time, "I want to be here."

Micah hated the thought of hiding Polly and Cedra at Lottie and Fay's house, but there was nowhere else. So far, though, it had worked. They had been here for three weeks, and there had been no sign of Sonny Pratt.

Micah had stalled as long as he could. But finally he'd had to admit to Blythe that Chester would not accept his offer, and he would not plead guilty.

That had been difficult for Micah. He was furious with Chester. Micah had screamed and threatened. He had begged and cajoled. But Chester was adamant. He would not plead guilty; he would stand trial.

"Why?" Micah shouted at Chester on the night before he went to Blythe's office to tell him the situation. "Why?"

"For Polly," Chester said. "I've told you that. Sonny has threatened to kill her *if* the truth comes out. I feel he'll kill her *unless* the truth comes out." They were in Chester's carriage house, and he was tinkering with the moto-cycle. He was always fussing with the damned contraption, and that also infuriated Micah. The temperature was in the single digits, much too cold for Chester to ride, but the only way Micah could talk to him was to stand in the bitter cold of the carriage house while Chester did whatever the hell it was he was doing. "That's one reason," Chester added. "There are others."

"Right, I know," Micah said. He paced back and forth, spewing plumes of frosty breath and slapping his arms together in a battle to keep his circulation going. He really hated the cold. "You think it's a bad law and you want to change it. Let me tell you something, Chester, getting convicted of a crime is not the way to change a law. Felons rotting in prison don't have a lot of influence with the legislature."

Chester was squatted beside the cycle and turning something with a wrench. "I do think it's a bad law," he allowed. "Any law that requires a woman to bear a rapist's baby is a bad law. But there's more to it than that." He slid a lamp closer to where he was working. "Do you realize, Micah, I've almost doubled the power this engine puts out? I expect I've got it well over three horsepower. I plan to write Uncle Oscar a letter explaining all the things I've done—"

Micah bent down and jerked the wrench from Chester's hand. "I do not give a god-damn about this toy of yours, Chester. You are about to go to prison. Don't you understand that? Prison for a long time. That's bad enough, but what makes it even worse is you don't have to. I want to understand why you are doing this, and the explanations you've given so far don't hold water, not to my thinking, anyway. So if you've got something more, I want to hear it, and I want to hear it right now."

Chester stood and wiped his hands on a rag. "You've become a pushy bastard since your admittance to the bar."

"I want some answers."

Chester smiled. "All right, all right. I know you don't understand my thinking, and I don't blame you. The truth is I have wanted to talk to you about all this," he said, "but to you it'll sound foolish, so I haven't."

"Since when did sounding foolish ever stop you, Chester?"

"I know there's a lot at stake. I'm about to be taken away for a long time. But it seems to me that's secondary."

"We're talking about fourteen years of your life here. What the hell could that be secondary to?"

Chester tossed the rag to the work bench and pulled his coat tighter. For the first time since Micah had come into the carriage house, Chester seemed to notice the cold. "The world's about to become a different place—"

"Oh, shit, Chester," Micah interrupted, "don't start in on this new-century stuff. It's become a joke, a bad joke."

Ignoring Micah's interruption, Chester went on. "The truth is, it's already changed, but no one's noticed it yet."

Micah began pacing again. "The wolf is at the door, Chester. I do not want to hear this."

"We have to be different, Micah. I love the complexity of this new century we're stepping in to, but because it'll be so complex, *we* have to simplify."

"Thank you for that insight, Mr. Thoreau."

Chester smiled again. He seemed to be having fun. "It does sound a bit Thoreau-like, doesn't it? But I've never had much regard for Thoreau. I've always thought not only was his message simple, so was a lot of his thinking." He shrugged. "I guess I still feel that way. I'm trained as an engineer, and I don't believe the machinery of modern society is a bad thing."

Micah clamped his gloved hands over his ears. "Damn it, Chester, I am not listening to this."

Chester went on. "Society's machinery is now about a hundred times more complicated than fifty years ago when Henry David was sitting around his pond. And soon, very soon, it'll be a thousand times more complicated."

"Jesus, Chester, we are not dealing with abstractions here. There's nothing abstract about hard labor in a state penitentiary."

"Hear me out on this. You asked why, and I'm telling you. I'm saying we can only succeed in this complex environment if we simplify things within ourselves." He tapped himself twice on the chest.

"Oh, God."

Chester waggled an index finger reproachfully. "You're not listening."

"I'm listening. I'm listening."

"The world—maybe Americans more than anyone—has always viewed things in black and white, but things're becoming grayer all the time. There are no clear lines between black and white anymore. You and Fay should realize that, Micah. But in some instances we need clear lines. It's our duty to decide where our own personal lines should be drawn, draw them, and refuse to go beyond them."

Micah had stopped his pacing and now only stood and stared at his friend with disbelief. This was all very interesting, but it was the sort of discussion they had with a brandy or a Scotch in their hands. This kind of talk was left in the parlor. It was not taken into the real world. Certainly not into a courtroom.

Micah would not hesitate to pick up one of the heavy wrenches and use it as a bludgeon if he thought it would do any good.

"Our lives are about to become so complex that there's a real potential for bad things to happen. Things unimaginable even for us in our own time, much less for Thoreau in his. But his ideas, some of them anyway, were right. Simplify. We'll never simplify the world around us—I wouldn't want to even if we could—but because we can't, we have to simplify ourselves." There was a stub of a cigar on the edge of the work bench. Chester picked it up and shoved it into his mouth, but didn't light it. "If we lose track of who we are, Micah, we'll look for only the most expedient ways to live, and we'll stop taking stands for those doomed but righteous endeavors that make being human special. It'll become a century populated by generation after generation of lost cynics." He grabbed Micah around the shoulder and, with a laugh, he added, "And, God knows, we wouldn't want that, would we? I mean, hell, there's only room for so many lawyers in the world."

Micah offered him a scowl.

"It'll be all right. Don't worry," Chester said. He gave Micah a reassuring shake, and with his big arm still around Micah's shoulder, he shuttled him toward the carriage house door. Come on," he said, "let's go inside, brew some coffee, and warm up. It's cold as shit out here. Didn't you notice?"

Micah tried to understand Chester's thinking, but he couldn't. As far as Micah could tell, the universe was divided into two categories: things that worked and things that did not. Accepting Blythe's offer worked; going to trial, losing, and Chester's ending up in prison did not work. No matter from what distorted angle Chester chose to view it, it did not work.

That conversation had taken place almost a month before. Now, as Micah stood in the back room of the house on First Street, he still didn't understand.

"I wish we could make love," Fay whispered.

That brought Micah out of his reverie. He could see a flush

in the coffee-and-cream color of Fay's cheeks. Although at night, in the dark of his room, her deeds were always pleasantly brazen, her speech never was, and he could see she had embarrassed herself. "I wish we could too," he said.

They relinquished privacy when they set up "The Tiny Fortress," as Jackson Clark called it. The house was small: a parlor, two bedrooms, a kitchen with a small dining area, and an enclosed back porch. During the day, Lottie and Fay would go to their café as always, and either Chester, Micah, or Jackson would stay with Polly and Cedra. At night they all stayed together. The four women slept in the two bedrooms; the men slept on mats in the parlor, and each man took a shift standing watch. Any time Micah began to question the necessity of such precautions, he remembered the slashed throat of Lester Jones.

"This is almost over," Micah said.

"Do you think we won't have to worry about Sonny after the trial?" Fay asked.

"Sonny's crazy. It's impossible to predict what he might do, but I have to agree with Chester. Once the story's out, even though there's not enough proof to convict Sonny of his crime against Polly, I don't think he'll bother her anymore. It would be too risky. If something happened to her after her testimony, even Brad Collins couldn't turn his back on a coincidence like that."

"Oh, he could turn his back on it all right," Fay said, "but, you're right. I can't believe he would once the whole town knew about it."

"You wouldn't think so, anyway." The feel of Fay next to him caused a tightness in Micah's groin. He lifted her chin, gave her a kiss, and said, "I think I'd better drink that coffee you brought in."

Fay straightened the collar of her dress and rubbed the back of her neck. "I miss our visits," she said. "Visits" had become the word they used to describe her late-night trips to the back door of Micah's office.

"I miss them too."

"It's all we have," she said as she dropped into the chair in front of the table where Micah had been working earlier. In a distant voice, more to herself than him, she added, "It's all we'll ever have."

She rarely mentioned their situation. Their inability to be together in the open was something they both were trying to accept. Talking about it didn't help. But Micah knew it bothered her. It bothered him.

"Only our visits," she said, "that's all."

Micah groped for something to say but came up with nothing.

"It's Christmas," Fay continued. "I guess a woman has a right to say silly things at Christmas." She pulled a handkerchief from the pocket of the large white apron she wore. She touched it to her lips, then with both hands clutched it in her lap. "I'm twenty-four years old, Micah, and I want more for us than our visits. I always feel that way, but sometimes I feel it more than others."

"I do too, Fay."

"I want to have your babies, but I know I never will. That makes me sad, especially at Christmastime." She held the handkerchief up for him to see. "I'm not crying," she said with what looked to be a forced smile, "but I got this out in case I did."

He came to her and lifted her out of the chair. "If you want to cry, you go ahead," he said, pulling her to him.

She lay her face against his chest and said, "I want us to have a big house with a yard and lots of children. I want a Christmas tree ten feet tall, with stacks of presents under it. I want to watch our babies crawling around that tree, shaking the presents, trying to guess what's inside." She looked up at him. "I want that, Micah, but it will never be."

Micah wanted to tell her, yes, it could happen, it would happen, but he knew it could not. His only response was to pull her closer.

"I wish we could make everyone disappear," she said. "That's the only way we'll ever be together is if the rest of the world would disappear."

"Hell, Fay, if we're going to make a wish, let's wish they would change. Let's wish they wouldn't think there was anything wrong with our being together."

She lay her head back on his chest. "No," she said, "that wouldn't work. There's a better chance they'd all disappear than there is they'll ever change."

CHAPTER TWENTY-TWO

When Jebediah Blake, Benjamin Walker's court reporter, came onto the stage with his pencils and pad, Micah knew the long months of waiting were over.

They were in Edwin Bury's Opera House. The courtroom's being so small, the county was forced to rent Mr. Bury's building every time Judge Walker came to Probity for a jury trial. There was always mumbling among the county commissioners about the need for a new courthouse whenever they received Mr. Bury's bill. Since Bury was a wily businessman and knew there was no other place in town suitable, he did not hesitate to test the limits of the commissioners' willingness to pay rent.

"Be ready," Jackson said to Micah under his breath, "whenever you see Jeb, you know Walker's not far behind."

Micah rubbed his stomach. For days now he'd felt a sick fluttering. He knew what it was, of course. He was scared out of his wits.

At least Jackson was with him. He took some comfort in that. Micah had never had a jury trial in his life. In fact, he'd never had a trial of any kind. Knowing this, when the word got out that Chester was not going to plead guilty and the case would go to court, Jackson had come to Micah and offered him his services as co-counsel *pro bono,* free of charge.

Micah jumped at the offer. "That would be wonderful," he said, not even trying to hide his relief at not having to defend Chester alone. Micah was confident in his abilities, but he knew there was much he did not know, and the assistance of someone who had been practicing law for as long as Jackson Clark would be invaluable.

Later Micah had asked Jackson why he wanted to help. "Three reasons," the old man said as they sipped beer in Buck's. "First, I like Chester Hedstrom—always have. Next, I think that abortion statute is poorly written and is bad law. And, third, but not last—" He poked Micah with his elbow. "—I want to teach that God-damned pompous ass Thomas Blythe a lesson."

Micah pointed out how it was doubtful Thomas Blythe would be taught any lessons in this case.

"Well, then," Jackson said, wiping foam from his mouth, "if by some miracle we should win, the humiliation alone would teach him something, and I know that you're an honorable enough young man that you would share the credit with me for helping out."

"And if we lose?" asked Micah.

Jackson laughed his high-pitched cackle. "I'll remind everyone you were lead counsel, and you'll take all the blame."

The court reporter was a man a bit older than Micah. He arranged his pencils in a neat row, opened his pad, and stood beside his chair with his hands behind his back.

"You watch the wing over yonder," Jackson said, nodding toward the left. "Walker's a fella who has a fondness for the trappings of being a judge. You'll get on his good side right off if you're the one who sees him coming first and calls out for everyone to stand up."

"That sounds a little petty," Micah said. Even Judge Pullum hadn't taken that sort of thing very seriously.

"Walker's not a petty man, I don't think, not about the important things, anyway, but he can be burdensome if your manner doesn't set right with him."

Micah looked into the stage's left wing. Though where they

sat was well lit, the wings were dark and it was difficult to see. Brad Collins stood off stage at the edge of the darkness. He was wearing a black suit and blended into the shadows, but Micah could tell where he was by the large white Stetson he held in front of him. The hat caught the light from the stage and stood out in the gloom.

Bury's Opera House, by opera house standards, was not a large place. There were only fifty seats in the audience, but they were all full, and spectators lined the walls and overflowed into the lobby.

The stage itself, though, was as fine as anything in Cheyenne or Casper. It was large and well constructed. It boasted thick velvet curtains. Upstage, a desk had been placed on an eight-inch-high pedestal. That would serve as Judge Walker's bench. Next to that sat a large oak chair for the witnesses. In front of the bench was a small writing table for the court reporter, and downstage were two larger tables for the prosecution and the defense. Stage-right, lined up in two rows of six, sat the jurymen. Micah didn't remember them looking as stern on Monday, when they were chosen to serve, as they looked now.

Micah peeked around Jackson to the prosecution's table. Both Thomas Blythe and Earl Anderson were elegant in their expensive suits and vests. The shine on Blythe's shoes was nearly blinding in the bright stage lights.

"Watch for the judge, now," Jackson said.

Micah looked left into the darkness of the wing. He stared past Collins and searched for some sign of movement.

The silence in the room was eerie. It seemed unnatural to have this many people in one place and have it be so quiet. It made Micah even more nervous than he already was, which surprised him. As he felt his innards churn, he didn't think it was possible to be more nervous than he was.

The lack of movement in the room was also strange. Blythe

and Anderson sat at their table, their hands folded, their eyes locked on the stage-left wing. Chester sat beside Micah like a rock. Jackson, the jury, the spectators, everyone could have as easily been pictures painted on canvas as real human beings. It was as though time had ticked to a standstill while the universe waited for Benjamin Walker to step onto the stage.

But then Brad Collins looked down at his hat, flicked something from the brim, and in a chorus, Earl Anderson and Thomas Blythe shouted, *"All rise!"* And the silence was shattered as every person in Bury's Opera House came to his feet.

With a majestic demeanor, Judge Walker ascended his bench, glanced down at Blythe and Anderson, bestowed upon them a quick nod, and said, "You may be seated."

As they resumed their chairs, Jackson made a sound like he was sucking something out of a tooth and whispered to Micah, "Damn, boy, you gotta be fast."

Benjamin Walker was a man in his late fifties who had read for the bar in Denver while supporting himself—in a meager way—as an actor. He possessed a rich baritone voice that had no difficulty reaching the "cheap seats" in the rear of the house.

"Court is in session," he said as he slipped his spectacles on. "We are here today in the matter of the State of Wyoming versus Chester Hedstrom, M.D." It was clear that the judge was speaking to the record as much as he was to the parties and spectators. He looked down at Jeb Blake, the court reporter, and said, "The date today is December 26, 1900. Court has been in recess since two o'clock on the twenty-fourth. A jury has been duly impaneled, sworn, and is now sitting in the box prepared to try this cause."

Walker turned his gaze upon the jury. "Dr. Hedstrom is charged, gentlemen, with the performance of an illegal abortion. I'll instruct you as to the specific law in this matter at the end of the evidence and before you retire to deliberate, but suffice it to say that in this state performing any abortion is a crime except when the health of the mother is at stake."

He turned to the prosecution's table. "With that, we will hear the state's opening statement. Mr. Anderson, you're the county attorney. Will you be making the opening?"

"No, sir, Judge. I will defer to Mr. Blythe."

"Very well, Mr. Blythe, you may proceed."

Blythe rose and started for the lectern that had been placed in front of the twelve jurors. As he crossed, he acknowledged Micah.

"Good morning, Mr. Blythe," Micah said in return, but he was shocked and embarrassed to hear the raspy quiver that came out. *Christ,* he thought, *I feel like a deer being stalked by a cougar.*

Micah was not sure how he felt about Thomas Blythe. It was clear Jackson Clark and Cedra both held a deep dislike for the man, and Micah could see why. Blythe was everything they said he was: a self-important, pompous ass. On the other hand, Micah believed Blythe was an honorable man, at least within the framework of Blythe's own definition of the term. Blythe would represent his client to the fullest. He would grant quarter if it was in his client's best interest to do so; if it was not, there would be no mercy.

When Micah had gone to Blythe's office to tell him that Chester would not accept the plea agreement, Blythe had shown surprise and what Micah believed to be genuine disappointment. After their discussion of the matter, Blythe walked Micah to the door. "You realize, don't you, Micah, what this means? The specific terms of the agreement were my idea. I wanted to make the offer so lenient Dr. Hedstrom would not dream of refusing. Since he has chosen to do so, however, I must change my approach. If this goes to trial, I will do everything within my ability to see that there is a conviction and that the doctor serves as much time in prison as the law will allow. It's not at all what I want to see happen, but I have agreed to take this case, and I have my reputation as a trial lawyer to consider." Micah said something to the effect that he would expect nothing less, and quickly left. He couldn't help thinking, though, that now they were worse off than they had been before. Before, their opponent had been an incompetent Earl Anderson. Now their opponent was a determined Thomas Blythe.

"Your Honor," Blythe began, "counsel, gentlemen of the jury." He paused, stared toward some spot in the near distance, and took in a deep breath. It was a quick gesture that communicated solemnity and the seriousness of the task he was about to perform. "Every case at bar," he said, "is a story involving real people. Real, flesh-and-blood people the same as all of you. The same as myself and Mr. Anderson. The same as young Mr. McConners there and Mr. Clark. We are all human beings. We shiver when we are cold. We perspire when we are hot. We love our children. We love our homes. The vilest criminal who has ever walked the face of the earth is also human. He was once a child. He had the innocence of a child. He had the ability of a child to love without condition. He had the hopes of a child.

"But occasionally as he grows something happens to that child. Sometimes it's the evil of the adults around him that turns that child astray. We have all seen it. It's an ugly thing, and it creates an ugly thing.

"Other times there can be a bad seed in a child that is present at the moment of his birth but takes time to grow before it manifests itself. That, gentlemen, can be ugly too."

Blythe moved to the side of the lectern and took a half-step closer to the jurors. In a soft and reasonable voice he said, "But evil does not *always* come in an ugly package. Sometimes—

oftentimes—it comes cloaked in finery. Sometimes it possesses wit and charm. Evil is not always an affliction of the low and the base. It is also capable of afflicting the high and the seemingly virtuous. That, my friends, is the situation we have before us."

He stepped in front of the lectern and shoved his hands into his pockets. A hint of a smile played at the edges of his mouth. "Those of us who have lived in small towns all our lives know the speed at which news can move from one place to another. I can still remember where I was when I first heard that Dr. Hedstrom had been charged with this horrible crime." He stopped and held up a finger. "By the way, I want you to remember those words, gentlemen: *horrible crime.* Because, as you will see, this is in fact a horrible, *horrible,* crime. A death has occurred here. It was the death of a nameless victim, but a painful, violent death has occurred. We must not ever allow ourselves to forget that."

He placed his weight on his left leg and assumed a casual stance. "But, as I was saying, I was in my own house when I heard the news. It was noon, and Ethel was serving some of her famous chicken." He patted himself on his still small but burgeoning abdomen. A number of the jurors chuckled. "Ethel had spent her morning perusing the shelves at the local millinery, which, as we all know, is a much more expedient source of information than the local newspaper." More jurors chuckled. "I was biting into a drumstick when she said, 'Thomas, isn't it awful about Dr. Hedstrom?' And she proceeded to tell me the story of what had occurred. And I assure you, gentlemen, the slightest breeze wafting through the open window could have knocked me over after I heard the horrid tale my good wife told."

He rounded the lectern and once again stood behind it. He turned his gaze to the defense table and raised his arm toward

Chester. "This is a special sort of man, my friends. He is a man who possesses a unique kind of evil. It is an evil of arrogance. It is an evil that sickens a man's mind to the point where he believes that he is above the law—all law, both man's and God's. It is an evil arrogance, gentlemen, which gives a man the ability and the stomach to insert cold steel into a girl and wrench and tear in bits and pieces the life from inside her young womb."

Blythe turned and walked back to the prosecution's table. For a moment Micah thought the man was finished, but Blythe only poured himself a tumbler of water, took a long drink, and returned to the lectern. When Blythe began again, Micah realized that during Blythe's pause for water, the violent image of cold steel in the young girl's womb had been turning over in Micah's mind. He expected the same image was at work in the mind of every juror, and by taking the time to pour himself a glass of water, Blythe had been clever enough to give it the opportunity to dig itself in.

"It is an evil unlike most we see," Blythe continued. "The man who kills in love, at least, has killed for passion. The man who kills in greed, at least, has killed for riches. In the presentation of our case, we will show you that this man has killed for nothing more than his own selfish arrogance, an arrogance that he feels allows him to decide who enters this world and who does not. And I say to you, that, gentlemen, is a decision only God can make, not Dr. Hedstrom."

Up to this point Blythe had been speaking extemporaneously. Now he returned to counsel table and came back with some notes. "The crime of abortion," he began again, "is not one that takes place in a crowded room. The state will be calling only three witnesses. I will list them for you now, although we will not necessarily call them in this order. One will be brief. Miss Polly Pratt. I will admit to a real fondness for Miss Pratt. I have known her most of her life. She is a wonderful girl. She has made some unfortunate decisions in the course of the last year. But if we search our hearts, who among us has not? Youth is a liquor so intoxicating it takes years to sober up. It is fortunate for most of us, the ramifications of our actions are never made as public as poor Polly's. But I am here to tell you, gentlemen—" Blythe turned to the spectators in the darkness beyond the stage. "—and I say to every member of this community— that I do not chasten Polly Pratt for what has happened. I do not blame Polly for the deeds of this man." Again, he jabbed a finger at Chester. "She was a girl in a desperate situation, and instead of offering her good Christian counseling, as any righteous man would have done, Dr. Hedstrom, in his arrogance, offered her his knife."

Blythe had brought his voice to a crescendo, and now he paused just the right length of time before beginning again. Micah was impressed.

"It is my belief the state could prove its case by asking Miss Pratt four simple questions. And we will ask those questions of her and no more. I am not here to bring shame to Polly Pratt. I will ask her four questions, and I will sit down. That, gentlemen, will prove our case, but we shall not stop there.

"We shall then call Mrs. Jane Eggers. Mrs. Eggers, you will see, is a woman of extreme courage and principle. She was a woman in Dr. Hedstrom's employ. She is a well-trained and highly skilled nurse who was accustomed to assisting in every procedure the doctor performed in his surgery. You can imagine her surprise when the doctor ordered her to prepare the surgery, but once she had done that, he dismissed her without explanation. Naturally, this good woman's suspicions were aroused, and she—" Blythe stopped. "No," he said. "I will allow Mrs. Eggers to tell what she observed in her own words.

"I submit to you, though, gentlemen, the State of Wyoming could prove its case with nothing more than the testimony of

Mrs. Eggers, but, again, we shall not stop there.

"Yes, there is even more." Blythe crossed once more to the prosecution's table and returned with a single sheet of paper. "Finally, we will call Sheriff Brad Collins. And he will describe to you, my friends, the ultimate arrogance. He will tell you how, bold-faced and without remorse, this man—" Again he aimed his finger at Chester. "—admitted to what he had done. The sheriff will describe to you how Dr. Hedstrom, in gloating defiance of his authority, told Mr. Anderson, the prosecuting attorney, of his crime. He will tell you how the doctor, while sitting in the clinic where the crime had taken place, described how he tore this innocent child from the body of its desperate young mother."

Without thinking, Micah found himself on his feet. "Objection, Your Honor," he called out. Micah knew that rarely did one attorney object during another's opening statement or closing argument. It wasn't prohibited, but it wasn't the sort of thing that was done. Certain leeway was allowed.

Walker peered over the tops of his spectacles. "Grounds, Mr. McConners?"

"Well, Your Honor, unless Mr. Blythe has in his possession something the defense has not been provided, he has misstated the evidence as we know it to exist. According to the affidavit the sheriff has provided to all counsel, there was no mention in the doctor's statement to the sheriff and the prosecutor of tearing a child from the young woman's body. He is attempting to inflame the jury against my client, and I object."

"Is that the sheriff's affidavit, Mr. Blythe?"

"Yes, Your Honor, it is."

"Let me see it," said the judge.

Blythe handed it over, and Walker scanned it, handed it back, and said matter-of-factly, "Sustained. The jury is to disregard the counsel's comments regarding the doctor's admitting to tearing the infant from the womb, or whatever it was he said. You may continue, Mr. Blythe."

"Thank you, Your Honor," Blythe said, and returned to the lectern.

As Micah sat down he realized the churning he'd felt in his stomach had stopped.

He took in a deep breath and slowly exhaled. For better or worse, he told himself, the battle was on.

Chapter Twenty-Three

The judge peered down at the woman and asked, "Madam, in the testimony you are about to give, do you swear to tell the truth, the whole truth, and nothing but the truth, so help you God?"

"Yes, sir, I surely do," she said.

Walker nodded toward the chair beside his bench. "You may take the stand."

Blythe lifted the lectern from in front of the jury and faced it toward the witness.

After the objection, Thomas Blythe's opening statement had continued for another hour. From Micah's perspective of the technical aspects of the opening, the man's demeanor and fervent choice of words were flawless. It was an exercise in eloquence, never once becoming boring. But Micah wondered if the jury felt the same. It was clear Blythe had them for at least the first forty-five minutes, but long before the end, Micah noticed many of the jurors were shifting in their seats. For that reason, Micah kept his own opening to less than fifteen minutes, and he could sense the gratitude of not only the jurors but the judge as well.

"Would you state your name for the record, please?" Blythe asked.

"My name is Jane Eggers."

"Is it Miss or Mrs. Eggers?"

"It is Mrs. I have been a widow now for going on fifteen years."

"I'm sorry to hear that, Mrs. Eggers. Tell us how you have supported yourself in those fifteen years."

"In many ways. I have been a housekeeper, cook, nurse, and matron in a school for young women. My most recent employment was with Dr. Hedstrom."

"Would that be Dr. Chester Hedstrom of Probity, Wyoming, Mrs. Eggers?"

"It would."

"Would you point to the doctor, please, if you see him in the courtroom?"

The woman hefted her flabby arm toward the defense table. "Right there," she said. "The big one."

Blythe asked the judge, "Your Honor, may the record reflect that the witness identified the defendant?"

The judge leaned forward in his chair, looked down at the reporter, and asked in his no-nonsense voice, "Jeb, did you write down what this woman said?"

"I sure did, Judge."

"I expected that you had." Walker turned his gaze to Blythe. "Mr. Blythe, there is no need to make superfluous requests of the court. Let's trust our reporter to do his job, shall we?"

"Of course, Judge. I was merely noting—" Blythe began, but he stopped when Walker's eyebrows rose an inch. "Yes, sir," he said. "Thank you, Your Honor."

Micah was aware that Blythe and Walker had known each other for years and were, according to the rumor, good friends, but there was no doubt who was in charge in the courtroom.

Blythe turned back to the witness. "Tell us, Mrs. Eggers, how long you were in the employ of Dr. Hedstrom."

"A little more than a year. A year and two months, to be exact."

"How did you come to leave his employ?"

The woman glared at Chester. "I was dismissed," she said. "Dismissed without so much as a warning."

"You were given no notice whatsoever?"

"None. In fact, I was thrown from the man's house in the middle of the night without even a change of clothes." She had taken the stand holding a lace handkerchief, which she now dabbed at her eyes.

"We will come back to that in a moment, Mrs. Eggers." Blythe added in a just-right solicitous tone, "Are you capable of proceeding? Would you care for some water?"

Mrs. Eggers sniffed and said, "Yes, please."

Blythe poured the woman a glass of water and waited until she composed herself. "Now, Mrs. Eggers," he began again, "what were your duties with Dr. Hedstrom?"

"Everything. I was his housekeeper, his cook."

"Did you have duties in his medical practice as well?"

"Oh, most definitely. I'm sure that was the main reason the doctor hired me in the first place, was my skills as a nurse, particularly a surgical nurse. But I did everything for him in his practice. I scheduled patients. Kept the records. Everything that was needed."

"Would you say the doctor respected your abilities as a nurse, Mrs. Eggers?"

Micah stood. "Objection, Your Honor. That calls for speculation on the part of the witness."

"Response, Mr. Blythe?" asked the judge.

"Yes, Your Honor. I suppose, in a sense, young Mr. McConners is correct. Arguably, at least on the surface, the question does ask the witness to speculate as to what is in the mind of her employer. But I would suggest, Judge, that it is the rare employee who does not have a feel for his position and place in the mind of the individual supervising him in his daily activities. I would suggest that—"

"That's enough, Mr. Blythe," the judge interrupted. "The objection is overruled." He turned to the witness. "You may answer the question."

"Would you repeat the question?" Mrs. Eggers asked.

Blythe looked to the reporter. "Mr. Blake?"

Jeb Blake flipped a page back in his notebook, scanned the notes, then read, " 'Would you say the doctor respected your abilities as a nurse, Mrs. Eggers?' "

Blythe turned back to the witness. "You may answer that, madam."

Mrs. Eggers's already voluminous breasts seemed to puff up. "Oh, yes," she said. "There were any number of times when he told me what a fine, fine nurse I was. He thought I was especially good at making the patients feel at ease—you know, making them feel comfortable."

"What horse shit," Chester whispered. Micah nodded but didn't respond.

"When was it that you were dismissed from the doctor's employ? What was the date?"

"August 27. I remember it well."

"Nineteen hundred?"

"Yes, sir, this August past."

"Describe that day for me, Mrs. Eggers. What you did. What the doctor did."

"Describe it?" she asked.

"Yes, did anything unusual happen that day?"

"Well, I'd say. I was sacked from my position. I thought that was unusual." Although the jury didn't react, there was a smattering of laughter among the spectators.

"Yes, of course," Blythe acknowledged, "but I mean other than that. Start when you woke that morning and take us in detail through your day."

"I woke at my usual time," Mrs. Eggers began. "I went downstairs, put on the coffee, prepared breakfast. On Mondays, Wednesdays, Fridays, and Sundays, the doctor likes oatmeal for his breakfast. On the other days he likes bacon and eggs. This was a Monday, I believe, so I prepared the oatmeal—"

"Pardon me, madam," Blythe said, "but you needn't provide quite so much detail." This time even the jury joined in the laughter. "Please provide us with a general overview of the day. If I want anything more, I will ask a specific question."

It was clear that Mrs. Eggers did not appreciate being the object of laughter to so many people. She pulled herself up straighter in the chair and folded her hands in her lap. "After I made the doctor's oatmeal," she said, "I called him down. Usually he was already down by the time breakfast was ready, but not on that day. When he still didn't come down after I called, I went upstairs and found he wasn't in his room."

"Did you find that odd?" Blythe asked.

"Yes, it wasn't like him at all. When I returned to the kitchen, though, I heard the sound of that motorized bicycle of his. I hate that thing," she said. "It scares the animals, and it makes—"

"Please, Mrs. Eggers, let's try to keep to the topic at hand."

Mrs. Eggers gave Blythe a disgusted look.

"Did you ask the doctor where he had been?"

"Well, Dr. Hedstrom is a man with a mind of his own. Everyone thinks he's a jovial, friendly fellow, but I can tell you, sir, that is not the case. In the privacy of his home, he can be a beast. You do not pry into his—"

Micah was on his feet. "I object, Your Honor. The answer in not responsive to the question."

"Sustained," Walker said.

"Let me try that again," said Mr. Blythe. "Did you ask the doctor where he'd been so early in the morning, Mrs. Eggers?"

"No, sir, I did not. I didn't want to get my head bitten off."

Micah considered letting that one go by, but Jackson nudged him with his elbow, and Micah rose. "Objection, Your—"

"Sustained," said the judge before Micah could say any more.

"Please, Mrs. Eggers," Blythe said, "listen to the question and answer only the question. Will you do that for me?"

Mrs. Eggers's bosom rose in a huff. "I thought that was what I was doing," she said.

"So the answer is, no, you did not ask the doctor where he had been or what he had been doing so early in the morning. Is that correct?"

"Yes," Mrs. Eggers said and pursed her lips together.

"Very good," said Blythe in a tone that suggested he was happy to be past that question. "Let's start at the time when the doctor began seeing patients. What time was that?"

"Patients are always scheduled between eight o'clock in the morning and four o'clock in the afternoon. As I recall, on that day the morning was full, but the only person scheduled for the afternoon was Polly Pratt."

"Was Miss Pratt ill?"

"She'd had some kind of an accident the week before, and the doctor had taken a couple of stitches. She was coming in to have the stitches removed."

"Did anything unusual happen during the course of the day up to the time of Miss Pratt's arrival?"

"No, not that I recall. The doctor was being moody, is all."

"Would you describe Dr. Hedstrom as a particularly moody man?"

"Objection, Your Honor," Micah said.

"Grounds?" asked the judge.

"Relevance."

The judge seemed to ponder that for a bit, and after giving it some thought, said, "Overruled."

Jackson tugged hard on Micah's sleeve, jerking him down so

he could whisper in his ear.

"Excuse me, Mr. Clark," Judge Walker said, "did you have an objection *you* wished to make?"

"Well, sir, Judge," Jackson said as he came to his feet, "I did have, but I supposed you didn't allow two lawyers making objections at the same time."

"As a rule I don't, but since I can still remember what it was like to be a young attorney, I expect that's Mr. McConner's only suit, and my guess is he would rather the sleeve not be torn off. What's your objection?"

"Foundation," Jackson said.

"Sustained," said the judge.

"Thank you, Your Honor," Blythe said. And Micah thought he could hear a speck of sarcasm.

"How long did you say you were in the doctor's employ?" asked Blythe.

"Over a year."

"And your duties were housekeeper, cook, and nurse?"

"That's right."

"You lived in the doctor's home."

"I had my rooms."

"Yes, and you spent the greatest portion of your day either in his clinic or his house; is that correct?"

"I spent most all of every day in one or the other of those places, except, of course, for church on Sundays and Wednesday nights."

"Would you say that over the course of the year you worked for Dr. Hedstrom you became acquainted with his manner?"

"I surely did, yes, sir."

"Would you describe him as a moody man?"

"I'd describe him as a mean man."

Micah was almost on his feet to object, when Walker's hand came up, stopping him. "Mrs. Eggers," the judge asked, "do you speak the English language?"

A baffled look fell across Mrs. Eggers's chubby face. For a moment she seemed lost for an answer. "Yes," she finally said, "of course I do."

"Well, I'm glad to hear it," said the judge, "because I was beginning to wonder. The question put to you was, 'Would you describe Dr. Hedstrom as a moody man?' As I understand the language myself, that requires a simple yes or a no answer. Either you would describe him as a moody man or you would not. Now which is it?"

Again Mrs. Eggers's lips pursed. "Yes," she said, "I would describe him as a moody man."

"Thank you," said the judge. "Now if you would listen to the question and answer only the question that is asked rather than some question you would like to be asked, maybe we could get this trial over before *next* Christmas."

There was tittering among the crowd.

"Did he seem to be any more or less moody on this day than any other?" asked Blythe.

"Well," said Mrs. Eggers, "he had been in one of his moods for days, but when he came in from riding that machine of his, he seemed right cheerful."

"When you say 'one of his moods,' are you saying he had been morose the few days prior to the day in question?"

"Yes."

"But he seemed to be feeling better that morning?"

"Yes."

"Now, did anything unusual happen up to the time of Miss Pratt's arrival at the clinic?"

"No."

"What time was Miss Pratt's appointment?"

"If I remember right, it was one-thirty."

"Did she arrive alone?"

"No, she came with her mother."

"Very well, now, Mrs. Eggers, did the doctor remove Miss Pratt's stitches?"

"I wasn't there during his examination of her, but the next time I saw her that afternoon, they had been removed, yes."

"When was the next time you saw her?" Blythe asked.

"When the doctor called me into the examination room and told me to prepare the surgery."

"Was there a surgery scheduled for that afternoon?"

"No, sir, there was not."

"Did it seem unusual to you that he should make such a request?"

"Yes, sir, it most certainly did."

"What did you do next?"

"Prepared the surgery."

"What did the doctor do next?"

"He told me my services as surgical nurse would not be required."

"Did you find that unusual?"

"Yes, I did."

"Why?"

"Because in all the time I worked for the doctor he never performed any surgical procedure without me being there."

"What did you do next, Mrs. Eggers?"

"I left."

"And after that?"

"I'm ashamed to say." She dropped her gaze to her lap.

"I realize this is difficult," Blythe said, "but, please, madam, it's important."

She took in a breath as though drawing in courage. "I waited until I knew the doctor had begun whatever he was planning to do in the surgery, and then I went into examination room two and peeked through the crack in the door."

"Why did you do that, Mrs. Eggers?" Blythe asked.

"Because I couldn't understand what he could be doing that he would not need assistance. Dr. Hedstrom would not lance a boil without an assistant present."

"What did you see when you peeked through the door?"

"Miss Pratt was on the table. Her legs were in the stirrups, and Dr. Hedstrom was using a curette to . . ." She paused.

"Yes," Blythe urged, "go on."

"He was scraping the baby out of her."

The jury remained stoic, but there were murmurs from the spectators.

"Could you see this from where you stood?"

"I could."

"Describe the specifics of what you saw that afternoon, Mrs. Eggers."

"Your Honor," Micah said, "may we approach the bench?"

"You may."

All four attorneys and the court reporter stepped to the bench and turned their backs to the jury. In a whisper, the judge asked, "You requested the side-bar, Mr. McConners. What is it?"

"Your Honor, I object to this line of inquiry. It is designed to elicit testimony of a grisly and macabre nature in yet another effort on the part of Mr. Blythe to inflame the passions of this jury. This area of testimony is highly prejudicial to my client."

"Judge," began Blythe, "The woman—"

Walker waved his hand, shooing away Blythe's attempt at a response. "Never mind," he said. "Young man, Mr. Blythe here has a right to prove his case. If this woman's testimony is grisly and macabre—very nice words, by the way—" He bestowed his compliment with half a smile. "—so be it. It is something she saw, and she has the right to tell the jury what she saw. As far as the testimony being prejudicial to your client, I disagree. I do expect it to be damaging to your client, but, my word, if the prosecutor didn't put on at least some testimony that was damaging to your client, he wouldn't be doing his job, would he? Your objection is overruled."

Everyone returned to their places, and Mr. Blythe resumed where he had left off. "Please describe, Mrs. Eggers, the specifics of what you saw as you watched Dr. Hedstrom performing the procedure on Polly Pratt."

Again the woman touched the handkerchief to her eyes. "It was awful," she whispered.

"You will need to speak up, madam," Blythe said.

"I had never seen such a thing done before," Mrs. Eggers said. "He inserted the curette into the girl's—into the girl and began to use it to scrape her out."

"Excuse me, Mrs. Eggers. This is the second time you mentioned the use of a curette. Could you explain to the jury exactly what a curette is?"

"It's a medical instrument. It usually has a long handle at one end and on the other it's shaped like a spoon; the edges are very sharp. It's inserted into the uterus and the fetus and placenta are scraped out."

"Do the contents of the uterus come out intact?"

"No, sir. There is a great deal of blood and tissue that comes out. It all comes out in pieces."

"Mrs. Eggers, when you say 'it' comes out in pieces, to what do you refer?"

"Why, the baby, sir. The baby comes out in pieces." Again, the woman brought the handkerchief up, this time to her mouth in an effort to suppress a sob. "It was awful. Awful."

"She does this very well," Chester whispered to Micah.

"I expect they've been rehearsing," Micah said.

"And you watched the procedure take place as you peered into the surgery?"

"I did, sir."

"Very well, Mrs. Eggers, what happened next?"

"When he was finished, I left and went about my chores in another part of the house. An anesthetic was used, and the doctor gave Miss Pratt time to rest. In a few hours, he drove the girl and her mother back to their boarding house."

"What did you do at the time?"

"I had been trying to decide all afternoon what I should do. A crime had been committed, I knew."

"Yes."

"I felt I should inform the authorities, but, too, I had a loyalty to my employer."

"Of course."

"I decided to confront the doctor with what I had seen when he returned."

"And did you do so, Mrs. Eggers?"

Once more, up came the handkerchief. "Yes, yes, I did."

"Tell us about that. What did he say, and what did you say?"

"When he returned, he came in demanding his supper. But I must admit, I was so distraught at what had happened I had not prepared his meal."

"Did this make him angry?"

"Oh, my, yes. Furious. Most times when he gets that way, I'm so frightened, I immediately do whatever it is he is demanding."

"Did you do so this time?"

"No, sir, this time I stood my ground."

"Did you tell him what you had seen take place in the surgery earlier in the afternoon?"

"Yes, sir, I did."

"What did he say?"

"At first he was very quiet. I had never seen him respond in that fashion, and I don't mind telling you, that was more frightening than when he shouted."

"Was there any conversation at all between you and the doctor regarding what he had done to Polly Pratt that afternoon?"

"Yes, sir. I asked him was there some problem with her pregnancy that required him to perform such a procedure."

"As the doctor's nurse and the keeper of his files, were you familiar with Miss Pratt as a patient?"

"Yes, sir."

"Were you aware of any specific health problem relating to the young woman?"

"No, sir, none."

"In fact, you were not even aware of her pregnancy, were you, Mrs. Eggers?"

"No, sir, I was not."

"The doctor had never entered that fact in her medical record, had he?"

"No, he had not."

Jackson whispered to Micah, "He's asking her leading questions."

"Yes," Micah agreed, "but it's helping to speed things along. The quicker we can get this woman off the stand, the better."

"You found it odd, didn't you, that he had not entered her pregnancy in her records?"

"Yes, sir, very."

"So, Mrs. Eggers, you asked Dr. Hedstrom if Miss Pratt had any life-threatening health problems regarding her pregnancy that would warrant performing the procedure; is that correct? You testified to that a moment ago; am I right about that?"

"Yes, I asked him that."

"What was his response?"

"He said the only thing wrong with her pregnancy was that it existed at all. He laughed and said, she was carrying some extra baggage, and all he did was help her get rid of it."

"Extra baggage? Is that how Dr. Hedstrom referred to this

baby, this child, as extra baggage?"

"Yes, sir. Extra baggage."

"What was your response to that, madam?"

"It is then, I'm sorry to say, that I lost my temper. I said if he didn't give me some sound, medical reason why he had done what he had done that it was my duty as a citizen and good Christian to inform the county attorney."

"His response?"

"He laughed once more. He said no one would take my word over his, and if I wished to reconsider, I was welcome to stay. Otherwise, I could seek employment elsewhere. I told him that what he had done was inexcusable, and I would seek employment elsewhere, and I gave him notice."

"What did he say to that?"

"He became enraged."

"What did he do?"

"He grabbed me by the hair, dragged me across the parlor, and threw me onto the porch. He told me to leave his house and never come back. He slammed the door in my face, not even allowing me time to collect my possessions."

"That was some four months ago, Mrs. Eggers. Was that the last time you have seen Dr. Hedstrom?"

"Today is the first time I have seen him since, and the last, I hope."

"Thank you, Mrs. Eggers," Blythe said. "No further questions, Your Honor."

"Mr. McConners," Judge Walker said, "we will begin your cross-examination after the noon break." He turned to the jury. "The jury is instructed not to discuss the case until it is submitted to you for deliberation. Court is in recess."

When the judge stood and turned to leave, Earl Anderson shouted, "All rise!"

As they came to their feet, Jackson Clark grumbled to Micah, "To be so damned young, you sure are slow."

CHAPTER TWENTY-FOUR

"Well, Micah," Jackson said, "we're halfway through the first witness. When are you going to tell me what the theory of our defense is?"

"Damn, Jackson," Chester pointed out, "didn't you listen to his opening statement? We don't have a defense."

"You know, that's what I thought he was saying. I guess I couldn't believe my ears."

"Believe them," Micah said. Micah didn't find Jackson's jokes at all funny. The two lawyers had discussed their strategy—or lack of it—many times.

Micah wasn't eating. The fluttering in his stomach was gone, and, to his surprise, his spirits were higher than he expected they would be—he had anticipated the blue devils to be pounding at his door long before now—but his insides still didn't feel steady enough to take on Lottie's noon special: cornbread, pinto beans, raw onion, and ham. "We're here to make a moral statement, remember? Not to defend an action at bar."

"My, my, aren't we touchy today?" As Chester said this, he shoveled a huge spoonful of pintos into his mouth. Some juice broke free, glanced off his chin, and landed back in the bowl. He blotted the dribble away with a checkered napkin and said, "You'd think *you* were the one going to prison."

Micah ignored the comment.

Chester continued, "Every third word Eggers uttered was a lie. She never watched me through the surgery door performing the abortion. If she had, she would've been more than pleased to let me know of that little fact when she tried to extort ten thousand dollars from me."

Micah slapped his forehead. "Well, damn, I'll bet you're right. It's all clear to me now. Mrs. Eggers made the whole thing up. It's a fabrication from top to bottom. You never even performed an abortion."

Chester gave him a quizzical look.

Although Micah was not eating, he was, against his better judgement, drinking perhaps his twentieth cup of coffee for the day. Now he dropped the cup into his saucer, sloshing coffee across the tablecloth. "Look," he said, "most of her testimony is lies, but it doesn't really matter, does it, Chester?"

"What do you mean?"

"You did perform the abortion, right?"

"Well, yes."

"The mother's health was fine, right?"

"You know it was."

Micah picked up the coffee, started to bring it to his mouth, and stopped. "We are now at the place I've been telling you we would be for the last month."

"Where's that?" Chester asked.

"In a courtroom with nothing to say." He drained his cup. "We can go in there and make some noise and maybe ruffle their feathers on a few bits of inconsistent information. But in the end, we have nothing to say to defend against what you're charged with."

"He's right, Chester," Jackson confirmed. "We have no hope with the jury."

Chester didn't respond, but he had stopped eating his ham and beans.

Jackson looked at Micah. "It's like you and I've been saying, Micah, for the last three weeks. We have to play things more to the judge than the jury. The jury's going to convict; there's nothing else they can do. But if we can humanize Chester, get Walker to recognize he's a good man, has never done this sort of thing before, and only did it because Polly was in a desperate situation, maybe when it comes time for sentencing, the judge'll be more lenient."

"It's all pretty damned thin," Micah pointed out.

Polly and Cedra were sitting at the next table over. Fay was standing, chatting with Cedra, holding a coffee pot. Micah held out his now-empty cup and said, "Fay, how about a little more?" She poured his coffee, gave him a quick smile that only the three men could see, and moved on to another crowded table.

Micah took a sip of the fresh coffee and asked, "Is the door to your clinic locked, Chester?"

"Yes, why?"

Micah checked his watch against the clock on the wall. "We still have half an hour before we need to get back. Let me have your keys."

Chester got that quizzical look again. "What're you doing?" he asked as he handed the keys over.

"I want to check something out. I'll meet you back at the opera house at one o'clock." Micah took another sip of coffee and left the café.

With his notes and a small file folder tucked under his arm, Micah rose from counsel table to begin his examination of Mrs. Eggers. "Remember," Jackson whispered, "get 'er off that damned witness stand as quick as you can. There's not a thing you can do to her that's going to help."

Micah grimaced, turned, and approached center stage. "With your permission, Judge," he said, "I'll move the lectern a little closer to the witness."

Walker nodded.

"Good afternoon, Mrs. Eggers," Micah said with a smile.

"Good afternoon."

"I trust you had a pleasant lunch."

"I did, thank you," the woman said.

"What was the noon special at the Glendale House?" Micah asked.

"Sirloin steak."

"Tasty, I bet."

"Yes, it was very good."

"I hope Mr. Anderson also treated you to some of their fine cobbler for dessert."

"He did," she answered with a broad smile.

Micah turned to the prosecution's table. "Mr. Anderson is well known for being a big spender." There was laughter throughout the room, not the least of which came from Anderson and Blythe. Turning back to the witness, Micah asked, "In fact, isn't it true, Mrs. Eggers, you've been allowed a suite of rooms at the Glendale House at taxpayers' expense since the day you reported this incident to the county attorney?"

"I object, Your Honor," Blythe said. "I fail to see how that is relevant."

"Overruled, Mr. Blythe."

Jackson had told Micah the judge allowed fairly wide latitude on cross-examination, particularly in criminal matters.

"You may answer that question, Mrs. Eggers," Micah said.

"I have been staying at the Glendale House, yes."

"Has that been at taxpayers' expense?"

"I'm not sure how the bills have been paid."

"You know that you haven't paid them; isn't that correct?"

"I have not paid them."

"You have assumed, have you not, that Mr. Anderson has been paying . . . Wait." Micah stopped himself and held up a finger. "Let me rephrase that," he said. "You have assumed,

212

have you not, that the bills have been paid for your rooms and your meals for some four months now by the office of the county attorney?"

Eggers didn't respond.

"Isn't that true, madam?"

"Yes," she finally said.

"Thank you." Micah scanned the notes he had taken during Mrs. Eggers's direct examination by Thomas Blythe. "Let me see here. I believe you said your husband passed on some fifteen years ago?"

"That's right."

"And you have been employed in one fashion or another ever since that time?"

"I have."

"Are you employed now?"

"Well, no."

"And you have not been employed since you left Dr. Hedstrom; isn't that true?"

Mrs. Eggers raised her chin. "I did not leave Dr. Hedstrom. I was dismissed and thrown into the street."

"Ah, yes, you were dismissed. You didn't think the doctor was very fair in the way he handled that, did you?"

"I most certainly did not."

"He was rather brusque, wasn't he?" Micah fired off this question as soon as Mrs. Eggers had answered his last.

"To say the least." She answered just as fast.

Immediately he asked, "Rude?"

"Very."

They were speaking with such speed there was a stream of scratching from the court reporter's pencil.

After the last answer, though, Micah paused. Finally, he said, "Yes, very rude," and paused again. "You were spending considerable time with the doctor, weren't you?"

"As his housekeeper and nurse, yes, a great deal of time."

"All day in his clinic," said Micah, "and all afternoon and evening in his living quarters?"

"That's correct."

Micah turned from the witness and faced his client. "The truth is, Mrs. Eggers, Dr. Hedstrom is a truly strange man, isn't he?"

"I'm sure I don't know what you mean, sir."

"Well, let's face it," Micah said, still looking at Chester, "this fella is one odd duck; isn't he?" He turned back to Mrs. Eggers. "I've known him since we were children. I expect I know him as well as anyone, and I'll say right here on the record, this man is the weirdest sack of beans I've ever run across."

Laughter filled the auditorium.

With a smile, Chester stood and shouted, "I object, Your Honor."

There was more laughter, this time even from the judge.

"Would you like to tell me where you're going with this, Mr. McConners?" Walker asked.

"Yes, Your Honor, I'd be glad to. Mrs. Eggers came to know the defendant well over the course of more than a year. She not only knew him in his professional capacity as his nurse, but from working as his housekeeper she knew him in his private life as well. I was wondering if she would agree with me that Dr. Hedstrom is—" Micah searched for a word "—well, that he's peculiar."

"I'll allow you to continue with that." The judge turned to Chester. "I guess I'll have to overrule your objection, Doctor. Sorry."

Chester gave Walker a little salute as he sat down. "That's all right, Judge."

"So, Mrs. Eggers," continued Micah, "would you agree that the doctor here is a bit peculiar in his ways?"

Now even Eggers seemed to be enjoying herself. "I'm not sure peculiar's the word. But I would go along with what you said earlier."

"What's that?"

"That he's the weirdest sack of beans I've ever run across."

Micah's smile widened. "His view of the world is different than yours and mine; would you agree with that?"

"I'd say he views the world different than everybody."

"Tell us more about that, Mrs. Eggers."

"Well, he's filled his house with machines, for one thing. He has gadgetry of every kind and description. He even has electricity wires running into the library. And he's always cranking up that—what do you call it—that big engine thing outside?"

"The generator?"

"Right. That thing sends electricity right into the house. I tell you, it's scary. You don't ever know what that stuff is going to do." There were rumblings of agreement from the spectator section. "I lived in constant fear that it was going to shoot out at me like lightning every time I passed by the library. And also, it's the way the man talks, the things he talks about. He's always trying to predict the future. He thinks he's some kind of fortune-teller or something—always talking about the twentieth century this and the twentieth century that. How grand it's all going to be. How human beings will be able to be something better than they've ever been before."

Micah nodded. "It gets a bit tiring," he said, not without some conviction of his own, "wouldn't you agree?"

"He's a know-it-all, is what he is."

"The truth is you don't like Dr. Hedstrom very much, do you?"

She leaned forward in her chair and said in a hard, even voice, "I have *never* liked that man." But seeming to realize how that sounded, she sat back and added, "I mean as an employer,

215

of course. As an employer, he was not a pleasant man to work for."

"Particularly at the end," Micah said.

"Yes."

"I take it the doctor was harsh in his behavior when he let you go."

"He was indeed."

Again Micah thumbed through his notes. "I believe you told Mr. Blythe you felt the primary reason the doctor hired you was because of your nursing skills; is that correct?"

"That is my belief from what he said."

"How extensive is your training, Mrs. Eggers?"

"Well, I can claim no formal training, sir, but I have had considerable training on-the-job, you might say."

"And where might that have been, Mrs. Eggers?"

"At the home for girls."

"Yes, you mentioned that place earlier. What exactly did you do there, ma'am, in terms of nursing?"

"Everything that was needed to be done. We had close to eighty girls, and there was always something or other that needed to be done. It was there I gained some training in the surgery as well, although it's true I've received most of my training for that from Dr. Hedstrom."

"What caused you to leave that position at the home?"

"I wished to return to Wyoming. I was sad to leave the girls. They had all become like my own daughters. The girls, the other staff members, the director, they all begged me to stay because we had become so much like family. But I missed Wyoming, and finally I gave my notice and left."

"I expect the rudeness of your dismissal by Dr. Hedstrom was difficult for you, particularly since your previous position had ended on such a high note."

"Yes, it was. I had never been fired in my life. Nor—" She

glared at Chester. "—have I ever been treated the way that man treated me on that night."

"I believe you said that the home for girls was in Omaha; is that correct?"

"I don't think I said it was in Omaha," Eggers said. Her brow wrinkled.

"Perhaps you didn't." Micah reached in his file folder and removed a set of papers held together with a paperclip. "I have here, Mrs. Eggers, a transcript of a statement you gave the county attorney some months ago. Have you had an opportunity to see this?" he handed her the transcript.

"Yes, I have seen it. Mr. Blythe showed it to me last week."

Micah took the papers back and returned to the lectern. "You say in here that you were employed at the Bowen Home for Wayward Girls; is that correct?"

Mrs. Eggers turned to the bench. "Judge," she asked, "what does this have to do with anything that Dr. Hedstrom did to that poor girl?"

"Please answer the questions, madam," Walker said. "If the prosecutors feel they need to make an objection, I'm sure they will."

"Was the home for girls in Omaha?" Micah repeated.

"Yes."

Micah pulled another sheet of paper from his folder and approached the witness. "I have here a carbon copy of a letter dated September 24, 1897. It carries the letterhead of the Bowen Home for Wayward Girls, Omaha, Nebraska. It is signed by Mr. Emerson Bowen. Can you tell me, Mrs. Eggers, to whom that letter is addressed?"

"It is addressed to me."

"Do you remember receiving it?"

Mrs. Eggers's eyes widened and she looked across the stage

to Blythe. Blythe didn't move. "I believe I've seen this at one time, yes."

"The letter itself has been typed, but if you will notice, there's a handwritten notation at the lower right-hand corner. Would you read that, please?"

Mrs. Eggers shifted in her seat. " 'Original letter hand-delivered to Mrs. Jane Eggers, September 25, 1897.' "

"I would like to offer this as Defendant's Exhibit A, Your Honor."

Blythe stood. "May I see it, Your Honor?"

Walker looked to Micah, jerked his head toward the prosecution table, and Micah handed the letter to Blythe.

Blythe took his time reading it. When he finally spoke it was in a tone that communicated it was silly that the letter should even be offered. "Your Honor," he said, "we would object. This has no relevance whatsoever."

"Let me see it," said the judge. He read it much faster than had Thomas Blythe. "Overruled," he said. "Defense Exhibit A'll be received."

Micah took the letter back to the witness stand and handed it to Mrs. Eggers. "Madam," he said, "would you be so kind as to read this document to the gentlemen of the jury?"

The woman gave Micah a scowl over the top of the paper, but after a moment, she lowered her eyes and began to read. " 'To Mrs. Jane Eggers,' " she began.

"I believe you'll need to speak up, ma'am. The jurymen seem to be having a difficult time hearing you."

She began again, a little louder this time. " 'To Mrs. Jane Eggers. Dear Mrs. Eggers, this is to inform you that as of your receipt of this writing your services as dorm maid and dishwasher at the Bowen Home for Wayward Girls will no longer be required.' "

Mrs. Eggers stopped. Her face had turned scarlet, and a vein bulged at her temple.

"Pardon me, ma'am," said Micah in a soft, polite tone, "but the letter goes on. Would you please continue?"

Mrs. Eggers cleared her throat and read on. " 'I feel as though I have done more than is required of any employer to assist you in maintaining your employment here at the home. I have overlooked your petty disputes with coworkers, your deleteriousness in the performance of your duties, and your prevarications to your superiors. I shall not, however, overlook your stealing the home's supplies and selling them on the streets of the city. Hence, your dismissal will be effective immediately. Signed, Emerson Bowen, Director, The Bowen Home for Wayward Girls.' "

Micah crossed and took the letter from Mrs. Eggers. He made a show of scanning its contents. "I may be wrong, Mrs. Eggers, but I don't believe Mr. Bowen mentioned that you had any duties as a nurse; am I right about that? Does this say anything about duties as a nurse?"

He handed the letter back to her, but she answered without looking at it. "No."

"And despite what you said earlier, I believe this letter indicates that you were dismissed from your position at the home for girls; is that correct?"

"Yes."

The woman muttered her answer, but Micah didn't ask her to repeat it. He knew the jury had heard. "Thank you," he said, and the theater was as still as a stone.

Micah took the letter to the court reporter's desk and placed it there. Jeb Blake was in charge of the exhibits once they were admitted into evidence.

"Let's move on to something else, Mrs. Eggers," Micah said as he crossed the stage to where there stood an easel that held a large pad of white paper. He carried the easel over to the witness stand, took his Conklin Crescent Filler fountain pen from his inside coat pocket, and unscrewed the cap. "On the day of the abortion, you saw a horrible sight; is that correct?"

"Yes."

Micah cupped his hand around his ear. "I'm sorry?"

"Yes," she said, "I did."

"You saw, if I understood your testimony, the doctor using that instrument—what did you call it?"

"The curette."

"Right, the curette. You actually saw him using the curette to scrape the fetus from the uterus of Polly Pratt."

"I did. It was dreadful."

"I can only imagine," said Micah. "Perhaps you can refresh my recollection and explain to the members of the jury how the doctor's clinic is laid out. Could you do that?"

"Yes, of course."

"If I'm not mistaken, you can enter the clinic both from Main Street—" Micah drew two parallel lines on the far right-hand side of the paper.

"That's right."

"—as well as from inside the house."

"Yes."

He drew a large rectangle that nearly filled the page. "We'll let this represent the house, okay? Are you still with me so far?"

"Yes."

He drew two horizontal, parallel lines along the bottom of the page. "Let's let this be Sixth Street."

"All right."

"Now I don't care how the living quarters of the house is laid out, Mrs. Eggers. All I'm interested in for the sake of our discussion this afternoon is the clinic." Micah drew a smaller rectangle within the larger rectangle. "Let's say this area is the clinic, all right?"

"All right."

"Now how many rooms comprise the clinic?"

"There's the waiting area and the doctor's office with the small examination table in it. There are examination rooms one and two. And, of course, the surgery."

"So, what, five rooms make up the clinic itself; is that correct?"

"Yes."

"Fine. I'll tell you what, Mrs. Eggers, rather than me standing here and trying to guess how all of those rooms are positioned, why don't you step down to the easel and within the smaller of these two rectangles show us how it all fits together? Would you do that?" Micah turned to the judge. "With leave of the court, of course."

"Go ahead," said Walker.

Mrs. Eggers hefted her ample frame from the witness chair and came over to where Micah stood. Micah handed her his pen and said, "Now, madam, please, take your time and draw in the rooms as you know them to exist in Dr. Hedstrom's clinic." Micah stepped back and watched as the woman drew in lines to represent the various rooms.

"There," she said when she was finished, "that looks about right."

Micah took the pen from her. "All right, I assume the room where you show the door going to the street would be the waiting area."

"Yes."

Micah wrote "waiting room" on the paper. "And this one?"

"Examination room one."

He wrote that in and pointed to the next place she had drawn.

"Examination room two. Next to that is the surgery and next to that is the doctor's private office."

"All right," said Micah, "and the area you have drawn here

would be the hallway connecting everything to the rest of the house; is that correct?"

"That's right."

"Very good. Thank you, ma'am. You may resume the stand." Mrs. Eggers started back to her chair. "Oh, excuse me, Mrs. Eggers, before you go, please draw in the surgical table in the surgery and show how it is situated in the room."

He handed her the pen once more, and she did so.

"Thank you. Now show the door in examination room two where you were standing when you watched the procedure."

She drew that as well.

"Excellent," said Micah. "Now you may resume the stand. I promise not to have you draw another thing." Micah turned his attention to the drawing. "May I assume, madam, that as you watched the procedure take place you were standing right here?" He pointed to a spot next to the door she had placed between examination room two and the surgery.

"That's right."

He marked an X at that location. "And as I understand the way it works—and I realize this is quite indelicate, Mrs. Eggers, so please forgive me—the patient is on the table and her legs are placed in what you earlier referred to as stirrups; is that correct?"

"Yes."

"And these stirrups are located at the end of the table closest to the door at which you were standing."

"That's right."

Micah spent a long moment eyeing the diagram. "Well," he said, nodding, "if you were standing at this door right here, that, as I see it, would allow you a clear, straight-line view of this end of the surgical table itself." He tapped the paper indicating where he meant.

"Yes, perfect."

"How far away would you say you were standing from the end of the table where the stirrups were located?"

"Oh, I don't know. I'm not too good with distances, but I would guess less than ten feet."

"Maybe as far away as I am from you?"

"I would say so," the woman agreed.

Micah marked "Defense Exhibit B" on the diagram and said, "I would like to offer the diagram at this time, Your Honor."

Blythe said, "No objection."

"It will be received," said Walker.

Micah screwed the cap on his pen and returned it to his coat pocket. "It must have been a horrible, horrible experience to watch something like that at such a proximity."

Mrs. Eggers looked down at her hands. "Yes," she said, "it was."

"All right," Micah said, "thank you, madam." He picked up his notes and tapped them into alignment on the lectern. Sliding the papers into the file folder, he walked to counsel table, placed the folder on the table, and said, "Oh, I guess I do have one more question. There's something I don't quite understand." He walked back to the easel. "We have you, Mrs. Eggers, standing right here, correct?" He pointed to the X. "And you were facing this end of the table, the end with the stirrups; isn't that right?"

"Yes."

"We have Miss Pratt on the table with her head at the opposite end of the table?"

"Yes."

"Where was Dr. Hedstrom?"

"Well, he was—" Eggers stopped short. Again her complexion changed, only this time instead of turning scarlet, the woman blanched. In an instant, as though some plug had been pulled, every ounce of color drained from her face.

Micah continued. "When Dr. Hedstrom was performing this procedure and you saw this horrific sight you've told us about in such detail, where was the doctor at that time?"

She didn't answer.

"Mrs. Eggers," Micah prodded, "isn't it true that the doctor would have had to have been standing at the end of the table, between the stirrups? Isn't it also true that he would have been *between* you at the exam room doorway and Polly Pratt, who was lying on the table?"

Still she was silent, and still Micah pushed. "Isn't it true that Dr. Hedstrom—all six feet two inches and two hundred and fifteen pounds of him—stood between you and what you, under oath, told this jury you observed?"

When she still did not answer, Judge Walker said, "Mrs. Eggers, you must respond to Mr. McConners's question."

Micah shook his head. "That's all right, Judge," he said. "I withdraw the question, and I have nothing further of the witness."

Micah walked to his chair and sat down.

CHAPTER TWENTY-FIVE

Though he had seen it many times, Fay's body always amazed him. She was moderately tall—five feet, four—at least four inches taller than Earl Anderson. But her body was thin. It was not the voluptuous body with enormous breasts and wide, full hips that many men considered the ideal. Fay was the opposite of that. She was Micah's ideal. Her breasts were small, but beautiful, firm, and high. Her hips arced in a feminine curve that melted into smooth thighs. But the thing that amazed him more than anything was Fay's waist. He could almost get his two hands around it—the thumbs touching in front and his fingertips almost touching at the small of her back. It dazzled him every time he saw her nude. It made him buzz as though the electricity from Chester's generator was coursing through him.

He felt that buzzing now as he lay smoking a cigarette and staring at the ceiling. Since they were in trial, Micah skipped his turn at standing watch. Jackson and Chester shared those duties so Micah could sleep. But sleep came hard.

Fay's head rested in the crook of his arm. She was quiet, but she was not asleep, either. Occasionally he could feel her light kisses on his chest. Occasionally he could hear her make the faintest of sounds: a sigh, perhaps—perhaps a moan.

It was very strange, their sleeping together here in this bed. After all, Polly and Cedra were in the bedroom down the hall, and Chester and Jackson slept on their pallets in the parlor. He and Fay had not done this before—not at Lottie's house—but today had been an eventful day.

On redirect examination, Thomas Blythe had done his best to try to salvage some of Jane Eggers's testimony, but for the most part it had been hopeless. Jackson was beside himself. He said he'd never seen a better cross-examination in his life. Micah felt good about it too. It was pure joy showing everyone what a liar the woman was, but he was not kidding himself. Ultimately it would not make a whit of difference. There was still Polly's testimony, and she would have to admit to the abortion. And, most of all, there was Chester's confession.

But Eggers's cross-examination had been fun. Micah was now what he had always wanted to be: a lawyer—more specifically a trial lawyer. And the trial was the thing.

He felt Fay's hand move up the inside of his thigh and brush against him. More electricity.

After Eggers's cross, Jackson was ecstatic. At the close of court that afternoon, he had stopped by Buck's, bought fifteen bottles of beer, and brought them to Lottie's Café. They were all taking every meal there now. They ate at the large table in a small but private back room off the kitchen. Even the women had each drunk one of Jackson's beers, although none of them but Cedra seemed to like it. Micah hadn't discouraged the celebration. He expected it was the only celebrating they would get a chance to do, so why not enjoy it?

He snubbed out the butt of his cigarette, rolled to his side, and scooted deep enough under the covers so that his and Fay's eyes were even. The moon was full, and the light coming through the window washed across her face. He pushed a loose strand away from her forehead so he could better see the arch of her eyebrow. He found even her eyebrows erotic. That was another thing that addled his brain when he was around Fay: the things about her he found sexually exciting that normally would not be considered sexual at all—like the arch of an eyebrow, the tiny lines at the edges of her eyes when she smiled, the flow of her neck.

"I can't believe this is happening," she whispered.

Micah smiled. "It is hard to believe." He nestled in closer to her.

"Even when I confronted her in September," Fay said, "she never admitted she knew we'd been together like this, but I knew she did."

"Well, that's clear now," he said, "but how did you know she knew it at the time?"

"The woman's not blind, Micah. She can see that stupid look you get every time I come around."

"My, my, aren't we proud of ourselves?"

Fay looked away from him, toward the ceiling, and the moonlight caught the line of her nose and the rise of her cheekbones. "Plus," she said, "she watched me pine away for you when you were gone so long." She looked back at him, their lips only inches apart. "She knows how much I love you." She kissed him. It was a soft kiss at first; then she kissed him harder, searching for his tongue.

In a day filled with the unusual, Lottie had called Micah aside after supper. "Micah," she had said and jerked her head toward the door. He followed her into the main room of the café. Their little party had run late, and all the customers were gone.

"What is it, Lottie?" When he saw the hard look on her face, he asked, "Is something wrong?"

"I like you, Micah."

"Why, thank you, Lottie. I'm fond of you too."

"And my little girl loves you."

This was the first time she'd ever acknowledged to Micah that there was anything at all between him and Fay. For a moment his glibness was gone. Finally, he said, "I love her too, Lottie. Damn, I've loved her for years."

"It's hard, ain't it?"

He nodded but didn't speak.

She turned and poured herself a cup of coffee but held it without drinking. "I figure there's two kinds of love in this world between a man and a woman. There's the practical, down-to-earth kind. That's the kind the lucky folks have, I reckon. They meet. They're drawn to each other. They feel a little lust, maybe. Maybe it's the time in their life it's time to get married, so they do. They share a few Christmases, a few good times and a few bad. After a while they're comfortable together. They make babies and watch them babies take their first steps. They raise up memories together like they was vegetables in a garden. They can those memories and stack 'em in the pantry. Before long what they have together is love. The best kind of love. The kind me and my first husband had. It's a real honest-to-God love, Micah, as real as anything ever was, and it's a practical, make-sense kind-a love. One they've built up over the years.

"What's the other kind, Lottie? You said there were two."

A little smile deepened her wrinkles. "The other kind," she said, "ahhh, that other kind, now it's a rude ol' boy. It's the kind-a love that walks into the room without knockin'. It's the kind that smacks you on the back of your head, and says, hey, you, look at me. It's something that's loud and pushy and makes its presence known. It's somethin' that won't take no for an answer. It'll go out of its way to disturb your sleep, your appetite, your work. It's something that will not be ignored."

Now her smile faded. She took a sip of coffee and crossed over and sat down at her "doing-books" table. "You never met Fay's Pappa. He was sick when we got to Probity, and a week later he was dead."

"No, I never met him, but I've heard a lot about him."

"I loved that man. I truly did. You may not believe it to know me now, but in my younger years I was a passionate, fiery woman. I left my home in the bayou, and I was ready to follow him all the way to the Yellowstone, but we only made 'er this far." She took another sip and said, "I'm sorry, Micah. Pour yourself a cup and come over here and sit down." It wasn't often Lottie invited anyone to sit at her table. He did as he was told. "Gaston was a white boy too, like yourself, 'cept he was a Frenchie. Not one of them Canadian Frenchies, neither. He was the real thing. Gaston was born and raised in the country of France. I was no child when we met. I had done buried me a husband and two sons. I knew the ways of the world all too well, but I tell you, Micah, that white boy done stole my heart away."

"Fay's shown me a picture of him. He was a handsome man."

"Yes, he was. He was beautiful. And he was as passionate and fiery as I was. What we had was a scorcher from the beginning to end. And I don't mean just the man and woman kind of thing." There was a twinkle in her eye. "Though, that was fine too. But there was fire in everything—our fightin' as well as our lovin'. We could sit for hours, him and me, holdin' hands like a couple of kids. We could talk to each other 'bout nothin', and the time would melt away. There was a magic how we could talk. Or," she said, staring into her coffee, "we could get us so furious at one another that you'd think all the furies of hell had been let loose. It could be an ugly thing, the way we could get sometimes." Her head rose. "It could be an ugly, ugly thing. It shames me now to think about it. We had us many, many hard times because of that, but we did love each other. At the end Gaston said to me, 'Lottie, I am dying. I can feel the death a-coming.' I told him I was with him, not to be afraid. And I *was* with him too. I climbed up in that bed beside him, and I put my mouth close to his ear and I began to whisper to him.

I told him how I loved him. How I had always loved him. I whispered love into that man nonstop until with a smile on his lips he closed his eyes and he was gone. He died, though, my man did, hearing how much I loved him. My whispers walked him off into that darkness, Micah, and he did not die alone."

Rufus, her little terrier, waddled up to her and nudged her leg. Without looking down, she reached and scratched behind his ears. "It was a fine kind of love we had," she continued, "but our life together was a harsh one." She looked up and fixed Micah with her black eyes.

"I know it was, Lottie."

"We had us none of the practical, comfortable things that life should offer to folks. The kind of things that helps folks get through the hard times. We could never grow us enough of them good memories, the kind the lucky folks grow and store away in their pantry. And that's what I want for my girl, Micah. I want her to have them things."

Micah looked away. "And you know she'll never have them with me."

Lottie's eyebrows moved toward each other. "You're wrong, boy. You misunderstand what I'm sayin'. You are the one person Fay can have 'em with. It weren't because his skin was one color and mine was another that Gaston and me didn't have them things. Well, that was part of it, sure; that was a big part of it. But the hardest part about our life was because we were too much alike, Gaston and me. You, Micah, you carry 'nough passion for two folks, and my Fay, that girl carries 'nough of the practical for a dozen. What you have, she needs, and what she has you need too. I done give up on her ever marryin' a nice Negro boy. She loves you. There's no denyin' that. She knows she could never be happy with anyone but you, and she is practical enough to admit it. Watchin' the two of you together these last weeks has finally convinced me of that too." She reached over and took Micah's hand. "I know what I'm talking about, so you listen to me. It's hard to mix white and black. That's why I've never wanted you and Fay to be together. Wyoming here ain't like the South, but it'd be hard here too. Maybe someday things'll change, but by then it'll be too late for the two of you."

"Yes, I know."

"It ain't right, you and Fay having to sneak around." Micah started to speak, but Lottie said, "Don't you even say it. And don't you be givin' me that innocent look, neither. Fay's told me how much the two of you loves each other. She tol' me that in no uncertain terms. And I'm not so old I can't remember that young people in love have to be together. I know part of the reason you've been havin' to sneak around to be together is because of me. I've known the two of you been sinnin', and I don't mind tellin' ya, I ain't liked it. But I was wrong. My Fay would choose to be your wife if the world was a different place, and I'd change this world if I could, but that ain't possible. I can change me, though. Tonight you and Fay can have my room at the house. I'll be sleepin' on the cot in the storage room here at the café."

"Lottie, I—"

She held up her finger and stopped him. She was not finished, and she would not be interrupted. "Gaston and me was married," she said, "and you would not believe what we went through. Once in New Iberia Parrish Gaston was tarred and feathered because he had taken hisself a nigger wife. It was fine to be with nigger women down in them parts, but you weren't supposed to marry one. He nearly died after that tarrin', but that time I nursed him back. I don't expect that'd happen here in Wyoming, not to you, anyhow, but there would be a hundred other ways they'd tar and feather you, Micah, a thousand ways. And Fay knows that. She would never bring that on you. But I know my girl and she can't let herself be with no other man. She considers herself your woman. You two might have to keep hidin' from the eyes of the world, but as of this minute, you don't have to hide from me no more."

"What about the others, Lottie? Jackson and Cedra, Polly—"

"For an intelligent man, you ain't too smart, are you? Didn't you see the way them people looked at you in there tonight? I saw it even if you didn't. They love you, Micah. They are your friends. And I saw them lookin' at you lookin' at Fay. You don't worry about them," she said. After a bit she repeated, "No, sir, don't worry about them." She reached up and patted his face. "You are a good man, and I want my Fay to have you in whatever ways she can. Except for the difference in your skin, you are perfect for each other. Fay needs some of your fire and although, God knows, you are more practical now than you was in your younger days, you could use some of Fay's practicality. She stood and tightened her apron. "You get on back in there, now. I have to finish my cleanin'.'"

He stood and drew the old woman to him, holding her close. He was surprised at how thin she was. He held her that way for a moment but didn't speak. After a bit, he let her go and returned to the back room.

Micah thought of Lottie and Gaston now as Fay lay beside him. He could tell by her even breathing that she was asleep. Coiling himself against her, he closed his eyes. It took a while, but eventually he too fell asleep.

CHAPTER TWENTY-SIX

Micah was asleep when the window exploded, but the second it happened, he knew what it was. "Fay, stay down!" he shouted. He ripped their top blanket away and threw it across the shattered glass that covered the floor. He rolled from the bed onto the blanket and grabbed the shotgun that leaned against the wall. He crawled over the blanket to the window and peered through.

The moon was gone, and it was too dark to even see the grove of cottonwoods by the river. Somewhere a dog barked, and Micah thought he heard a horse whinny, but nothing more.

There was a pounding on the bedroom door, and Chester called, "Micah, are you and Fay all right in there?"

"Yes, get back. Have everyone stay down. And watch the front." He turned to Fay, who was huddled in the corner of the room with the bed sheet wrapped around her. "Fay, throw me my pants." He knew it was irrational, but he didn't want to get into a gunfight without his pants. She tossed them to him, and he pulled them on.

"Can you see anything?" she whispered.

A thousand thoughts were rushing through Micah's mind, but Fay's whispering brought them all to a stop. There had been a shot fired, glass shattered, dogs barking, he and Chester shouting back and forth, and after all of that, Fay was whispering.

He would laugh if he weren't so damned scared. "No, nothing," he said. For five minutes he stared into the darkness, but he couldn't see or hear a thing. "Whoever it was is gone."

"Whoever it was?" said Fay, standing. "We know who it was."

Micah didn't respond, but she was right. Sonny Pratt had been outside the house tonight, and he had put a bullet through a bedroom window to let them know he was there.

Micah moved to the edge of the bed and sat down. He pulled on his boots and shirt. "Careful of the glass, Fay," he said as he crossed the room to the far wall. The bullet had blown out the window and torn into the wall. Micah opened the door and stepped through. Sure enough, there was an exit hole on this side of the wall.

"Is everybody okay in here?" he asked.

"Yes," Chester said. "A little shaky, but all right." They were clustered together in the center of the room.

"A *little* shaky?" Jackson asked. "*Very* shaky is what I am." He pointed to the floor next to the pallet where he had been sleeping. Micah crossed to the spot where he pointed. When the bullet exited the wall, it had done so in a downward trajectory, hitting the pinewood floor less than six inches from where Jackson's head had been. Micah pulled out his pocket knife and dug the slug from the plank. The bullet was distorted, but it looked to Micah to be a forty-four.

"It was Sonny," Polly said.

"He must not have liked your performance in court today," said Chester. "You showed him you meant business."

"Sonny doesn't give a damn whether you're convicted or not," said Micah. "But he doesn't want Polly to testify. This was his way of letting her know that one more time. So far his name hasn't come up in the trial. He wants to keep it that way."

"By God, he can't get away with firing a gun into a house full of sleeping people," Jackson said. His voice was still a little quivery.

"Oh, please, Jackson," said Cedra. "He's already gotten away with it. He gets away with everything. Isn't that why we're all hiding in this house together, because Sonny Pratt can do whatever he wants to do whenever he wants to do it?"

"It could never be proven that Sonny Pratt was the one who fired this shot," said Micah, "but there is some law in this town. There's supposed to be, anyway. And this time that son of a bitch Collins is at least going to question Pratt about it." Micah tore his coat from the hall tree. As he pulled it on, he said, "Chester, there's some wood in the shed behind the house. Cover that God-damned window in there before everyone freezes to death."

Brad Collins rented a small house on North Second Street, one block over and a couple of blocks south of Lottie's. Nora, his wife, had run off with a traveling salesman of pots and pans two years earlier, and Collins had lived alone in the house ever since.

Micah climbed Collins's front porch and pounded on the door. "Open up in there, Collins."

There was no response, and Micah pounded again. After a bit, there was the sound of curses, and Micah saw the flare of a match through the thin curtains as a lamp was lit. Collins pulled open the door. His hair was mussed and his eyes still looked a little out of focus. He wore pants and the top of his longjohns, but he was barefoot.

"Who is it?" he asked, holding the lamp up and rubbing his eye with the heel of his hand.

Micah stepped into the room, pushing Collins aside as he did.

"What the hell do you want, McConners? It's the middle of the damned night."

Micah held the piece of lead up to Collins's light. "Ten

minutes ago," he said, "this was fired through the bedroom window of Lottie Charbunneau's house."

Collins took it from him. He held both the lamp and the piece of lead as far from his eyes as the length of his arms would allow. "Anybody hurt?" he asked.

"No," said Micah, "by some miracle no one was."

Collins handed the lead back and placed the lamp on the table in front of the window. "What time is it, anyway?" he asked, rubbing his head.

"A little after five."

"Did you see anything?"

"No, it was too dark. But it had to've come from the freight yards behind the house."

"Probably some drunk cowboy."

"It was no drunk cowboy," said Micah.

"Now how the hell would you know that, McConners?"

"It was Sonny Pratt."

"What? Are you out of your mind?"

"You've been turning your back on Sonny's behavior ever since you've been in office. Now I'm telling you I have reason to believe he fired a gun into a house with six people in it."

"You got anything showing it's Sonny?" Collins asked.

"He's made threats to Polly to prevent her from testifying tomorrow."

"Well, now," said the sheriff, puffing his chest up, "this is the first I've ever heard about any threats being made."

"Polly and Cedra didn't want to inform the law. But I've had enough of it, and I'm here telling you now."

"I can't go out to the Pratt place and start making accusations with no more to go on than that."

Micah stared at the man. "Let me get this straight," he finally said, "a gunshot was fired into a house with six people in it.

One of the victims gives you the name of a person who's made threats against another of the victims to keep her from testifying in district court, and you won't even go out and question the person making the threats? Is that what I'm hearing?" Micah's anger was rising fast. "That's the way I'm reading the situation here, Collins. How close is that to accurate?"

Collins stuck a thick finger in Micah's face. "You listen to me, you pup. If you think you can come back into this town with the ink still wet on your license to play lawyer and start telling folks how to do their job, you are wrong." He jabbed Micah's shoulder. "Now you get out of here before you wish you had."

"Oh, for Christ sake, Collins, what's this? Are you getting tough with me?"

"You better watch yourself, boy. You're not in the courtroom now. You and me start scrapping, it won't be with words." He jabbed his big finger into Micah's shoulder again, this time hard enough to push him back a step.

"You know, I really wish you wouldn't do that," Micah said. He could feel a smile bloom but it felt too wide and too stiff.

"So you don't like that, huh? Let me tell you something, if you didn't like that, you're really going to hate this." He pulled his hand back for another jab, and when he did Micah's left fist lashed out, catching Collins on the right eye, making him stagger and turning his head to his left. Micah followed up with a right cross that also landed on Collins's right eye. This time the sheriff went down flat on his back, smacking his head with a clunk on the wooden floor. Collins was stunned, but still conscious.

Micah stood above him looking down. "Collins," he said with disgust, "you are about as worthless as any man I've ever run across." He tossed the bullet onto Collins's chest. It hit and bounced to the floor, rotated in one tight circle, and came to a stop. "I don't guess I ever expected anything from you, anyhow." He started for the door. "By the way," he said, turning back to face the sheriff, "you were wrong about me hating it." He watched as Collins lifted a hand to his eye. A little groan skittered through the man's clenched teeth. "Knocking you to the floor was the most fun I've had in years."

He stepped out into the cold late-December air. Although Micah had not accomplished a thing by his visit to the sheriff, as he walked back to Lottie's, he felt one hell of a lot better.

CHAPTER TWENTY-SEVEN

"I won't be taking long, Judge," whispered Thomas Blythe in a side-bar conference. As soon as the judge had entered, Blythe asked if they could approach the bench to take care of a few housekeeping matters. "I would say I have less than fifteen minutes with the sheriff, and then, as I mentioned in my opening, I have only four quick questions for Miss Pratt." Blythe turned to Micah. "Of course, Mr. McConners seems to do a rather extensive job at cross-examination, so I'm not positive we will be finishing up our case by midday, but I should anticipate we will."

Micah shook his head. "I won't be long, Judge. I'll take a little while with Miss Pratt, but I would think less than an hour."

"Fine. We'll finish the state's case, take a noon recess, then come back and begin the defense case. How long do you figure that'll take?"

"Not long, sir," Micah said. His response was an honest one, since he did not plan to put on a case at all. There was nothing he could do in a case-in-chief that he couldn't do as well on Polly's cross-examination. He didn't want to admit in front of the prosecutor, though, that he wasn't putting on any evidence. He doubted it would make a difference, but it was something he didn't want to do.

"Well, good," said Walker. "Maybe we can let the jury go a little early this afternoon, and all of us can get together and work out the law I'll be instructing them on. We can come back in the morning, I'll charge the jury, you fellas can give your closings, and we'll send them out to deliberate. How does that sound, gentlemen?"

Both Micah and Blythe agreed that would be fine, and everyone returned to their seats.

"Court'll come to order," Walker said. "I believe when we finished yesterday, Mr. Blythe, you were prepared to call your next witness."

"That's correct, Your Honor. The state would call Sheriff Bradley Collins."

"Come forward to be sworn, sheriff," said the judge.

Collins stepped up to the bench, and murmurs ran through the theater when everyone saw his red and swollen right eye.

Walker swore him in. "Take the stand there, please, sheriff," he said.

"Gracious," whispered Chester, "you did pop him, didn't you? I thought you'd learned to deal with that nasty temper of yours."

"He brought out the worst in me," Micah said.

Chester grimaced. "Maybe I'll start being nicer to you."

"Good morning, sheriff," said Blythe.

"Morning."

"Would you state for the record and the jury your name and your occupation?"

"Brad Collins. I was elected sheriff in the last election."

Blythe pointed out, "That's quite a shiner you're sporting there, sir." When Collins didn't respond, Blythe asked with a smile, "I suppose that is one of the many hazards of your job; is that right?"

"I reckon," Collins said in a flat voice.

"Yes, well, tell me, you said you were elected sheriff of this county in the last election. Would that have been the election a little over a month ago, or did you mean the general election in '98?"

"Ninety-eight."

"So," said Blythe, "I assume you held the position of sheriff of this county, then, on the twenty-eighth day of August, 1900."

"I did."

"Did you have occasion to make any arrests on that date?"

"Yes, sir."

"Can you tell us who it was you arrested?"

"I arrested Dr. Hedstrom there." He lifted his arm and pointed to the defense table.

Micah noticed Blythe did not ask the judge if the record would reflect that the witness had identified the defendant. A dog didn't have to bite the clever Thomas Blythe more than once.

"And," continued Blythe, "what were the circumstances surrounding that arrest?"

"I was called over to the county attorney's office that morning."

"How was that done?"

"Mr. Anderson sent a boy to my office with a message for me to come to the courthouse right away."

"Did you do so?"

"Sure."

"And once you arrived at the county attorney's office, what happened next?"

"That Mrs. Eggers who was here yesterday, she was at Mr. Anderson's office when I got there. Earl, he told her to tell me what she'd told him."

"Yes?"

"So I listened to her story, and me and Mr. Anderson decided we should go talk to the doctor. We walked up to his place—his clinic there—and asked him a few questions."

"Did you tell him your business—that is, the reason for your visit?"

"Yes—well, Mr. Anderson did."

"Tell us what was said."

"Earl told him we'd been informed that he had performed an abortion there in his clinic the day before."

"What was the doctor's response to that?"

"Well, he guessed right away who it was told us about it."

"You mean he knew it was Mrs. Eggers, the woman he had thrown into the street the night before when she had confronted him with his crime?"

"That's who he said, Mrs. Eggers, right."

"What else was said on that day?"

"Mr. Anderson asked him if that information was true."

"And what did the doctor say in response?" asked Blythe.

"He said that, yes, it certainly was true. He had performed the abortion."

"He never denied it at all?"

"No, sir, he never did. He admitted it right away."

"Thank you, sheriff," said Thomas Blythe. "Nothing further at this time, Judge."

"Mr. McConners, cross?" asked the judge.

Micah stood, but he stayed at the table rather than walk to the lectern. Collins gave him a scowl.

"Sheriff," began Micah, "isn't it true that the doctor asked what would happen if he did deny Mrs. Eggers's accusations?"

Collins nodded. "Yes, now that you mention it, I believe he did."

"What was either your or Mr. Anderson's response to that?"

"Seems like Earl said he'd have to go ask the Pratt women some questions. Maybe investigate their involvement in the situation."

"And wasn't it at that time that Dr. Hedstrom gave his

confession to you and the county attorney?"

"Yes, it was."

Micah started to sit down but stopped himself. He couldn't resist asking one more question. "So, sheriff, tell me, have you tried putting a steak on that eye of yours? I expect Mr. Anderson would be glad to buy you one."

Everyone laughed except Collins and Anderson. Even Blythe was chuckling when he made his relevancy objection. And the judge smiled too when he said, "Sustained."

"The state," said Thomas Blythe, "would now call to the stand its third and final witness, Miss Polly Pratt."

After Polly was sworn and gave her name, Blythe said, "Now don't be nervous, Miss Pratt. Would you care for some water?"

Polly said in a strong voice, "I don't need any water. Thank you, Mr. Blythe."

"Miss Pratt, it is not my desire to embarrass you. I have known you since your childhood. I know what a fine young woman you are."

"Thank you, sir."

"But as you know, there are certain questions I must ask."

"I realize that. You may ask your questions."

"Very well. Miss Pratt, were you with child on the date of August 27, 1900?"

Micah saw Polly swallow hard, but she turned to the jury and answered loudly, "Yes, Mr. Blythe, I was."

"On that same date, August 27, 1900, here in Probity, Wyoming, was there an abortion performed to rid you of that child?"

"Yes, there was."

"Did this pregnancy cause your health to be such that you were in danger of death?"

"No, Mr. Blythe, my health was fine."

Blythe moved from the lectern to the witness stand, and in what Micah assumed was his most solemn of voices, he asked, "By whom was this abortion performed, Miss Pratt?"

For the briefest instant, Polly looked down at her hands; then she raised her head, took a breath, and said, "It was performed, Mr. Blythe, by my doctor and my friend, Chester Hedstrom."

"Thank you, Miss Pratt. Your Honor, I have no further questions."

"Polly," Micah began, "I'll not be as brief as the attorney for the state, but I'll not take long, either. There are, however, a few things that I feel will help the gentlemen of the jury to put all of this in some kind of perspective."

"I understand, Mr. McConners." Polly's voice was not as strong with Micah as it had been with Blythe. Although she was the state's witness, Blythe had been an adversary. Micah was her friend, and with her resistance more relaxed, her nervousness showed.

Micah had given a great deal of thought to how he was going to handle this examination of Polly. Yet as he stood before the judge, the prosecution, and the heat of hundreds of eyes, he still was not sure of the best way to approach it. He knew that on a practical level it would not matter. In the end Polly would tell her story, and there would be a conviction. But perhaps Chester was right. We must establish our own personal lines, and once established, refuse to cross them no matter how impractical. It was odd. His conversation with Lottie last night hadn't been so different than his discussions with Chester. Both divided the world into two categories: the practical and the ardent. Both, like Micah, were passionate, sometimes too passionate for their own good. But still both also had great respect and admiration for the practical, more down-to-earth side of things . . . Lottie with her fond example of lovers storing memories in a pantry,

Chester with his excitement for all the practical advances the new century promised to bring about. Micah had learned in his own life that passion often had to give way to the practical, but he acknowledged sometimes it had to go the other way too.

"Polly," said Micah, "let's get right to the heart of the matter. How did you become pregnant?"

There was tittering and stirring among the spectators. For a moment Micah thought Polly was not going to answer. Finally, she said, "I was raped, Mr. McConners. I was raped on June 14, 1900."

There was more stirring in the theater, but not the sound of even one voice.

"And, Polly, who was it who raped you last spring?"

Blythe was on his feet. "Your Honor, I must object. This is totally irrelevant to the matter before the court. Whatever happened to this poor young woman is unfortunate, but, Judge, it has absolutely nothing to do with the charge against Chester Hedstrom."

"Response, Mr. McConners?"

"Your Honor, we're dealing with a tragic situation here. It's a situation in which a large number of lives were changed forever." He waved his hand in the direction of the jury. "We are asking these men to make a decision that will also affect lives—not only my client's life, but all of our lives to one degree or another. I will say to you, Your Honor, and as of this moment I will say to everyone who will care to listen—" He turned to face Earl Anderson and Brad Collins. "—that Probity has up to now not been a community in which the truth was welcome. It has been, in fact, a community that has hidden the truth—ignored the acts of certain individuals. Even, I'm afraid—" He faced Thomas Blythe. "—felt the truth was irrelevant." He turned back to Judge Walker. "It's sad, Your Honor, but right now this trial is the only forum the truth has in Probity, Wyoming. And I feel these jurymen must be provided all the truth before they're asked to make their decision."

Blythe was on his feet again. "That was a wonderful speech, Judge, but the fact remains that the question is irrelevant."

Walker poured himself a glass of water, took a sip, and replaced the tumbler beside the pitcher. "Well, Mr. McConners, the prosecutor is right. That question is irrelevant to the specific charge against your client."

Micah felt his insides drop. "Very well, Judge," he said. He hoped the defeat he was feeling didn't echo in his voice. "I'll move on to something else."

"Now, wait a minute. I haven't made my ruling yet." He took another sip of his water, again replaced the tumbler, looked down at Blythe, and said, "Overruled."

Micah felt a smile tug at the corners of his mouth. "You may answer the question, Miss Pratt. Who was it who raped you on June 14, 1900?"

"Hank Jones," said Polly, "and my stepbrother, Sonny Pratt."

This time there was more than a stirring in the room. There was the surprised exclamations of a couple of hundred voices.

Walker allowed it to go on for a few seconds. "All right," he finally said, "everybody hold it down."

"Polly," Micah said, "I'll not ask you details about the rape. But I do want to know, were there any threats made against you at that time?"

"Yes."

"Would you tell us about that?"

"As they were leaving, Sonny took his knife and held it up to my face. He said if I ever told anyone what had happened, he would cut my throat."

"Did you ever tell anyone, Polly?"

"Not right away, no. I was too afraid and ashamed."

"Did you tell anyone later?"

"Yes, eventually I did."

"Who?"

"My mother."

"At what point did you tell her?"

"A couple of months later, when I realized I was pregnant."

"Why didn't you go to the authorities, Polly? Why didn't you inform the law of this crime against you?"

Polly turned her gaze on Earl Anderson. "Because nothing would be done, and Sonny would have carried out his threat."

"Do you really believe Sonny Pratt would have killed you, Polly?"

"I am certain of it," she said. And in a near whisper she added, "I expect he will yet."

"Why do you say that, Polly?"

"Because I know he murdered Lester Jones, and last night he fired a shot into the house where I was sleeping."

"*Objection,* Your Honor," shouted Thomas Blythe. "This is irrelevant and absolute conjecture on the part of the witness."

"Sustained," ruled the judge.

"Polly," asked Micah, "have you seen Sonny Pratt since the day he raped you?"

"My mother and I moved out of the house after I told her what had happened. I've seen Sonny only twice since."

"Why did you move out?"

"My mother told my stepfather, Emmett, about the rape, and when he didn't believe her and wouldn't do anything about it, we moved into Mrs. Jordan's."

"You say you've seen Sonny twice since that time?"

"Yes."

"What were those circumstances?"

"Your Honor," said Blythe, "I have to object."

"Overruled," said the judge.

"The first time was on the day of your return, Mr. McConners. Late that afternoon, I left the party they had for you in the park to walk the few blocks back to our boarding house, and Sonny attacked me. He beat me so badly Dr. Hedstrom had to suture my face."

"Again, Your Honor," objected Blythe, "I must—"

"Overruled."

"In addition to the beating, did he threaten you again at that time?"

"He did. He said no one had better ever find out what he and Hank had done."

"Did he know of the pregnancy, Polly?"

"Yes, I told him that night. That's when he started to hit me. He said I should leave the county to have the baby, and once it was born, he said I'd better either give it away or throw it in the river. He said if anyone found out, he would kill me."

"He said he would kill you if anyone found out?"

"Yes, he did. He told me to leave town or he would kill me."

"And, again, you believed him when he said that?"

"Objection," said Blythe. "That question was asked and answered earlier."

"Sustained."

"All right, Polly," said Micah. "The other occasion you had to see Sonny Pratt since you moved out of your stepfather's house, when was that?"

"The afternoon Lester Jones's body was discovered."

"What were the circumstances surrounding that encounter?"

"We were all standing around the body, and I saw Sonny watching us from the alley. He looked right at me, and when he saw I had noticed him, he dragged his index finger across his throat in a cutting gesture."

"Did you consider this a threat to you, Miss Pratt?"

"I did."

Blythe started to his feet, but he seemed to reconsider his

objection—or the likelihood of having it sustained—and sat back down.

Micah scanned his notes, turned to the judge, and said, "Nothing further, Your Honor."

"Redirect examination, Mr. Blythe?"

"Yes, Your Honor. Miss Pratt, you say you were beaten by your stepbrother; is that correct?"

"Yes, sir."

"When did this beating take place relative to the abortion performed on you by Dr. Hedstrom?"

"I'm not sure. Maybe a week before. Dr. Hedstrom agreed to do the abortion on the day my mother and I returned to have him remove my stitches."

"Tell me, Miss Pratt, did this beating in any way affect your pregnancy?"

"I don't understand."

"By being beaten, as you say you were, did it affect your health in any way? I mean, other than the injuries to you from the beating itself, did that cause any complications in your pregnancy?"

Polly, obviously understanding where Blythe was going, shook her head and said, "No, sir, to be honest, it did not."

"And Dr. Hedstrom never told you that the beating had affected your health in terms of your pregnancy, did he?"

"No, Mr. Blythe, he did not."

"So, to your knowledge, the beating you allege was administered to you by Sonny Pratt did not affect your health and played no role in Dr. Hedstrom's decision to perform the abortion on August 27, last; am I correct?"

"I'm not sure I understand the question," Polly said.

"Let me simplify it a bit," said Blythe. "Would you agree that Sonny Pratt's actions played no role in Dr. Hedstrom's decision to perform the abortion on August 27?"

"I don't know the answer to that," said Polly, "but, no, he never said that the beating had affected the pregnancy in any way."

"Thank you, young lady," said Blythe with a satisfied smile. "No more questions from the state, Your Honor."

"Any recross, Mr. McConners?" Walker asked.

Micah had not intended to ask any more questions of Polly, but the tenor of Blythe's last question had caused a thought to cross his mind. He reached for his statute book, which was on the corner of his table. "May I have a moment, Your Honor?"

"You may."

Micah turned to the abortion statute, which was titled, "Attempted Miscarriage." It was a statute he had read many times over the course of the last four months, but now he wanted to read it again, perhaps in a different light. He did, and with his own satisfied smile, he stood, and to Judge Walker he said, "I do have one question, Judge."

"One question, is that all?"

"Yes, Your Honor."

"Should I hold him to that, Mr. Blythe?" asked the judge.

Blythe laughed, "You'll never get me to agree, Judge, that any lawyer should ever be held to just one question."

"I didn't think you would," Walker said. "Proceed, Mr. McConners."

"Polly, did you ever tell Dr. Hedstrom that you had been threatened by Sonny Pratt?"

"I didn't," Polly said, "but my mother did."

Micah turned to the judge. "I guess Mr. Blythe is right, Your Honor. A lawyer shouldn't be held to only one question."

"I expected you to change your mind, young man," said the judge. "Go ahead."

"How do you know your mother told him your life had been threatened by Sonny Pratt?"

"Because I was there when she did it. I was begging her not to tell. I knew if she told, Sonny would kill me."

"Well, Judge," said Micah, "only two questions; that wasn't too bad."

"No," agreed the judge, "it wasn't. Anything further, Mr. Blythe?"

"No, Your Honor. We have no further questions of Miss Pratt."

Walker turned to Polly. "You may step down. Call your next witness, Mr. Blythe."

Blythe did a quick conference with Earl Anderson, stood, and said, "Your Honor, we have no further witnesses, and the State of Wyoming would rest its case at this time."

"Very well, sir. Mr. McConners, are you prepared to proceed with the defendant's case-in-chief?"

"Your Honor," Micah said, "before we proceed, I would like the opportunity to make a motion outside the hearing of the jury."

Walker scratched his chin. "I assume it's the usual defense motion made at the close of the state's case." By usual defense motion, the judge was referring to the *pro forma* motion for acquittal as a matter of law on the grounds that the state had failed to prove all of the elements of the crime charged. Jackson had told Micah that Judge Walker, in order to save time, would often have counsel make the motion for the record; he would either take it under advisement or deny it outright and they would proceed with the defendant's case. If defense counsel wanted to flesh out the record with some brief argument, Walker would allow them to renew the motion and argue in chambers later.

"It is the usual motion, Judge," Micah said, "but I would like to be heard at this time, if I may." Micah knew the old judge had not been expecting this. Argument now would slow things down, and if there was anything Walker hated, it was some

251

frivolous lawyer throwing off his schedule. But Micah also knew in a criminal case such as this one, it was awkward for the judge to deny his request if Micah wanted to push it.

"All right, Sheriff, take the jury into the jury room." As the jury filed out, Walker instructed them not to discuss the case among themselves nor with anyone else until they were told it was time to do so.

Once they were gone, Walker turned to Micah and said, "All right, young fella, make it quick."

Micah stepped to the lectern, tried to gulp down the knot in his throat without much success, and said, "Judge Walker, I'd like to move the court to direct a verdict of acquittal in this case."

Earl Anderson snickered. Blythe shhh-ed him and sat forward in his chair.

Walker slid his spectacles to the tip of his nose and looked at Micah over the top. "Of course you would, Mr. McConners. What specific element or elements do you feel the state has failed to prove?"

"Well, Judge, I feel it's more than the failure to prove all the elements. I feel, Your Honor, that through one of the state's own witnesses, it's been shown that in fact no crime has been committed at all."

This time Blythe also snickered.

It appeared to Micah that Walker too was about to snicker, but for decorum's sake suppressed it. "All right, Mr. McConners, explain your position."

"Judge, my position is really a simple one. Since the beginning of this case we have all recognized that there is only one defense to a charge of causing a miscarriage or performing an abortion. And, of course, that is if the woman's pregnancy is causing such health concerns as to threaten her life."

"I believe that's the law, Mr. McConners," Walker said in a

matter-of-fact tone. "That's the way the statute reads, if I'm not mistaken."

"Yes, Your Honor, that is how I've read the statute as well."

"So what is your point, young man? Let's get to it."

"My point, sir, is that is how I've read the statute—how we've all read the statute, but that is not what the statute says . . . not at all. We have always assumed that's what it says, but we've been wrong. If you'll allow me, I'll read it to you verbatim." He held up his statute book. "I have here, Judge, the Revised Statutes of the State of Wyoming, 1900 edition."

"I see that," said the judge. "Start reading, Mr. McConners."

Micah's index finger held his place. He set the heavy book on the lectern and opened it up. "The heading is, 'Attempted Miscarriage.' It says, 'Whoever prescribes or administers to any pregnant woman, or any woman who he supposes to be pregnant, any drug, medicine, or substance whatever, with intent thereby to procure a miscarriage of such woman; or with like intent uses any instrument or means whatever, unless such miscarriage is necessary to preserve her life, shall, if the woman miscarries or dies in consequence thereof, be imprisoned in the penitentiary not more than fourteen years.' " Micah repeated with emphasis, " *'Unless such miscarriage is necessary to preserve her life.'* " Closing the book, he said, "I don't mean to play games or bandy words, sir." He tapped on the book's cover and repeated for the third time, " 'Unless such miscarriage is necessary to preserve her life.' " That is what the statute says, and that is all that it says, Judge Walker."

The theater was silent.

"It is our position, Your Honor, that Dr. Hedstrom complied with the law and did what he did in order to preserve Polly Pratt's life.

"Your Honor, it is an undisputed fact. The evidence in the state's case was that if Polly Pratt had been forced to carry this fetus to term, Sonny Pratt would have killed her. I admit this is a unique situation, but it is the situation before us. Mr. Blythe educed that testimony himself. Actually, Sonny would have killed her as soon as the pregnancy began to show. He'd already beaten her severely, threatened her with a knife after he and another man had raped her, and upon Lester Jones's death, threatened her yet again. She was convinced he would kill her. So was her mother. And my client, the defendant, Dr. Hedstrom, was convinced of this as well. Because of the nature of law enforcement in this community, they were at a loss as to what to do.

"The statute does not say one word, Judge, about it's being legal to perform an abortion only if complications of the pregnancy cause a risk of death to the mother. It simply says, 'Unless such miscarriage is necessary to preserve her life.' No more, no less. It is we, Judge, the readers of the statute, who have always added that interpretation . . . complications of the pregnancy . . . and I say to you, sir, we cannot go outside the plain language of the statute and make our own inferences."

"My statute book is in my chambers, Mr. McConners. Let me see that thing." He snapped his fingers and motioned for Micah to approach the bench. Micah did and handed him the book.

"Your Honor," said Blythe, "this motion comes as a complete surprise to the state. We would like to have the opportunity to brief this issue and argue it at a later time."

"Did you forget we have a jury waiting in the jury room, Mr. Blythe? You're more than welcome to make any arguments you can think of right now. I would welcome you to do so."

Blythe straightened his coat and cleared his throat. He seemed to be searching for words and having difficulty locating them—a situation Micah had never seen the man in before. "Well, sir," Blythe began, "I think it's obvious that the statute is referring to the health of the mother in terms of complications of the pregnancy. I mean, it is so patently obvious that it goes without saying."

"Mr. Blythe, things that are not said in statutes are not the law. But I will think about this over the noon hour." Walker called a recess even though the time was only a quarter past eleven.

At one o'clock that afternoon, the parties sat at their tables waiting for Judge Walker to enter. All eyes were locked on the stage-left wing. The instant Micah saw Brad Collins flick a piece of lint from the brim of his hat, a gesture Micah had finally figured out was a signal to Blythe and Anderson that the judge was about to enter, Micah was on his feet and shouted, *"All rise!"* in a ringing voice that brought everyone in the theater to their feet.

Anderson glared across at him, and Micah returned his glare with a smile.

"You may be seated," said the judge. Walker took even longer than usual to pull his spectacles from his pocket and slip the wire earpieces around his ears. He looked at Micah and said, "Here are your statutes, Mr. McConners. I neglected to return this to you before the break."

Micah stepped to the bench, retrieved his book, and hurried back to his seat.

"Mr. McConners raised an interesting and imaginative point in his motion this morning. Some might say a little too imaginative, perhaps; others might be quick to agree with his position. I have given it a great deal of consideration over the last—" He checked his watch. "—hour and forty-five minutes. And I find myself somewhere in the middle. I think a reasonable man could very easily read that statute and come away with no opinion other than the one Mr. Blythe proposes. As a matter of fact, I consider myself a reasonable man, and I have read that statute many, many times, and I have never concluded anything other than it was referring to the woman's physical condition as a result of complications in her pregnancy.

"Mr. McConners, though, with his youthful eye, has looked at what has always been obvious to this old lawyer and made at least an arguable point that this statute does not say what we who have spent our careers reading it have always thought it said.

"As a quick aside, let me mention that I have never liked this statute. I have always thought it was too narrow. At a minimum, in my opinion, it should allow for the termination of a pregnancy in a case of rape or incest. There are, I am sure, those who would hold an opinion contrary to that and could make compelling arguments in that regard.

"But that is not the question, and that is not what the defense is arguing. As much as I would like to see that language with respect to rape and incest in there, I cannot add it to the statute. Only the legislature can do that, and I would not presume to tell our legislators in their infinite wisdom what laws they should or should not enact.

"I can, I suppose, in a round-about way, tell them, however, how they should write the laws they choose to enact. In fact, arguably, it is my function to do so since I am the poor soul required to interpret their words' meaning. And as I said, in making my interpretation of what they are trying to enact with their statutes, I cannot consider something that they have apparently chosen not to write down on the paper.

"The pertinent part of the statute with which we are dealing in this case says, essentially, that it's a crime to abort a fetus by whatever means in a pregnant woman unless—and now I'm quoting. '—such miscarriage is necessary to preserve her life.' Period. That is the cause allowed by law for creating a miscarriage, the preservation of the pregnant woman's life. Adding words to the statute, as Mr. McConners has said, is precisely what I would be doing if I were to include at the end of the phrase, '. . . to preserve her life *due to complications in her pregnancy.*'"

He pulled off his spectacles. "I cannot do that. As a matter of fact, I would not be doing my job if I did do that.

"Likewise, I am not here to determine whether Miss Pratt was in fact in danger of losing her life. As I sit here, I don't know that Sonny Pratt planned to kill his stepsister. I have to assume that he would not. Sonny Pratt, like Dr. Hedstrom, is presumed to be innocent until proven otherwise.

"Also, if Miss Pratt's life had been threatened as a result of complications in her pregnancy, I would be forced to accept her word and the word of her physician that they felt that was the case.

"In our present situation, all that is necessary is that I accept as fact that she, and more importantly, Dr. Hedstrom, believed she was in fatal danger, and because of that belief the abortion was performed.

"After hearing Miss Pratt's testimony, I do believe that was their fear."

He looked down at Micah and added, "So, for those reasons, Mr. McConners, and based on the language of the statute *as written,* I will grant your motion. I will direct a verdict of acquittal for Dr. Chester Hedstrom, and I will order this case dismissed as a matter of law."

He turned toward the jury. "And I will also excuse the jury. Thank you, gentlemen, for your good service.

"Court will stand adjourned."

With that the judge rose, stepped from his bench, and left the stage.

Even before his exit was complete, the spectators in the opera house came to their feet with cheers.

★ ★ ★ ★ ★

PART FOUR:
MICAH'S DECISION

★ ★ ★ ★ ★

CHAPTER TWENTY-EIGHT

"Have a seat, gentlemen." Judge Walker motioned toward the chairs set up around the large table in the theater's backstage green room. Shortly after he had adjourned court, Walker called the lawyers into his makeshift chambers. Since Brad Collins had been acting as bailiff throughout the trial, he followed the attorneys into the room and stood by the door. Walker scrutinized him and said in a hard tone, "We won't be needing your services at this time, sheriff."

Collins cleared his throat and said, "Yes, sir," stepped out, and closed the door.

Walker eyed each one of the men, and in as harsh a tone as he had used with Collins, he said, "It seems we have ourselves a situation here, gentlemen." He turned to Earl Anderson. "I said a moment ago it wasn't necessary in order to reach my decision that I believe Miss Pratt's life actually was in danger, and that's true; it wasn't necessary." His back was stiff. His shoulders were squared. Still looking at Anderson, he added, "But I do believe it. I believe this Pratt kid raped her, and I believe he has threatened to kill her. Of course, if he were ever to be charged with anything by you, Mr. Anderson, which I doubt, I would re-cuse myself from his case and ensure that he was afforded his right to the presumption of innocence and all due process. We would have no trouble finding another judge to hear the matter."

Walker paused and for a brief instant Micah assumed he'd

said what he brought them in to say, and they were finished with the matter. But the judge continued.

"I've been judging in this district now for nearly ten years, and it's my opinion that the state of law enforcement in this county for the last two of those ten years has been deplorable. It was bad enough since your election in '94, Mr. Anderson, but since '98 when Collins was elected sheriff and the two of you have worked together, it has defied belief. I've been tempted to inform the State Attorney General of it on more than one occasion."

The earth's natural gravity seemed to double when the judge said that, at least in the area surrounding Earl Anderson. Everything about the little man drooped—his head, his shoulders. His entire body sank deeper into his chair. The monocle he wore fell from his eye and swung on its chain.

The judge went on, this time spreading his gaze among the others at the table. "The way I see it, an investigation needs to begin immediately into the accusations Miss Pratt made in court today. Now that her claims are out in the open, she may be in less danger than before. Then again, perhaps she's in even more danger. There's no way to know. But serious charges have been levied against this Pratt boy, and it needs to be looked into starting right now." Walker punctuated his last sentence by smacking the flat of his hand on the tabletop.

Everyone looked to Anderson to respond. He was the county attorney, and despite the judge's spreading the heat of his glare about the table, it was obviously Anderson to whom Walker was still speaking.

Finally, after a full minute of silence so thick it could be whittled, Thomas Blythe spoke up. "Judge," he began, "if I may be so presumptuous as to speak for the county attorney and the sheriff, in all honesty, today was the first either of these men had heard any of the accusations against Mr. Pratt. I assure you had they been informed, they would have promptly looked into the matter."

Walker looked from Anderson to Blythe without the heat dropping a degree. "Tom," he said, "it's one of the requirements of my job to listen to a certain amount of bullshit, but there's a limit to how much I'm willing to hear. You and I both know that because Sonny is Emmett Pratt's boy, not a God-damned thing would have been done if that girl and her mother had gone to either Collins or Anderson. Nothing. Not a thing. But I'm here to tell you that those days are done. They are over." He turned back to the county attorney. "Do you hear me, Mr. Anderson?"

Anderson gave a quick nod.

"Now, for some reason that I cannot fathom, you have been elected by the people of this county, not once but twice, and because of that I can't tell you how to do your job." Walker's usually pallid face had turned such a deep crimson Micah thought the man might be about to detonate. The judge reached inside his coat pocket and pulled out a sheet of paper. "But I will tell you, sir, before calling all of you in here, I drafted a telegram. It's to the AG explaining what's going on here in Probity. Unless you can give me one hell of a reason why I shouldn't, as soon as we leave this room, I will be going down the street to the telegraph office and sending this off. I expect the Attorney General can have a whole passel of lawyers and investigators here by tomorrow afternoon looking into the manner in which you and the sheriff perform your duties."

Micah saw a flash of panic hit Anderson's eyes. The little man's lips moved a couple of times before any sound came out. Once he found his voice, it was quivery and at least an octave higher than before Walker had called them in.

"Judge," Anderson said, "I—I promise you if you hold off on sending your wire, I'll have the sheriff make a full investigation.

I'll see to it he leaves no stone unturned, and if there's any truth to the allegations, I promise you, arrests will be made."

The judge seemed unconvinced. "There are multiple accusations here, Mr. Anderson. There's not only the accusation of rape, but the murder of that fellow—" He snapped his fingers trying to recall the name.

"Lester Jones," offered Micah.

"Lester Jones, right. There is threatening a witness, assault and battery, and from what I hear, at least six counts of aggravated assault, if not attempted murder, by firing a shot into a house full of people."

Micah had not mentioned the shot through the window to Walker, but apparently Jackson had before the rest of them made it in to chambers. Since it was out, Micah decided to let the judge know it all. He sat forward in his chair and said, "The sheriff knew of the shot being fired, Judge. I informed him of it myself." Micah was not one to enjoy another man's discomfort, but he had never had any fondness for Anderson or Collins, so even as he watched Anderson squirm from the heat of Judge Walker's anger, he could not help but toss another log on the fire.

"That does not surprise me," Walker said. "I would be hesitant to turn the investigation of anything over to you and your sheriff, Mr. Anderson."

"Judge," said Anderson in a near whisper, "I can assure you that the best effort would be made to get to the bottom of all of these things. In fact, I make you that promise."

"Not good enough," said the judge flatly.

"Your Honor," said Blythe, "perhaps I can make a suggestion."

"All right, let's hear it."

"It's an unpleasant embarrassment for everyone in the community to bring in people from Cheyenne—Cheyenne of all places—to rummage through our dirty laundry." He held his palm out as though making an effort to ward off contradiction even before it could be made. "Yes, Judge, I realize we have a situation here that may well warrant doing that very thing. But as you yourself pointed out, Mr. Anderson is an elected official, as is Sheriff Collins; perhaps we could give them one opportunity to show that they are prepared to fulfill the function of their offices." He paused, waiting for a response. When none came, he continued. "Perhaps we could go ahead and allow the investigation to be conducted locally, but put someone we know to be uninfluenced by the politics of the matter in charge— someone we can all trust."

Walker seemed to ponder that suggestion for a moment. "Did you have someone in mind, Thomas? Yourself, for instance?"

"Myself? Oh, my, Judge, no, certainly not." He shifted his eyes to the other end of the table. "I was thinking of young Mr. McConners."

At first Micah couldn't believe what he was hearing. He would be the last person he'd expect they would want. He was responsible for the accusations being made in the first place. Micah shook his head, fending off the idea. "No, Judge," he said, "I don't think so."

"Why not?" asked Blythe. "You wouldn't be conducting the investigation; the sheriff would. You would merely be there to ensure everything was being done the way it should be. You're already intimately familiar with the case. Who is there better than you to do this?"

For the first time since they entered the room, Judge Walker seemed to have relaxed. He reached to the ashtray in the center of the table and picked up a pipe. As he tamped tobacco into the bowl he said, "I tend to agree, Micah. I believe you are the man for the job. We'll have Collins swear you in as a deputy. That will keep you close enough to watch over things, give you the power of arrest, but at the same time we can appease Collins's pride as sheriff by at least allowing him to pretend to the townsfolk that he's in charge."

"Judge," said Micah, not liking at all the turn this was taking, "I can't work with Brad Collins on something like this."

"Oh, why's that?"

Micah considered for a moment how much he should admit. Deciding nothing could be worse than working with Collins in an investigation of Sonny Pratt, he said, "Well, Judge, I'd say there's a basic dislike between Collins and me."

"I guess you fellas'll have to set that aside to get this job done."

Micah shook his head. "That'll be difficult, I think, particularly for the sheriff."

"How so?"

"I'm the man who gave him the black eye he's wearing today."

Walker smiled as he struck a match and lit his pipe. "Excellent," he said. "Then Sheriff Collins already knows you're a man to be reckoned with."

Chapter Twenty-Nine

Nervousness was not a condition that came upon Emmett Pratt any too often. He liked to think he was a man who made other people nervous, not the other way around. But nervous was how he felt when he came into Thomas Blythe's office and Blythe explained the judge's ruling that ended the trial so abruptly the previous day.

After listening to the lawyer's rather long-winded explanation, Pratt nodded and acknowledged that the decision had been a fair one. It wasn't the outcome of the trial that made Pratt uneasy—to the contrary. He was pleased that the case had been dismissed. That was what he had wanted all along. "I never wanted anything to happen to that young doctor," Pratt said. "He's a fine man. A little strange, I reckon, but a fine man all the same."

Blythe smiled. "I never like to lose a case in court," he said, "but I admit I wasn't disappointed to hear the judge's decision." He waggled a finger at the ceiling to emphasize his point. "I think it was a blatant stretching of the law, but the truth is, I wasn't surprised by what he did. In this case, it was the right thing to do. And McConners gave the judge enough to hang his hat on so that Walker could make his ruling without looking foolish."

A box of cigars was on the corner of Blythe's desk, and he offered Pratt one.

"No thanks," Emmett said. He pulled the makings for a

cigarette from his vest pocket and rolled one with a deftness borne from years of practice. When a man was used to rolling a smoke on horseback in the Wyoming wind, twisting one up sitting in a lawyer's office was easy.

"There's more, though, Emmett," Blythe said.

"I figured there would be." That flutter he'd come in with hit his insides again.

"The judge is demanding an investigation of Sonny. He's ordered Micah McConners to oversee the whole thing."

Emmett pulled a match from the holder on Blythe's desk and lit his cigarette. He inhaled, filling his lungs, and let the smoke roll out slowly.

Emmett was no fool. He realized the law around here had been looking the other way every time Sonny rode by only because Sonny's last name was Pratt. He realized that, and even though he knew Sonny was getting meaner and wilder all the time, Emmett had done nothing about it. He had never asked for any favors from any man, but if favors had come his way without asking, he'd never turned them down.

That, he knew, had been wrong.

He tapped the ash from the end of his cigarette, took another drag, and asked, "So, Thomas, do you think all the things they're saying about my boy are true?" Blythe was both Emmett's lawyer and his friend. But even with their friendship, asking that question was a hard thing for Emmett Pratt to do. By asking, he was allowing for the possibility that Sonny was what Polly and Cedra and all the others said.

For the first time Emmett could remember, Blythe had been posed a question without providing an answer. Instead, a look of compassion filled the lawyer's eyes, and that look sunk into Emmett deeper than any words Blythe might have said.

"Damn," said Emmett as he came to his feet. He was not a sitter. How these God-damned city people could sit in their stores and offices hour after hour, day after day, was beyond him. He walked to the window, turned, and came back to the desk. "I did the best I could by Sonny," he said, "but somewhere along the line, he went sour. I could see it happening, but I didn't know what to do about it."

Blythe shook his head. "Emmett, I watched you raise that boy. You were a fine father to him. Alice was a fine mother, and so was Cedra when she came along." Thomas's cigar had gone out, but he didn't make any effort to relight it. As he spoke, his voice sounded different to Emmett. It was soft, without the usual deep resonance. The words were simple, and they seemed to come from a different place than his usual lawyerly words. "Sometimes," Thomas added, "people do turn sour. It's nobody's fault, but it happens, and there's no way ever to figure out why."

Emmett dropped back into the chair. "What does the sheriff and this McConners fellow have in mind for their investigation?" he asked.

"Oh, I don't know. Nothing very complicated. I expect they'll ask Sonny and Hank some questions—see what they have to say about all this. I heard Micah tell the sheriff yesterday when we left the judge that he wanted them to ride out to the Jones place this morning to talk to Hank and your place this afternoon."

"Where is this McConners's office?" Emmett asked.

"On the west side of Third, between Walnut and Main. Why do you ask?"

"Because," Emmett said, snuffing out his cigarette, "I expect it's high time I did the right thing."

CHAPTER THIRTY

Hank Jones pulled Lester's saddlebags from beneath his brother's bed. Being dead and all, Lester would not need them and, as it happened, Hank did. The bags weren't very good. They were old and the leather stiff, but Hank could only take with him what he could carry, and he wanted to be able to carry as much as possible. With his own bags and Lester's, he could haul most of what few clothes he owned and at least a couple of days' worth of food.

Hank was not a man given to sentiment, but a part of him hated to be leaving the place. It was where he was born, where he grew up. Probity and its surroundings were all Hank had ever known. But since that damned Polly Pratt took the witness stand and spilled her guts at the trial the day before, there was no choice but to run. And that was what Hank planned to do.

He pushed himself up from the floor and threw the bags over his shoulder. He'd load Lester's bags with some canned goods, jerky, and what was left of the batch of biscuits he'd made that morning. That should last him awhile.

He hadn't decided yet where he was going. First he thought about heading up into the mountains and waiting until all this blew over. But it was winter, and living in the mountains would be chilly. Hank Jones liked to avoid chilly living as much as possible. Besides, he wasn't sure things would ever blow over. There was a judge in it now and that new lawyer in town. Even if Sonny could convince the sheriff to forget about what Polly had said, Hank doubted the lawyer or judge would soon forget.

He had filled Lester's bags with the food and was now in his own room shoving clothes and shaving gear down into the other set of bags.

As he packed, Hank pondered where he should go. Making decisions had always been an inconvenience for Hank. For every reason he could think of to do something, he could always think of at least two good reasons not to do it. He was in the midst of debating the good and bad about heading east into Nebraska when he heard the clop of a horse's hooves. He felt his balls tighten at the sound. Hank wouldn't have thought any law would be out to his place this soon. With a shaky hand, he drew his revolver and rushed to the window.

The early morning was still cool. The rider was far enough away that Hank couldn't make out the face, but he recognized the thick buffalo-hide coat the man wore. It was only Sonny Pratt. Hank hadn't realized he'd been holding his breath until, in his relief that it was Sonny, he felt the air rush out of him.

He holstered his gun and returned to packing his things. After a bit there were footsteps on the porch. "Hey, Hank," Sonny called. "You in there?" The front door opened, and Hank heard Sonny come in.

"Back here, Sonny."

There was the jingle of spurs as Sonny moved through the house and came into the small bedroom. "What you doing?" he asked.

Hank had the things he was packing spread out over the bed. Lester's bags were at the foot of the bed on the floor. Sonny went over to them and looked down. The buckle was broken on one of the flaps, and Sonny lifted the flap with the toe of his boot. "So, Hank," he asked, "you going on a vacation or something?"

"I'm getting my ass outta here. That's what I'm doin'."

"You're leaving? How come?" Sonny crossed the room and leaned against the wall opposite Hank.

Hank lifted a pair of socks and brought them to eye level. There was a hole in one the size of a half-dollar. He checked the other one. There was no hole in it, so he shoved the pair into the bag. "How come?" Hank said. "Christ, Sonny, what d'ya think? You heard them boys talking in Buck's last night the same as me." He stopped his packing long enough to meet his friend's eyes. "They's coming after us, Sonny, for what we done to that damned sister of yours. Maybe for what you done to Lester too."

Lester had been a dumb one. And the truth was that Lester would rather go whoring than eat. Hank had always found that an aggravating flaw in his brother's character. But Hank had to admit he sometimes missed the kid. Not that Lester didn't have coming what Sonny gave him. He did. Lester knew better than to be talking to that lawyer fella the way he was. But still and all, from time to time Hank did miss the dumb bastard.

"They is coming after us this time," Hank said again, "and the thing to do is get."

Sonny shook his head. "Naw," he said, "you're being hasty, partner." He said it *pod-ner,* the way the old cowboys used to say it when he and Sonny were kids. "They don't have anything on us." Sonny's voice was soft the way it always was. Hank had never heard Sonny raise his voice to a soul. Hank knew the madder and more dangerous Sonny got, the softer his voice became. When he was his angriest, Sonny barely spoke above a whisper. Hank, on the other hand, was a screamer. When he got mad or upset, he would yell. That was the way average folks were, as far as Hank knew. But not Sonny Pratt. Sonny was the soft-spoken sort. "It's Polly's word against ours," Sonny said. "And as far as Lester's concerned, why, hell, they can't prove a thing."

"Remember, Sonny, it ain't the county attorney or Sheriff Collins who's in charge this time," Hank said. "That lawyer's in charge, and I hear he's a smart one." He resumed his packing. "I ain't sticking around to see if he can prove things or not. I'm gettin' the hell out."

"If you run," Sonny said, "that's as good as confessing."

"Not if they don't catch me, it ain't."

"Where are you planning to go?"

"I ain't decided. Nebraska. Maybe Colorado. Anywhere far away from here'd do."

Sonny took off his hat, shoved his hair back, then put the hat back on. "Well, Hank," he said, "I think you're making a mistake. You might as well be writing those folks a letter saying we're the ones who did the crimes."

Hank had finished with one bag and now began filling the bag on the other side. "Sonny," he said, "I've been doin' things your way ever since we was boys. I gotta admit, you are a faster thinker than me, and mostly your ways've been best. We've raised us some hell and had us some fun at every turn. But I got a feelin' that this time we're in deep. Let me finish up here, and then let's ride over to your place, get some of your things, and both of us light out. What d'ya say?"

Sonny gave a smile. "Now, you know I could never do that. Why, this is my home, the same as it is yours. I wouldn't be happy anywhere else, and you know deep in your heart you wouldn't be happy anywhere else neither."

"Well, I know I wouldn't be happy down in the state penitentiary," Hank pointed out. "That's for damned sure."

Sonny shook his head. "You are truly a worrier, aren't you? You always have been. No one's going to the penitentiary. I can handle this lawyer."

"That may be, but this time you'll be handlin' him without me. I am changin' my location as fast as that nag of mine'll get

273

me somewheres else."

"I wish you wouldn't do that, Hank. As your friend, I'm telling you it's not a wise thing. It'll make us both look bad if you run."

"Then you best come along. That's all I can say." Hank tucked his extra pair of long johns into the bag, buckled everything up, and bent to pick up the bags on the floor. He looked the man who'd been his boyhood friend right in the eye. "I'm right about this, Sonny." He tapped himself on the chest. "This time, I am right. We're in for a fall if we hang around here." He threw both sets of bags over his shoulders. "The only thing for us to do is leave."

Sonny made no comment, so Hank turned for the door. As he started to leave the room, though, he did hear his friend say something, but Sonny was behind him now, and he said it so softly, Hank couldn't make out what it was.

CHAPTER THIRTY-ONE

Micah's stomach did a quick flop as he cut into his fried eggs. He was eating a late breakfast this morning. Last night's victory celebration at Chester's—the one Micah had been certain they would never enjoy—had continued until . . . well, Micah wasn't certain how late it lasted. All he knew for sure was it had gone on until the numerals on the grandfather's clock in Chester's parlor had begun to blur.

Today was to be the last day of the trial, but since the judge brought that to an abrupt end, Micah had the day free. He had taken advantage of that fact by sleeping a couple of hours later than usual and coming to Lottie's for breakfast. As he left, he tacked a note on his office door saying where he was in case a client should wander by. He doubted that would happen since clients had been pretty scarce, but he left the note anyway.

Having a big breakfast was unusual for Micah. He seldom ate breakfast. His regular morning fare consisted of no more than two or three pots of coffee, swilled nonstop in his office from first light till noon. This morning, though, despite a headache, Micah felt good, and he decided to begin this fine day with a healthy breakfast of fried eggs and a rasher of bacon.

"Sit down, Fay," he whispered when she brought his food. "Let's eat breakfast together just this once. Who cares what people think?" This was not the sort of thing Micah ever joked about. Neither he nor Fay thought of it as a joking matter. But he felt frisky today. He knew she'd never do it. He expected he'd faint dead-away if she did. It was clear the town knew he and the Charbunneaus were friends. After all, he had stayed at Lottie's home before and during the trial. But it was all right to be friends with the colored as long as it went no further than that.

Fay shot him one of her looks. "Don't start with me, Micah," she said under her breath. She did, though, give him a smile, and with a furtive move, she traced her index finger along his wrist as she set his plate on the table.

Micah's victory in court had made him the hot topic of Probity conversation. He knew he'd always been well liked in the community—or at least his father had—but since Judge Walker made his ruling, people had looked at Micah in a different way. Before it didn't matter that he was now an attorney, everyone still thought of him as the rowdy youth he once had been. But since yesterday he sensed they viewed him with a kind of respect. It was what he wanted, but now that he was getting it, it made him uneasy. What might they expect of him next?

Micah wasn't kidding himself. He knew his victory in the courtroom the day before was in large part due to luck—the luck of trying the case before a judge who was as sensitive to the rules of justice as he was to the rules of law. Micah had pointed that out to Thomas Blythe and Earl Anderson after the trial yesterday afternoon, but Blythe had only smiled without comment, and Anderson didn't smile at all.

Micah watched the yellow of the eggs ooze out across the white plate, shuddered, and gave the plate a shove. Perhaps his stomach wasn't ready for this after all. He picked up his coffee and sat back in the chair. As he did, he saw Emmett Pratt enter the café. Pratt spoke to all the patrons he knew, which was everyone, and made his way toward Micah's table.

"Mr. McConners," Pratt said, "I'm Emmett Pratt." Micah

stood and they shook hands. "Would you mind if I join you?"

"No, sir, not at all." They sat down, and Micah started to motion to Fay to bring Pratt some coffee, but she was already on her way with the pot and another cup. Pratt accepted the coffee and told her he would not be ordering breakfast.

"Congratulations on your victory, young man," he said. "I was pleased with your success. I hear you were brilliant."

"Brilliant?" said Micah, embarrassed. "I think that's overstating it. Dr. Hedstrom didn't deserve what he was facing. I think the judge agreed."

Pratt spooned sugar into his coffee. "Well," he said, "*I* sure agree."

There was an awkward silence. Finally, Micah asked, "Was there something I could do for you, Mr. Pratt?"

"No, son," the man said, "not really. I was hoping I could do something for you." He dropped the spoon to the tablecloth and a brown stain began to spread. "Word is you'll be making an investigation on my boy."

"Yes, Judge Walker asked me to look into the allegations Polly made in the courtroom yesterday, and some others too."

Pratt stared down at the spot growing on the tablecloth and said in a low voice, "I fear it's true what she and her mother are saying."

Micah sat up straighter. "Do you know something about it?" he asked.

Pratt shook his head. "No, not for sure. Fact is, I still can't believe it. I do know, though, it was Sonny who fired that shot into the house you were staying at a couple of nights ago."

"How do you know that?"

"I was in the barn when he and Hank Jones rode in that morning. I heard them talking and laughing about it. They didn't know I was there, and I didn't let 'em know. But I listened."

Micah sat back in his chair. This was interesting. It didn't rise to the level of being proof of Polly's rape or Lester's murder, but it was evidence of guilt. Why else would Sonny fire the shot into the house except to frighten the witness who was about to testify against him? Plus, as the judge had mentioned by firing into a house like that, Sonny Pratt could at least be charged with six counts of aggravated assault—a count for every person inside. And perhaps six counts of attempted murder.

"I came into town that morning. I planned on telling Blythe or even Anderson what Sonny had done, but I found out no one had been hurt, so I—" He stopped without finishing.

"Would you be willing to testify in front of a jury about this, Mr. Pratt?" Micah asked.

There was a pause. This one was long enough Micah was convinced the man wasn't going to answer the question at all. "Yes, sir," Pratt finally said, "I would." He looked across the table and found Micah's eyes. "I'll do better than that," he added. "There'll be trouble if you and the sheriff come out to our place to arrest him. I'll bring the boy in myself."

"Are you sure that's wise?" Pratt seemed to have recognized at least some of the truth about his son, but Micah wondered if the man understood how dangerous Sonny was.

"I reckon I've been ignoring my duty long enough. It's time I did something about it."

Micah thought for a moment. Having a father who was willing to testify to his son's committing a crime changed things. They had enough with that alone to make an arrest on the aggravated assault charges. "I worry about you doing that, Mr. Pratt. That's the sheriff's job."

"That sheriff's a sniveling coward, and you know it. I expect the fact he's left Sonny alone to do his bad deeds all this time *is* partly because he's my boy. The other part is because Brad Collins didn't have the guts to arrest him."

Micah couldn't disagree. "Do you think you can do this, Mr. Pratt?" he asked.

A dampness brimmed the older man's eyes. "I believe there's a redeemable spot left somewhere in the boy. I'll persuade him to come in."

Micah was reluctant but said, "All right. You go on out to your place. The sheriff and I will go out to get Hank. You bring Sonny over to the Jones place. We'll meet you there at—" He checked his watch. "— noon. Then the three of us'll bring them both back to town."

Pratt nodded.

"Are you sure you're all right with this?" Micah asked. Emmett Pratt might believe there was still something redeemable in Sonny, but Micah wasn't convinced.

"Don't worry, son," he said, "I'll bring my boy to you. Everything's going to be fine. You'll see." The man forced a smile, but Micah could see a sadness chiseled into the lines of Emmett Pratt's face. It was a sadness cut deep enough that Micah expected it would never disappear.

"You want what?" Chester asked.

"To borrow a gun."

"Good, Christ, Micah, I can't imagine anything scarier than you with a loaded gun."

"I also need to borrow a horse."

"All right, so there *is* something scarier: you with a loaded gun sitting astride a horse."

"I'm serious, Chester."

They were standing in Chester's parlor. The place was still a mess from the party the night before, and snoring came from beneath a quilt spread across the sofa. Micah lifted the quilt's corner and saw Jackson Clark sound asleep.

"Jackson decided to stay for one more after you left," Chester said.

It was obvious Micah's pounding on the front door had awakened Chester, if not Jackson. Chester wore a dressing gown, and his hair spiked in a dozen different directions.

"I need to borrow a pistol and a horse," Micah repeated.

Chester rubbed his eyes with the heels of his hands, yawned, and asked, "Why?"

Micah hadn't spoken much about Judge Walker's naming him to oversee the investigation. He hadn't wanted his friends to worry. Now he was to meet Brad Collins in less than half an hour for the ride out to the Jones place. He knew he needed a horse, and he was afraid he might—God forbid—need a gun. He had no choice but to tell Chester everything that was happening.

"You're out of your mind," Chester said once Micah explained the assignment the judge had given him. "You're no policeman."

"All I'm doing, Chester, is riding along with Collins to ensure he does a thorough investigation. Walker doesn't want to allow too much independence on the part of local law enforcement in this matter."

"Well, that makes sense. What doesn't make sense is dumping it on you. Really, Micah, you have nothing to gain by getting mixed up in this thing. Hell, you could even get yourself killed. Sonny Pratt and Hank Jones are no one to fool with."

"It's too late for that. I'm already in it. Besides, I do have something to gain. I want to see Sonny and Hank brought to justice. I'd like nothing better."

Chester lifted a half-smoked cigar from an ashtray that brimmed with cigarette butts and even smaller cigar stubs than the one he'd plucked from the mess. "Well, all right, but it's crazy," he said, striking a match and holding it to the end of the cigar. "Wait here. I'll be back in a few minutes." Chester blew a stream of foul-smelling smoke into the air and started for the stairway. He stopped halfway there and turned to Micah. "And for God's sake, Micah," he said, "be quiet. I don't want Jackson to wake up. He'd probably insist we have another round of drinks."

Chester climbed the steps and disappeared into his upstairs bedroom.

While he waited, Micah wandered from the parlor into the library. Electric lamps were positioned around the room, but the generator wasn't running so there was no electricity. Micah opened the bank of draperies at the front of the room. The morning light streamed in low, stretching shadows across the flowered carpeting.

The library was its usual chaos. Micah walked to the large table that held Chester's various projects and was as amazed as always. "Projects" was the word Chester used. "Dismantlings" was what Micah called it. Or disasters. Chester spent a huge amount of money buying all the latest gadgets, but he seldom used them for their intended purpose. Instead, he'd take them apart to see how they worked.

Since his conversation with Lottie a couple of nights before, Micah had spent a lot of time thinking about the nature of the passionate life and the practical life. It was true he was sometimes an impetuous person who reacted before thinking a thing through. And it was also true that Fay was the practical one. But, he allowed, there was also a vein of the practical in him as well, and about certain things Fay could be as passionate as anyone.

Passionate or practical, no one was altogether one way or the other, but, Micah guessed, everyone was *primarily* one way or the other. That was as much a part of people as the color of their eyes.

His gaze moved about the room. What, he wondered, was Chester? Was Chester primarily passionate or primarily practical? Judging by the technology that fired his interest, he might be practical. Micah lifted the largest piece of a new Kodak "Snapshot" camera. There were a half-dozen smaller pieces scattered about the table. He smiled. Chester—an engineer, a physician, a man of science—was certainly practical, but he was a man passionate about his practicality.

"Careful, now, don't you be disturbing my projects." Chester said this as he sauntered into the library. His spirits seemed high right now. It was clear he'd expected to spend the next fourteen years of his life smashing rocks with a sledgehammer. Since that fear was now gone, he had been doing a great deal of sauntering.

Micah replaced the camera piece among the rest of the debris and turned toward his friend. "What are you dressed up for?" he asked.

Chester was shaved and his hair slicked down. He wore denims and a heavy wool shirt. The cigar, a bit smaller now, was still clenched between his teeth. Around his hip was strapped a six-gun. "I'm not going to let you go out there alone." He tossed another holster and revolver to Micah. "Here," he said, "try not to shoot yourself—or even worse, me."

Micah caught the gunbelt and buckled it on. Two pieces of rawhide hung from the bottom of the holster, but Micah didn't bother to tie them around his thigh. "Collins is coming with me," he said. "I'm not going out there alone."

Chester laughed and turned to leave the library. "Micah," he said over his shoulder as he headed toward the kitchen and the door at the rear of the house, "going with Brad Collins is the same as going alone."

★　★　★　★　★

The late-morning sky was the color of lead, and a steady northwest wind took the feel of the fifty-degree temperature down a notch or two. Micah turned up the collar of his jacket and was glad he'd worn gloves.

Collins hadn't said much on the ride out from town. When Micah arrived at the sheriff's office with Chester, Collins gave a grunt of displeasure and said, "I'll swear you in as a deputy, McConners, because Earl Anderson tells me that's what Judge Walker wants, but I ain't swearing in this doctor." Chester assured him he didn't wish to be deputized under any circumstances, and he promised to stay out of the way at all times. Collins gave another grunt and didn't look happy.

After he administered the oath to Micah, the three of them went outside and Collins looked even unhappier when he realized Chester intended on riding his moto-cycle. "You're not planning to ride that damned thing, are you?" he asked.

"Sure am," said Chester with a broad smile.

Collins shook his head. "Well, when it breaks down, you ain't riding double with me."

It had been more than ten years since Micah had been to this part of the county. When he was a kid, he and his father would often spend summer afternoons searching the ancient, dried-up watering holes in the area for arrowheads. They always made it a point to avoid the Jones place, though. Delbert Jones, Lester and Hank's father, had not been an affable sort, and if anyone rode up unannounced, old Del was as likely to shoot him out of his saddle as offer him shade and a cup of water.

Micah's memory of his father's caution regarding the Joneses was not lost on him now. He was glad to be wearing the Colt Chester had provided. There was a time in his late teens when Micah was pretty fair with a handgun—at least when it came to putting holes in tin cans. It had been a while since he'd used a gun, but he expected if it came right down to it, he could still handle one well enough if he had to.

At least well enough to avoid shooting himself in the foot. He hoped so, anyway.

They came over a rise, and below was the Joneses' ranch house. Things seemed quiet enough, but they waited and watched a bit before Micah said to Chester, "Collins and I will ride on down. I don't want that loud machine of yours to let him know we're coming any sooner than we have to."

Micah and Collins rode toward the house at a trot, but Micah was prepared to turn away and gig his horse into a gallop at the first sign of anything strange. There was nothing, though. They rode into the yard, right up to the front porch, without seeing a soul or hearing a sound from either the house or any of the outbuildings.

Collins looked to Micah, and Micah gave him a nod.

"Hank Jones," Collins called out, "are you in your house?"

There was no response.

Micah looked back toward the hill and waved Chester in.

"Hank, this is Sheriff Collins. If you're in there, come on out. We want to ask you some questions."

When there was still no response, Micah swung his right leg over the horse's rump and allowed his left foot to slip from the stirrup. He flipped his reins over the rail and stepped onto the porch. He knocked twice on the door. "Is anyone home?" he shouted.

Nothing.

Chester had pulled up in the yard as Micah called out. "Do you suppose he heard we were coming," Chester asked, "and ran off?"

"Anything's possible," said Micah. "I expect he knew someone'd be coming sooner or later. It's no secret what Polly had to say on the witness stand yesterday."

Micah tried the door and it was unlocked, but he didn't want to barge in before he had a better idea what he was barging into. He walked to a window and peered inside. It took a moment for his eyes to adjust to the dark of the room, but when they did, he felt them widen. He then heard someone shout, "Jesus Christ!" It was a second or two before he realized he was the one who'd done the shouting. He lurched back from the window.

"What is it, Micah?" Chester asked. "What did you see?"

Micah faced them, swallowed hard, but didn't say a word. He then spun back toward the door and ran as fast as he could into the house. He heard Collins and Chester run in behind him.

Hank lay on his belly in the doorway between the main room of the house and a small bedroom. Micah had run in at full tilt but skidded to a stop eight or ten feet short of the body. The others came up beside him.

A huge pool of dark, viscous blood covered the floor almost up to where the three men stood. Two sets of saddlebags lay beside Hank. One had popped open, and canned goods had come out and rolled about the floor, leaving aimless, swirling tracks in the gore.

There was a small hole in the back of Hank's head, but in front his face was almost gone. Teeth, bone fragments, and pieces of flesh were scattered around the floor like some grisly archipelago in a murky sea of blood.

Micah lifted his hand to his stomach and felt the tide of coffee he'd drunk earlier that morning rise. He stepped back to the open front door and inhaled a couple of chilly late-December breaths. After a bit he turned back to the other two who still stared down at Hank. "We don't have time to tend to the body right now," he said. "We'll have to come back for it later."

"Why's that?" asked Chester.

"Because," Micah said, "we have to get over to the Pratt place as fast as we can. Emmett Pratt planned on confronting

Sonny and bringing him over here to meet us so we could take Sonny and Hank back to town. Emmett thought he could bring Sonny in peacefully." He glanced at Hank's body. "But it doesn't look like Sonny plans on doing any of it peacefully."

All the color leached from Collins's gaunt face, and he backed away from the body. "I'm finished with this business," he said as he pushed his way past Micah and out onto the porch. "This whole damn thing has gotten way out of hand." He climbed on his horse. "I'm done."

"You're what?" Micah asked.

"I don't plan on getting killed by some crazy kid, not for a measly hundred and twenty-five dollars a month, I don't." He reached inside his jacket, unpinned his star, and tossed it onto the porch. It bounced across the planking and landed at Micah's feet. "Here," he said, "you can give this to the county commissioners for me." With that, he wheeled his horse and loped away.

"Christ," Micah mumbled under his breath as he picked up the badge. He shoved it into his pocket.

"Well," said Chester, leaning against the doorsill, his arms folded across his chest, "I told you if you'd gone out here only with Collins, it would have been a lot like going alone."

CHAPTER THIRTY-TWO

Sonny Pratt was not a man given to analyzing his motives, but he felt so good on the ride home after killing Hank Jones, he had to wonder why. Although he hadn't noticed it at the time, he remembered feeling the same way a few months earlier after cutting Lester's throat.

It has been a harsh winter for the Jones boys.

That thought made Sonny smile. Not counting the Mexican Sonny ran into last year outside of Casper, Lester had been the first man Sonny had ever killed. He supposed it wasn't the thing a fella should be doing, killing white folks. But, damn, he could not abide disloyalty. Sonny had been having to deal with disloyalty his entire life, and now that he was a full-grown man, he did not intend to take it anymore.

Looking back on it, it was clear that he should have killed Polly at the river last spring the way his good sense told him to. If he had, everything would've been all right. Hank and Lester would still be alive, and that God-damned trial would have never happened.

That thought dulled Sonny's good feelings some. It was a terrible mistake not killing Polly. She turned out to be the most disloyal of the bunch. But he shouldn't be too hard on himself. How could he have known she'd tell her mother and the doctor and that lawyer and in the end the whole God-damned town? Who would have expected it? After all, he did do his best to put a scare in the girl. Sonny had figured at the time what with the scare and the fact that she was family—not blood, of course, but family all the same—that Polly would keep their little adventure down by the river to herself.

He'd sure been wrong about that one.

Now, he guessed it was too late to kill her. Hell, she'd already done her damage. Now it came down to his word against hers. And if she turned up dead, he'd be the first one they'd suspect. He'd gotten away with killing Lester. With killing Hank, folks might be a little suspicious, but there was no way they could put him in the Jones house this morning. Polly, though, was a different story. If she turned up dead after her testimony yesterday, things could get pretty warm. Nope, he'd missed his chance with Polly. Next time he would not allow himself to be so damned careless.

Live and learn.

Sonny always enjoyed the ride home from the Jones place. It was a rough trail that went up over the breaks, but at one spot where the cliffs were the steepest, it looked out past La Prele Creek all the way to the North Platte and the rolling prairie beyond.

There was very little snow right now, except on the north side of some of the larger boulders where the sun never hit. It was a beautiful view, and Sonny stopped for a moment to appreciate it. It had been cold off and on so far this winter, but right now Sonny guessed it was upward of fifty degrees. The view here was nice, but he thought it was prettier when it was all covered in snow.

Sonny liked the winter. Most folks only bitched about the winter, but not Sonny. He looked up at the white disk of sun that shone through the gray clouds. This time of day in any other season, his old man would be giving him hell about calving or branding or harvesting or rounding up or . . . Christ, the list went on and on. But the winter was different. The winter slowed things down. Sonny liked that. Sonny liked things slow.

He nudged his right spur into his horse's flank and started off again.

The world was starting to move way too fast for Sonny's tastes. He'd been down in Cheyenne a few months back and there were telephones all over the place. Messenger boys were pretty much driven out of business. The talk was there would be phone lines strung up all over Probity here in the next few years.

He read somewhere that back East there were gas lines everywhere, and now everyone was talking about electricity.

Sonny didn't like it. He figured he'd been born about thirty years too late. He would have liked to have lived in the earlier times, the frontier days the old-timers talked about. Back then a fella could ride his horse in a straight line in any direction and never see a fence. Those were freer times without all the towns and people and rules. Rules and laws. Lawyers and lawmen. Judges and juries.

Sonny turned his head downwind, cleared his throat, and spit. The wind caught the spittle, lifted it, and carried it twenty feet before in finally came down in the rough arms of a dry piece of sage brush. Sonny expected the day would come when a man couldn't even spit when he wanted. There would always be someone around like that McConners fella telling a man whether he could or he couldn't.

McConners. Now that's the one who could use some killing. Smart, know-it-all son of a bitch. Holed up for three weeks before the trial in a nigger's house. What kind of a man would do that? Sonny figured McConners was screwing that nigger filly too. But he guessed he couldn't blame him. Fay Charbunneau was a fine one. He wouldn't mind having some of that himself.

When Sonny rode into the yard, he saw his father's gelding

tied at the front porch. That was strange. The old man had gone into town early that morning, and Sonny expected he'd stay there all day.

Sonny tied his sorrel next to the gelding, climbed the porch and went in the house.

"Where you been, Sonny?" Emmett asked before Sonny could even take off his hat.

"I took me a ride on this fine December morning," Sonny said. He hung his hat and coat on the hall tree, crossed the room, and sat in one of the easy chairs in front of the fire. He stretched his long legs out and felt the heat soak through the thin soles of his boots. These old things have about had it, he told himself, looking down at his beat-to-hell footwear. He'd get a new pair the next time he was in town. Right now, though, the heat soaking through felt pretty good. He liked the winter, but he hated when his toes got cold.

Sonny looked toward his father and said, "I figured you went into town."

"I did," said Emmett. "I had myself a conversation with Thomas Blythe."

Returning his gaze to the fireplace, Sonny watched as flames curled off a two-foot-long cottonwood log. "Why'd you want to waste your time talking to that fool? He couldn't get a man convicted who admitted to committing a crime. It's the damnedest thing I ever heard."

"I also had a visit with Micah McConners."

When Emmett said that, Sonny didn't turn his head away from the fire, but he did take his father in as much as possible out of the corner of his eye.

His father had been talking to McConners. That was interesting. Sonny had been wrong earlier. Polly wasn't the most disloyal of the bunch. This old bastard was. First he lets Sonny's mother die, then he marries that school teacher and brings her and her brat kid into their house. And now this. What was next?

"McConners, eh?" Sonny said. "Now there's another waste of time. What business could you have with that man?"

Emmett sat in the chair across from Sonny and leaned forward, resting his forearms on his knees. "McConners wants to visit with you and Hank about what Polly said in the courtroom. He wants to ask you boys a few questions."

"Ask a few questions, hell. He wants to see me in prison. That's what he wants."

The old man sat back in the chair and nodded. "Well, I expect he believes what Polly says, all right, but he strikes me as a fair man. If you tell him your side, he'll give it consideration. You've got to talk to him, boy. He's running the show on this, no one else. As far as this thing's concerned, McConners is the law."

"That's right," Sonny said. "McConners is the law. What have you been telling him, you old fool?"

Emmett looked away, ran a hand over his balding head, and said, "I haven't told him anything. I want you to talk with him. That's all."

His father was a fine rancher and businessman, but he was not accomplished at deception. Sonny knew he was lying as soon as the words toppled from the old bastard's mouth, but he kept his face impassive and allowed Emmett to talk.

"It may be hard, but you got to face this thing, Sonny. Whatever it is, I want you to know I'll stand beside you. Maybe I haven't always been there in the past, but I'm here now. McConners isn't the sort to let it go. He'll get to the bottom of it before he quits, so we have to deal with this thing. We have to go to him and talk it out."

"Go to him?"

Emmett nodded. "I told him I'd bring you in. I was afraid if he and the sheriff came after you, there'd be trouble."

The old man stood and started to pace. He was a great one

for pacing. "You've gone a little wild in the last couple of years, Sonny. I got to admit that. I expect you've done some bad things, but I still believe you're a good boy. I don't know if you did what Cedra and Polly say you did. The fact is no one knows except you, Polly, and I reckon Hank Jones. I do know what they accuse you of would be a hard thing for even a man as clever as Micah McConners to prove, especially at this late date."

Sonny held back his smile.

"It's a tough thing to know what to do," Emmett said. "I don't know for sure what's right. I guess I've spent my whole life sorta making things up as I went along."

With that one, Sonny had to clamp his jaw down and purse his lips to keep the smile off his face. "Me too, Pa," he said. "Me too."

"But I worry about you, son. I worry if something's not done to stop the direction you're headed, you'll be lost forever."

He and his pa had never had such a touching conversation.

The old man still paced as he spoke. He walked from one end of the large room to the other and back again. All the while he kept his hands in his pockets and his head down, staring at the floor.

"I lied to you a while ago, Sonny."

"No, Pa, you lie? That can't be."

"I know you're the one who fired the shot into the Charbunneau house the other night, and I told McConners about it."

Sonny felt his jaw clench again, only this time it was not to hide a smile.

"He's going to get you on some kind of charge, Sonny, before he's done. That's the kind of man he is. If you go in and admit to firing that shot, it may be that's as far as it'd go. Like I say, it'll be hard if not impossible for him to prove anything more than that."

Sonny stood and faced his father. "Let me get this straight," he said. "You told that lawyer that I'm the one who fired that shot at the window, and now you want to take me into town so he can lock me up?"

Emmett turned to his son as he spoke, but he continued to pace. "Sonny, firing into that house was a bad thing. It's pure luck no one was hurt." He looked back to the floor. "But no one *was* hurt. So if you go to prison, it wouldn't be for long, and I'd bet we could work it out for you to serve your time right here in the county jail."

"Golly, Pa, do you think so?"

"I know you're upset with what I've done, boy, but in the long run it's for the best. Besides, I don't know that he'd lock you up right away. He only wants to talk to you now. That's all. He wants to ask you a few questions. And we don't even have to go all the way into town."

"What do you mean we don't have to go into town?" Sonny asked.

"I agreed that you and me'd meet McConners at the Jones place."

"You what?"

"He and the sheriff were going there to talk to Hank. I told him I would bring you over and he could talk to you at the same time."

The situation was getting worse fast. Sonny wasn't sure what he should do now. McConners would find Hank's body, and he'd assume it was Sonny who killed him. Still, though, he couldn't prove anything. There was no way he could show Sonny had been at the Jones place that morning. On the other hand, Sonny had no alibi. If McConners even discovered Sonny had been away from home that morning, it would mean trouble.

But there was no way McConners could find that out—no way in the world.

Except . . .

As Emmett paced back toward Sonny, he spoke in a tone that suggested he was thinking out loud, going over it in his mind, making it all up as he went along. "We'll meet McConners at Hank's. You explain to him how it was you who fired the shot into that house." Emmett turned, started back the other way. He stared at the floor as he ran through what they would do. "You'll explain it to McConners. You'll have to take whatever's coming to you. That's all you can do. But once you've done that, Sonny, it'll all be over. Everything'll be fine."

Maybe if Sonny had made it back home this morning before Emmett had, there'd be another choice, but he hadn't. The old fool came back earlier than expected.

Well, Sonny resolved, that was his bad luck.

Sonny lifted his revolver from its holster, took two quick steps toward his father, and brought the barrel down hard on the base of Emmett's skull.

Like his pa, Sonny had to make things up as he went along.

Emmett hit the floor face down. Sonny nudged him a couple of times with his toe. Emmett was still breathing but out cold. There was a gash in the back of his head and a nasty-looking red spot above his eyebrow from where he hit the floor. The gash was bleeding some, but not a lot. Sonny was glad for that. Unlike at Hank's, whatever mess got made here, Sonny would have to clean it up.

The place was covered in blood at Hank's that morning. Hank's whole damn face came off. There was blood everywhere, and the son of a bitch fell in such a way he was blocking the door leading out of the bedroom. Sonny had to step over him to get out, and there was no way to do it without stepping in the mess. It was disgusting.

Here, though, things were pretty clean. Sonny hefted Emmett up onto his shoulder before the old man could bleed on the floor any more than he already had. The old man was lighter and bonier than Sonny thought. He even felt frail. The coot was probably going to die of some nasty-damn disease pretty soon anyway. Sonny expected he was doing Emmett a favor—saving him a lot of pain and strife. With a smile, he allowed as how Emmett might not see it that way, but what the hell.

He took Emmett outside and tied him across the saddle of the gelding, climbed aboard his own horse and, holding the gelding's reins, he headed toward the gate.

Sonny guessed he didn't have much time. Once McConners realized Sonny and Emmett weren't going to show at Hank's, he'd head to the Pratt place. If McConners was as shrewd as everyone said, he might even start out the minute he found Hank's body. Either way, Sonny had to move fast.

He held his horse to a lope. He had loosely tied Emmett to the saddle, and he doubted if he rode any faster the knots would hold. But it was less than a mile to the breaks, and Sonny figured with any luck there would be time.

When he got to the top, he reined in. The trail curved sharply here, and the ground was loose and treacherous. He climbed off his sorrel, went to the gelding, and pulled Emmett down. He carried his father to the edge of the cliff and laid him in the dirt. As he did, Emmett's eyes fluttered open, and he looked up at his son.

"So, you woke up, did you? That's more bad luck for you, I reckon."

"Sonny," Emmett whispered, "I'm cold." The old man was shivering, and he didn't look too good.

Sonny smiled. "You're about to get a lot colder, old man."

Emmett's gaze moved about as he realized where he was.

Sonny looked out at the view. "Pa," he said, "you're like me, aren't you? You've always liked this place. There's the creek running down yonder, and the river beyond. Hell, the way I figure, it's about the best place around to die."

Emmett winced as he touched his fingers to the back of his head. "You hit me, Sonny."

"By golly, old-timer, you are the smart one. There's no putting anything over on you."

"Why are you doing this, son?"

"Because you talk too damned much, old man. You should never have gone to McConners."

"It's true what they say about you, isn't it, boy? You did rape Polly. You killed Lester Jones." When Sonny only stared at him without answering, Emmett said, "I was wrong. There's not any good left in you. Somewhere along the line you went rotten, and the rot went all the way through." He said this without surprise, or anger, or recrimination.

Sonny felt himself quiver inside. There was a time when he'd thought this man lying in front of him was the greatest man who ever lived. There was a time when Sonny would have done anything the man said. But when his mother died, everything changed. Emmett had killed her. Sonny knew that. His mother had never been the kind of woman cut out for life on a ranch in Wyoming. She was from St. Louis—born and raised in city life. She knew about things no one else knew. She loved plays and music. She had taken Sonny to the opera once down in Denver, and although he had hated the thing himself, he'd loved how much his mother had enjoyed it—how taken she'd been with the clothes, and the carriages, and the people. She was like a girl, young and beautiful in her own green velvet dress. Alice Pratt had been a lady, and the life this selfish bastard had forced her into had killed her.

Sonny locked his eyes to Emmett's. He wanted to see inside the man at the moment Emmett realized what was going to happen. Sonny wanted to see the man's fear. Sonny wanted to watch as his father cowered at death.

Sonny bent low and put his mouth close to Emmett's ear. "You're going over, old man." He pointed past the edge of the cliff. "Them rocks down there, that's where you're going to die." Sonny looked deep into the old man's watery eyes, and search as he might—as much as he wanted it to be there—he could not find the fear he was after.

He could see something, though. Sonny saw something deep inside the blue of his father's eyes. He could not identify it, but it was there, and whatever it was, Sonny knew it wasn't fear.

Emmett lifted his hand to his son's face and ran his finger along Sonny's cheek. "I ache for what has happened to you, boy. I ache for whatever it is I've done, or whatever it is I've neglected to do."

With that, Emmett lifted his hands, placed them on the back of Sonny's neck, and pulled Sonny's face down toward his own. Sonny tried to resist, but Emmett was unbelievably strong. Sonny pushed against Emmett's chest as hard as he could, but still the old man drew Sonny's face closer and closer.

Through clenched teeth Sonny grimaced, "What the hell are you doing, you old fool. Let me go."

For a moment Sonny thought the son of a bitch was going to toss him over the cliff, and Sonny knew there was not a thing he could do to stop him. The old man's hands were like two vises. Sonny wriggled like a fish, but he could not break free.

Sonny was convinced he was a dead man. That he was going to be the one to die at the base of the cliff rather than his father. The hands grew tighter against the back of his neck and Sonny whimpered, "No, Pa, don't."

But Emmett didn't throw him over. Instead, he slowly brought Sonny's head down until their faces were two inches apart, and he reached up and kissed Sonny full on the mouth. Sonny struggled, but Emmett held him fast.

When Emmett let him go, Sonny scuttled back away from his

father, wiping his mouth with the back of his hand. "You crazy son of a bitch!" Sonny screamed. "I'll kill you, you bastard! I will kill you!" But rather than move toward his father, he crawled farther back until he was against the rocks on the far side of the trail.

Emmett stared at his son for a long moment. His gaze pinned Sonny to the dirt where the boy sat. "No, son," he said in a hollow voice, "You won't kill me. I'll not let you do that." Then without taking his eyes from his son, Emmett rolled himself over the cliff and in silence fell to the rocks below.

Sonny stared in disbelief at the spot where his father had been. He could still feel the strength of Emmett's hands on his neck and the pressure of Emmett's lips against his own.

His heart hammered into the walls of his chest. His knees were oozy and soft. He wondered if they would hold him as he struggled to his feet. When he was sure of his footing, he walked to the edge of the cliff and peered over. Emmett lay crumpled fifty feet below, not moving, and obviously dead.

Sonny was trying to sort out what had happened when he heard the buzzing of a fly. At least that was what his cloudy mind first told him it was: a huge, angry fly. But that didn't make sense, did it? He forced himself to listen with a more rational ear, and he realized it was not an insect at all. He had no idea what it was, but whatever it was, it was no fly.

He mounted his sorrel, rode the hundred feet to where the trail curved around, and he saw. A half-mile down and headed his way was Micah McConners. Next to him on his noisy two-wheeled machine was Dr. Hedstrom. There was no sign of the sheriff, but that didn't surprise Sonny. Brad Collins was a coward, and Sonny figured the sight of Hank's face in little chunks all over the floor was more than enough to send the sheriff packing.

Sonny had hoped for more time, but a man had to take things

as they came. He wheeled his horse, gave him his heel, and took off for home at a gallop.

Chapter Thirty-Three

Although he'd thought it was a dim-witted idea, Micah had not tried to talk Chester out of riding his moto-cycle. If there was less than a foot of snow on the ground and the temperature was in double digits, Chester was on his contraption. Nothing Micah could say would change that, so he didn't bother to try.

Micah watched as the machine climbed the steep and rocky terrain. It was impressive. He never expected the thing could make it, but it had no trouble at all. Micah was about to mention that to Chester, but he stopped when he saw the horse.

It was a handsome gelding, with four stockings and an expensive custom saddle. Micah had seen it earlier that morning through the window at Lottie's. It had been tied to the rail out front, and it belonged to Emmett Pratt.

The horse stood with its reins hanging from the bit. With indifference, it turned its head toward Micah and Chester as they rode up.

"This horse belongs to Emmett," Micah said as he dismounted.

Chester stopped the moto-cycle, but being unable to get the small stand to hold on the oddly canted ground, he leaned it against a boulder. "I wonder what he's doing out here," he said.

Micah checked the horse for injuries. The trail here was bad as it came around the curve, and it might be possible to take a fall on the loose ground if a rider wasn't careful. Micah could find nothing wrong with the gelding, but there was no sign of Emmett.

Reaching for the reins, Micah stroked the horse's neck and asked, "So, fella, what brings you out in these lonesome parts all by yourself?"

The gelding snorted a response and shook his mane.

"Micah," Chester said, "come over here." His voice was raspy and distant.

"What is it? What's wrong?"

Chester stood at the edge of the cliff. His face had gone chalk-white.

Micah went over and followed Chester's gaze down below. "God," he whispered but didn't say more.

For a moment they both stared at the body in silence. It was Chester who spoke first. "This is Sonny's doing," he said. He turned to look at the loose soil where the trail curved. "I suppose it could be an accident, but I don't believe for a second that's what it was. Sonny Pratt had a hand in this."

Micah knew Chester was right. There were things about it all that didn't add up. It was cold out here—maybe not so cold for late December, but chilly—yet Emmett wore no jacket or hat. Also, this was a route Emmett had traveled a thousand times. He knew it well. There was no way he would lose control of his mount and tumble over this cliff, particularly not in broad daylight.

No, this was no accident, but Micah knew it was another situation where it would be impossible to prove otherwise. It seemed Sonny Pratt had a knack for doing his deeds in a way that the law couldn't touch him.

"He has to be stopped," Micah said. He lifted his eyes from Emmett's broken body and looked up at his friend. "And it's left to us to do it," he said. "You and me."

Chester nodded. "I guess you're right, but I'm damned if I

can think of two more poorly equipped fellas for the job. A doctor and a lawyer going after a killer is not my idea of intelligent law enforcement."

"There is no law enforcement around here, Chester." Micah climbed on his horse and reached down for the gelding's reins. "Mount that contraption of yours," he said, "and let's tell young Mr. Pratt what we've found at the base of the cliff."

As they started off toward the Pratt place, Micah told Chester they would pick up Emmett's body on the way back. "Now," he said, "we'll be toting two dead ones into Probity. Emmett and Hank."

He hoped there would be no more.

There was no better-tended place in the county than Pratt Land and Livestock. Micah knew that during the spring, summer, and fall, the operation would be at a bustle, with dozens of farm hands and cowboys scrambling around. Now, though, in the dead of winter, things were quiet.

The house itself was a frame Victorian, similar in design to Chester's, although maybe half-again bigger. There was a large barn and five or six other outbuildings, all of which were in excellent repair and sported a coat of bright red paint that could not have been applied more than six months before.

Micah tried to devise some sort of plan as to what to do, but he came up with nothing. There was no proof that Sonny had done anything—none that would hold up in court, anyway. With the testimony of Emmett, Micah might have been able to make the charges stick with regard to firing the shot into Lottie's house. Now even that was gone.

But Micah meant what he'd said to Chester back at the breaks. Sonny Pratt had to be stopped. Micah feared Sonny now was killing as much for pleasure as he was for what he thought was a necessity.

"Do we just ride in?" Chester asked as they came toward the gate leading into the Pratt place. "We could leave the horses and cycle down in that cottonwood thicket, then sneak up on him from the south side of the house."

Micah had pondered the question of how to handle this situation himself. Although he was convinced Sonny was taking pleasure from the killing he was doing, there was still a certain sick logic in the murders. It was clear from the saddlebags Hank Jones carried when he was shot that it was Hank's plan to run. Sonny would have wanted to stop him from doing that because of the guilty light it would cast on them both. And Emmett had probably confronted Sonny about coming in to talk to Micah, and it was likely Emmett had admitted what he'd overheard between Sonny and Hank regarding the shot into the Charbunneau house. Sonny had killed his father to keep him quiet.

This all went to show that Sonny was desperate, but it also showed he was still making the effort to cover his tracks. It was likely he wouldn't do anything rash until he felt an immediate threat. Micah doubted Sonny would shoot them down as they rode in. He would at least try to talk his way out of his problems before he sought to fight his way out.

"We'll ride in," Micah said. "I don't think he'll start anything right away. Besides, if he does try something, I don't want my transportation out of his rifle sights to be all the way down by the creek in a thicket of cottonwoods, do you?"

Chester nodded his agreement. "That's for sure," he said.

"Sonny's expecting us, anyway." A wisp of smoke curled its way from the chimney at the main house. "My guess is he's sitting with his feet propped by a cozy fire waiting for us to wander into the yard."

"You think we should confront him with our suspicions right off?" Chester asked. Chester was a forward sort of man prone to getting to the point. He was a fine doctor, but Micah imagined he would have made a damn poor lawyer.

"No need for confrontation, if it can be avoided. We'll tell him we were riding out for a chat, and that's when we found his father."

"I'd wager us finding his father won't come as much of a surprise to the bastard. One thing puzzles me about all this," Chester said after a bit.

"What's that?"

"Why you got mixed up in it. Yes, yes, I know what the judge said, still this sort of quixotic thing I could picture you doing five or six years ago. You were pretty fiery back in those days. But it's clear since studying the law and getting older, you've been trying your best—until now, anyway—to put your youthful fervor behind you."

"What I've tried to put behind me is my old stupid behavior. Unlike some folks."

"What's that supposed to mean?"

"To me, your willingness to go to prison for no good reason was the stupidest thing I've ever seen."

"Maybe so," Chester allowed. "I often show symptoms of stupidity. But I like to think I choose my causes with at least some logic. A couple of tenderfoots riding in to arrest a killer doesn't seem too logical. It even seems stupid." He smiled and added, "But it does have a fiery kind of fervor."

They rode through the main gate of the Pratt ranch. "Do you have a point to all of this, doctor?"

"My point is that this adventure reminds me of the old, wild-eyed, crazy Micah."

"Who's to say I'm not doing the same as you, picking my cause?"

"You may be. Although I'd bet it's more than that."

"Why would you say that?"

"Because you hate Sonny Pratt."

"Hate? That's putting a little more of an edge on it than it needs, I'd say. I want to see the law deal with him. That's all."

"You said yourself there's no proof, so how's the law going to deal with him?"

"What the hell are you getting at?"

"I think you'd like to kill the bastard."

Micah was silent.

"You're a city boy," said Chester. "You haven't touched a handgun in years, but you've taken on the duties of a deputy sheriff, and you're going after some cold-blooded killer. Like the Micah of old, you're putting logic aside and running on pure fervor. I only hope when the time comes you know when you should pull the trigger. And equally important, I hope you know when not to."

"So you think I *want* to kill Sonny Pratt? That's why I'm mixed up in all this?"

Chester shrugged.

"Well, you're wrong. I don't want to kill Sonny."

There was half a minute of silence before Chester said, "I expect that's a decision you're going to have to make. But, hell, Micah. What do I know? I'm just making conversation. Besides, it doesn't matter what I think."

Micah doubted Chester ever felt that it didn't matter what he thought, but Micah played along. "No," he said, "it doesn't matter what you think. And do you know what I think? I think you think too damned much. You always have. What I'm doing out here has nothing to do with anything except it's a chore that's got to get done. That's all."

"A chore that's got to be done," Chester repeated. "That sounds like a pretty practical attitude to me, Mr. McConners."

"Thank you," Micah said.

"But, my goodness," Chester added with a smile, "you sure do say it with passion."

"I know you can make that machine go faster. How 'bout doing it?"

"Why, sure," said Chester. The cycle let out a deafening roar, and in an instant Chester was fifty yards ahead.

Sonny Pratt could not have helped but hear them coming. He was standing on the porch as Micah and Chester rode into the yard.

"Well, well," he said with a broad smile, "isn't this a nice surprise. Two of the county's most upright citizens coming all the way out here for a visit." Micah searched for the sarcasm in the boy's comment. He knew it was there, but he couldn't find it.

It had been some time since Micah had seen Sonny. He remembered him from when Sonny used to come into the store. He had always been a lean, wiry kid. Now he was tall, his shoulders wide. He wore his gun low on the right, not like a cowboy. On the left side of the gun belt was a sheath holding a large ivory-handled knife.

"Say," Sonny said, jerking his chin in Micah's direction, "that looks like Pa's horse you got there. What're you doing with him?" Sonny's tone was without deceit. It was innocent and sincere. It was the voice of a caring son.

"We found him up on the trail by the breaks," Chester said. "Emmett's down at the bottom of the cliff. I'm sorry to tell you this, but he's dead."

Sonny jerked his head toward Chester. "Pa's dead?" He inflected a flawless note of disbelief. "Dead?" He said again. "Are you sure?"

"We didn't go down and check," said Micah, "but we didn't have to. He's dead. There's no doubt about it."

Sonny slumped to the porch step in a heap and shoved the fingers of both hands into his hair. He sat like that, staring at the dirt. After exactly the right amount of time, he lifted his head and said, "It's that damned soft ground up yonder. It washed out last spring. I told Pa we needed to do some work on it. It's a dangerous spot, especially where it curves around."

Micah tried to imagine what it would sound like if Sonny was making that same statement from the witness stand, and he knew it would sound reasonable as hell. There was not a jury in the country that would think Sonny was telling anything less than the truth.

"We'll need a rope," Micah said.

Sonny looked up. There was confusion in his young eyes, and maybe fear. It was clear Micah made him uneasy. "Rope?" he asked, and a nervousness laced the edges of the word.

"We need a rope to get Emmett out."

"Oh, sure, a rope." He nodded and stood. "I'll run into the barn and fetch one."

"We could use your help up there too."

"Sure," Sonny said. "I won't even take time to saddle my horse. I'll ride Pa's gelding."

Sonny disappeared into the barn and a moment later came out with a coiled rope. "This is the longest one I could find," he said as he mounted up. He attached the rope to the saddle's hornstring.

"That's fine," said Chester, turning his moto-cycle toward the gate. "I expect we'll need it all." He gave the speed lever a shove, and the cycle's rear wheel whipped a whirlwind of dust into the midday air. The two men on horseback rode at a gallop, but Chester led all the way.

When they reached the top, Sonny dismounted, sidled his way to the cliff's edge, and peered over the side. Sonny wiped his mouth with the back of his gloved hand, and Micah watched as tears blossomed in Sonny's eyes. For a moment Micah questioned his own cynical attitude toward this boy. Perhaps what he saw in front of him was not the cold-blooded killer Micah believed Sonny to be. Perhaps Sonny was nothing more than a sad young man trying without success to hold back the tears that welled up at the sight of his father's body on the rocks below.

But then Micah looked deeper, past the tears, and what he saw within those blue eyes was an empty, frigid landscape. It was a barren world, locked in ice—cold and dead. And there was something else in there as well, and this was even more unsettling than the lifeless plain Micah saw at first. What he saw even deeper in Sonny's eyes was amusement. The boy enjoyed this little drama they played. With a shudder Micah realized Sonny Pratt was having fun.

Micah walked to a heavy piece of granite that was three feet high and half that in diameter. After suffering a few million cycles of heat and cold, it had broken away from the rocks that rose above and found itself a new home.

"Bring me the rope, Sonny," Micah said.

"Sure thing, Mr. McConners." Sonny pulled the rope from the saddle and took it to Micah.

Micah dropped a loop around the boulder, pulled it tight, and tossed the other end over the side of the cliff. The rope reached the bottom with a few feet to spare.

The first eight or ten feet of the cliff was ninety degrees straight down. For the remaining forty feet, it banked out to maybe eighty degrees.

"I'll go down," Micah said, "and tie the rope around Emmett. You fellas hoist him up, then toss the rope back down."

Chester glanced over the side. "You be careful, Micah. That looks pretty treacherous."

Micah followed Chester's gaze. "Oh, hell, Chester, don't you remember when we were kids? We used to do this all the time up in the Laramies."

"What I remember," Chester said, "is you spent the better part of a summer with your leg in splints, hobbling around on crutches."

"Now, isn't it like you to remind me of that as I'm about to shinny down a cliff?"

"I doubt you'd heal as fast as you did fifteen years ago, either," Chester added.

Micah pulled off his gloves, then his coat. He folded the coat and laid it on the ground. "You are full of encouraging words." He then took off his hat and dropped it on top of the coat. He picked up the rope that dangled over the side. It was a new, thick piece of hemp, as fine as any rope made. He leaned his weight back and felt it pull taut and stretch against the opposing weight of the boulder.

"Well," he said, putting his gloves back on, "here goes." He sat and dangled his legs over the edge, then took hold of the rope and lowered himself over. He let himself down hand over hand until the cliff's angle became less severe. He was then able to use his feet to take some of the weight off his arms. He'd been living a sedentary life for the last three years, but he still felt strong. He enjoyed the climb down the cliff's face and felt invigorated when his boots touched solid ground.

"Nice work," Chester called down. "You're as agile as a monkey."

Micah had to admit to a nervous tingle in the pit of his stomach when he'd first lowered himself over the edge. Now that nervous tingle in his stomach was replaced with a pleasant tingle in his arms and legs.

That pleasant feeling didn't last long. It vanished as soon as he attached the rope to Emmett. There was very little blood, much less than Micah would have expected, but when he lifted the old man to cinch him up, there was a soft, unnatural feel to him that told Micah more than he wanted to know about the damage the old man's body had suffered in the fall.

As Micah worked, he remembered it was only a few hours before when he and this man had shared a cup of coffee. As he had that thought, he made a point not to look into Emmett's face.

Once Emmett was secured with the rope, Micah called to Chester and Sonny, "Okay, you can haul him up now." First the rope went taut, creaked, and the body began to rise. Micah sat back and watched as it ascended in short little jerks.

Now Micah could not help but see Emmett's face. The man's eyes were wide and bulging, as though in death he was seeing at a much slower speed the reverse of the last thing he'd seen in life.

As Micah watched the body go up he also felt his anger rise, and he wondered if Chester's rambling speculation about Micah's wish to kill Sonny Pratt was true. Earlier he'd said without equivocation that it wasn't true. But what else would he say? When first confronted with the possibility that he'd enjoy killing another human being, of course he was going to deny it. Now, though, within the privacy of his own thoughts, he wondered.

No, no, he assured himself, he did not want to kill Sonny Pratt. Of course he didn't.

Micah was locked in his thoughts when the end of the rope, like a heavy, braided snake, hit the ground in front of him. "Grab hold," called Chester, "and we'll hoist you up."

Micah stood, looped the rope around an arm, and took hold with both hands.

"You ready?" Chester asked.

"Yes, go ahead."

No, what Micah wanted was to let the law handle Sonny, but there was no proof. There was never any proof.

He looked down and watched the rocks beneath him grow

smaller, then lifted his eyes to the spot where the rope disappeared above the cliff. He could see the tips of two boots protruding over the edge—Chester's left boot and Pratt's right—as they worked together pulling him in like some large fish.

He spun around as they brought him up. First he would see the granite wall inches in front of his face; then his view would open to the wide expanse of prairie stretching out to the horizon; then, again, he would face the rough wall of rock.

Someday Sonny Pratt would slip. Someday someone's bullet would find him, or he would end up dangling from hemp like the rope that held Micah now. That was Micah's hope, anyway. And he nursed the additional hope that he would be around to see it.

Micah was less than ten feet from the top when, again, he looked up. He could now hear Chester and Sonny grunting with their effort. He could hear the scrape of the rope against the rocks. He could see the toes of the men's boots extended over the edge of the cliff, and with every grunt and jerk the men made, their boots would dip with the effort, then rise, dip, and rise.

"Damn, Micah," Chester said, "I don't mind telling you, you're a lot heavier than you look."

Micah was less than three feet from the rim now, and that was when he saw it. At first what he was seeing didn't register, but then like a light coming on—one of Chester's electrical lights—Micah knew. The shock of it was damn near enough to cause him to lose his grip. But he held on until they had him all the way to the edge. He then threw his forearms over and pushed himself up the rest of the way, rolling onto his back. He gave out a sigh of relief and felt Chester's big hands under his arms lifting him to his feet.

"Well," Chester said, blotting the sweat from his forehead

with the back of his hand, "I'm glad that's over."

Both Chester and Sonny were breathing hard. As they tried to catch their breath, neither was paying much attention to Micah. Because of that, they both showed the same amount of surprise when Micah pulled his Colt, pointed it at the middle of Pratt's face, and said, "Chester, get his gun. I'm placing this shit under arrest."

Micah saw Sonny's right hand twitch. He was thinking about trying something, but Micah shook his head, and Sonny stood still as Chester pulled the forty-four from Sonny's holster and the knife from Sonny's sheath.

"What the hell's this all about, McConners?" The innocent tones of youth that Micah heard in Sonny's voice earlier were now replaced with harsher sounds.

Chester wore a kind of befuddled smile. "I was wondering that myself," he said. "What is this all about, Micah?"

"It's simple," Micah said. "I'm arresting Sonny here for the murder of Hank Jones."

Chester led the way to the Jones place. This time he was so far ahead of Micah and Sonny that he had time to go into the barn and hitch a team to a buckboard. They would use the buckboard to haul the bodies into town. Chester pulled the wagon in front of the ranch house and was sitting on the tailgate waiting as Sonny and Micah rode up.

Micah had tied Sonny's hands in front rather than behind. He'd done this so Sonny could handle his own reins, and that would allow Micah's hands to remain free to carry the Winchester he had taken from Emmett's saddle scabbard. Micah wasn't concerned about Sonny's trying anything—not on the ride over to the Jones place, anyway. They had also tied Emmett's body across the front of the gelding's saddle. That should slow Sonny down enough that he wouldn't be so foolish as to try to run, even if he was so foolish as to gamble on Micah's marksmanship with a rifle.

"Climb down," Micah said to Sonny once they were up to the house. To Chester he said, "Help me get Emmett into the wagon."

Sonny had been quiet on the ride over; now, as Micah and Chester loaded Emmett's body onto the buckboard, Sonny began to chatter. "I don't know what the hell makes you think I killed Hank. I didn't even know the son of a bitch was dead till you told me I was under arrest."

Chester still wore that befuddled smile, but he didn't say anything.

Micah, without responding to Sonny, jerked his head toward the porch and said, "Inside."

The room was the same as it had been, except that the pool of blood had dried into a black crust.

"Damn," said Sonny, "Hank's kind of a mess, ain't he?"

"Shut up," Micah said, "and take off your boots."

Sonny blinked twice and asked, "What?"

There were a couple of straight-back chairs next to an eating table. Micah placed his foot against one and shoved it in Sonny's direction. "Sit down," he said, "and take off your boots."

Sonny grumbled but did as he was told.

Once they were off, Micah lifted the right boot and turned it over. "You need to take better care of your footwear, Sonny." He pointed to a worn spot in the boot's sole that was shaped like a backward *S*. It was at the point where the ball of the foot rested, about an inch in from the side. It was not all the way through, but the first layer of leather was clearly worn out. "You've got a hole forming in your boot here."

"So what?"

"I noticed it when you and Chester were hauling me up the side of that cliff. I got to thinking I had seen something like that before, although not quite the same. At first I couldn't place it, and then it came to me."

"What came to you, Micah?" Chester asked.

Micah crossed to Hank's body, stood for a moment staring down at it, then said, "It's obvious the killer was standing in the bedroom in there, and he shot Hank in the back of the head as Hank was leaving that room to come in here. Hank fell blocking the doorway, and the shooter had to step over him to get out. When he did, he stepped in Hank's blood." Micah knelt down beside three undistinguishable marks on the floor. "These," Micah said, "are footprints. I didn't recognize them as that when we were here earlier, but that's what they are, all right. There wasn't as much blood right after the shooting as there is now, so the killer didn't leave much of a trail."

He pointed to the first track. It was the darkest of the three and consisted of an arcing six- or seven-inch line. The line was an eighth of an inch wide at the top of the arc and three inches wide at the bottom. "The way I figure it, when the man stepped out of the room into the blood, he didn't put his whole boot down, only the toe, and most of his weight was on the inside of his foot. The only part of the boot to leave a track was the inside edge of the sole. You can see it right here." He ran his finger along the arc of the first track. "The other two tracks get fainter with every step he made toward the front door, but the first one's pretty clear. You can see the arc of the boot's sole, and right here—" He pointed to a squiggly line inside the other line. "—is what looks like an *S*."

Micah took Sonny's boot, placed it on its edge beside the mark, then rolled it over. The line's arc exactly matched the curve of Sonny's boot sole. The worn-out spot fell on top of the squiggly line.

Micah looked toward Sonny. He sat in his chair silent and

impassive. Micah then turned to Chester and tossed his friend a smile.

Chester saw Micah's smile and raised it with a laugh. "I'll be damned," he said. "It looks like you're a pretty fair policeman after all."

CHAPTER THIRTY-FOUR

Micah dropped Brad Collins's star on the counter at the hardware store and told Reginald Barker, the store's owner and chairman of the board of county commissioners, that the county no longer had a sheriff.

"He handed over his badge and told me he was finished," Micah said.

Barker's head was as round as a ball. Micah figured a fella could probably play ten pins with Reginald Barker's head.

"What's the county to do for a sheriff, then?" Barker asked.

"The commissioners'll have to appoint someone to serve until the election next year."

"How 'bout you, Micah? We'll appoint you. I heard you brought in Sonny Pratt—gonna charge him with the murder of Hank Jones."

News could travel fast in Probity. The town's gossip line was quick if not always accurate.

"I'll not be your sheriff, Mr. Barker. As a matter of fact, as of right now, I'm resigning my position as deputy. I was deputized for about five hours, and that is plenty long enough for me." Micah headed for the door. "I'll check in on the prisoner from time to time and see that he's fed, at least until you appoint someone new." He stopped when he got to the door and turned back to face the man behind the counter. "Don't you be too long about doing it, though. I do not plan to make this my

316

career." He smiled, gave a quick tip of his hat, said, "Afternoon," and left.

Chester and Micah had split up when they first got to town. Micah left to deposit Sonny in the jail—a pleasant experience despite Sonny's threats—and Chester took the two bodies to the undertaker's. Micah and Chester were to meet afterward at Buck's for a beer, and Micah headed over there now.

The bar was busy for a weekday afternoon, but Buck always did a thriving business. The saloon business seemed to be about as profitable as any business around. About ninety percent of the matters to come before the court down in Cheyenne when Micah was studying the law had the use of alcoholic beverages mixed up in them in one way or another. As much as he enjoyed a beer—or even better, a glass of Chester's fine Scotch whisky—Micah sometimes thought the temperance people had the right idea. They described strong drink as a blight upon society. They wanted to ban its use in every state in the union. But even if the temperance folks got their way, Micah wondered if people would ever stop drinking.

Chester was at a table in the far corner away from the door. He was smoking a cigar and had a half-empty glass in front of him. Micah made his way to the bar, ordered two beers, and crossed to Chester's table.

"Thank you, sir," Chester said, accepting the beer Micah set before him. "Did you get your chores all done?"

"I did," Micah said. "And you?"

"Yes, the bodies are delivered to the undertaker. It was interesting too," Chester said, taking a long puff on the fat cigar he held between his teeth.

Micah lit a cigarette. Every time he did, he felt guilty. The trial was over, and he still hadn't stopped smoking. "What was interesting?" he asked.

"When John Summerhayes saw that one of the bodies was

Emmett, he actually sat down and cried."

"Summerhayes cried? I didn't think it was possible."

"Not cried so much as wept. It was all I could do to console him."

"That's not only interesting," Micah said, "it's unbelievable."

"I must know of a couple of hundred bodies that man has worked on over the years," said Chester, "and not once have I seen him show the first sign of emotion."

"Why with Emmett Pratt?" Micah wondered.

"I asked him the same question. Seems they grew up together back in Illinois. They were the best of friends. Even came west together."

"I didn't know that. I guess I wasn't even aware they knew each other."

"No one was aware of it," Chester said.

"What's the story?"

"They made the mistake of falling in love with the same woman, and Emmett won her hand."

"You mean Alice, Pratt's first wife?"

"That's the one. I guess Summerhayes wasn't a very good loser, and for twenty years he's refused to speak to Emmett. He told me today he wouldn't even acknowledge the man when they passed on the street."

"But," Micah asked, "he broke down and cried when Emmett was killed?"

"The nature of friendship is a strange thing indeed," Chester pointed out.

Micah nodded and sipped his beer. "I'm glad this week is about over."

"It has been eventful," Chester allowed. "Even exciting."

"Exciting, yes," Micah said. "Too exciting. I for one am finished with excitement for a while."

Chester smacked him on the shoulder. "Oh, hell," he said,

"stop being such a baby. Excitement's good for the soul."

"I suppose I've always liked excitement as much as the next fella." Micah felt he needed to defend himself. "But right now my soul could do with some boredom."

"Well," Chester said, "it's not going to happen."

"Oh, and why do you say that?"

"Because tomorrow morning, I'm going to teach you how to ride the moto-cycle."

"Not a chance," Micah said. "I'd rather be shot out of a cannon than ride that machine of yours."

Chester leaned forward and rested his big forearms on the table. "Look," he asked, "how well do you know me?" His large face hovered over Micah's.

"Too damned well," Micah said.

"Then you know that I will hound you, berate you, and mock you in front of pretty girls until you agree to my demands, right?"

Micah didn't answer.

"Right?" Chester repeated.

Micah still didn't answer, but he knew what he'd be doing tomorrow morning.

CHAPTER THIRTY-FIVE

If he ever got the chance, Sonny Pratt vowed to smash that God-damned clock. He'd had to listen to it make its noise every hour since McConners had thrown him in this cell the afternoon before. What the hell were they doing with a clock in a cell block anyway, Sonny wondered. Why would anybody in jail give a damn about the time?

The clock chimed eight, and Sonny draped his arm over his eyes. He'd been locked up now for over sixteen hours, and he hadn't slept at all. It wasn't only because of the clock, although, God knew, that was part of it. Mostly he hadn't slept because of his anger. It was a hot and painful anger. It made his insides ache and made his head feel like it would explode. It had been rare in Sonny's life when anyone was foolish enough to make him angry. But it was a simple fact that Sonny Pratt felt anger now.

The chiming of the clock always brought him back to this jail cell, but between the clock's chimes, Sonny allowed his mind to flow in whatever direction it chose. Its usual direction was what he planned to do to Micah McConners once he got out.

Micah McConners was going to die. That much was for sure. The only question was how would Sonny choose to kill him. It gave Sonny pleasure to ponder all his many choices. McConners had died a hundred deaths during the long night Sonny had spent lying on this bunk, and each was more grisly than the one before.

Sonny was deep into these thoughts when he heard a key being inserted in the door out front. McConners had come in and checked on Sonny a couple of times during the night. About thirty minutes earlier he'd brought Sonny in a breakfast of biscuits and gravy. The front door opening up was strange, though. Every time before when McConners came in, he'd used the back door off the alley.

Sonny sat up on his cot and pulled on his boots. They weren't his boots, of course. McConners said he was keeping Sonny's boots for evidence. These were Hank's boots. McConners pulled them off Hank's feet yesterday at the Jones place and gave them to Sonny to wear even though the damned things were two sizes too big.

"McConners," Sonny called as he crossed from the bunk to the cell door, "is that you? Come in here, you son of a bitch. You can help me decide how I'm going to kill you."

Sonny was past trying to hide his ways. He figured McConners had him pretty good on shooting Hank. The best Sonny could hope for was to figure out a way to escape and make it to another part of the country.

Before he left, though, by God, he would kill Micah McConners.

"McConners, God-damn you, get your ass in here. I want to make my threats right to your face."

No one answered, but Sonny heard footsteps. After a moment the door leading into the front office opened, and a man stood in the doorway. Because of the light coming from behind, Sonny couldn't see the man's face, but he looked too big to be McConners.

"Who's that? Come in here where I can see you better," Sonny said.

The man stepped into the cell block, and Sonny saw it was Brad Collins. "Well, I'll be," Sonny said, "if it isn't the ex-sheriff of this fine county. I heard you'd run off, Mr. Collins. Whatever brings you back?"

Collins ignored Sonny's comment about running off. "I came in to get my things," he said. "I'll be leaving directly." Collins pulled a chair up next to Sonny's cell and sat down. "It appears like they got you caught, son." He lifted a pouch of tobacco and some papers from his shirt pocket and rolled a cigarette.

"Well, don't you be enjoying it too much, you old coward," Sonny said. "I won't stay caught long, and when I get out, I just might kill you."

"My word, but you are full of killing talk, ain't you, Sonny?"

Sonny narrowed his eyes at Collins, and he could see his gaze made the older man uneasy.

Collins turned his head first this way and then that. "This is a finely built jail," he said, looking around. "I don't reckon you'll be getting out until someone opens that door you're leaning up against." He struck a match on the underside of the chair and lit his smoke. "If your plan is busting out, I got to warn you, son, them bars in front of you are solid steel imported from Pittsburgh, Pennsylvania, and that wall behind you's made of three layers of brick."

"What's your point, Collins?"

"My point's a simple one, Sonny. I am prepared to come to your rescue, if you are prepared to make it worth my while."

Sonny smiled. "Well, Mr. Collins, that depends," he said, "How much is your while worth?"

Collins flicked an ash toward Sonny's dirty breakfast dishes that were on the floor outside the cell. There was a slot in the bars at floor level to slide the dishes in and out. "I may be wrong, but it doesn't strike me like you're in much of a position to bargain, young fella." He jerked his thumb toward the front office. "In that room yonder, there's a set of keys in the desk drawer. For a price, I'll go in there, get them, and let you out."

"And what's the price?"

"One thousand dollars."

"A thousand dollars? Hell, it's only about forty feet from here to that desk. I'd say that's pretty damned fine pay for walking forty feet."

Collins rubbed his chin as though he was calculating something out. "Well, let's see," he said, "forty feet. That's about thirteen steps. Why, hell, that's the exact number of steps you'll be climbing to the gallows."

Sonny gave the man another smile—a wider smile this time. "Aren't you a clever old cuss, though."

"I'm betting you know where you can lay your hands on a thousand dollars, Sonny. Am I wrong?"

Sonny shook his head. "No," he said, "you're not wrong. We got a floor safe in the house out at the ranch. I expect there's a thousand dollars in it."

"So," Collins asked, "do we have us a deal?"

Sonny shrugged. "Now, wouldn't I be a fool to say no to such a tempting offer?"

Collins took a drag on his half-smoked cigarette and dropped it onto one of the dirty dishes. It hissed as the gravy soaked in. "I'll be back," he said. He walked down the aisle between the cells and into the outer office. After a bit he came in carrying a ring of keys. He inserted one in the lock and gave it a turn. There was a sound as the tumblers clinked that was as sweet as music to Sonny.

Sonny stepped out of the cell. "My God," he said, smiling at Collins and slapping the older man on the back, "to think it was as easy as all that. Ain't that the damnedest?" He then ran into the office and tore the desk drawers open.

Collins came to the doorway between the cell block and the office. "What you looking for?" he asked.

Sonny reached in the desk and pulled out the gunbelt that

held his pistol and knife. He held it up for Collins to see. "I wouldn't want to leave without this," he said as he strapped it on.

"No," agreed Collins, "I reckon not."

Sonny moved to the window and peeked outside. The sun was slow rising this time of year. It had been up only a half hour or so, which meant the town, too, was tardy starting its day. There was very little traffic, and what there was moved in a lazy manner. Sonny could tell the morning still held a nighttime chill by the steam that blew from the nostrils of Collins's horse tied to the rail in front.

"I'm going to need a mount," Sonny said as he came over to where Collins stood.

"Yep, I thought of that," Collins said. "I have an old plug at the livery I sometimes use as a pack horse. He'll do for our ride out to your place."

Sonny nodded. "That'd work, all right," he said, "but I was planning on using that fine-looking animal tied out front."

"What, you mean my horse?" Collins asked.

"That's the one," said Sonny. "He's wearing a mighty hand-some saddle, and from the window there, that Winchester in the scabbard looks to be brand-new."

Collins snickered a disbelieving little laugh. "No," he said, "I don't expect you'll be riding my horse."

"Well, sir," Sonny said in his softest voice, "I expect you're wrong." And with one quick move, he unsheathed his knife and drove it into Collins's throat all the way to the hilt.

Blood exploded over Sonny's arm in a gush. When it did, Sonny jerked out the knife and another explosion of blood came with it. "God-damn it, Collins, you're bleeding all over me." He gave the man a hard shove, and Collins toppled onto his back. He flopped about with his mouth opening and closing like a banked fish gasping for water. After a bit his eyes glazed over, and the flopping stopped.

There was a basin of water in the outer office, and Sonny cleaned up as best he could. He wasn't sure what his next move would be, but one thing was certain: by the end of the day, Lawyer McConners would be as dead as that fool Collins.

Sonny dried off, found his coat, and buttoned it on. He looked again out the window. There was an occasional passerby, but for the most part the street was empty. He pulled down his hat, turned up his collar, and started for the door. He was almost out when he stopped, turned, and walked back into the cell block. As he came through the doorway, he was careful not to step in any blood. He knew it didn't make any difference this time. McConners wouldn't have any trouble figuring out who stuck Brad Collins, but still, not stepping in blood seemed like a good idea.

He walked to the end of the cell block's aisle, reached up, and took down the Regulator clock that hung on the wall. Using both hands, he raised the clock above his head and smashed it to the floor. The chimes clanged crazily and the glass over the face shattered into a hundred pieces. Sonny lifted his boot and brought the heel down on the clock over and over again. Tiny wheels, gears, and springs soared in every direction. When it looked as though no more damage could be inflicted on the thing, Sonny stepped back and kicked it as hard as he could. The clock rose in the air, turned over once, and crashed into splinters against the jail's brick wall. Sonny looked at the debris and felt his lips blossom in a smile.

Man, he told himself as he walked from the jail into the brisk morning air to locate Micah McConners, maybe he'd start every day by smashing a clock. That felt pretty damned good.

CHAPTER THIRTY-SIX

"Pay the lady," Micah said.

"Wait. Didn't I buy the beer yesterday afternoon?"

"No, Chester, you did not." Under his breath he said, "Now pay her, you cheap bastard."

"What was that?"

"You heard me."

Chester handed Fay a dollar and said, "I apologize for my friend's language, miss. He embarrasses me everywhere we go."

"He is hard to take," Fay agreed.

Micah had come to Lottie's Café earlier, had gotten Sonny Pratt's breakfast, and had taken it to him at the jail. Afterward, he came back and joined Chester. They had agreed to meet at Lottie's, and after they'd had a bite of breakfast, they'd take the moto-cycle to the outskirts of town where Micah, against his better judgment, would learn to ride.

Chester always loved an audience, and he spoke loudly enough now for Cedra and Polly, who sat at the next table, to hear. "I might have thought, Mademoiselle Charbunneau, after all this time you would have taught this blackguard some manners." The regular breakfast crowd was gone, and except for Lottie, who was banging pots and pans in the back room, the five of them were alone in the café.

"I've tried," Fay said. She smiled and shook her head in apparent frustration, "But I'm afraid he's untrainable."

Micah saw Polly and her mother share a smile. The two

women wore casual clothing. It was their plan to drive Chester's buggy to the Pratt place to check on things. The few hands that Emmett kept on in the winter would handle the chores, but they would pay little attention to the house.

"Untrainable." Chester laughed. "Isn't that the truth. But I must be as bad," he added. "I know how dull he is, yet here I am taking him out in an attempt to teach him how to operate a piece of modern machinery. I expect before he's done, he'll wrap my beautiful moto-cycle around a tree."

Fay nodded. "It is risky." The joking that lined her voice a moment earlier was now replaced with concern. Micah heard it, and it seemed Chester did as well.

Chester waved his hand, brushing away her worry. "Only a little," he said. "Some risk is necessary if you want to accomplish anything." He lifted a piece of egg with his fork and shoveled it into his mouth. " 'Course, I don't suppose you and Micah would agree with that."

"What's that supposed to mean?" Micah asked.

Chester shrugged. "It seems to me the two of you don't want to take any risks at all—not even the risk of other folk's disapproval."

Micah was perturbed with himself before he even responded. He always rose to Chester's bait. He couldn't stop himself. "There's no risk to it," he said. "We know there'd be disapproval. There'd be scandal."

"Why, a little scandal would be fun. Now that Sonny's locked up, Collins is gone, and Anderson's hiding under a rock somewhere, what'll we have to talk about?" He took a sip of coffee. "I expect there are places in this country you'd be wise not to visit," he allowed, "but what does that matter? You wouldn't want to go to those places anyway. Yes, sir, I think you and Fay raising the eyebrows of the local citizenry is exactly what this town needs."

Micah met Fay's dark eyes. The sadness he always saw there seemed magnified. As usual, Chester made things sound so easy. He turned to Chester and asked, "Is there anything in this world that you do not have an opinion on?"

"Nope," Chester said, stabbing his last bite of egg, "not a thing. And what's more, I'm always happy to share my opinions with others."

"Yes," said Micah, "you're generous that way." He stood, offered the women a thin smile, and said to Chester, "Let's go. Breaking my neck on that fool machine promises to be less painful than listening to your perspectives on life." He nodded to Polly and Cedra. "Now, you be careful on your errand, ladies. And you should try to make it back before dark." Since they were taking the buggy out to Pratt's, they would have to go around the long way rather than over the breaks, which added more than an hour to the journey.

Cedra told them earlier she was not looking forward to going back to the house, but she felt it had to be done. "We will," she replied. "You be careful, too."

Once outside, Micah said, "I think I'll check on Pratt again before we leave."

"Oh, come on, Micah," said Chester, "you were over there less than an hour ago. Let's head out."

"I don't know. I think I should take a look."

Chester threw his leg over the moto-cycle. "He's fine—cloistered away like a monk." He patted the cycle's rail.

Micah grimaced and climbed on. "It seems to me," he said, "the last time I was on this thing I ended up in a horse trough."

"That was a fluke," said Chester. "It wouldn't happen again in a hundred years."

"Right."

"Besides, I'm a much more experienced rider now than I was back then."

As Chester said that, he started off so fast Micah felt his neck pop. "Yep," Micah agreed, "I can tell."

Micah said that with as much sarcasm as he could muster, but right away it was clear Chester was a better rider than he'd been on Micah's first day back in Probity. His acceleration was smoother, and he leaned into turns with an ease that was graceful. That's what it was. Micah would have never thought he'd use the word "graceful" to describe anything Chester Hedstrom did, but he had to admit that on this machine, big, lumbering Chester was graceful.

Not only had Chester's ability to handle the moto-cycle improved from the August before, but the machine itself was better. From Chester's tinkerings, it had more power and was more responsive. Chester, who had taken apart hundreds of devices in his life and, more often than not, never got them back together, had worked wonders on this particular device.

"It's amazing, isn't it?" Chester said into Micah's ear. He sounded like a father showing off a child.

They rode less than a mile south of Probity to an area that was flat for a few hundred yards before the terrain gave way to rolling prairie. Chester brought the cycle to a gentle stop about fifty feet out from a grove of cedar and pine. Since he would be riding next, Micah was glad to see that Chester pointed the machine away from the trees toward the open flat land.

"You, Mr. McConners, are about to be dragged into the modern world."

"Come on, Chester, I came out to ride this damned thing, not to listen to one of your discourses."

"All right, all right," Chester said with a frown, "let me tell you a little about what we have here." He pointed to the motor that was built into the cycle's front frame down-tube. "Uncle Oscar designed this beauty. It's an automatic inlet valve, two-hundred-and-eighty-eight cubic centimeter engine. I've since bored it out and—"

Micah held out both his hands, palms almost in Chester's face. "Stop right now, Chester," he said. "I don't have the slightest idea what the hell you're talking about."

Chester laughed. He was enjoying himself. "It doesn't matter. You don't need to know the details. All you need to know is that you ride it like a bicycle. You do ride a bicycle, don't you?"

"Of course," Micah answered. The truth was he just barely could ride a bicycle. He'd never owned one of his own. They used to sell them in their store, and Micah spent half of one summer trying to master the skill. He did learn, but he was never very artful at it.

"Good. You begin as you would on a bicycle. You start the motor by pedaling, and you control both the ignition and the speed with the speed lever right here." He tapped a small lever at the front of the cycle's cross bar. "You push it forward to go faster, pull it back to go slower, pull it all the way back to stop. It's as simple as that. There's nothing to it."

Micah doubted there was *nothing* to it, but it didn't look too complicated.

"Are you ready to give it a go?"

Micah swallowed. "All right."

Chester stepped out of the way, and Micah threw his leg over. He felt an odd nervousness sitting at the controls of this machine. He'd never had this sort of feeling before. He'd grown up riding horses, of course, and if he felt this same way the first time he'd climbed on a horse's back, he couldn't remember. He doubted he had. A horse was different. If some fool was about to ride a horse into a tree or over the side of a cliff, the horse would probably let him know this was not the smartest action to take. This thing, on the other hand, was indifferent to its rider's stupidity.

Micah thought what he was about to do might well be the

stupidest thing he'd ever done. He glanced toward Chester, and the big man's face radiated excitement and pleasure.

Micah took a deep breath and felt his own face curl into a grimace as he lifted his boot to the pedal and pushed down. The motor was already warm from their ride out from town. In short order it caught, and the moto-cycle took off. Micah's stomach leapt to his throat, and he traveled the first hundred feet careening out of control. He didn't crash, but he was no more steering this device than was President McKinley as he sat at his Executive Mansion desk.

"Whooooooooo weeee! Ride 'em, *cowboy!*" Chester shouted. His laughter now was a howl.

Micah tried to slow down by dragging his feet, but all he accomplished was to send two huge plumes of dust billowing into the morning air. The moto-cycle was gaining speed at an incredible rate. The only time he had ever felt such acceleration was the first time he had ridden this damned thing with Chester, and now he guessed he was going twice as fast as they had been going then.

Eventually, even through the red glare of his panic, he remembered the lever on the cross bar. He must have pushed it a little harder when he took off than was necessary. He looked down and realized he had the thing all the way forward. He pulled it back, and the moto-cycle began to slow.

"Sweet Christ," Micah said out loud. His mouth felt as dry as a desert. There had been a moment back there when he was convinced he was about to die. "*SweetHolyJesusChristinHeaven,*" he said in one nonstop gush. Micah had never been religious, but he was certain if he spent much time on this thing, he would become as pious as the Pope.

Although still coasting at what Micah felt was a dizzying speed, as the cycle slowed, it became more difficult to balance. It began to wobble, and again that red glow of terror filled

Micah's head.

At just the point when he knew he was going down, he gave the lever a shove. The motor roared. His head whipped back so fast his hat flew away, and he was off across the prairie once again. He spewed forth another flood of profanity, but this time he knew what to do. He eased the lever back, and, again, the cycle slowed. He gave it another push—gingerly—and the thing sped up.

Micah realized there was a strange paradox to this moto-cycle riding: the slower you went, the harder it was to control. It must be, he thought, that the wheels worked like a couple of gyroscopes helping to keep the machine upright. The faster the gyroscopes spun, the more stable it was.

He slowed more, the cycle started getting shaky, and he gave the lever a little push. Sure enough, the line of travel straightened. He gave it another push, and it was at that moment the panic he'd felt earlier vanished. His heart still pounded, his mouth was still as dry as a wad of Texas cotton, but the sheer terror was gone. For the first time Micah felt the smooth sensation of moving on a motorized vehicle over which he was exercising control.

He eased the lever back, and he slowed; he eased it forward, and he sped up. He soon discovered another paradox. When he pushed the left handlebar in order to turn the front wheel to the right, instead, the moto-cycle turned to the left. When he pushed on the right handlebar to turn the wheel to the left, the cycle went right. Micah realized a fella had to change his way of thinking if he was going to be successful riding one of these things.

He practiced these maneuvers around the field, and as hard as it might have been to believe, he was enjoying it. Riding was fun.

He put the machine into a big sweeping turn, and again his

stomach made a leap toward his throat. This time it was the thrill that caused his stomach to jump, not the fear. The cycle leaned in its wide arc, and the sagebrush scrubbed his boot. He inched the lever forward a little more, pushed harder on the handlebar, and the cycle leaned over far enough that the sagebrush scraped his pantleg. This was incredible. He hadn't felt excitement like this since . . . since when, he wondered. *When?* He thought about that, and all he could come up with was he hadn't felt excitement like this since his first kiss. Yes, sir, this was every bit as exciting as that.

He felt himself smile. Well, maybe not that exciting, but, damn, it sure was close.

As he brought the bike around, he looked back toward where he'd left Chester, but he was so far away he couldn't see him. It was hard to believe how far he'd gone in such a short time. From where he was now he could see both ends of the grove of evergreens. It covered a couple of acres of flat land before it climbed over the hill beyond.

He came out of his turn, brought the bike upright, and didn't even try to resist the temptation to increase the speed. The smooth flow of wind lifted his hair and blew it straight back.

It was a freedom like he had never felt. Micah was certain this was the feel of flight.

He spotted his hat off to the left, veered in that direction, and brought the cycle to a stop so close to the hat all he had to do was bend down to retrieve it. He stuck it onto his head far enough he was sure he wouldn't lose it again.

He looked back toward the grove of trees, but he still couldn't see Chester. At first Micah thought that odd. He was close enough now he should be able to see him. He decided Chester must have stepped into the trees to relieve himself. They'd had a lot of Lottie's coffee at breakfast.

Micah pedaled the cycle, the engine caught, and again he

was off. He wondered how much Uncle Oscar and his partner back in Springfield, Massachusetts, were planning on charging for one of these machines. For a couple of years now Micah had expected that someday—perhaps not in his lifetime, but someday—the automobile would replace the carriage for transporting small groups of people. Now, he was convinced the moto-cycle would replace riding horseback for individual transportation. Micah could see the day when everyone—man, woman, and child—would have their very own moto-cycle.

He gave the speed lever a hard shove and rode the machine as fast as it would go. The heat coming off the motor warmed his legs, and the vibrations caused his body to buzz. He squinted into the distance, but Chester was still out of sight.

Micah aimed the cycle into a shallow depression, and when he came out the other side, the machine left the ground and sailed fifteen feet through the air. Though they were bared in a smile, Micah's teeth rattled when he landed, and he decided it might be wise to ease off a bit.

He slowed to a more reasonable speed and brought the machine to a stop in the same place where he had started his lesson.

Although he had straddled the moto-cycle only a few minutes earlier, Micah knew in that short time something in him had changed. Before he'd had an intellectual understanding of what Chester meant with his endless, mind-numbing descriptions of the many coming wonders of the new century, but now he knew on a deeper level what Chester was talking about. It was exciting. For the first time he grasped in a visceral way—the way Chester did—the extent of possibilities that the coming twentieth century had to offer.

As he listened to the ticks and pops of the cycle's cooling motor, Micah knew he would never again be quite the same.

★ ★ ★ ★ ★

"Chester," he called, but there was no response. "Chester," he called again—still, no answer. Micah peered into the grove of trees. It was darker in there. The open land where Micah had been riding was dry, but snow covered the ground in the shadows of the big pines and cedars.

"Chester, damn you, stop fooling around."

Micah looked about to make sure this was the right spot. He had ridden quite a ways. Maybe he had misjudged the place where he started. He was about to fire the moto-cycle up and check farther down the line of trees, when Chester stepped into view.

"Well, there you are," Micah said. "I wondered where the hell you were." He ran his hand along the handlebars. "I have to admit, Chester. This is quite the thing. I've never—" He was about to go on, but the expression on his friend's face stopped him. "What's wrong with you? You look sick."

"He is sick," a soft voice from behind Chester said. "Fact is, he feels like he's about to swoon." Carrying a Winchester, Sonny Pratt stepped out from in back of a bushy cedar, and with one swift move he swung the rifle like a baseball bat, cracking the barrel against the back of Chester's skull. Chester dropped like a sack of rocks.

Micah moved for his Colt, but Sonny's rifle was on him before his hand was halfway there.

"Now, now, Mr. McConners," Sonny said, "are you trying to spoil my day? After I went to all the trouble to follow you two fellas out of town, I don't want to have to kill you outright. No, sir. I don't want that at all." Sonny had been smiling as he spoke, but the smile dissolved. "Now you get off that thing you're straddling."

Micah dropped the cycle's stand and threw his leg over.

"Very good," Sonny said. "Now take your left hand and reach

across and pull that shooter out of its holster. And," he added, "please, Mr. McConners, you do it real slow."

Micah did as he was told.

"Now toss 'er over."

Micah did. The gun bounced once and slid next to Sonny's boot. Sonny bent and picked it up by the barrel. Without taking his eyes off Micah, he threw it as far as he could. Micah watched it sail end over end out into the prairie.

"Golly," Sonny said, "that is so much better."

Micah wondered how Sonny had escaped from jail, but decided at the moment that didn't matter. He hooked his thumbs into his gun belt and asked, "So, what now?"

"What now? You know, I've been asking myself that same question ever since you tied my hands together back at the breaks yesterday afternoon. What now? What now?"

"If you've given it that much thought, Sonny, what did you come up with?"

Sonny grinned. "Oh, hell, I never could decide for sure. But with so many fine choices and interesting possibilities, how could a fella go wrong? I reckon I'll have to make it all up as I go along." He nodded toward Chester. "You drag that big ox back here into the trees."

Micah fixed Sonny with his eyes and stood his ground.

They stared at each other, neither blinking. At last Sonny said, "Do it," and his voice was a soft, hot, semi-liquid. His voice was molten steel.

Micah looked toward Chester. The big man stirred a bit, but he was still unconscious. Sonny might feel he had a lot of choices, but Micah's choices were few. He lifted Chester under the arms and with effort dragged him through the snow into the trees.

"Prop him up against that dead one yonder." Sonny jerked the barrel of his Winchester in the direction of the trunk of a half-fallen pine.

As Micah placed his friend against the rotting tree trunk, Chester's lids fluttered. He shook his head and brought the heels of his hands up to his eyes. "Damn," Chester said in a gravelly voice, "things are whirling some, Micah."

"You lay there and take it easy," Micah said.

Chester leaned his head back against the tree. "Looks like I got us in a pickle," he said.

"It's not your fault, Chester."

"I never saw him coming. I was watching you on the motocycle, and I never saw the son of a bitch coming. I should have been paying more attention."

"Don't talk. It's all right," Micah said.

"After he got the drop on me, I wanted to warn you, but there wasn't anything I could do."

"I know."

"You boys stop that whispering," Sonny said. "Don't you know how impolite that is? You, McConners, step away from there." He motioned to a large rock to the left. "And sit down."

Micah gave Chester's shoulder a squeeze, stood, backed toward the rock, and sat.

"Now," said Sonny with a cheery smile, "isn't this working out well? I don't know when I've felt more alive." Still smiling, he lifted the rifle and fired a bullet into Chester's right arm.

An explosion of blood blew onto Chester's neck and face. He screamed and fell to his side. Micah leaped from the rock and made a running dive at Sonny, but Sonny must have been expecting it. He turned cat-fast and caught Micah square in the jaw with the rifle butt. When the blow landed, Micah was in midair, and he was spun around and knocked to the ground.

He could taste hot copper in his mouth, and he felt the sting of the snow on his face.

Sonny stepped over to where Micah lay and kicked him in

the ribs, rolling him over onto his back. "Get up, McConners," Sonny said, "and pay attention. When I get done working on your friend with this—" He waggled the Winchester. "—I'm going to start slicing off parts of you with my knife." He leaned in closer. "I like knives," he said. "They're a lot more personal. Now, get up."

When Micah didn't stand, Sonny lifted him by the collar of his jacket and shoved him in the direction of the rock where he had told him to sit. Again, Micah's face hit the snow. This time, though, the cold of it felt good against his throbbing jaw.

"We have a lot of work ahead of us, Mr. McConners, and I can't have you interrupting me every few minutes in a fit of temper. Now, I don't have any rope, or I would tie you to that damned rock there. So I guess there's only one thing to do to slow you down."

He placed the muzzle of the rifle against Micah's thigh and pulled the trigger. Micah screamed and grabbed his leg. Sonny didn't fire straight in, but held the gun so the bullet grazed the outside edge of his thigh, gouging out a four-inch-long piece of meat.

Micah's eyes were clenched with the pain, but he could feel Sonny staring at him.

"I reckon that'll hold you for a while," Sonny said. He knelt down and checked the wound. "Hell, that's not so bad, really." He packed a fistful of snow into the bloody groove. "There. That'll make it feel better." He then stood and walked back to where he had been standing when Micah charged. Like a stern schoolmaster, he pointed a finger at Micah and said, "Now, you behave yourself, or I will be forced to deal with you harshly."

He then raised his rifle and quick-fired twice more, blowing both of Chester's knees to pieces.

"You bastard," shouted Micah. "I'll kill you."

"Oh, hush up," Sonny said, and he lifted the rifle and fired again. This time he put his bullet high into the right side of Chester's chest. It hit him three inches below the shoulder and passed all the way through, popping into the snow a bloody piece of cloth from Chester's jacket.

Chester grabbed his shoulder when the bullet hit, but this time he didn't scream. His eyes were glassy, but they were focused, and they followed Sonny as Sonny walked toward him.

"Damn, Doc," Sonny said as he lifted Chester and propped him back against the pine, "you are bleeding like a son of a bitch."

Chester turned his gaze to the red snow that surrounded him and said in a hoarse voice Micah could barely hear, "By God, Sonny, I believe you're right. You have a real eye for detail, don't you?"

Sonny gave a half-snicker, like he wasn't sure if maybe the doctor was poking fun at him.

"You know something, Sonny," Chester said, looking up, "you are a dead man."

"I'm a dead man?" Sonny laughed as he said it. "I'm a dead man? You're laying there against that tree with four holes in you that God never intended, and you're telling me that I'm a dead man? Goodness gracious, if you don't have more brass than any fella ever."

Micah tore his kerchief from his neck and tied it around his leg. It wasn't as bad as he had first thought. The wound was long, but narrow and not very deep. Though he was slow, he could move, and he decided not to lie there doing nothing. If he was going to stop this crazy bastard, he needed to think of something soon.

Micah picked up a rock that was half-again the size of his fist and pushed himself to his feet. He tried to keep his weight off his bad leg, but he was wobbly, and he felt light-headed. Right now he would be no match for Sonny Pratt even if Sonny wasn't holding a gun.

Chester lifted a hand to his chest-wound and said, "I expect you took out a sizable chunk of my lung here, Sonny." He hawked and spit a round wad of blood into the snow.

"Yep," Sonny said, "you are looking a bit sickly. That's for sure. I'm no doctor," he added with a smile, "but I'd say you're dying fast."

Chester returned Sonny's smile. His teeth were pink, and his gums were lined with red. "Well, Sonny, I am a doctor, and I'd have to concur. My lung's filling up, and I'm drowning in my own blood. I'd say even for an amateur, your prognosis is an accurate one. I am dying, all right, but you are already dead."

Chester's voice was raspy and wet-sounding, but it still carried its not-unusual mocking tone.

Micah saw that Sonny, like so many others before him, was losing patience with Chester's banter.

But Chester went on. "You may keep on breathing for a while longer, but you're dead all the same, Sonny. You are dead."

"I'm not as dead as you're about to be."

Sonny placed the muzzle of the rifle on the spot between Chester's eyebrows, but before he could pull the trigger, Chester lifted his hand and pointed toward Micah. Sonny turned around. Micah braced himself, but to his surprise Sonny did not seem to notice him. He looked right past Micah, and when he did, his face went dark.

Micah turned, and at first what he saw didn't quite register. Behind him and to his right was Cedra and Polly. Between them, stood Fay. Her left foot was planted in front of her. Her right foot planted behind. At her shoulder she held the shotgun she had used to bag their Christmas dinner. The shotgun was leveled at Sonny.

"Well, I'll be damned," Sonny said, "if it ain't the little nigger bitch acting like she's gonna shoot someone."

340

"Drop the rifle, Sonny," Fay said. "Drop it now. Then unbuckle your gun belt and let it go too."

If staring into the barrel of Fay's twelve-gauge made Sonny uneasy, he didn't show it. "And if I don't?" he asked.

Fay didn't answer, and the fact that she ignored his question was something that did seem to make Sonny uneasy.

"You ever kill anyone, girl?"

"Not yet."

"Not everyone's cut out for it. To some it comes natural. Others, hell, they couldn't do it if they had to."

Micah tossed the rock to the ground. "Do what she says, Sonny."

"Tell me, girlie, you got bird shot in that thing or buck shot?"

Again, Fay didn't respond.

Micah hoped it was bird shot. She was standing seventy feet away from Sonny. If she was loaded with bird shot, it would make for a tighter pattern.

"Move in closer, Fay," Micah said.

Before she could move, Sonny said, "Don't you do it, nigger."

Micah turned to Sonny. "What's the matter, Sonny? Getting a little edgy? My money says she's close enough to kill you now, but a little closer would damn near guarantee it."

Fay took a step forward.

"Hold it right there, God-damn it." He held the Winchester with his right hand, the barrel running down along his leg. His left arm was extended, palm out, toward Fay.

Sonny was fast. Micah knew that. His thoughts skittered over Sonny and Chester coming out of the trees, and how Sonny, in one blinding-quick motion, hit Chester, then turned his rifle on Micah. The thought of Sonny facing Fay soured Micah's insides.

But there was no other way.

"Come in closer, Fay," Micah said.

She took another step.

"No, stop right there," shouted Sonny.

"I'm betting she's close enough to kill you now for sure, Sonny, but maybe I'm wrong. Could be she'll just wound you real bad. If she does, you'll die. Chester's the only doctor in forty miles, and he's not going to be able to help you. I doubt I'd let him help you even if he could. And he's right, you know. You're the same as dead. Your only hope is to drop your iron."

Sonny's usual look of confidence was gone. Now, except for his eyes, his features were pinched. His eyes were wide and bulging. He clutched the rifle in a fist so tight his knuckles were white. And Micah could tell by the way the cuffs of his pants jiggled that Sonny's knees were beginning to shake.

"Come on in, Fay," Micah said again. And she did. She took five steps this time. Six. Seven. Ten. Now, Sonny's big eyes were locked on the twelve-gauge's gaping maw.

"She pulls that trigger now, Sonny, and your head becomes mush."

The trembling rose from Sonny's knees up into the rest of him, and he looked to be close to tears when he dropped the Winchester into the snow.

"The gun belt," Fay said. And Sonny loosened it and let it fall.

"Move over to the side, away from the guns," said Micah. Sonny did as he was told.

Fay kept the twelve-gauge leveled at his chest.

Micah moved to Chester as fast as his injured leg would allow, but he knew before he was halfway there that his friend was dead. Micah was numb as he dropped to the ground next to Chester's blood-drenched body. All his mind would allow in was the distant look in Chester's eyes. They were green eyes. How strange. Even though they'd known each other most of their lives, if someone had asked Micah earlier that day the color of Chester Hedstrom's eyes, Micah could not have said. But they were green.

And now those green eyes stared out into the distance, past Micah, past the three women, past the field where Micah had ridden the moto-cycle. They looked past the town and even past the horizon beyond.

Despite everything, Chester appeared pleased, satisfied, perhaps even a bit amused as he gazed with those green eyes out toward the universe's edge.

That was when the rage struck. It was illogical, but for whatever reason, as Micah sat there in the bloody snow looking into his friend's eyes, that was the moment when the fury hit him. It hit him like a tidal wave. It rose like a flood. It filled him up. It overflowed, and when he turned his own eyes away from Chester, he made no attempt to look out into those same vast regions Chester now saw. Micah looked no farther than the spot where Sonny Pratt now sat huddled in a ball, his legs drawn up to his chest.

Micah pushed himself up and limped his way to Fay. He took the shotgun and crossed to Sonny. Sonny lifted his head. When he did, Micah slammed the gun butt down with all his strength. It smashed into Sonny's nose, turning it into a shapeless, bloody mass. Micah hit him again and again. Sonny screamed and covered his head with his arms in a futile effort to block the heavy blows that rained down. Micah beat Sonny onto his back, then stopped, flipped the shotgun around, and put the muzzle flat against Sonny's brow.

Micah heard the shouts of Fay and Polly—Cedra was stone silent—but he could not understand what they said. It didn't matter what they said. Micah was going to kill Sonny Pratt. He was going to rid the world of this vermin.

He watched Sonny's mouth move. It was clear he was plead-ing for his life, but, like with the shouts of the women, Micah couldn't make out the words. Some dam in Micah's brain kept the sense of the words out. Some barrier kept everything out except the gun against Sonny's head and the trigger against Micah's finger.

Chester had told Sonny he was as good as dead. And Chester had been right. If she had to, Fay would have killed him. Since she didn't have to, the hangman would. Eventually.

But Micah had no intention of waiting for the hangman. Sonny Pratt was going to die. And he was going to die today.

Sonny, you are dead, Chester had said, and those were the only words Micah could now hear. In Micah's mind Chester kept repeating those words over and over again. *Sonny, you are dead. Sonny, you are dead.*

And those were still the words that echoed in Micah's head at the moment he pulled the trigger.

CHAPTER THIRTY-SEVEN

Micah lay in his bed and stared at a spot on the ceiling. Jackson's pounding at the office's front door had gone on now for a full five minutes. The man would not relent. Micah had allowed Jackson to rouse him yesterday, but only because of Chester's funeral. Going to the funeral was the last thing Micah had wanted to do, but other than lie in this bed with the blue devils, it was the only thing Micah had done since Chester was killed on Saturday.

Micah had stayed at the cemetery long after the service was over. Everyone else, including Jackson, Fay, and the others, had gone once the last hymn was sung and the last prayer intoned. Jackson had brought Micah out in his carriage, and he tried to get him to leave with him as well, but Micah refused.

"Come along now," Jackson had said as he gave Micah's elbow a tug. Micah wouldn't budge. Jackson lowered his voice so no one else could hear, "Fay's worried about you, son."

Micah turned toward the crowd that filed away from the grave site. Fay was watching them, her hands folded at her waist. A look of sadness cloaked her face.

It was the first he had seen Fay since Saturday. After he and Chester left the café Saturday morning, Fay had gone to the jail to retrieve Sonny's breakfast dishes. It was then she discovered Collins's body and Sonny's empty cell. She ran back for Cedra and Polly, and the three of them drove Chester's buggy to the field where they knew Micah and Chester were riding. But first they stopped for Fay's shotgun.

Throughout Chester's funeral Fay had been standing at the back, apart from the rest of the mourners. Except at the café, neither she nor Micah ever allowed themselves to be seen together in public.

"Fay wants me to take you back to town," said Jackson. "She doesn't think you should stay out here alone, and I agree. We need to go now, Micah."

Micah jerked his arm away from Jackson's grasp and turned back to the grave. To Micah, leaving Chester in this graveyard was the ultimate act of betrayal. After a bit, Jackson gave up and left.

Once everyone was gone, the two grave-diggers, who shoveled dirt into the hole, eyed Micah with suspicion. It was clear they resented his watching them work, but Micah didn't care. He stayed until long after the last spadeful of earth was patted onto the mound that covered Chester's body.

It was cold at the cemetery. The wind sliced in from the northwest, but Micah ignored its chill. When the grave-diggers were finished, they loaded the picks and shovels into their wagon. After that was done, the older of the two men asked Micah if he wanted a ride to town. When Micah didn't respond, the man repeated his question. Still Micah didn't answer, and the grave-digger gave a shrug, snapped his reins, and drove away.

It was dark before Micah—numbed by the cold—turned from the grave and limped the half mile back to Probity. Once he was home, he fell into bed still dressed. He had lain there staring at the same spot on the ceiling ever since.

Now, Tuesday morning, some fifteen hours after his return from the cemetery, there was one last volley of pounding on the office's front door, then silence. At another time Micah would have appreciated the silence, but now he was indifferent. He welcomed that indifference; he embraced it. He wanted to bathe himself with indifference—every nerve of him, every feeling. Lottie was wrong. The opposite of passion was not practicality; it was indifference.

Micah's mind turned that thought around, held it to the light, examined it. Indifference was the answer. For those who allowed themselves to feel, life was an endless flow of pain. Even if passion could be tempered with the practical, as Lottie would advise, ultimately there was still relentless pain and death.

Micah heard voices. At first he could not make out what they were saying, but he could tell it was Jackson and Fay.

After a bit, they were close enough he could understand them. They stopped at his back door. "Fay," Jackson said, "I don't think there's anything to worry about. I mean, I can't imagine Micah would—"

"I understand, Jackson."

"But he gets so low, and when he wouldn't come to the door—"

"You did right to get me, Jackson."

There was a knock. It was the same soft rapping he'd heard so many times before.

Micah still lay staring at the spot. He didn't even want to see Fay. Perhaps Fay was the last person he wanted to see. He had avoided her ever since the shooting. Except for the death of his father and now the death of Chester, it was Fay who was at the root of most of the pain Micah had felt in his life.

There was her rapping again. "Micah, open the door. Let me in."

"Go away," he said. At the sound of his voice he heard both Fay and Jackson sigh with relief. They had been afraid he'd killed himself. Done himself in.

Micah had considered suicide many times in the past. When the blue devils came to call, they always brought those thoughts along with them. It was odd, though. This time it had not crossed his mind. He wondered why. Indifference was what he wanted. It was what he ached for, and suicide was the purest form of indifference. Suicide was caring so little that a person could turn away from life entirely. Suicide was indifference at its most distilled.

Micah felt his brow furrow at the strange realization that this time there had been no thought of killing himself.

Maybe, he didn't deserve to stop the pain. Maybe, just as Chester had said of Sonny, Micah was already dead.

Sonny. Micah hadn't killed him.

With the sound of Chester's words crashing through his head, Micah had moved the shotgun's muzzle at the moment he pulled the trigger. The blast blew a hole six inches deep into the snow and frozen earth next to Sonny's head. In his terror, Sonny had screamed nonstop for a full twenty minutes; finally his voice box broke, and as far as Micah knew, Sonny had not made a sound since. Micah had decided the hangman could have Sonny after all.

Now he heard Fay tell Jackson to leave. "I'll see to him, Jackson," she said. "You go on."

"You know, Fay," the old lawyer said, "it'll be here in less than an hour."

"I know. We'll see how he feels. We'll see. Now, you go on."

With grumblings of reluctance, Micah heard Jackson leave. Again there was the rapping. "Micah, let me in. We need to talk."

Micah wanted to shout that they did not need to talk; there was nothing either of them could say, but the weight of his indifference kept the words inside. Instead, he responded in the only way he could, with silence.

"Micah, I know your sadness for Chester. He was a man who knew things. And he was brave. Braver than us by far. Nothing mattered to Chester except what was right. He was ready to sacrifice himself for whatever he felt was right. He was ready to go to prison for what he felt was right." There was a pause. When she began again, Micah could hear the tears in her voice. "You not killing Sonny, Micah, that was the right thing. And I'm guessing it was Chester who helped you know that. People like you and me, we're good enough people. The world needs us to protect it against people like Sonny. But sometimes even good people need to be shown the right thing to do. We need someone like Chester Hedstrom to point the way. Maybe even show us it's all right to sometimes take a risk. Chester could see things none of the rest of us could see. It was like we were all huddled in darkness, and ol' Chester, he stood up, and he walked out into the light."

She cleared her throat, and when she spoke again, in his mind's eye, Micah could see her straighten the front of her dress in that prim, no-nonsense way she had. "His passing is a sad thing, and we'll never forget him, but now, Micah McConners, it's time for you to open up this door and let me in."

CHAPTER THIRTY-EIGHT

Number Twenty was a coal-fired steam engine that, according to its builders, was the fastest train in America. On Tuesday, January 1, 1901, in celebration of the new year and the new century, a demonstration had been arranged for the Twenty to travel from Casper to Cheyenne, a distance of a hundred and eighty miles. It was claimed by the rail line they could make this journey in two hours and forty-five minutes. One railway official suggested if everything went as planned, it was possible they could make it in less than two and a half hours. They boasted that on many areas of the refurbished track, the Twenty would reach a speed of one hundred miles per hour.

In addition to the engine, the train would be made up of three cars: the coal car, which was, of course, behind the engine, a caboose at the end, and in between the coal car and caboose, the most luxurious of sitting-cars. In this sitting-car would ride the president of the railroad and the governor of the state, along with their wives and children.

For months beforehand, advertisements of the event had filled every paper in Wyoming. Half the dignitaries in the state had been invited to attend a huge luncheon in Casper on the day of the trip. Dignitaries not attending the luncheon had been invited to a midafternoon reception in Cheyenne upon the train's arrival.

The promise of seeing an object moving at such speeds proved to be a tremendous lure. On the morning of the Great

Ride, as it had come to be called, people began to line the track. Even though no stops were planned, and the train would be in and out of all the towns along the way in a matter of seconds, every community on the route planned its own celebration.

Probity was no different. A dais large enough to hold the mayor, city council, county commissioners, and all their wives had been erected on the depot's platform. The Twenty was scheduled to depart Casper at precisely one o'clock. Probity was fifty miles to the southeast, so the train might pass through as early as one-thirty.

Mayor Thompson, who was always loquacious, began his speech at one. He was in his finest form on this New Year's Day—New Century's Day, as he described it—but despite the mayor's skill at turning a phrase, the crowd's attention was divided—focused more on the track to the northwest than on anything the mayor had to say.

Jackson Clark's attention was also pointed up the track. For his entire life Jackson had been fascinated with trains. When he was a boy growing up on his father's Ohio farm, every afternoon at three-oh-eight the train that ran from Hillsboro to Chillicothe would pass through. And no matter what Jackson was doing, he would stop doing it long enough to wave at the train's engineer.

For all his sixty years, Jackson had watched the changing face of trains, but he never would have believed he'd live long enough to see one capable of traveling as fast as the Twenty. He admired the courage of the train's passengers. He would not dream of getting on anything that could go a hundred miles an hour. He questioned a person's ability to breathe moving at such speed. He feared the air would be passing so quickly it would be impossible to suck it in.

Mayor Thompson's speech droned on. He spoke of the power

of modern machinery and the promise the new century held. Jackson recognized all these sentiments, every single one, as ones the mayor had borrowed from Chester Hedstrom. At first he found that irritating, but then he decided it was a fine thing, indeed. Chester would be pleased.

Jackson kept his eyes on the track. He had a clear view from where he stood. He could see all the way down First Street, past Antelope Flats, farther even than Lottie Charbunneau's. He checked his watch: one-twenty-six, and the Twenty was not in sight.

It was exciting for Jackson waiting for this mighty train to roar into their town, but it was a hollow excitement. Chester had looked forward to this day. He'd followed all the newspaper stories about the train. There were dozens of articles written, some of which even included schematics of the engine's design. Being educated as an engineer and having once even worked in a factory that built locomotives, Chester understood a great deal about the Twenty's construction. Prior to the trial, when it was assumed he would be going to prison, Chester had told Micah and Jackson that one of the things he regretted most was that he would miss the coming of the Twenty. It would be, Chester had said, quite a sight.

One-thirty-three. Jackson squinted toward the northwest. Still there was no sign of the train. He expected younger eyes than his would see it first, and he'd only know it was coming by the sounds made by the crowd.

Even as he had that thought, Jackson heard gasps and whispers. He squinted harder up the track, but still his old eyes couldn't see a thing.

The whispers grew louder, and there was a stirring from the other side of the dais. Jackson turned and saw why. Coming toward him—the crowd stepping back out of their way—was Micah McConners and Fay Charbunneau. Jackson smiled when he saw the surprised disbelief that draped the face of everyone who watched.

As Micah and Fay came toward him, they did so holding hands. The pale fingers interlaced with the dark was a sight never seen by the eyes that saw it now.

The crowd's attention was no longer divided. Not a soul looked toward Mayor Thompson—not even his wife, Muriel—as he delivered his windy oration. After a bit, he too had to turn to see what was happening. What he saw stopped him in midsentence. His practiced rhetoric was transformed to stammers and stutters as he grappled for something to say.

But before the mayor could find his words, a shrill scream ripped the afternoon air. It hit the buildings, rattled windows, and ricocheted through the town. Sparrows wheeled in panic from their perches by the river.

The stirring among the crowd stopped. Now they faced up-track, wide-eyed and mouths agape.

The Twenty was coming. A tornado of black smoke billowed from its stack. It was still a mile away, but the rails hummed with its power. It was a roaring juggernaut, the blast of its whistle growing louder with every second.

It came like an army toward them, a massive, inexorable force.

In moments it was there. The heat of it made the people in front shove back hard against those behind. The air in front of it was pushed aside. It blew hats from heads and caused women's hair to fly.

In the brief instant the train was parallel to the station, the engineer again blew the Twenty's whistle, and terrified children cupped their hands to their ears. To Jackson the shriek of it seemed loud enough to rend the sky and open up the heavens.

There was a quick blur of waves as the sitting-car blasted past. Then a two-fingered salute came from the brakeman who stood at the back of the diminishing caboose.

As fast as the Twenty came, it was gone, and the sudden quiet was engulfing.

Dust and papers whirled in circles. For a full fifteen seconds—more than three times as long as it took the great train to pass—the citizens of Probity, Wyoming, stood in total silence.

But then as if on cue—as if as one, they burst into cheers. They yahooed and yippeed. The Probity Brass Band began to play. The people laughed and hugged. They spun and danced. It was as though this mighty engine screaming across the winter prairie had left a field of pure energy in its wake.

Jackson felt it as much as anyone, and he began to do a jig. He knew it looked strange and old-fashioned, but the old lawyer didn't give a damn. It was a jig he'd learned back in Ohio as a boy in the middle of what was now the previous century. And despite his years and the crick that always plagued his back, Jackson Clark was certain he had never done it better.

He grabbed Fay and twirled her around, then grabbed Micah and twirled him too.

Jackson could still see the sadness in Micah. It was thick and hung in his eyes like a storm. Micah felt things stronger than most folks. Jackson would wager that was one of the things that would make him a fine attorney—and a fine man to boot.

He gave the boy another spin, then let him go. Micah smiled at Jackson, then moved to his lovely dark-skinned woman.

Yes, the sadness was there all right—it probably always would be—but Jackson saw it soften some when Micah looked at Fay.

ABOUT THE AUTHOR

Robert D. McKee has had a number of jobs in his life, including four years in the military. He has also been employed as a warehouse worker, radio announcer, disc jockey, copywriter, court reporter, and municipal court judge.

After school in Texas, Bob settled in Wyoming, where he lived for over thirty years. He and his wife Kathy now make their home along the Front Range in Colorado.

His short fiction has appeared in more than twenty commercial and literary publications. One of his stories was selected to appear in the prestigious annual publication *Best American Mystery Stories,* edited that year by Otto Penzler and Michael Connelly. He is also a recipient of the Wyoming Art Council's Literary Fellowship Award, as well as a three-time first-place winner of Wyoming Writers, Incorporated's adult fiction contest and a two-time first-place winner of the National Writers Association's short fiction contest. His first novel, *Dakota Trails,* was awarded the 2016 Will Rogers Silver Medallion for Best Western.

The employees of Five Star Publishing hope you have enjoyed this book.

Our Five Star novels explore little-known chapters from America's history, stories told from unique perspectives that will entertain a broad range of readers.

Other Five Star books are available at your local library, bookstore, all major book distributors, and directly from Five Star/Gale.

Connect with Five Star Publishing

Visit us on Facebook:
   https://www.facebook.com/FiveStarCengage

Email:
   FiveStar@cengage.com

For information about titles and placing orders:
   (800) 223-1244
   gale.orders@cengage.com

To share your comments, write to us:
   Five Star Publishing
   Attn: Publisher
   10 Water St., Suite 310
   Waterville, ME 04901